# THE LOST EMPRESS

A Jefferson Tayte Genealogical Mystery

**Other books in this series:**

*In the Blood*
*To the Grave*
*The Last Queen of England*

# THE LOST EMPRESS

A Jefferson Tayte Genealogical Mystery

by

## STEVE ROBINSON

Text copyright © 2014 Steve Robinson

Published by Thomas & Mercer, Seattle

www.apub.com

Amazon, the Amazon logo, and Thomas & Mercer are trademarks of Amazon.com, Inc., or its affiliates.

ISBN-13: 9781477825839
ISBN-10: 1477825835

Designer: bürosüd° München, www.buerosued.de

Library of Congress Control Number: 2014940222

Printed in the United States of America

*For my wife Karen*

# Preface

On 20 June 1908, Anglo-French journalist and diplomat William Le Queux returned from his travels to Berlin with report of an alleged secret speech delivered by Kaiser Wilhelm II at a Council held at Potsdam Palace on 2 June 1908. Below is a transcript of an article as it was published in *The Dominion*, volume 8, issue 2558, on 4 September 1915.

*The speech took over three hours to deliver, and for five hours afterwards was discussed. The report he brought home was placed before the meeting of the British Cabinet, and discussed. At first some little suspicion was cast upon it—had the speech ever been delivered? So further inquiry was made, and there was no doubt it was perfectly genuine. The gentleman who handed it to him (the lecturer) was a high official, very near to the Kaiser's person, an official to whom we should all be very deeply grateful, for he had furnished us with much important information. He was friendly disposed towards England and had no sympathy with the present war. If his name were revealed he would be arrested, and probably shot. In the course of the speech, the Kaiser said: 'We shall strike as soon as I have a sufficiently large fleet of Zeppelins at my disposal. I have given orders for the hurried construction of more airships of the Zeppelin type. When these are ready, we shall destroy England's North Sea, Channel, and Atlantic fleets, after which nothing on earth can prevent the landing of our army on British soil and its triumphant march to London.' He went on to say: 'You will desire to know how the outbreak of hostilities will be brought about. I can assure you on this point. Certainly we shall not have to go far to find a cause for war. My army of spies scattered over Great Britain and France, as it is over North and South America as well as all the other parts of the world, will take good care of that. I have issued already secret orders that will at the proper moment accomplish what we desire.' The concluding sentence was: 'With Great Britain and France in the dust, with Russia and the United States at my mercy, I shall set a new course to the destinies of the world, a course that will ensure to Germany for all time to come the leading power among nations of the globe.'*

Fact or fiction?

There is much speculation as to the authenticity of William Le Queux's report, which was not taken seriously by the newspaper editors Le Queux initially took his report to. Mr Le Queux later went on record to say that he had handed the report to the British government for its consideration, where it remained in confidential archives for several years. Further research has shown what some might consider to be an opportunistic publication of the report in newspapers around the world, several months after the outbreak of the First World War, to coincide with the publication of Le Queux's book, *German Spies in England*. Or was the timing simply good marketing sense?

# Prologue

Kent, England. Three weeks ago.

This would be his first murder, and he hoped it would be his last. His mouth felt dry despite having just been sick. He could still feel the gastric acid burning his throat—still smell the sweet bile that now stained his clothes. He wanted nothing more than to withdraw back into the shadows where he'd been waiting for the right moment, psyching himself up. But he knew he had to do it. There was no turning back now. He put on a pair of thin gloves and pulled a grey ski mask over his head as he continued across the moonlit yard, checking to his left and right as he went. It was quiet—no one else around. The owner of the workshop-cum-warehouse he was heading for didn't even have a guard dog, which would have complicated things because he liked dogs.

There was a light on inside, just a single lamp by his reckoning. That was where his victim would be, working late for the last time. He reached the door and pulled a sleek carving knife from inside his jacket, which he'd bought from the local supermarket that afternoon. He'd thought long and hard about how he would do it, concluding that a knife would be quick and quiet and easy to obtain, even if it did mean getting closer to his victim than he wanted to.

He went around to the side of the building, heading away from the light, and began to prise the tip of his knife beneath each window frame as he passed, waiting for one to pop open. It was an old building, as old as the antiques the man inside liked to restore, for all he knew. The windows were covered in a film of dirt, their old metal frames chipped and rusty. The fourth window he came to lifted easily, and he stopped beneath it. It was time. He took a deep breath to calm his nerves as he eased it open. Then he pulled himself up and slipped inside.

He could just make out the shapes of crates and boxes in the dim moonlight, and he cursed himself for not thinking to bring a torch. *You're such an amateur,* he thought as he fought the dry cough that was rising in his throat from all the dust he'd kicked up. He stepped further in, feeling his way around the crates, looking for the door. Then he heard music, classical music that was faint and tinny, as though coming from a small radio. The sound guided him, and as his eyes adjusted, he began to make out the glow beneath the door from the room beyond.

The heady smell of polish and linseed oil hit him as he teased the door open. The man he had gone there to kill had his back to him. He was bent over an old pedestal desk twenty feet away, rubbing the surface with a cloth in smooth, even strokes that seemed to keep time with the string section that was playing on the radio. That was good. He thought it would help to mask his approach as he crept up behind the man, but after taking two steps, his nerves got the better of him, and he ran to the desk, knife in hand. He grabbed the man by the collar of his overalls and pushed him back onto the desk, quickly showing him the knife so there was no mistaking his intention.

'The notebook!' he shouted. 'Where is it?'

The man's eyes were wide with fear. 'Who are you?'

'Just tell me where the notebook is, or you're dead!'

The man shook his head only slightly at first, and then more emphatically. 'I—I don't have it.'

'Don't lie to me. I know you've got it.'

The man continued to shake his head. 'No, I swear. I thought I was close, that's all. I can't get to it.'

'Really?'

The man in the ski mask flicked the tip of his knife across the other man's jaw line, drawing blood. 'You've got one last chance to change your mind. Now, do you have it, or don't you?'

'No, but I'll find a way to get it. It's just a matter of time. Please!'

'It's too late for all that.'

The man in the ski mask drew the knife back, ready for the kill. Whether this man had the notebook or not, he knew he had to do this. But he hesitated. The knife began to shake in his hand as he fought with his conscience, one voice in his head screaming, 'Do it! Do it!' while the other promised an eternity of damnation if he did.

He hesitated too long.

The man beneath him shifted suddenly, unbalancing him. A heavy blow caught him below his left ear, and he felt the heel of the man's shoe kick into his chest, pushing him away. He staggered back, and as he put his hands out to soften his fall, he dropped the knife, and it clattered away from him, out of sight and out of reach. Before he could get to his feet again, the man he had gone there to kill now came at him with an antique short-sword, which he seemed to produce out of nowhere, the polished brass hand guard glinting in the lamplight. He cut the air with the blade, and the air whistled around it.

'Tell me who you are. How do you know about the notebook?'

The man in the ski mask gave no reply. His heart was thumping hard, and all he could think about was where his knife was. He scrabbled across the floor to where he thought it had fallen, but as he reached into the shadows to feel for it, the sword cut him off, hacking into the floorboards ahead of him. He kicked his legs to push himself away, heels slipping and sliding until he was backed up against a sideboard. Then the other man swiped the blade at him again, narrowly missing him.

'Tell me how you know!'

Unrelenting, the man swung the sword for a third time, and now it cut into the sideboard, lodging deep into the wood. The man in the ski mask grabbed the hand guard and used it to pull himself up, dislodging the blade as he rose. Their hands locked around the antique weapon, each man pulling and twisting as he fought to gain control, but the masked man knew he was the stronger of the two. He bent the other's wrist back until the man was forced to let go. Then, in the midst of his kill-or-be-killed frenzy, he shoved the man away and ran the blade clean through his chest.

# Chapter One

Quebec, Canada. Present day.

Jefferson Tayte was standing in a stiff breeze at Pointe-au-Père, Rimouski, 157 nautical miles northeast of Quebec City, on the south bank of the wide St Lawrence River. It was a Sunday, and he was visiting an exhibition at the Site historique maritime, which commemorated the centenary of the sinking of the RMS *Empress of Ireland* and—according to the Canadian Pacific Railway index he'd found online—the loss of 1,015 passengers and crew.

The man Tayte had gone to see was a local historian who also worked part-time at the centre on a voluntary basis. His name was Emile Girard. He was a thin, grey-haired man with a weathered, perennially tanned face and a gently spoken French-Canadian accent, whom Tayte thought looked several years past retirement age. He wore a thick, cable-knit jumper over his shirt despite the sunny June afternoon that had Tayte feeling hot in his shirtsleeves. Girard was proving to be very knowledgeable in his specialist field, which came as no surprise to Tayte given that Girard had already informed him that he was a descendant of one of the survivors who had sailed aboard the *Empress of Ireland* on its fateful ninety-sixth voyage to Liverpool on 28 May 1914.

'It could be said that Father Time was her ultimate enemy,' Girard continued as they crossed the quiet Rue du Phare outside the museum, ambling into the breeze towards a white and red painted lighthouse that stood close to the rocky riverbank. 'The fog on the St Lawrence River that night was undoubtedly the catalyst for the disaster, but it was the lack of time that ultimately caused the loss of so many souls. The *Empress of Ireland* sank just fourteen minutes after the Norwegian collier *Storstad* rammed into her starboard side, tearing a four-metre-wide hole in her hull that was over seven metres deep. With around sixty thousand gallons of water pouring into her every second, there was only time to launch a few of the forty-two lifeboats she carried.'

The detailed manner of Girard's account made Tayte feel as if he were on a guided tour. 'And the time of day, or night in this case, would no doubt have contributed to that.'

Tayte had done his homework before leaving DC, covering the basics. He might have talked himself out of the visit altogether, sparing himself the personal trauma of the flight, were it not for his need to prove the information he'd found. The assignment that had brought him to Rimouski concerned a woman who, according to every record he could find, had drowned one hundred years ago, and yet his client's very existence seemed evidence to the contrary. He had to be sure about his findings before going any further, and he knew from experience that visiting locations and talking to local experts such as Girard often yielded more clues than could be found on the Internet alone.

'No doubt at all,' Girard said. 'She was struck soon after one thirty on the morning after she set sail, when most of the passengers and many of the crew would have been asleep in their cabins.'

Girard stopped beside the base of the lighthouse and pointed out across the expansive river to the northeast. 'She lies four miles off land in forty metres of water. Her loss has been greatly overshadowed by that of the *Titanic* two years earlier and of the sinking of the *Lusitania* a year later, and indeed by the outbreak of the First

World War a few months after she sank, but she deserves an equal place in our memories. Including the crew, more lives were lost when the *Titianic* went down, but did you know that more *passengers* lost their lives when the *Empress of Ireland* sank than on either the *Titanic* or the *Lusitania*?'

'No, I didn't,' Tayte said, thinking that he hadn't even heard of the *Empress of Ireland* until he'd taken the assignment, which was clearly the point Girard was making. In comparative terms the disaster had been all but forgotten.

'You'll see many items at the exhibition that have been recovered from the wreck over the years,' Girard continued. 'But of course, that's not why you're here, is it?'

'No,' Tayte said again, swapping the heavy briefcase he was holding in one hand with the tan suit jacket he had in the other, to give his arm a rest. 'But I'll be sure to take everything in before I leave. As I explained on the phone, I'd like to find out what I can about one of the passengers.'

'Ah, yes. Mrs Stilwell.'

Tayte nodded. 'According to the CPR passenger list I found, the woman I believe to be my client's grandmother, Alice Maria Stilwell, was aboard the *Empress* when she sank. Her death record tells me she died on May 29th, 1914, which tallies, but the problem I have with that is that my client's mother wasn't born until 1925, eleven years after Alice Stilwell is supposed to have died.'

'I see,' Girard said. 'But what then makes you so sure that your client is descended from Alice Stilwell at all?'

Tayte's thoughts skipped back to that first meeting with his client a few weeks ago. She was a wealthy entrepreneur called Kathleen Olson, who had contacted him barely a week after he'd started running advertisements for work again, because after several months of trying to break down the latest brick wall in his own ancestry, his reserve funds had almost run dry.

'Spare no expense,' Kathleen had told him as they were leaving her offices in Downtown DC. 'Grandma Alice was a wonderful, caring woman, but I always sensed there was a sadness about her. Perhaps you can find out why, Mr Tayte.' She had stopped walking then, and she'd turned to him and squeezed his forearm. 'I want to know the truth,' she'd added, the intensity in her expression growing with every word she spoke. 'I want to know everything there is to know about Alice Stillwell.'

Returning to his conversation with Girard, Tayte said, 'My client's father, her last remaining parent, died recently. The house and belongings were left to her, and when it came to getting the place ready to sell, she came across a gold locket she recalled her grandmother always used to wear. She knew her grandmother as Alice Dixon, no middle name, and I've confirmed that's what it says on my client's mother's birth record, yet on the back of that locket there's an inscription bearing the name Alice Stilwell.'

Girard looked unconvinced. 'But it could have been bought second-hand.'

'Yes, it could have, and the fact that they shared the same given name could be pure coincidence, but it's also interesting that I've been unable to find a single record that I could positively match to this particular Alice Dixon prior to 1925. No census entries, no birth record, and no record of marriage to the man she's supposed to have been married to.'

'And so you suppose that Alice Dixon and Alice Stilwell are, or were, one and the same person? That she was harbouring a secret past?'

'Yes, I do,' Tayte said, wondering, as he had wondered many times since taking the assignment, why Alice might have felt the need to leave her past behind. 'You see, that's not all. Inside the locket there's an old photograph of two small children, and that begs the question of why anyone who bought a second-hand locket, and who was known to have always worn that locket, would carry pictures of someone else's children inside it?'

Girard smiled, exaggerating the lines on his face. 'It sounds as though you have a fascinating puzzle to solve, Mr Tayte. Let's take a look at those records, shall we? I've already prepared some information I'm sure you'll find of interest. Perhaps it will shed some light on the matter. But then again, what I have to show you might just deepen the mystery further.'

Tayte and Girard went back into the Site historique maritime building where they had first met, which was itself a monument to the *Empress of Ireland*, with its twin glass light portals shaped like funnels rising from the roof, half of the building leaning to starboard as the *Empress* had leaned after she was struck. Girard took Tayte through a bright and airy space, past the exhibition visitors and the many displays and information boards, to a room that was not open to the general public. They exchanged smiles and nods with a female member of staff as they passed her and went inside.

'Please, have a seat,' Girard said, indicating a chair by the desk that was further into the office-like room.

Tayte put his jacket over the back of the chair and sat down. His eyes followed Girard as he went to a cabinet and returned a few moments later carrying a clear plastic folder. He sat in the chair beside Tayte and set the folder down on the desk in front of them.

'I have several things to show you,' Girard said. He slid a sheet of paper closer to Tayte. 'This is from the second-class passenger list for the *Empress of Ireland*'s last voyage, confirming information you will already have seen on the Internet.'

Tayte studied the familiar record, following Girard's bony finger to Alice Stilwell's name. His eyes scanned across to the word 'lost' on the right, and then to the blank space where other entries had 'body identified' written in.

'This I think you have not seen,' Girard said, 'or I'm sure you would already have mentioned the anomaly it represents.'

He slid another record in front of Tayte. It was another extract from the passenger list, this time for first-class passengers. Tayte saw the name before Girard pointed it out.

'Henry Stilwell,' Tayte said, furrowing his brow and noting that, like Alice, he was recorded as lost, his body unrecovered.

'I thought that would interest you, Mr Tayte. I'm sure you'll be able to confirm whether Henry Stilwell was related to Alice. Maybe that will shed some light on why they were travelling in different classes.'

'It only makes me more confused,' Tayte said. 'Henry Stilwell was the name of Alice Stilwell's husband.'

Tayte's focus so far had been on Alice and her side of the family. He knew whom she was married to—and more besides—but he hadn't delved into the lives of anyone else just yet. When he'd seen Alice's name on the passenger list as the only Stilwell travelling in second class, he hadn't thought to look for other family members aboard. The lists were ordered alphabetically, showing members of the same families together, as expected. Alice had appeared to be travelling alone.

Girard looked pleased with his find. 'Of course, it cannot be ruled out that our two Stilwells may not be related at all, but it's a curious thing, don't you think?'

'Yes, I do,' Tayte said. 'It's not a common name. What are the odds of another Henry Stilwell being aboard the same voyage?'

'I would say they were very slim.'

'As would I,' Tayte agreed. 'But why would husband and wife be travelling in different classes? Why didn't they share a cabin on the same deck?'

'Who knows? Perhaps they had fallen out over something.'

'Maybe,' Tayte said, wondering at the reasons and drawing no obvious conclusion other than that this new piece of information had indeed deepened the mystery of Alice Stilwell's life, as Girard had earlier supposed it might. Both Alice and Henry were recorded as 'lost,' and that set Tayte thinking about the likelihood of neither body being found.

'Do you know how many bodies went unrecovered?'

'A great many,' Girard said. Then, as if knowing where Tayte's question was leading, he answered it for him. 'Nothing can really be drawn from the fact that neither of the Stilwells were found, Mr Tayte. Not when you consider that only around one-fifth of all those who died were identified. The statistics show that it was far more typical not to be found. Many bodies would have been carried out into the Atlantic, and many remained within the ship itself and are now buried beneath the silt on the riverbed.'

Girard slid another piece of paper towards Tayte. I don't know if this will be of any interest to you, but I thought I'd show it to you just in case. It shows which cabin Henry Stilwell was travelling in. Perhaps more importantly, it shows whom he was sharing that cabin with.

Tayte scanned the information. 'Albrecht, Mr W,' he said, noting that the man was also listed as lost. The information meant little more to him than that Henry Stilwell had shared a cabin on that voyage with another man, with whom he may or may not have been acquainted. He suspected the former and wrote the details in his notebook.

'That's about everything I managed to find for you,' Girard said. 'I hope it has been of some use.'

'I'm sure it has,' Tayte said, considering that the trip had been very useful indeed.

That Alice's husband was in all probability aboard the ship with her, and in particular that he was sharing a cabin on a different deck with a man named Albrecht, led Tayte to suspect that it was of some importance to the reason why Alice had chosen to leave her old life behind when the opportunity presented itself. But there were other facts about Alice, about her family, that he just could not get past. The children pictured in the locket were Alice Stilwell's children—of that he was certain. He had already identified the birth records of Chester and Charlotte Stilwell, who were born in Kent, England, in 1910 and 1912, respectively, the son and daughter of Alice and Henry. The thing he couldn't get past—despite his own situation—was how any mother could wilfully choose to abandon her children. What could have happened in her young life that was so terrible that she felt she had no other choice? Having been abandoned by his own mother when he was just a few months old, Tayte's need to understand the reasons made the assignment all the more personal to him.

Turning to Girard, Tayte smiled and thanked him. He stood up and collected the records together. 'Can I keep these?'

'Of course,' Girard said, rising from his seat with Tayte. 'The copies are for you.'

Tayte lifted his briefcase onto the desk and slid the records inside between his laptop and all the other information he'd gathered so far. They made for the door, and as Girard opened it, he paused.

'I wonder whether perhaps you would contact me again once your assignment is finished. I should like to know how it all turns out.'

'Sure. I'd be delighted to.'

'And do you know where your investigation will take you next?'

Tayte knew where he was going next long before he arrived in Canada. If he was to have any chance of unravelling the secret life of Alice Stilwell for his client, he had to go and talk to the family.

'I'm booked on an overnight flight to England,' he said, trying hard not to think about getting on another plane again so soon.

Losing both of his adoptive parents in a plane crash when he was a teenager had put him off flying in ways he knew he would never fully overcome, but this time the degree of anxiety he always felt whenever he thought about boarding an aeroplane was mollified by the idea of seeing Professor Jean Summer again.

Their whirlwind romance had blossomed in the wake of the murder of the man who had brought them together, and it had come to an abrupt pause as soon as Tayte read through the contents of the safety deposit box Marcus had bequeathed to him in his will. Tayte hadn't seen Jean since that day. He'd been so excited to have a lead on his own ancestry again after so long that he'd returned to Washington and gone deep into his own family history research, to the exclusion of everything and everyone else. Tayte had so much to tell her about the recent discoveries he'd made—that is, if she still wanted to see him after the way he'd treated her since he was last in England.

'I've managed to locate a few descendants of Alice's family,' he said, steering his thoughts back to the assignment at hand. 'I'm sure they're going to be a valuable source of information once I can get to speak to them.'

He thought about the calls he'd made and the messages he'd left, letting people know he was coming and why. He hoped it might ease his introduction once he arrived, and his client had let him hold on to her grandmother's locket with the photograph of the Stilwell children inside, which he thought might also help. He had a photograph of Alice Dixon, too. His client had told him it was one of only a very few early photographs she'd seen of her grandmother. It was a faded black and white postcard portrait that Tayte thought had been taken around 1930, when Alice would have been forty years old—the same age he was now. He imagined that photographs of Alice were sure to exist in England. If he could get to see one, he would be able to confirm beyond doubt that Alice Dixon and Alice Stilwell were the same person.

Emile Girard followed Tayte back out into the exhibition. 'I'll wish you a safe flight to England then, Mr Tayte, and I shall look forward to hearing from you again someday.'

Tayte thanked him and was left standing with his briefcase beside a display cabinet, looking through his dark-haired reflection at the first artefact to have been recovered from the wreck of the *Empress of Ireland* after its rediscovery in 1964: a steel double pulley that was orange with rust. He always thought it curious how such inanimate objects could form a connection to the past. He knew it was all in his head, but he felt it just the same as he stood looking at it. He wished he could touch it—feel the flaking rust beneath his fingertips. It had been a part of the ship Alice had boarded a hundred years ago. He wondered then whether she had touched it, or used any of the china or glass dishes he could see in the other cabinets. His thoughts began to drift, and he wondered again who Alice Stilwell was and why she had felt the need to escape her past life so completely as to begin it over again.

# Chapter Two

South Holland, Netherlands. Monday, 13 April 1914.

The Stilwell family was staying at the Hotel Des Indes on Lange Voorhout, a former nineteenth-century palace in the heart of The Hague. Alice shut off the basin taps in her room and watched the steam dissipate, thinking it a very modern establishment to have hot and cold running water and a bath for every room; there was even a hydraulic elevator that she had been informed worked by the pressure of water from the North Sea. Although it was rare to accompany Henry on one of his business trips, Alice had readily agreed that it would be good for the children to spend more time with their father, and Henry had been keen for Chester to see more of the textiles business he hoped his son would one day succeed him in—although as Chester was only four, Alice supposed there would be plenty of time for that. To Alice, who was still in her early twenties, time seemed as a boundless entity that spring, caught up as she was in the dream that had become her family life since meeting Henry five years ago.

She went back to the dressing table, and for the umpteenth time she readjusted the wide-brimmed hat she was wearing. She frowned at her reflection and flicked at her chestnut hair again. Maybe that was it. After all, it was not the hat that was new, but the hairstyle beneath it. At Henry's insistence, and much to her parents' disapproval, she had had her hair styled short because, according to Henry, it was the height of fashion in New York City, and if they were going to settle their lives in America, then they should make every effort to keep up with the times. Alice wasn't particularly keen on the look, but Henry had said it suited her very well, so she went along with it more to please her husband than herself. She didn't mind half as much as her hats seemed to.

'Darling!'

It was Henry, calling from the adjoining room where he'd been waiting more patiently with the children than she felt she had any right to expect of him. There was a faint knock at the door, and in the mirror Alice saw it nudge open—and there he was, standing tall in the frame, freshly shaved in his light-grey sack suit and felt Homburg. She thought he looked as dapper as ever she had seen him. He was smiling as he spoke, his soft American accent as alluring to her now as it had been the first day they met.

'Whatever's keeping you?' he said. 'If we don't leave soon, I shall be late for my meeting with Mr Van Heusen.'

Alice swung around as Chester and Charlotte followed their father into the room: Chester in the sailor's suit her own father had bought for him, and Charlotte in white lace. They were holding hands, or rather Chester was holding Charlotte's hand, having taken it upon himself to look after his younger sister because, with Henry away so often, Chester had come to see it as his duty.

'I'm afraid it's this hat,' Alice said. 'I can't decide whether it looks best with the brim tilted to the left or to the right.'

'You look lovely, Mummy,' Chester said, and Charlotte just smiled and nodded.

'Yes, I'm sure it looks wonderful either way,' Henry added, a little impatiently Alice thought. He stepped closer, grabbed her hand, and pulled her to her feet as he checked the time on his pocket watch. 'We really must be going.'

'Can we play in the park?' Chester asked.

'I'm sure we can,' Alice said, looking to Henry for confirmation.

Henry squatted until his eyes were level with the children's. 'First I thought you might like to see what keeps your father away from home so often,' he said. 'Then afterwards we can do whatever you wish.'

'Even sailing?' Chester asked, his face full of hope.

Henry laughed as he got to his feet again. 'Sailing?' He paused as though considering the idea. 'I don't see why not, as long as we go out first thing in the morning. I'm not expected in Rotterdam until the afternoon. I'm sure you'll like Rotterdam. It has the largest seaport in Europe, and you know what that means.'

'More boats!' Chester said, wide eyed.

Their rooms were on the first floor, but they rode the elevator to the lobby, more for its novelty value than convenience, because the children were fascinated by it. Alice hadn't said so, but she was glad she didn't have to take the stairs to the lobby. Henry had bought her a purple-and-cream-striped dress for the trip, and like her new hairstyle, the appropriately named 'hobble' dress was all the rage in New York. It was fitted to her knees where a purple band wrapped around them to intentionally limit movement. As the elevator attendant opened the cage for them and the Stilwell family stepped inside, Alice thought that if they had taken the stairs she would most likely have embarrassed herself by falling into the lobby rather than arriving gracefully as intended.

With the attendant's permission, Henry lifted Charlotte so she could help move the crank handle to take them down, and moments later the bell pinged and the attendant pulled the cage door open. Alice held back and watched her family go on ahead of her. She smiled to herself and silently wished they could remain together like this forever, but she knew they would only be in Holland for a few more days. After that, they would spend several more days with her parents in England, and then they would return to America. As much as she tried to accept it, she still felt so out of place and alone in New York whenever Henry was away, despite the children and having Henry's parents living close by.

She watched her children run from the elevator as soon as the way was clear, and she was pleased to see that Henry soon had a strong hold on their hands. Even so, he lurched forward with them, and Alice smiled and thought how glad she was that Henry was not as strict with their children as her own father had been with her. They were soon in the middle of the lobby, which was richly decorated with marble pillars and red stuccoed walls illuminated by soft golden lighting. Alice made no attempt to keep up. She knew it was hopeless to try in her hobble dress, and she thought it too fine a morning to rush anywhere. She would be glad of her parasol today.

When Henry and the children reached the doors, Henry looked back to Alice and smiled at her with a look that was as much to say, 'Whatever can I do?' Alice would have liked to be on Henry's arm, but she didn't mind. This trip was for the children, and she imagined there would be plenty of time for them to steal a moment or two together, perhaps in the park later, when their children could run and dance circles around them until the little darlings felt giddy. She watched the doorman hold the door open for them as they went outside, so full of life and energy that it sparked Alice into quickening her step.

Outside, she saw colourful painted buildings, and parked before them were several black motorcars in stark contrast. She wondered if one of the vehicles was for them, and then she saw Henry and the children further along the street. She followed after them and saw that another car had pulled up. It was a sizeable cream-coloured machine with bright chrome headlights, wire wheels, and whitewall tyres, which she thought was more to Henry's liking. Two men got out, and Henry and the children stopped walking. One of the men put a hand on her son's shoulder, and the gesture struck Alice as being far too forward.

'Excuse me, madam.'

The voice startled Alice, and she wheeled around. She had to catch her breath when she saw the fair-haired man who had spoken. He towered above her and would even have towered above Henry were he beside her. The man touched his cap, smiled amiably and in the Dutch accent she had heard so many times since her arrival in Holland, he simply asked, 'Do you know the way to Alexanderstraat?'

The question took Alice aback. She shook her head. 'No, I'm sorry.' She smiled politely and turned back to her family. The children were getting into the car, and now one of the men was holding Henry's arms. She started walking again, and when she saw her husband begin to struggle, concern engulfed her. She quickened her pace until she could feel the purple band at the knees of her dress tighten like a strap that bit into her skin as she tried to run. Then she saw something that forced her to stop altogether.

As Henry freed himself from the man who had tried to restrain him, the man produced a gun. Alice saw it stab into Henry's ribs. Words were exchanged, but she couldn't hear them. Then Henry turned to her without expression and climbed into the car beside their children, who were smiling, as though they had seen nothing of what had just happened.

'Henry!'

She called out to him and began to move again, but it was too late. The car pulled away, and within seconds her family was gone.

She turned back, thinking only that she must report what had happened to the police—that she must get help. But when she did so, the man who had just asked her for directions was still there, and he was still smiling, even though he, too, must have witnessed what had just happened. Now she saw his smile for what it was.

'Please, do not alarm yourself, Mrs Stilwell. Your husband and children are quite safe.'

Alice tried to pass him, but she made so little progress in that ridiculous dress that she knew any attempt to escape the man would be utterly futile. The man made no effort to stop her. His words were enough.

'If you want to see your family again, Mrs Stilwell, you will do exactly as I tell you.'

Alice froze. She turned back and stared up into his eyes. 'Who are you? What do you want with my family?' She felt close to tears, but she fought them. Her dress now seemed two sizes too small, and she found it hard to breathe.

The man stepped closer, and suddenly he was towering over her again. 'I am Raskin,' he stated. 'And it is not your family we want.'

'Then who?' Alice began, but she already saw the answer reflected in the man's eyes. 'Me?' she asked, at a loss to understand why. 'You want *me*?'

Raskin nodded, but he made no attempt to elaborate. 'You are over-excited,' he said. 'You need to lie down. Look at your hands. They are shaking.'

Alice made fists with them.

'In one hour,' Raskin continued, 'the telephone in your room will ring three times. When it does, you must go down to the hotel reception desk. There will be a letter waiting for you. Collect it and take it back to your room, and do not let anyone else see it.' He stared down at Alice until she could feel his eyes boring into her. 'If you want to see your children again, Mrs Stilwell, you will follow your instructions exactly. Do you understand?'

Alice sniffed back a tear and nodded, and with that the Dutchman turned and walked briskly away.

# Chapter Three

Kent. Present day.

'Get off my property!'

It wasn't the first time Jefferson Tayte had heard that line, but its delivery on this occasion was among the most aggressive. It made the usual trials of his flight to England seem calm by comparison. As soon as the man knew who Tayte was and why he was there, he'd deliberately made a show of rolling up his shirtsleeves, as if he was bruising for a fight. Every word he'd spoken since was punctuated by jabbing an index finger at Tayte, almost making contact several times. But Tayte wasn't giving up just yet. Right now he had very few leads, and the Metcalfe family were key to his assignment. He looked along the drive, trying to catch a glimpse of the house, but his view was blocked by the sunlit trees that lined the way, and more immediately by the man standing like an ox in front of him.

'I'd just like to speak with Reginald Metcalfe for a few minutes,' Tayte said. He began to smile, but quickly decided that a show of charm was ill-advised under the circumstances. 'I believe he's the current owner of the Hamberley estate.'

'It's *Lord* Metcalfe to you. Now piss off before I throw you off!'

The ox was called Raife Metcalfe. Tayte had managed to get that much information from him when he'd met him by the gate-house, before he'd introduced himself. Tayte thought he looked to be in his mid-thirties, and at around six feet tall he was a few inches shorter than Tayte, but heavyset and muscular. He had wavy brown hair and thick, wiry sideburns, the likes of which Tayte thought belonged in a period drama.

'Alice Stilwell was Lord Metcalfe's grandmother,' Tayte persisted. 'She was your ancestor, too.'

'Yes, that's right. *My* ancestor—and none of *your* damned business!'

'Don't you even want to know what it is about her that brought me here?'

'No, quite frankly, I don't, and neither does my grandfather. Now get off our property, or I'll set the dogs on you. I won't tell you again.'

Tayte put his hands up. 'Okay, I'm going. But give him this, will you?' He offered out a calling card, which Raife Metcalfe took and tore up and threw back in his face.

'You're not welcome. If you come around here again, I'll see you off with the lead from my shotgun.'

Ten minutes later, Tayte was in his hire car, driving through the Kent countryside towards the centre of Rochester. It was mid-afternoon and he was already beginning to feel tired from the travelling and the jet lag, so he'd put some music on and turned the volume up to help keep him going. He was listening to 'Mr Mistoffelees' from the *Cats* soundtrack he'd packed for the trip along with several other show-tune CDs, although on this occasion he didn't feel much like singing along.

As his journey progressed and the view beyond his windows changed from the green of the countryside to the grey of town, he began to wonder whether his first day in England could get any worse. The door he'd hoped would lead to many answers about Alice Stilwell had been slammed, none too delicately, in his face. Now his already tentative connection to the Scanlon side of the family through Alice's Aunt Cordelia, who, according to the 1911 census, had lived at Hamberley, looked to be heading the same way.

Tayte had no home address for the present-day Scanlon family. As soon as he'd got back into his car, he'd called the phone number of the business premises he'd previously identified as belonging to a Mr Lionel Scanlon, whom he believed was a descendant of Alice Stilwell's aunt and uncle, Cordelia and Oscar Scanlon. Receiving no answer, he'd left another message, but he wasn't holding his breath. The business was located in Rainham. It was less than ten miles away according to the car's navigation system, so that's where he was heading now. He hoped he might at least find someone he could talk to about the Scanlons. Maybe then the day would end on a brighter note.

He pulled up at a junction with the main road he needed to take towards Chatham, and the traffic became busy to the point of congestion. He sat listening to his CD and the plink-plink of the indicator until a few cars began to build up behind him. Then he saw his gap and put his foot down, pulling out and joining the flow of traffic. Somehow the car behind him managed to squeeze out, too, and Tayte made a mental note that he had to be more assertive with his driving in England if he wanted to get anywhere.

Several minutes later, as he left Chatham and the pace began to pick up again, he considered that his day had really started going wrong as soon as he'd stepped off the plane and called Jean. The surprise visit he was hoping to drop in her lap had backfired when she'd told him she was in Spain and wouldn't be back in London until the weekend, which, as it was now only Monday, seemed a long time off. Jean had told him she was attending a series of royal history seminars on the kings and queens of Spain, with someone called Nigel, whom, Tayte noted with great interest, she had mentioned more than once during their conversation. But what did he expect? If he'd called Jean more often—if he hadn't let his research take over his life like it always did—he would have known she was away this week.

Tayte had apologised to her for being so aloof in recent months, and with great enthusiasm he'd told her he was finally making progress with his own research and that although he'd hit another brick wall, he was waiting on a phone call he hoped would bring that wall tumbling down—as if any of that justified his behaviour. She had sounded genuinely pleased that he was making progress at last, but there was something in her tone throughout the conversation that told him he'd blown it. When he'd added that he hoped to go into the details with her in person when he next saw her, she had given him no reply.

'So, can I see you when you get back from Spain?' he'd asked her.

'I don't know, JT. I need some time to think. I'll call you when I get back to London.'

'When exactly is that?'

'Next Saturday afternoon.'

'And you'll call me then?'

'Yes, JT. I'll call you then. I promise.'

And they had left it there.

Tayte couldn't help going over the conversation again and again. He tried to focus on the road, but try as he did, he couldn't stop thinking about Jean and whether she wanted to see him again. And there was Nigel. Tayte hadn't been able to get that name out of his head since he'd heard it. He figured he was just a colleague—a like-minded associate whom Jean knew through her work. *That's all he is,* he told himself, but it didn't matter how many times he did so, he still couldn't help picturing the two of them together, staying in the same hotel, seeing each other every day. He sighed as he navigated a roundabout, watching for his turn, wishing he could be there in Nigel's place—not that he thought he deserved to be. He knew that now and only hoped it wasn't a lesson learned too late.

The traffic had thinned, and Tayte supposed from all the houses he could see beyond the street lamps and neatly trimmed hedges to either side of him that he was passing through a residential area. He'd become so lost in his thoughts about Jean and how he was going to win her affections back that he hadn't realised he was driving so fast. He slowed down and began to reminisce, picturing the goofy expression Jean had pulled for the photograph he'd taken of the two of them outside Buckingham Palace on his last visit. He smiled to himself, and then his smile suddenly dropped as a flash of silver coachwork shot past his side window, slamming into his front wing, knocking all thoughts of Jean Summer from his head.

Tayte's hands tightened like a pair of vices on the wheel as he tried to control the car, but the force of the other vehicle as it careened into him made it impossible. A split second later he was forced half onto the verge, wheels spinning and the car sliding out of control. He saw the other car briefly as it sped past him. The driver clearly had no intention of stopping. Then as Tayte's car fully mounted the verge and began to spin, he couldn't help but stare at the steel lamppost he knew he was about to hit.

# Chapter Four

Kent. Saturday, 18 April 1914.

Five days had passed since Alice Stilwell's objectionable encounter with the Dutchman known to her only as Raskin. She had followed his instructions, trusting and hoping that if she complied, then he would be true to his word, and her family would be safe. She still had no idea how she'd managed to compose herself enough to go down to reception that morning to collect the letter that was left for her, precisely one hour after the ordeal, as Raskin had said. She had been shaking violently and crying until the moment the telephone rang, and she was shaking again by the time she got back to her room with the letter and opened it. What she read immediately lifted her spirits, causing her to laugh and cry at the same time. Her children were to be returned to the hotel that afternoon, but as she read on she learned that her husband was not.

The letter contained little by way of an explanation as to why her husband and children had been taken from her, simply stating that she must return to England at the earliest opportunity, and once there await further instructions. It gave no clue this time as to how contact would be made, only that it would. She was to tell no one of what had happened, and to anyone who asked, she would say that her husband had to remain in the Netherlands on unexpected business. The letter also reiterated that her husband's life, and the lives of her children, depended on her full cooperation.

As Alice sat in her old bedroom at Hamberley, her parent's home near Rochester, purposefully delaying her appearance at the dinner party her father had thrown for a few friends and family, she recalled the last part of the letter again, and it sent a shiver through her. It was clear that her children, who were now safely asleep in their beds, had been taken in order to scare her, and she had little doubt that these people could get to them again if they so wished. She had, of course, asked Chester and Charlotte—almost to the point of interrogation—what had happened that day, and she had come to realise that Henry had cooperated for their sakes, because the men who had taken them had caused the children no apparent distress. To the contrary, she was surprised to receive them back so full of joy. The children had by all accounts enjoyed a grand outing, having been told that that Mummy wasn't coming with them so they could spend more time with their father.

Alice pictured the towering image of Raskin again, as he had stood in the hotel lobby, holding her children's tiny hands in his, as though having throughout the course of the day formed a bond of friendship with them. It made her feel sick just thinking about it. She wondered again who Raskin was and more importantly, whom he was working for. She had gone over their brief conversation outside the Hotel Des Indes many times since her return to England, and she distinctly recalled him using the word 'we' rather than 'I,' suggesting that he was perhaps as much a pawn in these terrible events as the men who had arrived in that cream-coloured car and more directly stolen her family.

A knock at Alice's door preceded the appearance of her mother, who had no doubt come to find out what was keeping her daughter from the dinner guests. She came into the room as full of smiles as she had been since Alice first arrived at Hamberley, and it had forced Alice to realise that her mother, who always seemed to have her best interests at heart, must have missed her and the children a great deal since they had made the decision to settle in America. Alice returned her mother's smile, but it was tainted by her thoughts and all the dark possibilities she could not block from her mind.

'Oh, dear,' her mother said. 'Don't you want to come down? Are you missing Henry? Is that it?'

*Henry . . .*

Alice could neither hear nor think his name without feeling her stomach cramp with worry. Instinctively, she clutched at the engraved picture locket she wore on a chain around her neck: a wedding gift from Henry.

'I heard you again last night,' her mother added. 'Will you at least let me call for the doctor? I'm sure he could prescribe a tonic to help you sleep.'

'No, I'm well enough,' Alice said. 'Really, I am. It's as you say— I'm missing Henry, that's all.'

'Well, come along then. Stand up and let me have a better look at you.'

Alice drew a deep breath as she rose, and then she smiled more fully as she looked at her mother properly for the first time since she had entered the room. Her hair was pinned up in a tight roll, and her dress was dark grey below the waist and white above it. She wore nothing bright or colourful, and Alice blamed her father's influence for that—not that Alice felt like wearing any of her own colourful dresses any more, but they were all she had packed.

'Your father has invited someone special along this evening,' Alice's mother said. 'Someone to see you.'

Alice could only think of one person in the world her father would invite to dinner specifically to see her.

'Archie?' she said, already knowing the answer.

Her mother nodded. 'It wasn't my idea. You know how your father is.'

Alice knew very well. Archie Ashcroft had been introduced to her before her memories began, which she supposed was on her third birthday because she could vividly remember the rocking horse her parents gave her, with its long black mane and its bright red and gold painted stand. She couldn't recall anything before that day, when she had been guided into her bedroom with her hands over her eyes. 'No peeking,' her father had said, but she had. Perhaps she was just a baby when she and Archie first met, neither having any clue as to what their parents had planned for them.

*Those were such carefree times,* she thought, and her memories made her smile. 'It's quite all right, Mother,' she said. 'I shall be glad to see him again.'

'It's been awhile, hasn't it? I don't believe you've seen him since the wedding.'

'No, I'm sure I haven't,' Alice said. 'I suppose he'll barely recognise me.'

Her mother gave a small laugh. 'Oh, I'm certain he will.'

---

Dinner was at eight, although the guests at Hamberley had all arrived by six thirty for canapés and cocktails, and Alice, who wasn't in any kind of mood for small talk was glad to have missed it. She arrived in the dining room along with the creamed chicken soup, and without looking at anyone, she followed her mother to the head of the table, where they each took a seat beside her father, Lord Charles Metcalfe.

'I'm sorry I'm late, Father,' Alice said.

'Are you? I was beginning to think you weren't coming to your own dinner party at all.'

There was more than a hint of sourness in his tone, and Alice, when she glanced at him, could see that pinched expression she knew so well, hiding beneath his beard. It told her to choose her words carefully, or better still to say nothing at all.

'Charles.'

It was her mother, speaking softly. Alice saw her pale hand land as gentle as a butterfly on her father's arm, and it seemed that all the tension drained from him. He sat back in his seat, and Alice turned away, thankfully distracted by the bowl of soup that had been set before her. She was aware that the general conversation, which had been lively when she first entered the room, had now stopped, and as she forced a smile and nodded to each of the guests in their dinner jackets and evening gowns, she saw that the reason was because everyone was already smiling back at her. The dining room, with its many old family portraits, always felt overcrowded to Alice, no matter how many guests had been invited to dinner. Tonight, though, the attention of all those eyes, which now seemed to stare at her, was close to unbearable.

'How have you been, Alice?'

Frank Saxby's silky tones drew Alice's eye, and she turned to him.

'We don't see much of you these days, do we, Bea?' Saxby continued, addressing her as he turned to his wife, Beatrice, who was sitting opposite him.

'No,' Beatrice said. 'Hardly at all since the wedding.'

'I'm very well,' Alice said, smiling politely to disguise the truth.

She knew Frank as Uncle Frank, although he was no relation— just a good friend of her father's since long before she was born. She had never directly asked, but Alice was of the impression that their friendship harked back to their school days. Saxby was a businessman who had made his money selling asbestos to the building industry, and according to her father, was someone so adept at his profession that he could sell snow to Eskimos.

At the opposite end of the table were Lord Abridge and his wife, whom Alice had only met a few times at one event or another in connection with the Admiralty. Then there was her Aunt Cordelia and her husband, Oscar Scanlon, whose poorly advised business ventures had all but left them in financial ruin, and was the reason why they had now been in residence at Hamberley going on five years—much to her father's displeasure. They had a son, Edwin, whom Alice thought as disagreeable as his father. Thankfully, he was away at university, which was something else her father's estate was paying for.

Archie was sitting immediately to Alice's right, and the years since she'd last seen him had done little to alter his appearance. He was still the same slim-figured boy she had known all her life, with tidy medium-brown hair and dimples in his cheeks whenever he smiled. She had teased him about his dimples so many times as they were growing up, but in truth she had always thought them quite a charming feature. Seeing him again brought back so many fond memories of their time growing up together that she felt her spirits lift, if only for a moment. As soon as he spoke, he seemed to inject the life back into the room as everyone continued their conversations and began the first course.

'It's awfully good to see you again, Alice. You look very well.'

'Thank you, Archie. It's good to see you, too. You haven't changed a bit.'

'Really?' He sounded disappointed. 'But surely my sideburns must have grown a little by now? You know how I've always wanted a pair.'

Alice picked up her spoon and laughed to herself as she tested the soup. There had always been laughter between them, and she welcomed it now. 'I'm sure they're very fetching.'

Missing from the gathering were Admiral Waverley and his wife. He was another close friend of Alice's father, and she couldn't imagine why they wouldn't have been invited. She thought the Admiral must have been otherwise engaged on important naval business.

'No Admiral Waverley this evening?' she asked, and the room fell silent.

Alice looked around the table at all the faces that were now staring at her as though she had just asked her father to explain something as inappropriate as how a steam turbine worked.

Her father's beard twitched several times before he spoke. 'I'm sorry, Alice. I should have told you before now.' He paused.

'Whatever is it?' Alice asked.

Her father sighed. 'Our good friend Christopher Waverley has passed on.'

Alice's face dropped. 'He died? When?'

'Barely two weeks ago.'

'But how? What happened?'

'They said it was a heart attack, although what he was doing near Tilbury Docks in the middle of the night is beyond my reckoning.'

Lord Abridge spoke then. 'He was found on the muddy riverbank between the docks and Tilbury Fort, poor fellow. It was lucky the tide didn't take him.'

'Quite,' her father said. 'Another half an hour and his body might never have been found.'

'That's terrible news,' Alice said.

'Yes, and I'm afraid that's not all of it. His wife is missing.'

'Missing?' Alice said, scrunching her brow. This was all too much to take in.

Alice's mother joined the conversation. 'Florence hasn't been seen since her husband's death,' she said. 'It's all very peculiar.'

Lord Abridge cleared his throat and said, 'There's something fishy about the whole bally business if you ask me.'

Alice's father placed a hand on hers. 'I hope you'll forgive me for not breaking the news to you sooner.'

'Of course, Father.'

Everyone continued eating again, but without speaking for a few minutes as though out of respect for their friend departed. When the silence broke, it was Lord Metcalfe, speaking to Archie.

'I should have liked your father and mother to attend this evening, Archie. But duty first, eh?'

'Of course, but His Majesty's Navy has always been my father's first mistress.'

'As well I know. And yours, too, no doubt?'

'My first and only mistress at this time, sir,' Archie said, stealing an awkward glance at Alice.

'And how are you finding things in Whitehall?'

'In all honesty, sir, I'd sooner be a fighting man again, serving aboard one of His Majesty's warships.'

Lord Metcalfe laughed. 'I admire your spirit, Archie, but you're still boxing for the Navy aren't you?'

'Yes, but it's not quite the—'

'Well then,' Lord Metcalfe cut in. 'And you shouldn't underestimate the work that goes on at the Admiralty. Battles are rarely won on the front line these days. And our defensive strategies, particularly when it comes to our homeland, are just as important as our offensive strategies.'

'Hear, hear!' Lord Abridge chipped in.

'You've a sharp mind,' Lord Metcalfe continued. 'Both your father and myself are in agreement that you are best placed to serve our great nation where you are for the time being.'

Archie smiled uncomfortably. 'Yes, of course, sir.'

'That's the stuff, lad. You'll make us all proud, I'm sure.'

The Royal Navy dominated life at Hamberley. Alice had never really minded. She supposed she had become used to it because it was all she had known, but meeting Henry had been like a breath of fresh air to her. Everything about the dashing American was so different and so welcome. She thought about him all through the rest of the main course, treading around the general conversation so as not to be drawn in. It was the not knowing that kept Alice awake at night, and which caused her to cry out in those rare moments of sleep. How was Henry being treated? Was he still in Holland, or even still alive for that matter? She had no way of knowing. Plates of food came and went with the conversations that drifted over her, as unheeded as the tick-tock of the mantle clock, until one voice caught her attention. It was Oscar Scanlon, ruddy faced and almost shouting, as though he'd made too freely with her father's claret again—which Alice had seen him do most days since her arrival.

'I heard a painting was attacked in London not so long ago. I was out of the country at the time and missed the details.'

'I read about it,' Saxby said, twisting the tip of his moustache. 'It was by one of the Old Masters.'

'Blasted suffragettes,' Alice's father added. 'That confounded Richardson woman smuggled a hatchet into the National Gallery and tried to destroy one of Velázquez's masterpieces. Quite what a three-hundred-year-old painting has to do with women's suffrage is beyond me.'

'It was the *Rokeby Venus*,' Alice said casually, still thinking more about her husband than the conversation. 'Mary Richardson told the press afterwards that she wanted to destroy the picture of the most beautiful woman in mythological history as a protest against the government for destroying Mrs Pankhurst, who, according to Richardson, is the most beautiful character in modern history.'

Alice felt the room close in around her as she finished speaking. In the ensuing silence the clock on the mantle sounded louder than ever. 'With all the rain, I've had plenty of time to go over old newspapers this week,' she added, as though she felt the need to apologise for something, no doubt because of her father's longstanding disagreement with her interest in politics and current affairs.

Her father coughed loudly into his hand. 'I've arranged to take my grandson into Chatham to see the dockyard tomorrow,' he said, changing the subject. 'Chester is old enough to appreciate a proper visit now, and there's something I want to show him. It will be good education for him.' He paused and began to pull at his beard. 'Just the two of us, you understand? I'm sure it would be of no interest to you.'

'Of course,' Alice said, knowing that it was unlikely to be of any interest to her at all. 'I'm sure Chester would like that very much.'

Saxby leaned in. 'We were sorry to hear about Henry,' he said, glancing at his wife and confirming to Alice that her father must have told everyone the story of how she and the children came to be there at Hamberley without him. A part of her was thankful because it would save her the discomfort of repeating the lie, and it would lessen the chances of her tripping herself up in the process.

'It's a shame for the children, isn't it?' Mrs Saxby added, and the other women around the table nodded their agreement.

Mention of Henry's name made Alice think of him more than ever, and she wondered how much longer it would be before she was contacted again. She was eager now for that to happen. All she wanted was to get through this and go back to normal life again; to get Henry back and remove the threat that hung over her children's head like the Grim Reaper's scythe.

Her father drained his wine glass and leaned towards Saxby. 'Personally, I think there's more to it,' he said under his breath, clearly hoping that Alice wouldn't hear him, but she did. She wanted to say so many things in response to the remark, but instead she just stared at the individual chocolate soufflé in front of her, which she had barely touched.

'Had your first proper row, have you?' her father continued, directly to Alice now. 'I always said—'

Alice's mother cut him short. 'Charles, not now. Please.' To Alice she added, 'I'm sorry, dear.'

That Alice knew Henry could never live up to her father's expectations was not news to her. She had no doubt this was why her bedroom was kept ready for her, just as she had left it, in the hope that she would fall out with Henry and return home again. Henry was new money and an American, and such a match would never do for her father. She silently wished the meal would end so she could return to her room, but her father would not be silenced on the matter.

'Well, what sort of husband lets his wife and children travel by themselves anyway? Our daughter and our grandchildren!' he added. 'And I don't know why you insist on bringing them up all by yourself. Every respectable mother has at least one nanny.'

Alice would have made her excuses and left the room there and then had Archie not spoken.

'Tell me, Lord Abridge, do you see Germany building many new Dreadnoughts this year? Or in your opinion is that now a one-horse race?'

Abridge scoffed. 'After conceding three such ships to our seven last year,' he said. 'I should think we've got the Germans entirely demoralised.'

'And we have the jump on them again this year,' Alice's father added. 'I'd say the race was as good as won.'

Both men began to laugh, and as they continued the conversation between themselves, Archie edged closer to Alice and whispered, 'Get a pair of old sea dogs talking about the naval arms race, and they won't talk about anything else for hours. Would you care for some fresh air before leaving us to our port and cigars?'

Alice sighed and returned his smile. 'Yes, I'd like that very much.'

'Good. I could do with a stretch.'

They both stood up together, momentarily pausing the conversation.

'Would you excuse us?' Archie said, addressing the room. 'Alice has kindly agreed to accompany me on the terrace for a few minutes before taking her coffee in the drawing room with the rest of you fine ladies. I'm afraid that last glass of wine has left me feeling in need of some air.'

'Of course, Archie,' Alice's father said. 'And I'm sure you two have plenty to catch up on while you're out there, eh?'

Alice caught the wink her father gave Archie, who just smiled politely as they turned and left the room.

⌣

As soon as they were outside, Alice threw her head to the stars and breathed as though it were the first breath she had taken all evening. She thought it was cold for the time of year, but she didn't mind.

'Thank you, Archie.'

'Not at all,' Archie said. 'It was the least I could do for an old friend.' He threw her a smile, accentuating his dimples. 'The truth is that I couldn't bear to see your father torture you like that. I'm sure he didn't mean to.'

'Oh, I'm sure he did.'

'Well, perhaps it was the wine. It's changed many a good man and left him aching with regret afterwards. Cigarette? Or haven't you started smoking yet?'

'No, I did try it once, but it just made me cough.'

They were laughing at the idea as they walked to the low balustrade that bordered the terrace, where shrubs that were black against the moonlight framed wide stone steps that led down to the lawns and the countryside beyond. Alice felt suddenly dizzy. She sat on the stonework, unsure whether it was from her lack of sleep and general state of mind or the sudden intake of all that fresh air.

'Are you well?' Archie asked, concern in his voice.

Alice took a slow and purposeful breath. 'I'm sure I'll be fine in a moment or two. Are you still living in Gillingham?'

Archie nodded. 'Same old place, except I've had a small part of the house to myself since Ernest left.'

'Your brother moved out?'

'Yes, he married the year before last—child on the way. He lives in Sittingbourne now.'

'You didn't have too far to travel then. How did you get here this evening?'

'I have my own motorcar now,' Archie said with pride. 'It's a Vauxhall C10—the four-litre model. I must say she's rather sporty with it, too. I only got her last year.'

Alice smiled playfully. 'Four litres,' she mimicked, as though she knew what that meant. 'You must be moving up in the world.'

Archie snorted. 'I don't know about that, but it certainly makes getting up to Town more agreeable. I'll introduce you to her before I head home. Maybe I can take you for a spin sometime?'

'I'd like that.'

Archie sat beside Alice. 'Look, I must apologise to you. I've been waiting a long time for the opportunity, and many's the day I've thought I might never have another chance. I'm sure I'd given up all hope of ever seeing you again when you left Hamberley—all my fault of course.'

'You're not the one who went off to live in America,' Alice said.

'No, but I shouldn't have left so soon after the wedding. It was rude of me and entirely unforgivable not to call on you and Henry afterwards. I just—' Archie stopped himself and turned away, looking back to the house with its tall windows glowing like sheets of silver in the moonlight.

Alice put her hand on the back of his. 'You have nothing to apologise for. If any apology is necessary between us, it should come from me, for keeping my feelings for Henry such a secret from you. It all happened so fast, despite my father. One moment Henry and I were smiling at each other across a busy restaurant, and the next we were married. At least, that's how it seems to me now. That first year passed so quickly, and then Chester was born. Our second year together went by even faster.'

Alice was about to ask Archie why he hadn't called to see them, but she realised she already knew the answer. She had always known. Her mother had said that it was the Royal Navy that had kept him away, but she knew it was really because he didn't want to see her with Henry, which she supposed was the reason he had left their wedding so soon after the ceremony. She was in no doubt that Archie had stayed away because he couldn't come to terms with their marriage and the fact that the woman who had been promised to him, albeit without her consent, now belonged to another man. It wasn't that Alice didn't love Archie, but their parents had done such a good job of bringing them together at so early an age that by the time she was old enough to consider marriage, she had come to love him more as a brother. She wondered if he still felt the same way about her and decided it was best to talk about something else.

'You must call again and meet the children,' she said, realising as soon as she had spoken that that too might be difficult for Archie.

To contradict her thoughts, Archie's face lit up. 'I'd like that very much,' he said, and Alice felt at ease again.

She showed him her picture locket, unclipping it and holding it up as he leaned closer to her. On the side that was not concealed by her fingers, it showed a small portrait of Chester and Charlotte, side by side, holding hands.

'I had the photograph made on Charlotte's first birthday,' she said. 'I'm sure you'll adore her, and I know Chester would love to talk about all the ships you've served on. Henry tries to indulge his interest in the sea, but I'm afraid his grandfather has spoilt him.'

Archie laughed. 'Few men can live up to your father's tales of life on the ocean wave,' he said, 'but I'll certainly do my best.'

Alice found herself smiling again, and she was thankful. 'You're so sweet, Archie. You always have been.'

'I don't know about that,' Archie said, giving another small laugh as though he was embarrassed by the suggestion. 'I'm sure Henry must be far sweeter. You do love him, don't you?' He rushed the words out as though he'd been waiting to do so for some time.

'Yes, of course. I love him very much.'

'And does he return your love? I mean, is he kind to you?'

Alice gave no answer. Her earlier discomfort rekindled inside her.

'And what your father said just now,' Archie continued. 'About you and Henry quarrelling . . .' He paused. 'There's no truth to it?'

Alice could not believe that Archie could be so insensitive as to save her from her father's interrogation one minute, only to continue it himself the next. But he had done just that, and the reason was clear: Archie wasn't over her marriage to Henry any more than her father was. She stood up and Archie stood with her.

'I'm sorry,' he offered. 'Always putting my foot in it, aren't I?'

But it was too late. Alice turned away and gazed into the distance, across a lawn that was like a shimmering ocean in the moonlight, the grass shifting this way and that in the breeze, like the rolling of the sea.

'I'd like to be alone now if you don't mind.'

'I'm so sorry,' Archie repeated.

Out of the corner of her eye, Alice saw him move away, heading back to the house, and a part of her felt deeply sorry for him, this man who had been promised her love and clearly could not get over its denial. She heard the door open and close again as Archie went back inside, and she sighed to herself as she walked to the steps and slowly began to descend them, wondering why they couldn't just be friends as they used to be, yet knowing now that the time for that had passed.

She sat halfway down the steps, out of sight of the lower windows of the house, and wondered whether her life was destined to ever be simple and happy again. She sank her head into her hands and closed her eyes, not wanting to go back inside, but knowing she must. When she sat up and opened her eyes again, her breath caught in her chest. Sitting cross-legged on the grass below her was a man she immediately recognised. His fair hair shone bright beneath the moon, and even sitting down he appeared as tall as some men.

It was the Dutchman, Raskin.

# Chapter Five

Present day.

Described by the press as a state-of-the-art flagship police station when it was officially opened in 2007, the North Kent and Medway Division police headquarters was located close to the River Medway, where once a busy dockyard stood. Two hours after some-one ran Tayte off the road, he was standing inside the police station in the front counter area, talking to one of the duty officers, having waited his turn for close to an hour. The officer was a heavily set, grey-haired man in his early fifties, who spoke in tones that con-veyed little emotion.

'Were you injured, sir?'

'No, but it was a close call,' Tayte said over the general hubbub that he imagined was a perennial attribute of the police station's front counter area.

'Were you able to drive your car after you came to a stop?'

'Yes, it's outside now. I was mad enough to try and give chase, but by the time I managed to get the car back onto the road, the other car was long gone.'

'Did anyone stop? Any witnesses?'

'A car pulled up to check that I was okay. The driver said he saw me sliding across the verge. I was heading for a streetlamp, but

I managed to get the car sideways, which slowed it down enough to limit the damage.'

'But the man who stopped didn't see who caused the incident?'

'No, he was too far back when it happened.'

'Can you tell me where you were going at the time of the incident?'

'I was travelling to see a Mr Lionel Scanlon at his business premises in a place called Rainham.'

Tayte was aware then that another man was standing beside the duty officer—a plainclothes detective, judging from the fitted grey suit he was wearing, which accentuated his lean physique. He didn't say anything. He just looked at Tayte and listened.

'And you say you believe it was deliberate, sir?' The duty officer continued. 'A hit-and-run?'

'Yes, I do,' Tayte said, 'and I'm pretty sure I know who it was. If you're quick, you might find the car that hit me on his premises.'

'What type of car was it, sir?'

'A silver one.'

'Make and model?'

'I don't know. It was just a regular sedan, I guess.'

'Registration?'

'No, I didn't get that either. I was too busy trying to stay alive. Look, if you send a unit over to—'

'I'm sorry to interrupt,' the other man cut in. 'You say you were on your way to see someone called Lionel Scanlon?'

Tayte sighed. 'Yes, that's correct.'

The man in the suit turned to the duty officer. 'I'll take it from here,' he said. Then to Tayte, he added, 'Would you mind coming with me, Mr . . .?'

'Tayte. Jefferson Tayte.'

In a sparsely furnished private room adjacent to the front counter area, the man who had led Tayte there closed the door behind him and introduced himself as Detective Inspector Bishop. Tayte put him in his late thirties. He was clean-shaven, with a pale, freckled complexion and short auburn hair that carried enough red as to appear slightly ginger.

'Have a seat,' Bishop said.

Tayte's eyes wandered with distraction to the crime-prevention posters on the walls, his mind busy with thoughts about the man he had been on his way to see and why the man sitting opposite him had become interested as soon as Tayte had mentioned Lionel Scanlon's name. Bishop gave Tayte a half smile as he settled into the chair opposite him.

'I'd like to ask you a few basic questions to begin with and take a few notes, if you don't mind, Mr Tayte.'

'Not at all—go right ahead.'

Bishop readied his pencil, and then he addressed Tayte again. 'Are you currently residing in the UK?'

Tayte shook his head. 'No, I live in Washington, DC.'

'Is your visit one of business or pleasure?'

'Business,' Tayte said, thinking that the latter would be a welcome change after all the trouble his various UK assignments had caused him over the years.

'And what line of business are you in?'

'I'm a genealogist.'

'Can you expand on that?'

'Sure,' Tayte said. 'Using various means and records available to me, I typically look back through time to build my clients' family history. Sometimes you're thrown a curve ball, and things don't add up, which is why I'm here in England.'

Tayte then briefly explained the enigma that was his client's grandmother, and how he was in the UK to try to prove she was really Alice Stilwell, née Metcalfe, and to find out all he could about her life before the *Empress of Ireland* sank in 1914.

'And as my first line of enquiry with the Metcalfe family failed so miserably,' Tayte continued, 'I was on my way to Mr Scanlon's business address in the hope of seeing him. I wasn't able to get an answer when I tried to call before. I guess someone didn't want me to do that.'

'So you believe someone deliberately ran your car off the road?'

'I know they did, and I believe that person was Raife Metcalfe. As soon as I told him who I was and why I was there, his behaviour became very threatening.'

'I know Raife Metcalfe,' Bishop said. 'And I know he's got a temper, but from what I gather it's all just hot air. Did he know you were on your way to Mr Scanlon's business premises? Did anyone else know?'

'No, I had no cause to say where I was heading next, and I only arrived in England this morning. The Hamberley estate is the only place I've been to in relation to my assignment, and Raife Metcalfe is the only person I've spoken to. I believe that he, or someone acting on his behalf, must have followed me after I left.'

Tayte thought about the car that had pulled out onto the busy main road behind him, not long after he'd left Hamberley. He hadn't really paid much attention to it, but on reflection he thought now that it was also a silver car—probably the same car—and the driver had seemed very keen to stay with him as he turned out onto the main road.

'It had to have been someone from the Hamberley Estate,' Tayte added. 'Who else could it have been?'

Bishop gave no answer. Instead, he came back with another question. 'What were you hoping to ask Lionel Scanlon?'

Tayte sat back and let out a sigh as he thought about it. 'I was just going to ask the usual questions for now, I guess. Like whether he'd heard of Alice Stilwell, or if he had any old photos from the time period I'm interested in. You can often make other family connections through old photos, particularly wedding photos. If he didn't know anything about Alice, I'd have tried to make another connection through him to someone else in the family who might.'

'I see,' Bishop said. 'So just routine stuff?'

Tayte nodded. 'Just routine.'

They both seemed to pause for thought then, until Tayte asked the question that had been on his mind since he'd met DI Bishop.

'Do you mind if I ask what your interest in Lionel Scanlon is?'

Bishop pressed his fingers together and rolled his head back, staring at the ceiling momentarily. When he looked down again, he said, 'Lionel Scanlon was murdered a few weeks ago, at the very premises you were travelling to.'

'Murdered? What happened?'

'I'm afraid I'm not at liberty to discuss the details.'

'No, of course not,' Tayte said, thinking it little wonder he'd received no answer when he tried to contact Mr Scanlon, and understanding now why his calls hadn't been returned. 'Do you think there might be a connection between the murder and my assignment?'

'Who knows at this point?' Bishop said. 'But when a man is murdered, and a few weeks later there's a hit-and-run against someone trying to visit that man, you've got to question the odds, haven't you?'

Tayte agreed. 'Although, if someone wanted to stop me from seeing Mr Scanlon, surely that person can't have known he was dead.'

'That's a good observation, Mr Tayte. So, assuming for now that your traffic incident wasn't random, whoever was driving the other car either wanted to stop you from visiting Scanlon's premises, or simply wanted to stop you, period. Do you get that much in your line of work?'

Tayte thought back over some of his more adventurous assignments. 'It certainly wouldn't be the first time,' he said. 'Folks don't always appreciate me digging up the past.'

'Do you know why anyone might want to stop you on this occasion?'

Tayte thought about it. Then he shook his head. 'No, not yet. My best guess is that it has something to do with the reason Alice Stilwell felt she had to abandon her old life and start over, but with all my contacts dried up, I'm a long way from knowing why anyone would want to stop me from finding out.'

Thinking about past assignments gave Tayte an idea. He wasn't convinced it was a good idea, but he now had so little to go on with his current assignment that he thought it was worth a shot. 'If there's any chance there could be a connection between my assignment and Mr Scanlon's murder, maybe I can help.'

Bishop didn't say as much, but Tayte could see from his slightly amused expression that he was sceptical. 'It wouldn't be the first time I've assisted the British authorities with a murder investigation,' Tayte added. 'I can give you references from your Devon and Cornwall police, and from the Metropolitan Police in London.'

Bishop's expression changed at hearing that. He began tapping his pencil on his notepad, as if he was now giving the proposal consideration. A moment later, he said, 'And how exactly do you believe you can help?'

Tayte didn't need to think about that. He would do what he always did. 'I'll keep digging,' he said. 'Someone's already tried to stop me. If there is a connection and I keep going, my own experience tells me that sooner or later we'll find out what that connection is. Then maybe you'll find your killer.'

Bishop sat back and drew a long breath, his eyes fixed on Tayte's. 'We do employ specialists for all kinds of reasons,' he said, thoughtfully.

'I'd keep out of your way,' Tayte added. 'Most of the time I'd just be getting along with my research.' Now that the idea had taken hold of him, Tayte was all the more keen to gain Bishop's approval. He knew their collaboration could open doors—doors which were currently closed to him.

Bishop sat forward on his elbows. 'Okay, why not?' he said. 'It's uncertain whether there's a connection between Mr Scanlon's murder and your hit-and-run incident this afternoon, and in all truth I'm not entirely convinced that your assignment really can help solve my case, but I'm prepared to keep an open mind for now. I'd like to see where your research leads.'

'Great,' Tayte said. 'Can you help with the people I need to see? Can you get the Metcalfe family to talk to me?'

'I can't make anyone talk to you, Mr Tayte, least of all a family like the Metcalfes. But yes, we can go and see them. Anyway, I didn't have them in mind just yet. I was thinking about Mrs Scanlon, the deceased's wife. I'm sure she'd be only too happy to talk to you if she thought it could help to find her husband's killer.' He paused and flashed his eyebrows at Tayte. 'If you do, you might even earn a little extra on the side for your trouble. Mrs Scanlon's offered a reward for information leading to a conviction. I'll call to see whether it's okay to pop round for a chat. She might not be up to it, of course.'

'No,' Tayte said, thinking that it hadn't been long since she'd buried her husband.

Tayte's naturally inquisitive nature got the better of him then, and he asked Bishop about the case details again. This time the chief inspector was both open and very matter-of-fact with his answer.

'At face value it looks like a random burglary attempt gone wrong. A chancer trying his luck finds an unsecured window. He enters the premises to see if there's anything worth stealing, but instead he finds Mr Scanlon, working late.'

'Do you have any suspects?' If so, Tayte thought it would be good to ask them what they were doing earlier that afternoon when his hire car was run off the road.

'None,' Bishop said, nipping that idea in the bud. 'Human vomit was found outside the premises, but we've been unable to match the DNA with anyone on our records. A supermarket-branded kitchen knife was found at the scene, but there were no prints on it, so it's unlikely to have belonged to Mr Scanlon. I suspect the killer was carrying it, although it wasn't the murder weapon.'

'What was?'

'An antique sword. Mrs Scanlon identified it as her husband's, stating that he kept it at his workshop for protection because he often worked late—much good that did him.'

'Was anything stolen?'

If there was a connection between Lionel Scanlon's murder and Tayte's desire to speak to him, then past experience told him that the perpetrator of the crime was usually looking for something.

'Nothing that we're aware of. Mrs Scanlon runs the business side of things, working to source antiques for private clients most of the time. She says she keeps a tight inventory and that everything's accounted for.'

Bishop stood up. 'Do you mind waiting in the front counter area? Or I can meet you outside if you'd prefer. I've just got a couple of things to do—shouldn't take a minute. Then hopefully we can go and see Mrs Scanlon.'

Tayte got up as Bishop went for the door. 'You don't think it would be better to go to Hamberley and talk to Raife Metcalfe first? The car that hit me might be on the premises. You can check for damage—match the paint marks. Tomorrow could be too late.'

'Believe me, Mr Tayte. Even if Raife Metcalfe was behind your accident this afternoon, we wouldn't find the other vehicle at Hamberley. He's not the kind of man to make an error like that. I'd like to ascertain why you were run off the road in the first place.'

Davina Scanlon lived in a detached house near Foxburrow Wood, just a few miles southwest from the workshop where her husband had been murdered. She met Tayte and DI Bishop at the front door, and she had opened it before either of them had the chance to knock. Her sombre smile as she greeted them reminded Tayte that more than a modicum of sensitivity and tact was required. Talking about a past ancestor was one thing; a past husband whose grave had barely settled was entirely another.

'Good evening, Mrs Scanlon,' Bishop said as they were invited in. 'I hope we're not putting you out. This is the gentleman I spoke to you about on the phone.'

Tayte offered his hand. 'I'm pleased to meet you, Mrs Scanlon. I'm Jefferson Tayte.'

'Yes, the genealogist. I'm intrigued to know how your profession relates to my husband's murder.'

Bishop answered. 'I think at this stage we all are, Mrs Scanlon. That's if it's related at all.'

'Yes, of course,' Mrs Scanlon said, 'and please call me Davina.'

She was a well-spoken, attractive woman, with short blonde hair, classic high cheekbones, and a slender frame. Tayte thought she looked about his age, or more likely she was a little older but was aging better. She looked settled in for the night, in jeans and a long jumper that hugged her figure, and she wore little to no makeup, which was another plus to Tayte's mind. Overtly beautiful women had always made him feel uncomfortable for some reason, and Davina Scanlon was no exception.

She led them into the sitting room, which was a modern space with exposed wooden flooring and a leather three-piece suite, plain walls adorned with colourful abstract paintings, and here and there an item of antique furniture that threw the environment into contrast. They sat around a glass coffee table, and Davina curled her legs up beside her. A glass of red wine sat on the occasional table at her elbow. She picked it up and swirled the wine.

'Can I offer either of you a glass?'

Tayte would have loved a strong black coffee, but he got the idea that it was wine or nothing.

'No, thank you,' both men said together.

Davina sipped her wine and held on to it. She looked across at Tayte, studying him momentarily. 'So, what did you want to talk to Lionel about?'

Tayte realised that he was still on the edge of his seat, briefcase between his legs. He put it to one side and settled back. 'I wanted to ask whether he knew anything about a past relative called Alice Stilwell. Your husband's great-grandfather was Alice's uncle by marriage to a woman called Cordelia Metcalfe.'

Tayte went on to explain again the curious situation that had brought him to England, wondering as he did so this time what it was about Alice Stilwell's life—and perhaps more importantly, her apparent death—that someone today seemed keen to leave buried in the past. He concluded with his account at the gates of Hamberley earlier that day, where Raife Metcalfe had so vehemently turned him away.

'Ah, Raife Metcalfe,' Davina said. She stared into her wine as though the mention of his name had distracted her. Her next words made it apparent to Tayte that it had. 'I was with Raife and his wife the night Lionel was murdered.' She looked up. 'They've gone all Palladian and wanted Lionel and me to source some pieces for them—for Hamberley. Early Georgian and Chippendale from the middle period, Hepplewhite from the latter. Lionel should have been with us that night. If he had—' Davina paused and looked away, raising the back of her hand to her eye as if to catch a tear. 'Excuse me.'

'Please take your time,' Bishop said. 'If it's too difficult, just say so. We can come back another time.'

'No, it's all right. I want to talk about it—want to help if I can. You just keep going over the alternative scenarios, don't you? 'What if' this and 'if only' that. But nothing changes. If only Lionel had got along with Raife like he used to. That's why he didn't want to go with me that night—why he wanted me to handle everything.'

'Do you know why they didn't get along?' Bishop asked. Clearly the suggestion that a level of enmity existed between the two men was news to the detective.

Davina shook her head. 'No, and it's too late to ask Lionel now, of course. You'll have to see what Raife has to say about it.'

'I will,' Bishop said, casting a glance at Tayte.

Having met Raife Metcalfe once was enough for Tayte to want to avoid sharing a dinner table with him. He pulled the conversation back to the reason he was there.

'I discovered from the 1911 census for England and Wales that your husband's great-grandfather, Oscar Scanlon, was living at Hamberley at the time.'

'Yes, I know.'

'You know?' Tayte hadn't expected that. For Davina to know where her husband's great-grandparents lived a hundred years ago indicated a special interest. Tayte thought it also showed great promise, and he wondered whether Davina might know something about Alice Stilwell. He found himself smiling as he asked her how she knew Oscar Scanlon was living at Hamberley.

'Family history used to be something of a hobby,' Davina said, 'although I've not dabbled for a few years now.'

'In your research, did you come across Alice Stilwell née Metcalfe?'

'Yes, of course. Her time wasn't so long ago, was it.'

'No, barely beyond living memory.'

Tayte pulled his briefcase up onto his knees and opened it. From inside he withdrew an envelope, and from inside that he produced the gold picture locket his client had let him hold on to. He held it up by the chain and watched it spin for a moment as it drew everyone's attention. Then he opened it and passed it to Davina.

'One side's empty, as you can see,' he said. 'The picture on the other side shows who I believe are Alice's children, Chester and Charlotte.'

Tayte watched as Davina studied the locket. She turned it over and read the inscription.

'True love will hold on to those whom it has held.'

Tayte thought he heard Davina sigh as she read it, and he imagined the words had rekindled thoughts of her husband. He hadn't thought about whether such a sentiment might upset her, but now that she'd read it, he hoped she might take comfort from it.

'It's a lovely phrase,' she said as she handed the locket back.

'Yes, it is,' Tayte agreed. 'I looked it up. It's from a love poem by a Roman philosopher called Lucius Annaeus Seneca.'

'Do you mind?' Bishop said, holding out his hand for a closer look. 'Great words can really stand the test of time, can't they?'

Tayte passed it to him. Then he handed Davina a photograph. 'This is my client's grandmother, Alice Dixon. Do you have any photos of Alice Stilwell I could compare it with?'

Davina took the photograph and gazed at it for a few seconds. 'I do have some old photographs somewhere, but I doubt there are any of Alice.'

'Do you recall ever seeing any? Maybe you recognise her from a picture you might have seen somewhere? At Hamberley perhaps?'

'At Hamberley?'

Tayte thought she almost laughed at the notion.

'No,' she added. 'I'm sorry.'

Tayte took the photograph and the locket back and put them away again. 'I should like to see those old photographs you mentioned. Your research, too, if that's okay.'

'Yes, of course, but I can't think where it all is at the moment. You'll have to come back once I've had time to look. Tomorrow afternoon should be okay.'

'That's great,' Tayte said. He thought Davina could prove to be a mine of information about Alice and her family, and he wanted to keep the line of communication going now that DI Bishop had opened the door. He reached inside his jacket and handed Davina a business card. 'My cell number's right there in case you want to call me in the meantime. I'm staying locally at the Holiday Inn.'

Bishop stood up. 'Well, thanks for seeing us, Mrs Scanlon.'

Tayte rose after him, but he didn't want to leave things there. He was hopeful that tomorrow afternoon would prove to be very fruitful, but tomorrow seemed too long to wait with nothing new to go on, and from the way Davina had reacted when he'd asked whether she'd seen any photographs of Alice at Hamberley, he sensed she had some idea as to why Raife Metcalfe had reacted the way he had towards him.

'Before we go,' he said. 'Do you have any idea why I received such a cold reception at Hamberley when I went there earlier? Specifically, when I asked about Alice Stilwell?'

Davina drew a deep breath and slowly let it go again. 'Yes, I'm sure I do. If there's any truth to what I once heard about Alice Stilwell, I expect Raife Metcalfe thought he had a very good reason to turn you away.'

# Chapter Six

Sunday, 19 April 1914.

After her unexpected encounter with the Dutchman the previous night, before returning to the dinner party, Alice Stilwell had rushed to her children to make sure they were still safe in their beds. After Raskin's bold appearance at her family home, she fully believed that whoever was holding her husband hostage could get to her children again wherever they were. The encounter had also made it imperative that she change her mind about accompanying her son on his day out to the dockyard. Chester had been pleased that she wanted to go—her father had not. At first he would hear none of it.

'But you've never shown any genuine interest,' he'd said, 'and besides, I no longer consider the dockyard to be a place for girls.'

The exchange had made it clear to Alice that her father still could not, or stubbornly would not, regard her as the woman she had become since leaving Hamberley, so in reply Alice had stamped her motherly right on the matter.

'If my son is to go at all, I really must insist on accompanying him,' she had said, and there was nothing Admiral Lord Charles Metcalfe, for all his authority, could say about it. If he wanted to take Chester to the dockyard, Alice was going with them.

It was mid-morning by the time they arrived, and the fog that had greeted Alice from her bedroom window when she first rose was still present. It made the day feel colder than it might otherwise have been, and given the lack of any discernible breeze, Alice supposed it would linger. She pulled the astrakhan collar on her overcoat closer to her neck as they walked, Chester holding his grandfather's hand while she trailed a pace or two behind with a young naval officer who had been assigned to them for the duration of their visit.

Alice thought him no more than Archie's age, and thinking about Archie again made her wonder how he was today. He hadn't remained long at Hamberley after dinner, declining a glass of brandy in the smoking room and making what Alice thought was far too hasty a departure. After the words that had passed between them on the terrace, he had clearly felt too embarrassed to stay, and Alice was sorry that there had been no chance to mend things between them. If there had been, she would have said that none of it mattered; that they were good friends and always would be. She supposed that however Archie felt today, he would have felt better if she'd had the chance to tell him that.

'The dockyard is quite old,' the young officer said, interrupting her thoughts.

Alice hadn't caught his name because she wasn't really paying attention when they'd first arrived. Her nerves had got the better of her as soon as they had passed through the main gates.

'It was established as a royal dockyard by Queen Elizabeth I in 1567,' the officer continued.

Alice already knew most of the dockyard's history. She was no stranger to the place, and her father had been thorough with her education. But that was when she was a child. Now her father would repeat that education with Chester, the son Alice knew her father had always hoped for. She watched Chester's little boots switch back and forth, wishing she had insisted he wear a coat over his sailor's suit, yet understanding that he wanted to show it off in a place such as this.

As they continued, Alice tried to take the dockyard in through the veil of fog, but all she could discern were the dockworkers coming and going in their dark work suits and flat caps, and the indistinct shapes of those buildings that were once familiar to her: the huts and other structures where she knew a great many more people were busy earning their wage. Now and then she could see the disembodied heads of the dockside cranes as they came and went with the shifting fog.

Beyond the dry docks to their left, which were alive with activity, they passed an impressive block of structures that ran out to the edge of the River Medway. She heard her father then, who had been pointing out anything of interest to Chester, telling him now that they were the covered slips, No. 3 slip to No. 7, and that they were built in the days of sail to protect the wooden ships from the elements while they were being built.

'The ship I thought you'd like to see, my boy, is just ahead,' he said. 'HMS *Calliope*. She's too big for the covered slips.'

'Where is she?' Chester asked, peering into the fog. Then after a few more steps, his question was answered: No. 8 slip began to emerge, causing everyone to gaze skyward as first the support beams that loomed above the construction came into view, and then the ship itself.

Lord Metcalfe nodded and smiled to himself as though the sight of a Royal Navy ship being built from the keel up would never cease to impress him. He stopped walking and turned to Chester. 'There she is, lad. It won't be long now before the hull's complete. What do you make of her?'

'She's very big.'

'Big for Chatham these days,' Lord Metcalfe agreed. 'Her displacement will be nearly four thousand tons by the time she's in the water, but she's no more than a light cruiser.'

'When are they going to launch her?' Chester asked.

'Not for several months yet, and of course she'll have to be fitted out before she's commissioned.' Alice's father turned to her now and continued to address them both. 'Her keel was only laid down in January. It's incredible what can be achieved in just a couple of months and round-the-clock shifts—even on a Sunday. In the House of Commons recently, I heard our First Lord of the Admiralty, the estimable Mr Churchill, say that there are currently around thirteen thousand workers employed in the Royal Dockyards.'

Alice just smiled, feigning interest so as not to dampen her father's enthusiasm, but now that they had reached their intended destination, her thoughts were focused on how she was going to get away and go about her business. For the first time she began to question whether she could really bring herself to do what the Dutchman had asked of her. But given the stakes, how could she not?

Chester was still staring up at the side of the ship, clearly as impressed as his grandfather hoped he would be. 'Are there any battleships?'

'No, lad, and more's the pity. But that's progress for you. They outgrew Chatham several years ago. The Medway is too shallow and too difficult for the new Dreadnoughts to navigate.'

When Alice's father moved on again, still holding Chester's hand as they went, Alice deliberately slowed down. 'I suppose you've been in the Royal Navy since you were old enough to join up,' she asked the young naval officer.

Her sudden interest seemed to take him aback. He smiled keenly. 'Yes, I was fifteen,' he said. 'Family tradition, I suppose. I don't think I had much choice in the matter, other than running away from home.'

'Have you ever dreamed of doing something else?'

The officer drew a thoughtful breath. 'No, I can't say I have. The Navy treats me well enough.'

'And what do you do when you're not escorting admirals and their daughters around the dockyard?' Alice asked, but she didn't wait for an answer. 'Don't tell me. Let me guess.' A moment later, she added, 'I know. You must be in charge of the whole dockyard, is that it?'

'You flatter me.'

'Well, maybe you're only passing through, and you're really the captain of a submarine.'

The young officer laughed at the idea. 'Now you're getting carried away. Besides, I'm too tall. I'd be forever bashing my head.'

Alice laughed with him. Then she asked the question she'd been steering him towards answering. 'I suppose submarines are being built here now?'

'Yes, indeed, and Chatham is well up to the task. New submarines have been coming out of No. 7 slip since *C17* was laid down in 1907.'

At hearing that, Alice quickened her pace, and they soon caught up with her father and Chester again.

'She'll have a top speed of twenty-eight and a half knots,' her father said, continuing to further Chester's education of the C class light cruiser that was to be HMS *Calliope*.

At that point, Alice tripped over a rusty length of chain and fell onto her side. Both the young officer and her father were beside her at once.

'Are you hurt?' the officer asked.

'Get up with you,' Alice's father said, showing no concern and very little patience.

Together, they helped Alice to stand again, but when she put her weight on her left foot, she winced. 'I think I might have sprained my ankle.'

She put her foot down again, and this time she winced more loudly and started to hop on her other foot.

'Blast it!' her father said. 'I told you, you shouldn't have come. Didn't I say that?'

'Yes, Father. I'm sorry.'

'It's too late for apologies now. You'll have to go and get it looked at.' He addressed the young officer. 'Fetch some help, and have my daughter taken to the medical hut.'

'I'm sure I can manage to take her there by myself, sir,' the officer said a little too eagerly.

'You'll do what you were instructed to do and remain here with my grandson and me,' Lord Metcalfe said. To Alice he added, 'We'll collect you when we're ready to leave. And for Heaven's sake, look where you're going in future.'

———

Alice did not have to wait more than a few minutes for the young officer to return with help, which came in the form of a nurse and her orderly.

'Be a good little sailor for your grandfather,' she told Chester.

Then she limped away, keeping up the pretence until she was lost to the fog, which although persistent was gradually beginning to lift. They passed the Mast Pond on their left, where once the wooden masts and spars were seasoned in salt water to prevent the resin from setting and making the wood brittle. Ahead and to her right, she could see pale sunlight on the roofs of the covered slips, reflecting in the many windows that were designed to flood the interiors with daylight to work by.

'We'll soon have that ankle seen to,' the nurse said as they went. 'If it's anything more than a sprain, we'll have to run you to the hospital for an X-ray.'

When they drew level with No. 7 slip, which was the largest and rightmost of the five covered slips when looking towards the River

Medway, Alice tried to take measure of the activity. This was where the young officer had said they built their submarines. She knew she would have to find a way to get inside unnoticed, and once there remain undetected if she was to go ahead with her plan. She could see that the area was busy with dockworkers, and once again she questioned her resolve to do what she had really gone there to do. She waited until they had passed the covered slips before making her move. Then gradually she began to limp less until she was walking normally again.

'Do you know, I think my ankle is much better now,' she said to the nurse. 'The pain's almost completely gone.'

She stood unaided and took a few light steps before walking more briskly back to the nurse again.

'There,' she added, smiling. 'It was nothing.'

'It should be looked at,' the nurse said. 'And you should at least rest it until your father comes to collect you.'

The nurse seemed insistent, but bringing up two small children whose father was often absent had taught Alice how to be insistent herself.

'I'm sure it's fine, really,' she said, a little more haughtily than she meant to. Then she started hopping on her supposedly injured ankle as if to prove it. 'You see, it really was nothing.'

'Well, I don't—' the nurse began, but Alice cut in.

'Thank you kindly for you assistance,' she said, stepping away. 'I can find my own way back.'

With that, Alice turned on her heel and headed back the way she had come, hoping that the nurse and her orderly would leave it at that, and wishing the fog would thicken around her again and make her disappear all the more quickly from sight.

Now that she was alone, Alice felt the urge to run as far from the dockyard as her legs could carry her. She became suddenly aware of her heartbeat for the first time that day, and of a dryness in her throat for which she imagined there was no other cure than to remove herself from the situation in which she now found herself. She had stopped adjacent to No. 7 slip, with its high, metal-trussed roof and wrought-iron framework, and was now staring at the opening, where the coming and going of dockworkers and the clamour of activity from within appeared to be ceaseless. Her head was spinning with doubt as to whether she could go on, and it caused her to question whether she could even get the information Raskin had asked for. Was she really going to carry out the Dutchman's instructions—or at least try to—and spy on her own country? To continue was certain madness. She knew her life would be forfeit if she was caught, but to abandon her task without trying carried unthinkable consequences.

She was under no misconception as to whom she would be spying for. If the newspapers and general gossip were to be believed, then Raskin was in the pay of Kaiser Wilhelm II, and she, an admiral's daughter, had been unwillingly recruited as a 'fixed post,' as Raskin had called it, to give up British naval secrets to Germany—or else put her family's lives in danger. Surely, it was too much to expect any mother to choose between her family and her country? Or, as it now seemed to Alice, that was precisely why they had chosen her. She concluded that for now, at least, she would have to go on.

As she continued to watch the activity, she knew she would have to time her entry well. Then once inside, it would be darker, with only the light from the openings and the windows, which, although plentiful, could not light the entire covered area. Surely there would be shadows where she could conceal herself, and she thought her dark overcoat would help. So with a dry a throat and clammy palms, she made to continue, but when she tried to move off again, she found her legs unwilling to carry her another step.

'Everything all right, miss?'

The voice startled Alice, and she turned sharply to see a bearded man carrying a heavy-looking coil of rope across his chest.

'Y-yes,' she said, stammering a little. She coughed into her hand. 'I'm perfectly fine.' She offered a smile and felt the tremor in her lips as she did so. 'I was just trying to get my bearings in this fog. I'm looking for my father, Admiral Metcalfe. He's showing my son how a light cruiser is built.'

'That would be the *Calliope*, miss. No. 8 slip.' The man pointed ahead in the direction Alice had been walking. 'I'd be happy to take you there if you'd care to follow me.'

Alice drew a quick breath. 'No, no, that's quite all right. I can manage, thank you. I wouldn't want to keep you from your duties.'

'Very well, miss.' The man pointed again. 'Just keep going in that direction. You'll soon see the *Calliope* once you get closer.'

'Thank you,' Alice said again, and then she moved off at a pace, not changing her course until she felt certain the man could no longer see her.

There were several smaller buildings and sheds before the river to her left, which were next to No. 7 slip. Alice made for them, hoping they would offer her cover and a place to rest briefly while she calmed her nerves. She could feel her legs shaking as she went, and she supposed that was largely because she knew that from this point on, she would be committed to her task and would have to avoid contact with anyone. She would not be able to offer the same excuse as to why she was there again.

Making her way alongside one of the huts, Alice thought it would be better if she blended in better. Her hair being dark and short was a good start, and it was easy enough to smudge the powder from her cheeks, but her hat would easily give her away, so she removed it and ruffled her hair. Once behind the hut, she set her hat down and took off her coat, which was plain on the inside, so she turned it inside out to hide the collar. There was nothing she could do about her ankle boots, but they were black with a low heel and were only just visible beneath the hem of her coat. She didn't think anyone would notice them.

There was an annexe on the side of No. 7 slip. Alice took three deep breaths while watching to make sure the way was clear, and then she crossed the open ground towards it, keeping her head down as she made her way alongside the corrugated steel walls, heading for the opening. When she peered around the corner, she had to pull herself back again as three men came out. She turned towards the river as they passed, keeping her back to them with one eye over her shoulder. Once they had gone, she looked again, and this time she kept going, passing several stacks of crates and boxes. The opening was no more than a few feet away now, and every step she took towards it made her heart thump harder.

Another man, in that same style of dull, sagging suit jacket that everyone seemed to be wearing, came out of the slip as two other men approached the entrance. All Alice could think to do was to busy herself with the boxes beside her. She turned away and stooped as if to pick one up. Then rising again, on legs that felt too weak to stand on, she followed the two men inside, staying close enough so as to appear to be with them and praying that neither man turned around to see the fear in her eyes.

Inside the slip, it seemed brighter to Alice than it had looked from the outside. The lifting fog was rapidly giving way to sunlight, which came in bright beams across the windows high in the walls and the roof, and to Alice it was as if a searchlight were periodically passing over the building, seeking her out. She knew she would have to hurry. It wouldn't be long before the fog lifted altogether, and then there would be few shadows within which to hide.

She saw a rack of coats and hats against the wall just inside the slip. As she passed it, she grabbed a cloth cap to complete her disguise, thinking she would have to return it again on her way out, if indeed a way out was open to her by then. She imagined herself being caught and having to explain herself to the police, or worse still, to her father. She knew he would never forgive her for spying on the country he loved so much, and she would not blame him. How could she ever forgive herself?

Whether she failed or succeeded, the possible consequences of her actions all seemed to hit her at once, and her breath caught in her chest. She rushed to the nearest of the wide, H-section support columns that ran all around the slipway and leaned her back against it. Her senses were so heightened that she could smell the sweet tang of the ironwork in the air, mingled with the heady odour of the mud banks and the river, which, with hardly any breeze, lingered inside the slip, adding to Alice's nausea.

Knowing she would soon draw attention to herself if she did not move again, she went further in. There were two submarines under construction: dark iron hulks lying before her in varying states of build, effectively dividing the slipway in two. She had to remind herself what Raskin had said: *Experimental submarine, HMS F1*. He wanted to know her dimensions and propulsion, her speed and armament. Even if she truly did want to obtain this information for the Dutchman, it seemed an impossible task to Alice now she was here. What did she know about submarines? She had only shown interest in the dockyard as a child to please her father, and there were no submarines being built at Chatham then. Neither had she shown any interest in her father's collection of books about such things.

She shook her head, keeping to the shadows as best she could, turning away whenever anyone came within ten feet of her, which was often. There were iron stairways on either side of the slipway, which provided access to the gantry cranes. Looking up, Alice could see there was less activity above her, so she waited until she had a clear path to the nearest stairway and then walked out towards it. She hoped that from above she'd have a better view of the submarines and of the layout of the slip, so as to have a better idea of where she might go to find out what she needed to know. The steps clanked with her every footfall, and several times she thought she would get her heel stuck. Then it would all be over—and how she wished it were!

Halfway up, her attention was drawn to a man wheeling a barrow into the slip. At first it was the squeaking wheel that made her stop and look, and then immediately below her she heard the man who was pushing it speak.

'Where do you want it?'

The man he had asked had a clipboard in his hands. Alice saw him turn a few pages before pointing in the direction of the river.

'That's for *E13*,' he said. He shook his head. 'Should have been here first thing this morning.'

'I just do as I'm told,' the man with the wheelbarrow said, and then he went on his way, and the squeaking started up again.

*E13*, Alice thought, knowing now that the designation belonged to the submarine closest to the water. The submarine she was there to find out about, the *F1*, had to be the submarine that was right in front of her.

'Don't stand around gawping!'

The voice startled Alice. Someone was descending the steps behind her, but she did not turn to see who it was. She dropped to her knees and pretended that she had paused briefly to tie her bootlace. She kept her head down, her face turned away from the approaching man's gaze.

'Well, jump to it, lad! Quick about it!'

As the man passed her, Alice crouched lower and gave a nod, but she couldn't move. Fear had locked her to the spot, and it took all of her strength and will to stand again and continue up the stairway, which she did very slowly and deliberately, knowing now that she could not go on. She was not cut out to be a spy, and her heart was certainly not in it. She heard the man continue on his way again, clanking down the iron steps at a jaunt, and she knew she would soon have to turn around and follow after him. How could she hope to get the information the Dutchman wanted? And even if she could, would her conscience really allow her to hand it over and betray her country?

As she contemplated her options, it occurred to Alice that it surely didn't matter what she told Raskin. Her father's many books could give her all the information she required to make her report at least seem believable. Raskin would be satisfied that she had done as asked, and her family would be safe. She could be seen to cooperate, yet in reality she would simply feed the Dutchman misinformation, and he would be none the wiser, or why else would he task her to do what he and his associates could not?

Alice turned back and began to descend the stairway. By the time she reached the last step, her pace had quickened, and she ran to the opening, pausing only to return the hat she had taken. She no longer sought the shadows or cared whether anyone saw her. If she kept going, she would be outside again before anyone had the chance to question her. Her focus was now on her father and on getting back to the medical hut, so she could intercept him on his way to collect her. As she ran back around the side of the slip, to the huts and sheds where she had left her own hat, her thoughts were only of her children and how much she wanted to see them again, to hold them in her arms and know they were safe.

# Chapter Seven

Present day.

Fresh from his early morning shower, Jefferson Tayte stood in front of the full-length mirror in his hotel room, sucked his stomach in and tried again. *Better,* he thought, but he could hardly walk around like a puffed-out pigeon all day. He relaxed and everything sagged back to reality, telling him that despite all the jogging he'd pushed himself through back home in Lincoln Park, he was still an overweight forty-year-old with no hope of looking fit before he saw Jean again.

'Must be heavy boned,' he told his reflection. 'That's all it is.'

He'd even managed to cut back on the Hershey's chocolate miniatures he was so fond of—not that he'd stopped buying them. He'd just eaten less, stashing the remainders of the packets out of sight to the point where he'd managed to fill two whole bags solely with his favourite, Mr Goodbar, one bag of which he'd brought with him. He'd intended to 'break seal only in case of emergency' but that idea hadn't lasted beyond the flight over.

He looked at himself again. 'Anyway,' he said to his reflection. 'You feel better on the inside, don't you?'

His reflection nodded back.

'Well, then, that's what matters. And Jean's too nice a person to worry about all that.'

His eyes fell to his star-spangled boxer shorts, and as he thought of home, he wondered where that really was. Certainly not here at the Holiday Inn, although he thought it might as well be. What was home to him anyway but another four walls somewhere else?

*Home is where the heart is,* he reminded himself.

He hadn't really given that phrase much thought before now, but if it was true, then right now he figured home was in Spain— or wherever else Jean Summer happened to be. He wanted to call her, to let her know how he still felt about her, despite how distant and uncaring he knew he must have seemed to her of late, but he resisted the urge. She'd told him she needed time to think. She'd said she would call him when she was back in London on Saturday. He had to respect her wishes and wait until then. He felt himself begin to sink at the idea of Jean not wanting to see him again, and he tried to shut those thoughts out.

*It's going to be okay, JT,* he told himself. *It has to be okay.*

He turned his thoughts back to his assignment and Alice Stilwell, recalling the few words Davina Scanlon had imparted before he'd left her house the night before. Was there any truth to the rumour? Had Alice really been involved in spying against her own country before the First World War? *No smoke without fire,* he thought, but he suspected there had to be more to it. He took a clean shirt from the wardrobe, carefully chose which of his almost identical tan suits to wear, and dressed: white shirt, tan suit, and loafers. He'd never felt the need to complicate his wardrobe with anything else. To Tayte, it was something simple in an otherwise complicated world, and that was just the way he liked it.

He was meeting DI Bishop in a few hours. They were going to Hamberley, and if he was honest with himself, he was nervous about the visit given that he knew he was not welcome. In light of this new, if as yet unfounded, information about Alice, he could understand why Raife Metcalfe didn't want to talk to him. Such families have often gone to great lengths to protect their good name and the family honour. If Alice was a traitor to her country and a disgrace to her family, such a prestigious family might well take steps to guard their family secret. And yet, he wondered what damage such a revelation could really cause today, a hundred years on. He thought there had to be more to that, too. Someone had run him off the road. Clearly it had been a warning. Or had they tried to kill him? If they had, and if Lionel Scanlon's murder was in some way connected, then surely there was no justification in the name of family honour after all this time for such extreme measures.

Tayte finished dressing and took his laptop out. There was enough time for a little research before meeting Bishop, and his interest in spying in Britain before the First World War had been well and truly ignited. One way or another, it seemed highly likely to have played a part in the reason why Alice felt she had to abandon her old life and start again. He booted the machine up and fixed himself a coffee while he waited for his laptop to settle down. Then he sat at the desk and googled 'spying in Britain pre-WWI.'

The first result was a link to The National Archives, concerning espionage. He followed it and read how the mounting threat of war with Germany during the pre-war years created a degree of paranoia in Britain, fuelled as it was by journalistic fantasy and such books as *The Riddle of the Sands* by Erskine Childers and several works by journalist and diplomat William Le Queux. The truth of it, he discovered as he read on, was that only ten arrests for spying had been made before the war by the Secret Service Bureau—as the British Secret Intelligence Service was then known—although twenty-one bona fide German spies were arrested on the day Britain declared war on Germany.

He went back to his search. Second on the list was a review of a book entitled *Spies of the Kaiser* by Thomas Boghardt, a historian at the International Spy Museum in Tayte's home city of Washington, DC.

He read about German naval spying, which seemed to be the focus of Germany's naval intelligence agency before the war. He read plenty more about the 'spy fever' that had gripped Britain at the time, before turning to the third search result on the list.

This interested Tayte greatly because, although it concerned itself more with the period after the outbreak of the First World War, it was about the lives of those individuals who were caught and executed under the High Treason Act. There were almost a dozen names on the list. Tayte scanned them briefly and then he clicked the first entry, opening another page of information about the arrest, trial and execution of a German called Carl Lody, the first spy to be executed during the First World War and the first person to be executed in the Tower of London in 150 years.

Tayte read through the account, becoming more and more absorbed. Letters had been intercepted, and Lody had been found guilty of 'passing information useful to an enemy' to an address in Berlin. When later asked about his mission to gather information for Germany, he had said that it would hopefully save his country, but probably not him. Tayte also read that he had said he was an unwilling agent but that he had his orders to carry out. Tayte moved on to the verdict and sentence, and he read how Lody had been shot by a firing squad at the Tower's miniature rifle range: a single volley from members of the Third Battalion of Grenadier Guards. Going back to the index of names, Tayte eagerly clicked another, this time at random, and he began to read through the account of a Swede called Ernst Melin.

Then his phone rang. It was over on the bedside table between the photograph he had of his birth mother and a picture he'd taken of Jean. He got up to answer the call, noting the time as he went. He thought it was too early for a social call—and who called him socially anyway?

*Jean . . .*

Tayte sprinted the last few feet and picked up the call without looking to see who it was, in case the delay might cause her to hang up.

'Jean!'

The call was silent for a few seconds.

'Mr Tayte? Is that you?'

Tayte recognised the voice immediately. It was Davina Scanlon.

'Mrs Scanlon. Sorry—I thought you were someone else.'

'You must call me Davina, remember?'

'Yes, of course—Davina. How can I help you?'

Tayte thought he heard Davina laugh to herself.

'And there I was thinking I was helping you, Mr Tayte. Do you mind if I call you by your first name, too?'

'Not at all. It's Jefferson, but I prefer JT.'

'Very well then, JT. You're probably wondering why I'm calling you so early. It's just to let you know where to find me later because I'm moving out of my house.'

'Moving out?'

'Yes, I've had a night prowler, and it's unnerved me. I've worked myself up into thinking that whoever killed Lionel wanted something from him, and now they're coming after me. It's ridiculous, I'm sure, but you now how it is once the idea's been planted. I've got an apartment at Gillingham Marina that few people know about. I thought I'd stay there for a while, and I just wanted to give you the address.'

Tayte went back to the desk and wrote the details down on the hotel notepad.

'Did you report the prowler to the police?'

'Of course, but what can they can do? It's not as if a crime has been committed—not yet anyway. I just don't want to be there when whoever it was comes back.'

'No,' Tayte said. 'It's good thinking. So when—'

'Come over whenever you like,' Davina cut in. 'I'm going to the marina now, and I don't have any plans. I managed to find all my family history paraphernalia, and I have one photograph in particular I'm sure you'll find interesting.'

'That's great.'

'Yes, fortunately I went on the hunt for everything soon after you left yesterday. It was no bother.'

'I'm looking forward to seeing it all,' Tayte said. 'I should be able to get there soon after lunch.'

The call went silent for a few seconds.

'Look, why don't you come and have lunch with me?' Davina said. 'There's a restaurant at the marina. We can get to know each other better before we start on the research.'

Tayte found himself nodding without saying anything, as though he were reticent to commit.

'Fabulous,' Davina said, clearly taking his silence as confirmation. 'I'll see you later then.'

The call ended, and Tayte went back to his laptop, already feeling uncomfortable, as he always did, at the idea of having to engage in small talk over lunch with someone he'd only just met. The fact that Davina was such an attractive woman just made him feel more uneasy, and a big part of him felt guilty about having lunch with another woman while he was in a relationship, albeit distant, with someone else. A moment later he laughed at himself. *It's just a business lunch,* he thought. *People have to eat.* He closed his laptop and put it back in his briefcase, deciding to worry about the small talk later. Right now he wanted breakfast. Changing time zones had given him an appetite the likes of which he could no longer ignore.

# Chapter Eight

It was mid-morning and the sun was already high over the River Medway as DI Bishop drove up to the gates of Hamberley in his unmarked black Audi saloon. Tayte was sitting beside him in the passenger seat. His briefcase was in his lap, and he was already glad of the air conditioning; with a hazy sky and no discernible breeze, it promised to be a hot day. Bishop, who had called ahead to arrange the visit with the elderly Lord Reginald Metcalfe, lowered his window, reached out to the intercom, and pressed the call button, glancing up at the security camera as he did so. A couple of seconds later, the gates eased open with a metallic squeal, and Tayte wished he felt more welcome. This wasn't at all how he liked to go about his business, but given that he knew so many answers must lie beyond these gates, and especially because someone had potentially tried to kill him the day before, he was glad to have any opportunity to talk to this particular family.

'I shouldn't expect too much from our visit this morning, Mr Tayte,' Bishop said as the car headed along the drive, which was flanked by tall poplar trees.

'Sure,' Tayte said. He figured that any information the Metcalfes could give him about Alice Stilwell would be a bonus after the reception Raife Metcalfe had given him.

'I've a few lines of enquiry to follow,' Bishop added. 'I'll introduce you, and when it's appropriate, I'll give you a nod, and you can ask a few questions. Other than that, you'd best leave the talking to me.'

'You won't know I'm there,' Tayte said, and Bishop turned to him and eyed him up and down in his bright tan suit, as if to suggest there was no way anyone could miss him.

When they came in sight of Hamberley, Tayte drew a deep breath and held on to it for several seconds, thinking that the late nineteenth-century mansion was very stately indeed. It was bathed in sunlight, which was reflected in the many stone-mullioned windows that formed a shimmering matrix three rows high by at least a dozen across.

'How the other half live, eh?' Bishop said.

Tayte nodded and wondered how many of the current Metcalfe family members lived in such a vast dwelling. 'Do you know much about the family?'

'The Medway area's been my patch long enough to learn a little about most of them over the years. They've always given their support to the community, I'll say that much for them.'

'Do you know who else lives here, apart from the current Lord Metcalfe and his grandson Raife?'

'Not as many people as you'd think,' Bishop said. 'Lord Metcalfe lives here with his second wife, Vivienne, and their son Alastair. He's a good few years younger than Raife, and there's plenty of rivalry between the two of them. It's no secret that Alastair is likely to inherit the estate, if not the titles, when the current Lord Metcalfe dies, and I'm sure Raife's none too keen on becoming a penniless lord. The first Lady Metcalfe died some years ago, as did her son Robert—Raife's father. He was a naval man, as most of the Medway Metcalfes have been, although not Raife.'

'Why's that?'

'Who can say? Maybe it was because he lost his father during the Falklands War. Raife would have been a young boy then. I can see how that might have influenced his decision not to follow in his father's footsteps. Or perhaps it was his mother's influence. Maybe losing her husband to the Royal Navy was enough. Either way, Lord Metcalfe doesn't seem to hold a very high opinion of his grandson because he didn't "man up and join up," as it were.'

'So, what does Raife do?'

'He manages the estate with his wife, Miranda, and that's about it, as far as I know. Mind you, I'm sure it's a full-time job, not that any of the family needs to work. There's a lot of money tied up in all this.' Bishop waved a hand in front of him, indicating the house they were now almost upon. 'Raife and his wife must do well enough out of it. I suppose that's one of the perks of managing the place. Their two boys are both away at university, last I heard. Raife's mother lives locally, but not at Hamberley.'

Bishop turned the car around a stone fountain, where four oversized verdigris fish were spouting water back into the pond from which they appeared to have leaped. Tayte thought the inspector was about to stop the car, but the roar of an engine to the right of the house drew their attention, and Bishop kept going.

'Sounds like someone's in one of the garages,' he said. 'Might be a good opportunity to take a look. Although, as I've said, I wouldn't expect to find the car we're looking for here.'

They approached a block of garages that had been sympathetically built to blend in with the architecture of the house, and then the sound came again. It was a deep, rough sound, rising and falling in pitch as if someone was revving an engine.

'That motor's not firing on all cylinders,' Tayte said.

'Something of a mechanic as well as a genealogist, are you, Mr Tayte?'

'I'm more of an enthusiast really. I've picked up a thing or two keeping my old '55 T-bird on the road. I guess if you spend enough time around old cars like that, you develop an ear for what sounds right.'

As Bishop pulled the car up alongside the garages, the revving suddenly stopped, and a man Tayte recognised stepped out into the sunlight. It was Raife Metcalfe in blue overalls. He was holding a rag, which he was wiping his hands on as he came out to meet them.

Bishop began to open his door, but he paused and turned to Tayte. 'As I said, Mr Tayte—let me do the talking.'

'Don't worry—he's all yours,' Tayte said as he followed the detective out.

'Good morning, Mr Metcalfe,' Bishop said.

Metcalfe nodded back. 'Morning, Inspector,' he said, making it clear to Tayte that the two men knew one another enough to need no further introduction. 'What brings you to Hamberley?' he added, eying Tayte with a narrowing of his eyes and more than a hint of displeasure.

'We have an appointment to see your grandfather this morning,' Bishop said, 'but I'm glad to find you home. I'd like to speak to you as well, if you can spare a few minutes.'

'What's *he* doing here?' Metcalfe said, flicking his nose towards Tayte, his sour expression deepening into one of blatant disdain.

'Mr Tayte is assisting me with a murder investigation.'

'Is he now?' Metcalfe said. 'Well, well. Fancy that.'

'I'd appreciate your cooperation,' Bishop said before the other man could protest. 'It shouldn't take long.'

Tayte set his briefcase down beside the Audi and stepped closer, smiling slightly, as if to suggest there was no ill feeling on his part. He peered into the garages, looking for the car that had run him off the road the day before. He saw several expensive-looking cars, and the only silver vehicle in the garage was a two-seater Mercedes that was too low and altogether too sleek and sporty to be mistaken for the car that had hit him. His eyes were quickly drawn to the vehicle Raife Metcalfe was working on. Its bonnet was up, engine idling roughly, as if it might cut out any minute. Tayte recognised it as an Aston Martin DB4, forerunner to the car Ian Fleming had given to his character James Bond in *Goldfinger*.

'Hobby, is it?' Bishop asked, indicating the Aston.

'More like a challenge,' Metcalfe said. 'It's something I've always fancied having a go at. She's never run well, and I've become too bloody-minded about fixing her up myself to call a mechanic in.'

'I hear that,' Tayte said, gravitating towards the open engine bay and the gleam of polished Racing Green coachwork. 'I'm the same with my old motor. It's like you can't let it beat you—man versus machine.' He looked in at the straight-six engine as it rocked back and forth on its mounts. 'Very nice,' he said. 'Is it the GT model or the Vantage?'

'Both,' Raife said. 'And it's rare and quite valuable, so don't touch anything.'

Bishop pulled Metcalfe's attention back to his enquiry. He indicated the silver Mercedes, and Tayte discreetly shook his head. 'Is that the only silver car you or your family own, Mr Metcalfe?'

'The Merc? Yes, it belongs to Alastair—my grandfather's son by his second marriage. Don't ask me what relation he is to me. I'm still trying to work it out.'

'He's your step-uncle,' Tayte called from beneath the Aston's bonnet.

'Yes, well, the Merc belongs to him. Nice birthday present it was, too, not that he shows much gratitude.'

'And are these the only garages at Hamberley?' Bishop asked.

Raife smirked. 'Not enough horsepower here for you, Inspector?'

'No, it's not that. I just wondered if there were any other cars on the estate, or perhaps they're not all here just now. I see one of the bays is empty.'

'This is the only garage block at Hamberley,' Metcalfe said. 'That's the Landrover's space. It's in regular use, so it's rarely there. My groundskeeper's out on the estate with it now. Why are you interested in our cars?'

'It's just a routine enquiry, Mr Metcalfe. Mr Tayte here was run of the road after he left Hamberley yesterday.'

Metcalfe laughed to himself. 'Just routine, eh? You think I had something to do with it because I didn't want to talk to the man about my family history?'

Tayte heard 'the man' and felt as if Raife Metcalfe had forgotten he was there, despite still having his head buried in the Aston's engine bay. He was studying the ignition and timing components. He picked up a rag and reached in and pulled one of the high-tension leads from the spark plug it was attached to. The idling engine maintained the same rough beat.

'I think everything and I think nothing,' Bishop said. 'As I just told you, it's just a routine enquiry for now. Primarily, I came here to talk to your grandfather about your family history because there's a chance it might be connected in some way with the murder of Lionel Scanlon three weeks ago. I wanted to talk to you because I've heard that you and Mr Scanlon had recently fallen out over something. Can you tell me what that was?'

'I don't know what you're talking about. Who said we'd fallen out?'

'Mrs Scanlon, with whom you and your wife were at dinner the night her husband was murdered. She said she believed this falling out was the reason Lionel was in his workshop that night, rather than out having dinner with the rest of you. She said you'd asked them to source some antique furniture for you and that Lionel didn't want to go along because of you.'

Raife Metcalfe turned away. 'Well, I can't think why Lionel would have said that. If he had a reason, he didn't share it with me. Families don't always get along, do they?'

'No, they certainly don't,' Bishop agreed. 'I just wanted to ascertain whether the two of you had argued about anything specific recently.'

'No,' Metcalfe said. 'Maybe he just didn't like me.'

Tayte scoffed to himself. *I really can't think why.* He pulled another high tension lead, and this time the engine note became rougher still, letting him know that this cylinder had been firing okay. He quickly reattached that lead in place of the first one he'd pulled, and the engine returned to its former uneven idle.

'Well, thanks for your time,' Bishop said. 'Is it okay to leave the car here while we go in to see Lord Metcalfe?'

'Yes, of course.'

'Mr Tayte,' Bishop called, and Tayte came back out into the sunlight.

As he passed Raife Metcalfe, whose scowling eyes were on him again as soon as he turned away from the Aston, he handed him the high tension cable he'd removed and said, 'You've got a bad plug wire. I'd get a whole new set if I were you, and it's probably worth replacing the timing belt, too.'

Tayte felt the cable tear from his hand as Raife snatched it from him. The man's features began to twist, and Tayte thought he was about to say something unpleasant, when Bishop called to him again, this time with more urgency.

'Mr Tayte!'

Tayte turned on his heel and collected his briefcase. He quickened his step to catch up with Bishop, and they made their way towards the house.

Tayte and DI Bishop were met at the entrance to Hamberley by a thin woman in a black dress, who introduced herself to them as Mrs Tenby, the housekeeper.

'I've been wondering what was keeping you,' she said as she led them across a white marble floor to the main staircase. 'Lord Metcalfe doesn't like to be kept waiting.'

She spoke quickly in a precise manner and with such an air of superiority that Tayte felt as if they were being told off, but he figured her attitude and general lack of emotion was just part of the job.

'Please remove your shoes,' Tenby said, and Tayte slipped his loafers off while Bishop untied his laces. Then they began to climb the stairs. 'When you meet Lord Metcalfe,' Tenby continued, 'you'll have to speak up. His Lordship's hearing is not what it was.'

Tenby led them to the upper landing, where she indicated a small settee. 'Wait here,' she said. 'I'll let Her Ladyship know you've arrived.' Then she left along a poorly lit corridor, her black dress quickly fading into the shadows.

'I wouldn't like to get on the wrong side of her,' Tayte whispered as he sat back and took in the austere surroundings: the oak panelling and the twinkling chandeliers, the period furniture and the myriad family portraits of people whom Tayte supposed were past generations of the Metcalfe family. His eyes flitted from one painting to another as he wondered whether Alice's image was among them—although, given what he'd heard about her, he very much doubted it.

'Did you buy the answer Raife Metcalfe gave you about Lionel Scanlon?' he asked Bishop.

Bishop drew a long and thoughtful breath. 'It's possible that Mr Scanlon just didn't like the man, of course, but I suspect there's more to it. Either way, I'm afraid Mr Scanlon's reasons for disliking Raife Metcalfe might have died along with him.'

'Are you going to make any further enquiries into the car that hit me?'

'Not here. You saw for yourself the kind of vehicles this family runs. When you came into the police station yesterday, you said you thought it was just a regular sedan—a saloon as we call them. I'm not ruling anyone here out, but it would have been foolish to go after you so soon after being turned off the estate. I'd certainly credit Raife Metcalfe with more sense than that.'

'He didn't have sense enough to check the plug wires on that old Aston.'

Bishop just shook his head and smiled. Then something drew his attention, and he stood up. Instinctively, Tayte stood with him, turning as he rose to see a tall, dark-haired woman in a lime-green knee-length dress and a beige bolero cardigan. She was approaching along the corridor opposite that by which the housekeeper had previously left.

'I'm Lady Vivienne Metcalfe,' the woman said. 'Welcome to Hamberley.'

'Detective Inspector Bishop, your Ladyship.'

Bishop offered his hand, but Lady Metcalfe declined to shake it.

'Please don't think it rude of me,' she said, 'but my husband is in ill health, and as I care for him full time now, I try to remain as germ free as possible. I'm sure you understand.'

'Of course,' Bishop said. He turned to Tayte. 'This is Mr Tayte.'

'I'm pleased to meet you, ma'am.'

'Likewise, I'm sure.'

'Mr Tayte's a genealogist, your Ladyship. He's assisting with my investigation in a specialist capacity.'

Tayte had done his research on most of the immediate family, and he already knew that Lady Vivienne Metcalfe was the younger woman Lord Reginald Metcalfe had married after his first wife died. She was fifty-seven years old to her husband's eighty, and it came as no surprise to Tayte to hear that Lord Metcalfe's wife was now also his nurse.

Lady Metcalfe led them back along the corridor she had arrived by. 'I hear you're conducting a murder investigation, Inspector. It all sounds very exciting, but I'm intrigued to know how my husband might be able to help.'

'As am I at this stage,' Bishop said as they walked.

Lady Metcalfe stopped before a door on their left and opened it, instantly flooding the corridor with sunlight. 'Please, go in,' she said. 'My husband isn't exactly bedridden, but he prefers to stay in his room most days now.'

Tayte followed DI Bishop into the room, and Lady Metcalfe closed the door behind them. Lord Metcalfe was sitting in a wing chair by one of several tall mullioned widows that looked out over the grounds to the back of the house. He was wrapped in a blue velvet dressing gown, reading a book, which he lowered into his lap as his visitors stepped further into what had evidently been made up into a small sitting room. Tayte supposed it was annexed to the master bedroom and bathroom via the doors he could see leading off to his right. It was a warm room, despite most of the windows being open.

'The policeman I told you about is here to see you, dear,' Lady Metcalfe said, speaking louder for her husband's benefit.

Lord Metcalfe sat up and changed his reading glasses for another pair that were on the table beside him. 'Only too happy to help the police,' he said with a throaty, almost gargling voice.

Tayte doubted Lord Metcalfe would feel the same way when he learned that Tayte was there to ask him about his ancestor, Alice Stilwell.

Lady Metcalfe leaned in and straightened the blanket that was covering her husband's legs. Then she combed a hand through his wispy white hair to straighten that, too.

'That's my Vivienne,' Lord Metcalfe said. 'Always fussing over me, aren't you, dear?' He smiled, and then he began to cough. He waved a bony, arthritic finger towards the settee opposite him as he tried to recover himself. 'Well, don't make the rest of the place look untidy,' he said. 'Sit down, sit down.'

'Would either of you gentlemen like something to drink?' Lady Metcalfe asked. 'Tea or coffee? Or perhaps something cold?'

'Tea would be great, thank you,' Bishop said.

'Black coffee for me, please,' Tayte said as he sat beside Bishop on the settee.

Lady Metcalfe went to the table beside her husband's chair and picked up an electronic tablet device, into which she began entering what Tayte supposed was the drinks order.

'This was our son's idea of bringing Hamberley into the twenty-first century,' Lady Metcalfe said. 'Alastair calls it the modern equivalent of the bell pull. I just type or dictate a message into any of these devices around the house, or even into my mobile phone, and the housekeeper picks it up straightaway.' She finished tapping the screen and set the tablet down again. 'Oh, to be twenty-two again,' she added. 'Young people pick it all up so much faster.'

'Is Alastair at home?' Bishop asked.

'No, he set off for Wales yesterday afternoon. He's training for the three-peaks challenge.'

'I still can't work the bloody thing,' Lord Metcalfe added, as he seemed to catch up with the previous line of conversation.

Lady Metcalfe smiled at him and sat down. 'The drinks won't be long,' she said. 'Now, tell us all about your murder investigation, Inspector, and how my husband might be able to help.'

Bishop sat forward as he addressed Lord Metcalfe, and in a loud, clear voice he explained who Tayte was and why they were there, connecting the murder of Lionel Scanlon three weeks ago to the possible attempt on Tayte's life after he left Hamberley less than twenty-four hours ago.

'Mr Tayte was on his way to see Mr Scanlon when the incident occurred,' Bishop said. 'At least, he was hoping to see him. The common factor between the hit-and-run and Mr Scanlon's murder could well be linked to Mr Tayte's assignment.'

Lady Metcalfe eyed Tayte questioningly. 'What exactly is your assignment, Mr Tayte?'

Tayte popped his briefcase open and pulled some papers out, which he set on his lap. He didn't want to talk about Alice right away. He'd learned that lesson with Raife the day before. This time he proceeded with more caution, although he knew it was always going to come down to Alice, her being the subject of his assignment.

He began at the beginning and told them all about his client back home in DC, and about the mysterious life of her grandmother, keeping Alice's name out of it for now. He went on to talk about his visit to Quebec before coming to England, turning to his interest in the ship that sailed from Quebec on 28 May 1914 and sank several hours later with a loss of 1,015 lives.

'So many,' Lady Metcalfe exclaimed. She sounded genuinely shocked. 'I had no idea.'

'Relatively few people do,' Tayte said. 'The tragedy of the *Empress of Ireland* was overshadowed by the outbreak of the Great War and the loss of the *Titanic* and the *Lusitania* around that time.'

He glanced at Lord Metcalfe, whose pinkish eyes were already on him. He seemed either not to register the great loss of life or was unmoved by it. Or perhaps, as Tayte suspected, the statistics came as less of a surprise to him because he already knew them.

'I'm particularly interested in this period of your ancestry,' Tayte said. 'Specifically 1914, just prior to the outbreak of the Great War.'

He handed Lord Metcalfe a postcard he'd picked up at the Empress of Ireland Museum in Rimouski. It was a reproduction of the postcards that would have been in circulation in 1907, showing the ship as it had looked then, with the words 'Hands across the sea' written above the image of two hands joined in greeting. Lord Metcalfe took it and looked at it all too briefly before handing it back. Then he turned away and looked out of the window.

'Your father, Chester,' Tayte continued, addressing Lord Metcalfe directly, 'was just a young boy when the *Empress of Ireland* sank. His mother, your paternal grandmother, died that year, having been aboard the *Empress* on its fateful last voyage—or so it seemed at the time.'

Tayte could see that Lady Metcalfe was becoming more and more interested, whereas Lord Metcalfe was growing more uncomfortable.

'What I'm trying to confirm initially is whether my client's grandmother and your grandmother were one and the same person. With your help, Lord Metcalfe, I believe I'll be able to do that. If they are, it means you have family in America you've previously known nothing about.'

Tayte was smiling as he finished speaking, but he could see that the pleasure he always felt whenever he delivered a line like that was not shared by Lord Metcalfe. As Tayte came to the question of Alice Stilwell more specifically, he knew the signs were bad, but he didn't have anywhere else to take the conversation, so he took the locket out of his pocket, opened it and showed Lord Metcalfe the small image inside, hoping that seeing a picture of his father as a young boy would at least bring a hint of warmth to his face.

'This locket was in the possession of my client's grandmother when she died. The young boy in the picture is your father, Chester.'

Lord Metcalfe took the locket, and Tayte noticed his hand was shaking. He changed his glasses and studied the image more closely, but his expression remained unchanged, giving nothing away.

'Is the locket at all familiar to you?' Tayte asked. 'Maybe you've seen it in a family photograph or a portrait painting of your grandmother, Alice.' He kept his eyes on Lord Metcalfe, trying to read the situation as best he could as he picked up the photograph he had of his client's grandmother from the papers on his lap. He offered it to Lord Metcalfe, breaking the spell the locket seemed to have over him. 'Is this woman your paternal grandmother, Alice Maria Stilwell née Metcalfe?'

Lord Metcalfe's eyes drifted very slowly towards Alice's image. He dropped the locket when he saw it, and in that moment Tayte knew he was right—Alice Stilwell and his client's grandmother had to be one and the same person.

Lord Metcalfe began coughing again, until he was bent double in his chair. When he sat up, he was red-faced, and as he spoke, his words were seething. 'Do not mention that name here!'

'I'm sorry,' Tayte offered. 'I didn't mean to upset you. It's just that—'

Lord Metcalfe's head began to shake from the anger that was clearly building inside him. 'She's a traitor best forgotten!' he yelled, and then he started coughing again.

Lady Metcalfe was already on her feet, and judging by the anxious and confused expression on her face, she was clearly more surprised by her husband's outburst than Tayte was.

'Reginald?' she said as she picked up the locket and handed it back to Tayte. 'Whatever's the matter?'

Lord Metcalfe didn't seem to hear her; at least if he did, he gave no indication as he fought to control his coughing. Once he'd sufficiently composed himself, he fixed his eyes on Tayte. 'Alice Stilwell drowned in 1914,' he said, as if he would accept no other possibility. 'To my mind, as to my father's, it was the best thing that could have happened to her!'

'Reginald!' Lady Metcalfe said.

Bishop stood up. 'I think it's time we were on our way, Mr Tayte.' He turned to Lord and Lady Metcalfe. 'My sincere apologies to you both.'

As Tayte and Bishop left the room, passing the housekeeper who was on her way in with a tray of hot drinks, Tayte's thoughts were fixed on what Lord Metcalfe had just said: *To my mind, as to my father's . . .* It was unsettling to Tayte to think that Alice's son, Chester, had come to think of his mother in that way, and he could only conclude that the young Chester had been turned against his mother so completely because of what had happened that the blackening of Alice's name had lasted to the present day.

Heading in silence down the staircase, trying to keep up with Bishop, Tayte thought it was easy to see where Raife Metcalfe got his attitude from when it came to talking about Alice Stilwell. Whatever course her life had taken in 1914, in the eyes of her loyal and patriotic family she had become a black sheep and had been branded a traitor because of what she had done.

Tayte began to wonder at the circumstances that had steered Alice's life onto such a damning course, and he considered again why a young woman such as Alice would spy against her own country, especially being an admiral's daughter. He thought then that the reason might have been because of who her father was. Thinking back to his earlier research on spying in Britain before the First World War, he recalled how Carl Lody had said in one of his letters that he had been an unwilling agent. As he and Bishop left the house and made for the car, Tayte wondered whether it had been the same for Alice. Had she also been an unwilling agent of the kaiser? If so, he thought that someone must have had a strong hold over her back in 1914.

# Chapter Nine

Monday, 20 April 1914.

It was a bright day, if still rather cool for the time of year. Alice Stilwell had spent most of the morning and a good part of the early afternoon out on the estate at Hamberley, trying to distract herself with the box of watercolour paints she'd found in her room. She had long forgotten about the mahogany box she was once so fond of, but which was now just another relic from her childhood that her father had so painstakingly preserved for her inevitable return, as he saw it. She hadn't picked up a paintbrush since Henry and the children came into her life, and she thought her lack of practice showed, but at least it had helped to take her mind off her plight for a few hours.

As she walked the gravel path back to the house, beside the long and narrow ornamental pond in which she and Archie had raced a great many paper boats over the years, she recalled that she had been quite good with a paintbrush once. Or maybe she'd just imagined she was, because although there were many paintings in the forty-eight rooms at Hamberley, she could not recall ever seeing any of her own beyond the walls of her bedroom.

Completed in 1889, Hamberley had been commissioned by Alice's father so that, rather than growing up in London, she would grow up in the clean air of the countryside, along with all the other children he had hoped for, but who were never to be. Alice had always thought the house a grand gesture on his part, but she also knew now that it was because he had wanted to have a residence closer to his beloved Chatham.

Three days had passed since Alice's ordeal at the dockyard, and the Dutchman known to her as Raskin had come to her for his report the very next day, allowing her little time to prepare. But Alice had been ready. After spending time with her children, she had retired to Hamberley's great library under the pretence of having found a new interest in geography, as Henry's business forced him to travel abroad so often. The family atlas in the library was too vast a tome to take to her room, so her father had had it laid out on the reading desk for her. It had made access to her father's naval books all the more easy, and she had spent hours looking through them, eventually coming to a wealth of information on the early C-class submarines, dating from 1905 to 1908.

She had read that C-class submarines were the first class to have been built at Chatham, and she supposed that was why her father had taken particular interest in collecting the information for his library. All Alice thought she had to do was to take the general characteristics of those older class submarines and add a few embellishments, such as increased size, more powerful propulsion, and armament. As long as this new 'experimental' F-class submarine appeared to be an improvement, she couldn't see how Raskin would be any the wiser.

So when the Dutchman found her alone with her thoughts at the bottom of the garden late that afternoon, Alice, having first established that Henry was alive and well, had felt very pleased with herself as she fetched her report from her room. She had written it in lemon juice between the lines of several pages of sheet music, as Raskin had instructed her to do, and she had handed it to him knowing that she had done her country no disservice. She had hoped that would be the last of it—that her husband would now be released—but even though Raskin had not said as much, she knew the Dutchman would visit her again.

Alice reached the house and made for the side entrance as usual. She rarely used the front door because it had always seemed too grand an entrance to her, with its wide pillared portico and heavy double doors. She had promised to take the children for a ride on the horse omnibus into Rochester for ice cream, and while she was there, she hoped to go shopping for some much-needed casual attire: a tweed suit and a simple straw boater would do.

'Chester! Charlotte!'

She called for them as she entered the house, stepping into a small hallway that had a single staircase leading up to the staff accommodation, and a passageway at the far end that led into the heart of the house via the kitchen and the butler's pantry. She called for them again and looked into the kitchen as she passed, in case Mrs Morris the cook was keeping them amused in her absence. She had left them with her mother, but she supposed they had long since tired her out.

'Children!'

There was no sign of either the children or Mrs Morris, so Alice continued into the house, calling their names and looking into this room and that as she went. She reached the main hall in the centre of the house, and voices drew her to another door. It was the door to her father's study. She opened it, knowing better to knock first. When she entered, she saw her father with two other gentlemen whom she had not seen before.

'I'm sorry for the intrusion,' Alice offered. 'I'm looking for Chester and Charlotte.' To her father, she added, 'Have you seen them?'

'Not since late this morning,' her father said. 'They were with old Mrs Chetwood. Your mother contracted one of her headaches and went to lie down.'

Old Mrs Chetwood was the longstanding housekeeper at Hamberley, having been in the family's service since the house was built. She had been referred to as 'old' Mrs Chetwood ever since her daughter came to work at Hamberley, so there would be no confusion between them. Alice didn't know exactly how old she was, but the title suited her well enough as she had always seemed old to Alice, with her grey hair and thin hands that reminded Alice of gnarled tree roots.

'I see,' Alice said. 'Well, I'm sure they must have worn old Mrs Chetwood out, too, by now.'

She gave a polite smile and turned to leave, but her father stopped her.

'I wanted to see you, Alice,' he said, his voice taking on a sombre tone. 'These two gentlemen are detectives from a special branch of the police service at New Scotland Yard.'

Alice swallowed dryly and turned back into the room. 'How do you do?'

Her father indicated the man to her left. He was a tall man with a thick, black moustache that covered his lips. He wore a high-buttoned, three-piece suit with a stiff white collar that seemed to cut into his neck, forcing his chin proud.

'This is Inspector George Watts,' Alice's father said. 'And beside him is Sergeant John Hooper.'

Both men nodded, but only the sergeant smiled. He was an older man with wiry sideburns, who was thicker set and shorter than the other. He was similarly dressed, but in a suit of coarser fabric that held its shape far less precisely than the inspector's. They each carried a black bowler hat.

Alice could only think of one reason why two detectives from London were now standing in front of her: someone must have seen her in the slipway at the dockyard and reported her to her father, who had then summoned these men to interrogate her. She looked at her father, and a wave of anxiety washed over her. She wanted to speak out in her defence, hoping to quash the inevitable proceedings before they began. She yearned to tell someone what had happened, to share the burden, and why not with her own father? The matter would be taken out of her hands then, and perhaps that was for the better. She had done nothing wrong so far. It wasn't too late. She was about to tell them everything and risk all, but her father's next words stopped her.

'There have been further developments concerning the death of Admiral Waverley.'

Alice caught her breath.

'We suspect foul play,' Inspector Watts said, his voice conveying the elocution of a first-class education.

'Possibly murder, miss,' Sergeant Hooper added in coarser tones.

Alice let her breath go, and she felt the tension inside her go with it.

'I wanted to see you,' her father said, 'because these gentlemen would like me to accompany them back to London, and it's unlikely I'll be home before supper. I didn't want to disturb your mother, but I couldn't just leave without explaining my absence.'

'Of course,' Alice said, feeling guilty now for having been so relieved by the announcement that poor Admiral Waverley might have been murdered. 'I was going to take the children into Rochester, but we can go tomorrow.'

'No, no,' her father insisted. 'There's no need to change your plans. I wouldn't want you to disappoint the children. I'm sure your mother will sleep through until you return.'

At that moment, Alice heard scampering footsteps out in the hallway, and then she heard the housekeeper calling, 'You're not to go in there, children.' But it was too late. Alice turned as the study door shot open, and Chester and Charlotte appeared in the frame with Mrs Chetwood close behind them, carrying an armful of yellow tulips.

'I'm ever so sorry,' the housekeeper offered. Her cheeks were flushed, partly with embarrassment, Alice supposed, but mostly from trying to keep up with the children.

'We were out picking flowers for the rooms,' she continued, still catching her breath. 'They must have heard you talking. Well, there was no stopping them. They got themselves all excited and ran off saying something about ice cream.'

Lord Metcalfe laughed. 'That's quite all right, Mrs Chetwood. We've concluded our business here anyway.'

Alice watched her father go to the children, his face still full of smiles. He knelt in front of them and from his waistcoat pocket he produced two shiny pennies.

'Here,' he said, holding them up in front of the children's beaming faces. 'Get yourselves an extra penny lick from your old grandfather, but don't tell your grandmother when you see her, or I'll be for the chop!'

# Chapter Ten

Ancient Rochester was located on the River Medway near Chatham, approximately thirty miles southeast of London. It boasted a twelfth-century cathedral and a medieval castle, which, during the period of the Angevin kings, was one of Southeast England's most strategic fortresses, guarding the junction of the River Medway with the Roman road that ran between London and the port of Dover.

Alice gazed up at the castle's imposing Norman keep as she and the children walked through the castle grounds towards it. Upon their arrival in Rochester, the children's hunger for the promised ice cream had been satisfied with a penny lick apiece, which had kept them amused while Alice bought the simple items of clothing she had wanted, along with the straw boater hat she was now wearing to keep the sun out of her eyes. Before leaving the High Street, the children had spent the money their grandfather had given them on two more ice creams, which they were now busily licking from their glass dishes as they walked.

'Eat them slowly, or you'll be sick,' Alice warned, getting no answer.

Slatted benches lined either side of the wide walkway, where tidy lawns gave way to trees that were heavy with pink blossoms. Alice stopped beside a vacant bench and sat opposite an elderly man who was feeding crumbs to the pigeons from a brown paper bag.

'I've finished mine,' Chester said, offering out an empty dish that was so clean it looked as if it had never been used.

Charlotte held hers out. It was still half full.

'Don't you want any more?'

Charlotte shook her head, rocking her shoulders as she did so, and Chester took it from her. He finished it off with a grin that was exaggerated by the lines of melted ice cream the dish had left on his cheeks.

Alice wiped the ice cream off with her thumb and set the dishes down on the bench beside her. 'We mustn't forget to return them on our way back through the High Street,' she said, and then she sat back and watched Chester and Charlotte play with the pigeons. She laughed to herself when she saw Charlotte repeatedly trying to touch one, only for it to hop out of reach every time.

The castle grounds were busy with people enjoying their afternoon recreation. Two ladies in long white gowns and wide-rimmed hats nodded to her as they passed, and there were several other small children here and there with their families or their nannies. The couples she could see made her think of Henry and how much she longed to walk hand in hand with him again. She hoped that time would be soon. On the bench to her left sat a man reading a newspaper. It was a copy of the *Daily Mail*, which her father had often cited as being overtly warmongering. The headline certainly offered nothing to contradict his opinion. It immediately caught Alice's attention.

'KAISER PLANS TO CRUSH BRITISH EMPIRE!'

It was certainly sensational, and Alice supposed it had achieved its goal in helping to sell more newspapers. But warmongering? Given what the Dutchman had wanted her to do at the dockyard recently, she thought there might be more truth to it than she cared to admit. She read the words again and wondered what else Raskin would ask of her before this ordeal was over. Surely he hadn't gone to such lengths merely to have her gather information about submarines. She imagined just about anyone could be recruited to do that, and someone with a much greater degree of skill and courage than she possessed. No, she had already decided that Raskin must have other plans for her—something perhaps only she could achieve as an admiral's daughter, or more specifically as the daughter of Admiral Lord Charles Metcalfe. But what?

'Would you care to read it? I'm almost finished.'

The voice startled Alice. She had become lost in her thoughts, all the while staring at that headline as if it were her own newspaper.

'I'm sorry. You must think me terribly rude.'

The man offered a smile. 'Not at all. Here.' He folded the newspaper flat and handed it to her.

'No, it's quite all right, really. I was just daydreaming.'

The man got up. 'Well, a very good afternoon to you.'

Alice watched him go, and she laughed to herself, thinking he must have thought her quite the fool. She turned back to the children and saw Chester on his hands and knees. He was scrutinising something at the edge of the grass that she supposed, from Chester's predilection for such things, was an insect of some sort. When she turned to her daughter, expecting to see her among the pigeons as before, her face dropped. Charlotte was no longer there.

Alice shot to her feet, noting that the man who had been feeding the pigeons when they arrived was also nowhere to be seen.

'Charlotte!'

Chester looked over and Alice ran to him.

'Where's your sister?'

Chester just stared blankly back at her.

'Stay here,' Alice said, and she ran to the middle of the walkway and called for her daughter again. She looked one way along the path and then the other. Then a bright red ribbon caught her eye as it danced in spirals above the heads of the people who were otherwise blocking her view. Someone moved aside and Alice ran towards the ribbon. A moment later she saw Charlotte staring up at it, transfixed and mesmerised. Alice dropped to her knees and pulled her daughter into her arms.

'Wherever were you going?' she asked. She stared into Charlotte's eyes. 'Promise you'll always stay close to me,' she added, silently berating herself for her stupidity and lack of concentration.

'I'm sorry, miss,' the man with the ribbon offered.

Alice looked up and saw that the man carried several such ribbons, and she realised then that he was a street vendor.

'I only just saw the little mite was following me,' the vendor added. 'I'd have stopped sooner if I'd known.' He twirled the ribbon again and Charlotte's head followed its dance. He laughed as if to make light of the situation. 'Here,' he said, still smiling broadly as he offered the ribbon to Charlotte by the stick it was attached to.

'How much is it?' Alice asked.

'That's quite all right, miss. Least I can do for causing you such a scare.'

Alice returned his smile and nodded to Charlotte, who then took the stick from the vendor and began to make the ribbon dance for herself.

'Thank you,' Alice said.

'Not at all, miss. My pleasure. You have a good day now.'

Alice led Charlotte with her new dancing ribbon back to Chester, whom she was pleased to see was waiting close to where she had left him. He was sitting on one of the benches beside a well-dressed man in a grey top hat, who was holding a paper bag in his hand, much like the elderly man who had been feeding the pigeons when they first arrived, although the pigeons now seemed disinterested and had moved away. The man rose as Alice arrived, and without acknowledging her, he walked off in the opposite direction.

Alice held her free hand out for Chester to hold, thinking that she never wanted to let go of either of her children again.

'We must get back now,' she said, noting that the light had started to fade, thinking that she had had quite enough excitement for one day.

She collected the ice-cream dishes, and they left the castle grounds, taking the tram back through the High Street and further on past the museum, where they picked up the horse omnibus for their return to Hamberley. It was a quiet and uneventful journey until they had almost reached their destination, at which point Chester said he felt sick.

'You've eaten too much ice cream this afternoon,' Alice said, ruffling his hair. 'That's all it is. I'm sure you'll be fine once the omnibus stops.'

The carriage fell quiet again. They were the only people aboard now, all other passengers having disembarked by the time they reached the outskirts of Rochester. Outside the window, Alice continued to watch the countryside: the abundance of trees—some full of blossom and others just coming into leaf; a white weatherboard windmill on the horizon; and the oast houses that were so common to the area, with their conical red-tiled roofs beneath which the hop harvests would later be set to dry.

'My tummy really hurts,' Chester said.

When Alice turned to him again, she thought his complexion was a shade or two paler than before. It made the skin around his eyes appear red, his lips darker than usual. She placed a palm on his forehead. It was hot and clammy to the touch.

'Perhaps you're not very well,' Alice said, worrying now whether it really was the ice cream and the journey that was upsetting him. She went to the window and opened it more fully. She leaned out and had to hold on to her hat as the breeze hit her.

'Driver!' she called. 'My son is unwell.'

'Do you want me to stop?' the driver called back.

'No, I think perhaps if you could go a little faster and take us all the way to Hamberley. We're almost there. I'll pay extra.'

'Hamberley. Right you are.'

A whip cracked as Alice came back into the carriage, and the omnibus picked up speed.

'Not long to go now, darling,' Alice said, stroking Chester's forehead, and at the same time wondering why his lips looked so dark. They were almost black in places. 'You'll soon feel yourself again, you'll see,' she added, as much to reassure herself as her son.

Alice hoped that what she had told Chester was true, but by the time the omnibus slowed down again, Chester had become very quiet and still, and he was soon visibly sweating. By the time Hamberley came into view, he had deteriorated to the point of having lost consciousness, and he could not be woken.

# Chapter Eleven

Later that evening, Alice waited with her mother and Mrs Chetwood in one of the sitting rooms at Hamberley, clutching her picture locket and praying for good news from Dr Shackleton, who for the past two hours had been in attendance with Chester in his room. She finished the second of the herbal tonics Mrs Chetwood had prepared to help calm her nerves and began to pace the room again, wondering what could possibly be wrong with her son. She had long since dismissed the idea that Chester had eaten too much ice cream, or that there had been anything wrong with it, because Charlotte had suffered no such ill effect.

Her father's return from London could not have come soon enough.

'Terrible news!' he proclaimed as Alice and her mother ran out to meet him.

Alice did not wait to hear it, considering nothing more terrible than her son's condition. She launched straight into a rambling account of everything that had happened that afternoon and was joined with equal passion by her mother halfway through.

'Now calm down, both of you,' Lord Metcalfe said. 'If Dr Shackleton is here, then Chester is in good hands. And my news from London can wait until morning.'

They came into the main hallway: a well-lit space served by two large chandeliers, and another above the grand mahogany staircase that swept away to the floor above, with its plush crimson carpet and brass handrails.

'I noticed his lips looked quite black,' Alice continued. 'I've never seen or heard of anything like it.'

'Neither have I,' her father said. 'But then we are not physicians, are we?'

'Will you go up, Charles?' Alice's mother asked as she helped her husband out of his coat. 'The good doctor has asked us not to disturb him, but it's been too long. We're beside ourselves with worry.'

'I'm sure that's precisely why the good doctor considered it best to be left alone with the boy.'

'Please go up, Father,' Alice said.

Her father reached inside his jacket and glanced at the fob watch he carried in his waistcoat pocket. 'Two hours, you say?'

Alice nodded. 'More or less.'

'Then of course I shall go up. Two hours is an hour too long to expect any mother to worry about the well-being of her child.'

Lord Metcalfe had only placed one foot on the staircase when other footsteps on the floorboards above stopped him. Everyone looked up as Dr Shackleton appeared with his little medical bag, and Alice ran to him, meeting him halfway.

'How is he, doctor?' she asked, his anticipated response bringing her close to panic. 'Is he all right? Please tell me he's going to be all right.'

The stolid expression on Dr Shackleton's face gave nothing away. 'He would appear to be over the worst of it,' he said. 'I gave him something to help lower his temperature, and his fever has broken at last. He's sleeping now.'

'What must we do?' Alice's mother asked as the doctor reached the bottom of the stairs.

'We must wait. Rest is the best medicine I can prescribe for him now.'

'Do you know what's wrong with him?' Alice's father asked.

The doctor shook his head. 'A fever such as this can be brought on by many things.'

'What about the blackening of his lips?' Alice said. 'Surely that must provide some clue as to the cause.'

'Liquorice. Nothing more. On closer inspection I noted that the boy's teeth and gums showed the same discolouration. I'm partial to it myself. The smell is unmistakable.'

*Liquorice?* Alice thought, confused. She was about to say that she had been with Chester all afternoon and that she would have known if her son had eaten any liquorice, but she stopped herself when she recalled that she had not been with Chester all afternoon—not quite. She had left him alone when she went to find Charlotte. She remembered the man sitting beside Chester in the castle grounds then, and a shiver ran through her when she pictured the paper bag he was holding. She recalled how quick he was to leave when she returned, and she thought it no wonder that the pigeons had been so disinterested. Why would they show any interest if the bag the man was holding contained not breadcrumbs, but liquorice?

*Poisoned liquorice . . .*

It was too abhorrent to think that anyone would give such a thing to a child. She wanted to tell the doctor that he was wrong to suppose it was liquorice and nothing more, but she had no proof, and to voice her suspicions would force her to explain why she thought anyone would want to harm Chester in the first place. She wondered now whether the street vender with his dancing ribbons had also been party to the setup, wilfully luring Charlotte away so as to separate them and leave Chester vulnerable.

Alice bit her lip until she tasted blood. How could she have been so foolish? She could only think that her plan to provide false information to the Dutchman on the experimental submarine at Chatham had been discovered for the misinformation it was. It was clear to Alice now that Raskin and the people he was working for were resourceful enough to get to her children wherever they were, and clearly they were prepared to go to any lengths for their cause, however unthinkable. Or was she simply being paranoid? Perhaps there was another, more innocent explanation. Alice wished that were true, but she could not believe it was.

Dr Shackleton made for the door, and she drifted after him, thinking now of her husband and hoping that no harm had come to him as a result of her misjudgement.

'Keep a watch over young Chester tonight,' the doctor said. 'While he's sleeping, leave him to it. If he becomes delirious again, apply cold towels and call me at once. I'll return in the morning.'

Lord Metcalfe opened the door. 'Thank you, James. We are once again in your debt.'

'Not at all, sir. Not at all.'

The doctor turned back from the door then and smiled at Alice. 'I know it's an impossible thing to ask a mother, but try not to worry too much,' he said. 'I'm sure Chester will be as bright as a new penny again in a day or two.'

Alice could not bring herself to return the doctor's kindly smile. She simply gave a small nod and silently prayed that he was right.

It was almost four in the morning, and because Alice had watched over Chester tirelessly since Dr Shackleton left the house, her mother had insisted she now try to sleep. But Alice could not sleep. She lay awake on her bed, wrapped in her housecoat and her thoughts, staring at the shifting shadows that her bedside candle cast on the ceiling. On top of everything else, she was as worried now about what evil deed the Dutchman might sanction against her children next, and when she thought about her little Charlotte, it brought tears to her eyes. Raskin was the last man in the world Alice wanted to see, but she knew she had to find him, to assure him that she would cooperate fully from now on. And she had to know she was right about the man on the bench with his paper bag, and that what he had given to her son to teach her a lesson would not cause Chester any irreparable harm.

Alice swung her legs off the bed and put on a pair of flat shoes, supposing that the Dutchman could not come to her in her own bedroom, although she would not put it past him to try. She tied her housecoat more securely at her waist and then took up her candle and went to the door. The house was still. All she could hear was the sound of the grandfather clock keeping time in the main hallway below. She stepped out, guarding the light from her candle with her free hand as she went towards the stairs. When she came to Chester's room, she paused and trod extra carefully past so as not to alert her mother. When she passed Charlotte's room, she looked in momentarily, just to know that she was still sleeping peacefully.

As she made her way down the stairs, all the while peering into the near darkness beyond the candle's glow, in case anyone else was about, she supposed that Raskin would not be far from Hamberley on this night of all nights—if indeed any night. She knew that he or one of his spies must have followed her into Rochester. How else could he know her every move? She reached the bottom step and went to the dining room, thinking to go out on the terrace as she had that night with Archie. Raskin had come to her there, and she hoped he would do so again tonight.

It was colder than Alice imagined it would be after so fine a spring day. She wrapped her arms around herself and gazed up into the night, where stars pricked the black sky and the moon was nowhere to be seen. She went to the balustrade and gazed out across the lawns, and then a breeze arrived unannounced and extinguished her candle.

'Raskin,' she called under her breath.

She looked down into the shrubbery below, but it was too dark to see anything, so she went to the steps and began to descend them as she had before. Somewhere far off an owl screeched, breaking the silence. She called out again, a little louder this time.

'Raskin!'

At the bottom of the steps, Alice ventured further around the house, and gradually her eyes became better accustomed to the dark, but it served her no purpose. Raskin was nowhere to be found, or perhaps he did not wish to be found, meaning to let her suffer all the longer for her deceit.

Alice did not call out again. She could feel the cold biting at her ankles now, and she had begun to shiver. She thought it would not do to catch a chill and fall ill herself with Chester in such need of her, so she returned to the terrace and went back into the house. She closed the door behind her and wished she had a match with which to relight her candle, but she knew the way well enough. She was about to move off when a familiar voice startled her.

'Here, let me light that for you.'

Alice spun around as a match struck up, and there in the flame's glow was Raskin. He was dressed in a long sheepskin coat, sitting back in her father's chair with his boots up on the table. Just being near him again made her skin crawl, but Alice went to him just the same and offered out her candle. His pale blue eyes commanded her attention as he lit it, and Alice could no longer avoid them.

'If you had called my name any louder, you might have woken the whole household.'

Alice thought that might not have been such a bad thing. Perhaps then this monster would be caught and made to free her husband and end the terror he had brought upon her family. But she knew his capture would make no difference. He would simply be replaced by another who would torture her emotions all the more for it.

'You've got a nerve coming in here,' Alice said.

The Dutchman smiled wryly. 'Strong nerves are very handy in my line of work.'

'Don't you sleep?'

'Of course. By day, when it suits me. A few hours here, a few hours there.'

'What have you done to my son?'

'What have *I* done?' Raskin gave a condescending laugh. 'You know very well it is because of what you have done that your son is now fighting for his life.'

At hearing that, Alice felt a rage inside her that she had never felt before. The candle she was still holding began to shake in her hand.

'You gave him poisoned liquorice,' she said. It was no longer a question in her mind.

'Not I, personally,' Raskin said. 'But yes, he was given a substance. The taste can be quite bitter. The liquorice helps to disguise it.'

The Dutchman's matter-of-fact coldness made Alice fear what he was capable of all the more. She set the candle down on the table and made a fist with her hand as she withdrew it to hide the fact that it was shaking.

'Will he die? I have to know.'

'The amount was not sufficient to kill him,' Raskin said. He leaned closer and added, 'Not this time.'

Were Alice a man, she thought, she would have used her fists to lash out at the Dutchman there and then, despite his size and obvious strength. Instead, her rage turned to tears as she pictured Chester lying in his room trying to fight off the poison.

'He's only four years old,' she said, pleading without hope to a sense of compassion she knew did not exist. She choked back her tears. 'How could you?'

Raskin offered her no sympathy. 'You were tested and you failed.'

'Tested?'

He gave a slow nod. 'We already know about your experimental F-class submarine. It has a double hull, which will accommodate the ballast tanks, making the vessel more streamlined. Length—151 feet. Expected range—three thousand nautical miles. She will have three 18-inch torpedo tubes—two bow, one stern. I could go on, but you already know how completely absurd your report was. The *F1* will be nothing more than a coastal patrol submarine of little importance to us. What is important to us is that we trust you. Can we trust you, Alice Stilwell?'

Alice swallowed the lump that had risen in her throat. She nodded.

'Are you quite sure? Because from now on there will be no more chances.'

'Yes, I'm very sure,' Alice said. She was never more sure of anything in her life. 'I'll do everything you ask of me. Just promise you won't harm my children again.'

'That is not a promise I am at liberty to make,' Raskin said. 'As I hope you now fully understand. The fate of your children depends entirely on you.'

'And my husband? Is Henry well? Tell me you haven't harmed him because of me.'

'He is quite comfortable, I assure you. And your son will make a speedy recovery. Now we must press on.'

'Where is all this leading?' Alice asked. 'Why me? Is it because of who my father is? What do you really want?'

'So many questions,' Raskin said. 'And they will be answered—that I do promise you. But not now. Now I have another task for you. Tomorrow you must go to the Burlington Hotel in Dover and speak to the head waiter, Raimund Drescher. Ask him how his mother is. Say you hope she is well. He will then tell you what you must do.'

'His mother?'

'His mother is dead. If you say this, he will know I sent you.'

'I see.'

Raskin produced a notebook and pencil from inside his coat. 'There is something I have to show you.' He began to write into the notebook, and a moment later he held it to the candlelight so Alice could see what he'd written.

'Alice is a good girl,' she read aloud, confusion furrowing her brow.

Raskin didn't elaborate. Instead he wrote something else into the notepad, taking longer this time. He showed her again, and Alice just stared at it. What he had written looked like unreadable nonsense. 'Lac iie aso gdo igl r.'

'It's a cipher, Alice. A code if you like. I want you to use it for all further communication between us.'

Alice was still looking at it. 'How does it work?'

'It's really very simple. Just swap each pair of letters around. Then write them out in blocks of three, which merely serves to confuse the eye. It's called a transition cipher. There are many variants and some quite complex, but this will be sufficient.'

Alice looked at the text again and found she was able to read the original sentence quite easily now she knew how it worked. 'It's very clever,' she said. 'But what if I can't do what Drescher asks of me?' She knew from her experience in the slipway at the dockyard that she was ill suited to this.

'You must do it.'

'But what if I fail again?'

The question seemed to amuse the Dutchman. 'Don't you see, my dear Alice. It is the very fear of failure that will ensure your success. It doesn't matter how you do it—what or whom you use to accomplish the task is irrelevant. But you must accomplish it. Do you understand?'

'Yes,' Alice said. She understood very well.

# Chapter Twelve

Present day.

It was just before midday when Jefferson Tayte arrived at Gillingham Marina, where Davina Scanlon had said she would meet him for lunch. He was earlier than expected and somewhat confused because the restaurant he had just entered was the only restaurant at the marina, and the tanned young man who had introduced himself to Tayte as the restaurant manager had just informed him that they had no lunch reservation in Davina's name.

'I guess there must have been some mix-up,' Tayte said. 'Thanks for checking.'

He picked up his briefcase and was about to leave, but as he turned around, he saw her through the floor-to-ceiling windows. She was standing outside, smiling and waving at him in a low-cut summer dress. The sight of her made Tayte's palms clammy. She was an unquestionably striking woman, and he couldn't deny his attraction to her, which only made him feel worse because of Jean—not that he planned on trying to do anything about it. To the contrary, he wanted to run the other way. They met at the door to a chorus of crying seagulls.

'You're early,' Davina said, still smiling. 'You must be keen, is that it?'

Tayte's mouth cracked into a nervous smile. 'Actually, my visit with Lord Metcalfe didn't go so well,' he said, thinking that it was quite a setback in light of the fact that he already knew from his research that Alice's daughter Charlotte had borne no children, making her brother's bloodline the only Metcalfe line available to him. 'I wasn't at Hamberley half as long as I'd expected to be.' He turned back to the restaurant. 'I just checked, and they told me they don't have a reservation. Maybe they can still fit us in, though.'

'No need,' Davina said. 'I changed my mind. It's such a nice day that I thought . . .' her words trailed off as a playful grin danced across her glossy lips. She took Tayte's arm. 'Come with me and I'll show you,' she added. 'You do like surprises, don't you?'

Tayte snorted uneasily. 'Who doesn't?' he said, already wishing he were back at his hotel having a room-service meal for one.

Davina led Tayte down towards the water, where reflections of the sun, now at its zenith, twinkled and shimmered between the yachts and the cruisers that were moored there. They took a pontoon walkway and were soon between the boats, and it didn't take long for Tayte to realise where Davina was taking him.

'Which one's yours?' he asked, showing his impatience to find out where Davina's change of plan was going.

'We're coming to it. She's call the *Osprey*.'

Seeing all those boats only brought bad memories to Tayte's mind, most of which stemmed from his first assignment in England, when he'd almost drowned. 'What did you have in mind?' he asked when his impatience to know the answer got the better of him.

Davina turned to him as they walked. Her playful grin had returned. 'Don't worry,' she said, clearly sensing his unease. 'I wasn't planning to take you for a ride.' She winked. 'Not today anyway. I just thought that, as the weather's so nice, we'd have lunch on the boat instead of at the restaurant.'

'Oh, okay,' Tayte said, thinking that this was all going to be far more intimate than he wanted it to be.

Davina stopped beside a gleaming white cruiser that looked to be around forty feet in length. Its marine blue canopy was folded down, revealing a white leather lounge deck around a table set for two, flowers and all. Tayte's eyes fell on the bright red rose in the table centre and the beads of condensation on the ice bucket, which just made his throat feel all the more dry.

Davina stepped aboard. Then she turned and offered Tayte her hand. 'Welcome to the *Osprey*.'

Tayte whistled. 'She's a lovely craft.'

'She was my husband's pride and joy.'

'I'm sorry,' Tayte said. 'I didn't mean to—'

'It's okay,' Davina interrupted, saving Tayte from an awkward apology. 'Actually, I like being here. I like being close to the things that remind me of him.'

Tayte stepped aboard, and the boat swayed and settled again.

'Everything's ready,' Davina said. 'I've even brought my research down so we can go over everything here.'

'Great,' Tayte said, glad to know that he no longer had to find uncomfortable small talk to fill the conversation with. Or so he thought.

'You don't mind if we save all that for after lunch, though, do you?' Davina added. 'I'd like to find out all about you first.' She indicated the table. 'Have a seat. I'll be right back.'

With that, Davina opened a small door beneath the cockpit and disappeared below deck. Tayte took his jacket off, carefully folded it, and laid it over his briefcase. He sat down and tried to think of something interesting to say that wasn't about his latest assignment, coming up blank as he knew he would by the time Davina returned. She was carrying two plates, which she set on the table.

'I hope you like seafood?'

'Sure. See food and eat it,' Tayte said, eying the plates of dressed crab and brown shrimp, salad, and baby potatoes. 'There isn't much I don't eat,' he added, and immediately wished he hadn't.

Davina smiled. 'I like a man who likes his food.' She reached for the ice bucket, pulled the bottle out and showed Tayte the label, cradling it in a cloth napkin to catch the drips. 'I bought us a nice Sauvignon blanc—Pouilly-Fumé,' she said. 'Would you like some?' She pouted her lips at him. 'Please say you would. I really don't like drinking on my own.'

Tayte gave the label a cursory glance, knowing he would have had a glass, whatever it was, just to settle his nerves. 'That would be very nice. Thank you.'

Davina poured the wine and sat in the curve of the seat beside Tayte, shifting around until their knees were touching. 'Cosy, isn't it?' she said, and Tayte just smiled and unfurled his napkin.

'So, tell me something about yourself,' Davina said as they started on the meal.

Tayte laughed through his nose. 'I'm afraid there really isn't much to tell.'

'I don't believe that for a minute. Let's start with where you're from.'

Tayte wanted to say that he wished he knew, but he didn't want to get into the mystery of his own ancestry right now. He just wanted to get on with his assignment. 'Washington, DC,' he said. Then to save time, he rattled off just about everything else about him he could think of, holding back anything he thought could lead to deeper questions about himself and his lifelong search for his biological family. 'I'm a Redskins fan, and I like Broadway shows. Beyond that, I seem to spend my waking hours with my nose buried in my work.'

Davina sat back and stared at him with a look of mild surprise. 'Broadway? I adore musicals. What was the last show you saw?'

*Jersey Boys.*'

'I love that show,' Davina said. 'I saw it in the West End a couple of months ago. So you're a Valli fan, too?'

'I wouldn't say that. I just like the shows.'

Davina topped up the wine, and they ate and drank and talked about musicals all through lunch, during which time Tayte felt himself becoming more and more relaxed in Davina's company. She'd bought a New York cheesecake for dessert, which she'd said was to make him feel more at home, and Tayte thought that was a nice gesture.

'So what was that about having nothing much to say about yourself?' Davina said with a smile as she topped up Tayte's wine glass again. 'We've found something in common and haven't stopped talking about it since.'

Tayte smiled along with her, thinking that maybe small talk wasn't so difficult after all, or maybe he'd just got lucky this time around. He finished his cheesecake and sat back, having waited until Davina had finished hers so as not to appear too eager to devour it.

'That was a fine lunch in a fine setting, Davina. Thank you.'

'You're welcome,' Davina said. 'It was nice to have someone to share it with.'

There was a solemnity in her tone as she finished speaking. Tayte was so used to dining alone that he never gave it much thought, but he imagined that mealtimes had been difficult for Davina since her husband's death. He didn't want her mood to slip, so a moment later he grinned and said, 'So, can we talk about my assignment now? I'm dying to go over your research.'

'I don't see why not,' Davina said. 'You've been very patient with me. I suppose it's only fair. Let's go inside. As lovely as it is out here, I think I could use some shade. I'm melting.'

'That sounds good,' Tayte said. 'Let me help you clear up the table.'

The space inside the *Osprey*'s cabin was small, but it was bright and airy because of the white leather and cherry wood furniture that had been designed to maximise the space. All the same, Tayte couldn't stand up without stooping, but he was pleased he hadn't had to squeeze through or around anything to get to the table he and Davina were now sitting at by one of the starboard portholes. On the table, Davina had a lever arch file containing her research. Tayte had his briefcase open beside him.

'Looks like someone needs a new briefcase,' Davina said, casting a studious eye over Tayte's long-serving travel companion.

'Oh, I don't know,' Tayte said. He looked over the battered leather edges and at the handle that he'd worn to a high shine. Then his gaze drifted to the repair he'd made to the bullet hole in the side, which he'd picked up on a previous assignment. 'We've been through so much over the years, I'm sure I couldn't bear to part with it.'

Davina smiled at him. 'So you're the sentimental type?'

Tayte shrugged. 'I guess, maybe.'

Davina opened her file and removed the contents, which comprised several loose sheets of paper and a few folders. 'So, what happened at Hamberley?' she asked. 'You said your visit hadn't gone too well.'

'Not well at all,' Tayte said. 'I tiptoed around Alice for as long as I could, but when I mentioned her name and showed Lord Metcalfe the photo I have of my client's grandmother, he became very upset about it—much as Raife Metcalfe did when I asked him about Alice.'

'You shouldn't be too surprised,' Davina said. 'They're an old and proud family, as devoted to their country as I should think anyone can be.'

'It's hardly scandalous news today, though, is it?'

'No, perhaps not, but you have to remember that Reginald Metcalfe is of a generation when such things were highly scandalous. I don't imagine his views have changed much with the times.'

'But what about Raife? He's a young man. He was just as upset, if not more so.'

'I'm sure most of the family who know about Alice have had the need to forget her drummed into them over the years. Knowing how his grandfather is about the black sheep of the family, I'm sure Raife was simply reflecting Lord Metcalfe's wishes.'

'You're probably right,' Tayte said. 'He just seemed to go a bit over the top about it, threatening to see me off the property with his shotgun like he did. Anyway, it's clear that I'm not going to get any assistance from the Metcalfe family anytime soon.' He indicated Davina's research. 'You said on the phone this morning that you had a photograph you thought would be of particular interest to me.'

Davina flicked through her papers, nodding as she did so. 'Here we are,' she said. She slid an old sepia photograph in front of Tayte. 'It's a family-and-friends gathering, circa early 1900s, I should think.'

Tayte studied the image, and his eyes were immediately drawn to the young girl on the knee of the bearded naval officer in the foreground.

'I believe that must be Alice,' Davina added, 'because that's her father, Charles Metcalfe. Her mother Lilian is standing beside them.'

'Can you put names to all these faces?'

'No, not all,' Davina said. 'Although I've tried to. My husband was able to help with some, and I managed to connect others by talking to the family over the years.' She leaned closer to Tayte and put a finger on one of the figures to the side. 'That's Alice's Aunt Cordelia and her Uncle Oscar, who as you know is my husband's great-grandfather.' She laughed to herself. 'Chancers and wheeler-dealers, the lot of them by all accounts. I suppose that's why Lionel was so well suited to the antiques business.'

'Who are these gentlemen?' Tayte asked, pointing to a line of highly decorated naval uniforms in the background.

'I don't know all their names,' Davina said. She indicated a white-haired man with wiry sideburns. 'His name's Waverley—he was another admiral I believe, like Lord Charles Metcalfe. To his right is Lord Ashcroft. I'm sure they're all friends of Charles through their connection to the Royal Navy.'

'And who's this smart young fella?' Tayte asked, indicating a boy who looked no more than a few years older than Alice, standing straight as a ship's mast before the naval officer who Davina had informed him was Lord Ashcroft.

Davina paused before answering. Then she nodded to herself and said, 'That's Archibald Ashcroft—Archie, I believe he was called.'

'Do you know whether the Ashcrofts were from around here?'

'Yes, I'm sure they were, although I've no idea where they live now. I think the two families lost touch over the years. I did hear that Archibald and Alice were to be married. At least, that was the hope of their parents, but it never happened.' Davina caught Tayte's eyes. 'Love should come from the heart. Don't you think?'

Tayte swallowed dryly and looked back at the photograph. 'Yes, I suppose so,' he said, keen to move on. He pointed to another figure—this time to a man in a sharp business suit on the left side of the photograph. 'And what about this man here?'

'My husband told me his name was Frank Saxby,' Davina said. 'He was a friend of the family with connections to the Metcalfe family through a failed partnership with my husband's great-grandfather, Oscar Scanlon.' She paused and stared into space for a moment. 'I do know that one of Frank Saxby's descendants lives locally—a young man called Dean Saxby.'

Tayte was writing names into his notepad. He looked up. 'How do you know him?'

'I don't. I went to the workshop to collect something for a client about a month ago, and I almost bumped into him as he was coming out. Lionel told me who he was.'

'Do you know how your husband knew him?'

'I'm not sure he really knew him. At least, he'd never mentioned him. I was running late, and I was in such a hurry that I didn't think to ask why he was there. I'd forgotten all about him until now. Come to think of it,' she added, 'he seemed a far cry from the sort of people we usually do business with.'

'How do you mean?'

'Well, they're typically older and well heeled. Dean Saxby can't have been more than twenty-five, and he was wearing sportswear—shabby with it, too.'

'Maybe he'd been jogging,' Tayte said, wondering why Dean Saxby had gone to see Lionel Scanlon. He thought it would be good to pay him a visit, both to find out and to see if he knew anything that might prove useful about his ancestors and about Frank Saxby's connection to the Metcalfe family. 'Do you have his address? Maybe it's on file somewhere.'

'I'll check for you,' Davina said. 'Lionel might have written it down. We keep business contacts and customer details in books, the old-fashioned way.'

'Great,' Tayte said, and then he turned his thoughts back to Alice. He gazed at the image of the young girl again, and then he took the photograph of his client's grandmother out from his briefcase. He set the two images side by side, and he could see little resemblance between them—not that he'd really expected to see much of a likeness. The photographs were old and faded, and there were clearly a few decades between the two Alices when the photographs were taken. As expected as it was, Tayte's disappointment must have been written all over his face.

'No good?' Davina said.

Tayte shook his head and slid both photographs across so that Davina could get a better look. 'It's possible to see how the young Alice might have grown up to look like the older Alice, but it's hardly conclusive, is it?'

'No, it's not conclusive at all. I'm sorry. When I saw the photo and knew the girl must be Alice, I really thought it would help.'

'That's okay,' Tayte said. 'It's still a great photo. I'll just have to keep looking. Lord Reginald Metcalfe's reaction when I showed him the locket and this photo of Alice Dixon was certainly enough to keep me going for now. I'm sure that proving they're the same person is only going to be a matter of time.'

Davina showed Tayte a few more photographs. They were largely of her late husband's ancestors and were too recent to hold any significance to Tayte's assignment.

'Does all your research concern the Scanlon line?'

'Most of it,' Davina said. 'I'm sure you're not interested in that, though, are you? I started with my own line of course, but I soon got stuck, so I switched to Lionel's family, then I started hitting brick walls there, too.'

'Is your husband's father or grandfather still alive?'

'No, my Lionel was the last of his line.'

'That's too bad,' Tayte said, considering that it looked as though Davina's research was going to prove less valuable than he'd hoped. He went back to the only photograph she'd been able to show him from the time when Alice was around, and his eyes drifted to the man Davina had called Frank Saxby. 'You said this man was a friend of the family, connected to your husband's ancestor, Oscar Scanlon, through business.'

'Yes, that's right.' Davina went through her folders and pulled out a few documents. 'I was particularly interested in the various businesses my husband's ancestors had been involved in over the years. I researched quite a few at The National Archives, and the

British Library was a good source of information, too. Going further back to the time period you're interested in, I came across one of those rewarding family history finds that gives you goose bumps.'

'The connection to Oscar Scanlon?'

Davina nodded. 'I got my lead from the Historical Directories of England and Wales—specifically from an entry in Kelly's Directory of Kent, covering the period from 1900 to 1909. Here it is.'

Davina slid a sheet of paper in front of Tayte that looked as if it had been printed from an online scan. It showed a page full of names and businesses, complete with addresses. Tayte's eyes shot straight to the line that had been highlighted.

'Oscar Scanlon and Frank Saxby,' Tayte said.

'They co-owned a shoe factory in Dartford. I found out that they began their business partnership in 1908, and it was only when I began looking into what became of the business that things started getting interesting.'

Davina placed another sheet of paper in front of Tayte. This time it was a copy of a newspaper archive dated 11 June 1912, taken from the *Kent Messenger*.

Tayte read the headline aloud. 'Factory Blaze Kills Six.'

'Now look at this.' Davina showed Tayte another newspaper archive copy, this one from *The Times*. It was dated two months later.

'"Insurance fraud,"' Tayte read out.

He went on to read the verdict that had followed the inquest into the shoe factory fire in Dartford, which reported that the company was in financial difficulty at the time of the fire and that arson was suspected. Further down he read that no proof against the owners could be produced and that subsequently no charges were brought against them.

'That's a great piece of research,' Tayte said, 'and it certainly leaves suspicion hanging over your husband's great-grandfather and his business partner.'

'Yes, it does. It's a shame I couldn't find out any more about it. If it's true, it doesn't say much for the character of either of them, does it?'

Tayte agreed. 'If it's true.' he repeated. 'As nothing was proved, then as far as my assignment goes, we can't draw any more conclusion from it other than that Oscar Scanlon and Frank Saxby were once business partners.'

'No, I suppose not.' Davina went to pour more wine and found the bottle all but empty. 'Shall I open another one?'

'That sounds good, but I've got my car.'

'You could always get a taxi.'

'Yes, I could, but you've given me some research ideas. I'd like to follow up while they're fresh.'

'I could help,' Davina said, and Tayte could see the eagerness in her eyes. He was about to give her his usual line about preferring to work alone, when she added, 'If there's any chance your assignment could help to find my husband's killer, I need to be a part of it. You can understand that, can't you?'

Tayte understood all too well. He'd felt exactly the same way when his good friend Marcus Brown was murdered. Understanding why had meant everything to him. He smiled at Davina and gave a small nod. 'Sure,' he said. 'I don't see why not.'

Davina's eyes lit up. 'Thank you. I won't get in the way.' She stood up. 'Let's go up to my apartment. It's a little cramped in here, and I've got a laptop and a fast Internet connection. Two laptops might be better than one.'

# Chapter Thirteen

Davina's apartment was located in one of six conjoined units that formed a crescent rising in tiers amid landscaped gardens facing the moorings and the River Medway. Tayte followed Davina into a lift that was in one of the taller sections of the building and watched her press the button for the top floor.

'We splashed out and were lucky enough to get one of the penthouses,' she said. 'Oh, dear. You probably think I'm rich now, don't you? New boat and a second property on the river.' She laughed. 'I wish.'

'You can't take it with you,' Tayte said, and he immediately regretted it. 'Sorry,' he offered, thinking about her husband. Davina seemed to be handling Lionel's death so well on the outside that Tayte had forgotten to be careful with this choice of words. 'I'm afraid I'm always putting my foot in it. Can't seem to help myself.'

'That's okay,' Davina said as the lift door opened. 'I like that about you. What you see is what you get. No pretence.'

'I never really thought about it.'

'No, you wouldn't, would you? That's what I mean.'

They stepped out onto a bright, sunlit landing, and Tayte began to think about his next line of research.

'I think I'd like to find out some more about Lord Charles Metcalfe,' he said as they walked. 'He seems pivotal to everyone I'm interested in from the time before Alice Stilwell supposedly died. We can go over what we already know about him first. Then see what else we can find.'

They arrived at the apartment, and Davina took out her key. 'Sounds like a plan.'

She went to put her key into the lock, but as she did so, the door nudged open, and she froze. They stared at each other for a moment. Then Tayte put a finger to his lips and moved in front of her, noticing as he did so that the lock had been forced.

'Is there another way out of the apartment besides this door?' he whispered.

Davina shook her head. 'Only the balcony, but it's a long way down.'

Tayte eased the door further open and called through the gap. 'Hello?'

He stepped back again, taking Davina aside with him. If anyone was still in the apartment, he thought he'd rather the intruder knew he was there. He also hoped the person would choose to bolt rather than stick around to fight it out, but no sound followed. Tayte called again, and this time he pushed the door fully open. What he saw made him feel for Davina all the more. He shook his head.

'You don't want to see this,' he said, but Davina was already beside him, her mouth agape.

'Who did this?' she said. She looked close to tears. 'Why?'

The place was a mess. Tayte scanned the room, from the internal doors that led off to his left to the glass doors that looked out past the balcony over the river to his right. It seemed as if everything that could be knocked over or flipped upside down had been. The sofa and chair cushions were strewn across the wood flooring, and the dining table had been turned on its side. Even the pictures on the walls were either crooked or lying on the floor below their hooks. Tayte thought the place looked more like a chalk pastel abstract painting than a living space.

'It looks like whoever did this has gone,' he said, 'but I should check the rooms, just to be sure. Do you mind?'

'I'd feel safer if you did,' Davina said, and Tayte could see that she was shaking.

'Do you need to sit down?'

Davina looked around as if to ask where? 'No, I'm okay. It's just the realisation that someone probably was at my house last night, and that whoever it was must have been watching me this morning. He must have followed me here and waited for the opportunity to break in while we were on the boat.' She shuddered. 'It gives me the creeps.'

'I'll call Inspector Bishop,' Tayte said, reaching for his phone as he began to pick his way through the debris. 'We'd better not touch anything until he gets here.'

Soon after Tayte had called DI Bishop, the Inspector arrived at Davina's apartment with a small forensics team. The Scenes of Crime Officers went straight to work, and after taking a look around the apartment for himself, Bishop led Tayte and Davina back outside.

'I want to be thorough with this,' Bishop said. 'The break-in could be linked to your husband's murder, Mrs Scanlon, so the team will be in there awhile. Shall we grab a coffee?'

They went to the Marina restaurant, which was quiet now, during that in-between time after lunch and before dinner. The tanned young restaurant manager Tayte had met when he first arrived at the marina seemed to be the only person on duty. He showed them to a table by a window that was like a large round porthole, looking out onto the marina.

'Luca here makes the best coffee, don't you, Luca?' Davina said.

'For you, Mrs Scanlon, always my very best,' Luca said with a practiced smile and an exaggerated Italian accent that seemed to complement his slick persona.

As soon as Luca left with their order, Bishop got straight down to business. 'This looks bad just now, but it gives me hope that we'll catch your husband's killer, Mrs Scanlon.'

'How do you mean?'

'I mean he's still active—assuming for now that what's happened here is connected to the case, which I think is a pretty safe bet.'

'He's clearly looking for something,' Tayte said.

Bishop nodded. 'And that also tells me that your husband's murder, Mrs Scanlon, wasn't random. It wasn't just some burglary attempt gone wrong, as we'd previously supposed. Your husband's killer wanted something he thought your husband had, but he didn't get it. He's still looking.'

'And now he thinks I have it,' Davina said.

'Seems that way. Do you have any idea what it could be?'

Davina drew a blank expression. 'No, none at all. An antique of some kind perhaps? I suppose it would have to be something valuable to kill my husband over it.'

'Given the nature of your business, that would seem to be the obvious answer,' Bishop said. 'Was anything of particular value or interest acquired by you or your husband recently?'

Davina took a moment to think about it. Then she began to shake her head. 'I can't be sure whether Lionel had come across anything, of course, but we usually only buy to order, in which case I'd know about it. Our most valuable pieces tend to be items of furniture, but whoever broke into my apartment was clearly looking for something small, or why make such a mess?'

'Perhaps it's not something with an obvious face value,' Tayte said.

Bishop nodded. 'Whatever it is, it's clearly valuable to someone for some reason. Was there anything in your apartment that might fit the bill, Mrs Scanlon? Anything that was taken there recently by you or your husband?'

Again Davina shook her head. 'We've always kept the place quite minimalist. Nothing's old or worth anything—just some seascape paintings by local artists and a few cheap sculptures, mainly of seabirds. We bought everything new when we bought the apartment.'

'Good,' Bishop said. 'So it's unlikely that whoever broke in got what he came for.'

'I should say it's highly unlikely,' Davina said.

The coffee arrived, momentarily pausing the conversation. When it started up again, Bishop sipped his drink and thoughtfully said, 'Why now?' He turned to Tayte. 'My investigation was in danger of stagnating before you arrived. Then someone runs you off the road.' He paused and turned to Davina. 'And now your apartment's been ransacked, Mrs Scanlon. I mean, whoever did this could have done it weeks ago, so why now?'

'It backs up the idea that all this has something to do with my assignment,' Tayte said. 'Something I might turn up if I keep digging.'

Bishop agreed. 'But what does any of this have to do with your research into Alice Stilwell? Have you got any ideas yet? If you have, I'd love to hear them.'

Tayte quickly thought about what he had so far, and even more quickly concluded that he had next to nothing. 'It's too early to say, but there are some leads from Davina's research I want to follow up on. I'd like to find out what I can about the people who were around Alice Stilwell before she boarded that ill-fated ship in 1914.'

'Well, keep at it,' Bishop said. 'If whatever you're looking for really is connected to what our killer's looking for, maybe he's worried your research will lead you to it first.' He turned to Davina then and asked, 'Is your apartment alarmed? Was it set?'

'Yes, and no,' Davina said. 'It has one, but it wasn't set. The marina has gated security. We never set the alarm while we're here, only when we leave. That is, Lionel would set it. I'm hopeless when it comes to security. I'm sure there are security cameras, though. Perhaps you could check those.'

'I will,' Mrs Scanlon. 'Who else knows you own an apartment here? I mean, apart from various marina staff and the estate agency you bought it through.'

'Very few people as far as I know,' Davina said. 'It was a private weekend retreat, and I wanted to keep it that way.'

'And what about your husband?' Bishop asked. 'Do you think he could have told any friends or family members?'

'He might have, I suppose, but not to my knowledge.'

Tayte was already thinking about Raife Metcalfe. 'Did any of the Metcalfe family know about it?'

'Not from me,' Davina said. 'I've told no one except my parents. That's why I came here this morning after my scare last night.'

'Ah, yes, your prowler,' Bishop said. 'I saw the report a few hours ago. You said you were woken at around four this morning and that when you went to your bedroom window, you saw someone running across your front lawn.'

'I was beginning to think I'd imagined it until this happened,' Davina said. 'As I told JT before you arrived, Inspector, whoever was watching my house last night must have still been there this morning, and he must have followed me here.' Davina looked suddenly alarmed. 'Christ,' she said, standing up. 'My house . . . I need to go and make sure everything's okay. Can you drive me there, Inspector?'

'Yes, of course,' Bishop said. 'You have a house alarm, I suppose?'

Davina nodded, but there was something apologetic about it.

'Don't tell me,' Bishop said. 'It wasn't set either.'

'No, I'm sorry. Lionel was always telling me off for not setting it, and I was in such a hurry to come here this morning. I never gave it a thought until now.'

Bishop knocked his coffee back. To Tayte he said, 'Do you want to come along?'

'Sure,' Tayte said. He wasn't one to abandon people in their hour of need, however much he wanted to get on with the research.

# Chapter Fourteen

It was early evening by the time Davina was allowed back into her apartment. The police had left, but Tayte was still with her, knowing she would be glad of his company for a while longer. Visiting her house near Foxburrow Wood had realised Davina's fears that it, too, had been broken into earlier that day, and the chaos and sense of violation that had greeted her as she opened her front door and walked into her second nightmare, so soon after the first, made her feel so light-headed she had to sit down for a few minutes.

It had taken DI Bishop little time to discover that access to the property had been gained through a downstairs window at the back of the house: the glass was broken, and the latch had been lifted in order to fully open the window and climb inside, unobserved and unhindered. Davina's insurance had covered the twenty-four-hour tradesmen who had promptly been dispatched to make both of her homes secure again.

'You should stay with family tonight,' Tayte said as soon as the locksmith had left. He was helping Davina straighten the place up, and they had almost finished. Surprisingly, Davina had reported nothing broken.

'I don't have anyone within two hundred miles of here,' Davina said as she moved closer, straightening one of the sofa cushions on the way.

'Well, maybe you could stay with friends, or book into a hotel—anywhere but here.'

'I won't be chased away from my own home, JT. Besides, if whoever did this wanted to harm me, he could have done so last night.'

Tayte didn't doubt that was true under the circumstances, and it seemed unlikely to him that anyone would come back to the apartment tonight, especially given that by now the intruder already knew that what he was looking for wasn't there. He straightened the last of the crooked paintings and said, 'Okay, so why don't I come by again in the morning and see how you are?'

Davina looked horrified by the thought. 'What about our research?' She checked her watch. 'It's only just after six.'

Tayte had thought the research would have been the last thing on Davina's mind right now. He fully intended to continue himself, but he'd supposed, given everything that had happened, that he'd be doing it alone in his hotel room. 'You want to carry on as if none of this happened?'

Davina's eyes widened into a resolute stare. 'More than ever. What's happened today has only made me more determined.'

Tayte liked her spirit, and he wasn't about to pour cold water over it. He went to his briefcase, which he'd left inside the door, and brought it back with him. 'Shall we set up at the dining table?'

Davina gave a small smile—the first Tayte had seen since they'd left her boat that afternoon. 'Thank you,' she said, pulling out a chair for Tayte to sit on. 'I've lost my appetite, and I don't suppose I'll get it back tonight, but I can order you a take-away later if you're hungry.'

All the excitement had made Tayte feel very hungry, but he thought he could hold out until he was back at his hotel. 'No, I'm fine, thanks.'

'A drink then?' Davina said. 'I'm definitely having one of those—probably several. I've got wine, gin, Jack Daniels . . .'

A part of Tayte knew it was a bad idea, but the thought of a JD over ice right now was too much for him to resist. Davina left him briefly and came back with two large tumblers full of ice in one hand and a half full bottle of Jack Daniels in the other. She poured two large measures and raised her glass.

'Cheers,' Tayte said, and they both took a mouthful. Then as Davina sat beside him at the table, facing the picture windows and the shimmering early evening view of the estuary, he opened his laptop and logged in. 'We might as well just use mine for now. Can we take a look at that group photo you showed me on the *Osprey* again?'

Davina fetched her research files and laid them out on the table. She handed Tayte the photograph showing Alice on her father's knee, with her mother standing beside them, Oscar Scanlon and his wife Cordelia to the right, Frank Saxby to the left, and a line of highly decorated naval uniforms in the background.

'So, what are we looking for?' Tayte said. 'I find it's good to focus on something specific and see where it leads.'

'You said you were looking to prove that Alice Stilwell and your client's grandmother, Alice Dixon, were one and the same person.'

'Yes, and if that's true—as I believe it is—I also want to find out why she felt she had to leave her old life and her young family behind her when the *Empress of Ireland* sank. Those are the main answers I hope to find—the big picture if you like—but to see it clearly, I think it might help if we first try to put some of the smaller pieces of the puzzle into place.'

'The people in the photo?' Davina said.

Tayte tapped the image, nodding thoughtfully. 'All these people knew Alice. Most of them would have been around her in the years before she's supposed to have died. What do you know about Alice's father, Lord Charles Metcalfe?'

'Not much, I'm afraid. As I said earlier, most of my research has been about my husband's and my direct family history.' She tapped the image of Cordelia Scanlon née Metcalfe as she finished speaking. 'My husband's ancestry is only connected to the

Metcalfe family through Oscar Scanlon's marriage to Alice's Aunt Cordelia here.'

'I just wondered whether you knew anything about Charles Metcalfe from his descendants, since you're in touch—whether you'd heard any stories over the years.'

'No, I can't say I have,' Davina said as she topped up her drink. 'He was something of a British bulldog, by all accounts—very patriotic and pro British Empire. He served in the Royal Navy most of his life, extended service in the Admiralty before dabbling in politics after that. What do you know about him?'

'Only as much as Wikipedia and his vital records tell me, and what I've learned since arriving in England, which so far isn't much.' Tayte entered 'Lord Charles Metcalfe' into his Internet browser. 'The current family's attitude towards Alice must stem from her father, though. He's as good a place as any to start digging.'

The search came back with too many results for Tayte to get interested in anything. Most were for a first baron, Charles Theophilus Metcalfe, who was a British colonial administrator in the early Victorian period.

'It's not him,' Tayte said as he added 'Admiral' to the search, which brought up the Wikipedia link he'd previously looked at.

'There's another entry for him,' Davina said a moment later, pointing a long polished fingernail at an entry partway down the screen.

'House of Commons speeches,' Tayte said. 'We could be here all night wading through those for anything useful.' He ran through the results, page by page, skipping over what appeared to be several minor connections to the Charles Metcalfe they were interested in, most of which were political. Then he saw a familiar entry that never failed to excite him. 'Here we are.' He clicked on the link. '*The Times* Digital Archive. It's one of my favourite resources.'

Tayte logged in via his paid subscription to the online newspaper archive that contained scanned images of every complete page from the newspaper dating from recent years back to its creation in 1785. Available to search online for close to a decade, it had helped him to break through many brick walls, and as he finished entering his information and the page he had requested came up, he hoped it might do so again now.

The article was dated December 1911, which Tayte thought was perhaps a little early to be of any interest. It concerned the Admiralty, in particular a memo from Winston Churchill, the First Lord of the Admiralty at the time, proposing that, because of the Anglo-German arms race, British merchant ships should be armed for their own protection, in case the need to defend themselves should arise. Reading on, Tayte saw only a passing mention of Charles Metcalfe in connection with the establishment of a committee to explore the matter further.

'That's no good,' Tayte said, but he hadn't expected to get lucky with the first hit. He knew he had to be more specific.

Returning to the archive's main search screen, he entered the date range he was interested in, which was between January and June 1914, covering those months of the year up until the date of death on Alice Stilwell's death certificate—29 May 1914. He entered 'Charles Metcalfe' into the search keywords field and clicked the search button. Several entries came back, and most seemed to be in connection with general Admiralty business as before, but not all.

'Admiral Christopher Waverley,' Tayte said to Davina. 'You mentioned that name before.' He brought Davina's photograph closer and singled out the man standing in the background with white hair and wiry sideburns.

'That's him,' Davina said. 'It looks like his obituary.'

'It is.' Tayte quickly found the entry in the right-hand column of the scanned newspaper page he was looking at.

'You're pretty good at this, aren't you?' Davina said.

Tayte zoomed in on the information they were interested in. 'I guess I've been in the business long enough to develop some kind of nose for it. There's so much information out there. It really helps if you know where to look.'

'You'll have to give me some pointers before you go home,' Davina said. 'You've certainly rekindled my interest.'

Tayte just smiled and continued the research. 'Waverley died on April 6th, 1914,' he said as he read on. 'Caring husband and loving father to two sons . . . A few names are mentioned.' He took out his notepad and wrote them all down. 'Charles Metcalfe is noted here as being a friend, which we already know from the photograph. Apart from a few name connections, it doesn't really tell us much.'

He went back to the search results, and as he scrolled down, Davina drew a sharp breath and pointed at the screen. 'That's got to be important.'

Tayte saw the entry, dated 20 April 1914, and he felt a tingle at the back of his neck. It concerned a discovery that had been made the day before the article was published, and it carried the title 'Body Found in River Thames!' He clicked the entry, wondering as he did so how it was connected to Lord Charles Metcalfe, the subject of his search, and whether it might be connected to Alice Stilwell. His thoughts drifted back to the accounts he'd read of those spies who were executed at the start of the First World War.

*Executed for passing information useful to an enemy . . .*

Tayte still knew very little about the nature of Alice's spying activity in 1914, but he supposed that her involvement was along the same lines. Whatever Alice was doing, and for whatever reasons, the timing and the nature of this article from *The Times*, published barely more than a month before Alice was supposed to have died, was close enough to make Tayte feel excited about it. When the corresponding page from *The Times* displayed on his laptop screen and he began to read the article, every instinct in his body told him that he was on to something.

# Chapter Fifteen

Tuesday, 21 April 1914.

It was just after ten in the morning, and with breakfast at Hamberley finished, Alice Stilwell sensed that her father was as keen to share the details of his trip to London with the police as the rest of the family were to hear about it. Lord Metcalfe ushered them into the front sitting room, where he asked everyone to be seated while he remained standing. Alice and her mother, Lilian, sat together on one settee, while her aunt and uncle, Cordelia and Oscar Scanlon, sat on the settee opposite them. Chester, though much improved after having being poisoned by Raskin's liquorice, was to remain in bed for the rest of the day under doctor's orders, and Charlotte had been placed in the care of Mrs Morris the cook, because, as Alice's father had said, his 'terrible news' was not for the ears of children.

Lord Metcalfe paced the rug that was laid out between the two settees, tapping his fingers together as though contemplating where to start. He reached the fireplace and wheeled around. 'I'll not leave you to your own suppositions a moment longer,' he said. 'The good admiral's wife, Florence Waverley, is dead!'

Oscar Scanlon was the only person in the room who didn't gasp at hearing the news. 'Dead?' he repeated.

'That is correct. Her body was found two days ago on the south bank of the River Thames. Beneath Blackfriars Bridge to be precise.'

'That really is terrible news,' Alice said.

'Indeed. Just as I said it was.'

Lilian Metcalfe's hand had been raised to her mouth since hearing the news. She slowly lowered it and said, 'What happened, Charles? Did the police say?'

'For the moment it's assumed she drowned, although I'm told the precise cause of death was difficult to establish because the body was so badly decomposed.'

'She must have died awhile ago, then,' Alice said. 'Perhaps around the time Admiral Waverley had his heart attack.'

'Yes,' her father said. 'And a connection between the two deaths seems highly likely, which is one of the reasons I was asked to go to London—to help the police establish a motive for why Admiral Waverley should want to murder his own wife.'

'That's preposterous,' Lilian said. 'They've been married nearly forty years.'

'I told them exactly that,' Lord Metcalfe said.

Oscar Scanlon sat forward. 'You said that was *one* of the reasons you were asked to go to London. What was the other?'

'Indeed, there were two reasons,' Lord Metcalfe said, 'and together they have helped the police to form a theory that is damnably hard to refute. One is that certain documents were discovered at Admiral Waverley's house—the details of which I am not at liberty to divulge, but suffice it to say that I was able to confirm that the contents of these documents was of a most secret nature. The other is that Admiral Waverley's sidearm is missing.'

'Secret documents?' Scanlon said.

'Most secret,' Lord Metcalfe corrected. 'The recently formed Secret Service Bureau is also involved, not least because the proposed theory is that Admiral Waverley was in the pay of Kaiser Wilhelm II. Their suggestion is that his wife discovered his traitorous activities, so he took her out to Tilbury to drown her, taking his sidearm with him as a precaution in case he had to use it on her. They're supposing that performing this dark deed was all too much for him—hence the heart attack that followed.'

'But why is his gun missing?' Alice asked. 'Surely it would have been found on his person or beside his body where he fell.'

'A simple matter. Someone else must have discovered the body prior to the alarm being raised and taken the revolver. It's a reasonable explanation, I suppose, but I can't think it of Waverley. He was a good man. I knew him too long and too well to doubt his allegiance. Christopher Waverley, a spy for the kaiser? I can't think of a single person besides myself least likely to do such a lowly and unpatriotic thing.'

In light of Alice's current situation, another theory was running through her mind, but she didn't dare voice it. What if Florence Waverley had been kidnapped, just as her husband had been? What if she had been held to ransom in exchange for naval secrets? Perhaps the Admiral had removed the documents, ready for the exchange, but had chosen to take his revolver instead, hoping to free his wife. But the excitement had proven too much for him. His revolver might have been taken after he dropped it, and his wife later drowned and her body cast into the Thames. It was just another theory, but given what she knew, Alice thought it the more likely of the two.

*Lowly and unpatriotic . . .*

Alice felt just that as she got to her feet and delivered the lie that, between bouts of fitful sleep, it had taken her most of the night to invent.

'If you'll all excuse me,' she said. 'I have to go out and won't be back until this evening.'

'Where are you going?' Alice's mother asked.

'To Margate. I saw an old friend in Rochester yesterday who told me that my good friend Violet is very sick. I must go and see her. You remember Violet, don't you?'

Lilian looked confused. 'Yes, dear, but I didn't know you two were still friends. You've not seen her since the family moved away, have you? You were still children then.'

Alice took a step towards the door. 'Which is all the more reason I must go and see her now. Suppose she dies?'

'Yes, well, of course you must go and see her.'

'How will you get there?' her father asked.

Alice made a point of eying the mantle clock. 'I'm going by train, and I really must be getting along, or I'll miss it. I want to look in on Chester and Charlotte first.'

She felt bad about leaving Chester while he was still confined to his bed, but he was making a speedy recovery, just as Raskin had said he would, and to not go to Dover as he had instructed her to would only put her son in danger again. Raskin had been very clear about that.

Alice's Aunt Cordelia spoke then for the first time since breakfast. 'Oscar will drive you to the train station, won't you Oscar?'

'Yes, of course. I was going out anyway. I've got to see a man about a camera. It won't be any bother.'

'It's a new business idea,' Cordelia said. 'Oscar wants to open a photographic studio, don't you Oscar?'

'Well, I—'

Alice cut in, not wishing to be detained any longer. 'Thank you,' she said, thinking that her lie, which had perhaps slipped too easily from her lips, had worked very well.

# Chapter Sixteen

Originally opened in 1865 as the Clarence Hotel, the Burlington Hotel, as it had later been named, stood in a prominent position in Dover Bay, facing the seafront directly in line with Promenade Pier. Alice had hired a bicycle as soon as she got off the train, and after she'd asked for directions, the hotel had been easy to find. She was standing in the breeze on the pier. The white cliffs of Dover rose in the distance to either side of the bay, with the medieval fortress that was Dover Castle, 'the key to England,' sitting atop the cliffs to her right, the Western Docks and tidal harbour to her left. It was already late morning, and the sky was patchy with high, bright clouds that Alice thought posed no threat of rain. For the past fifteen minutes, she had been gazing across Clarence Lawn, up at the letters that spelled out the hotel's name, telling herself every now and then that everything would be all right and that she really could do this.

On the train journey she'd had plenty of time to think about the events surrounding the deaths of Admiral Waverley and his wife, and during that time, with nothing else to do but watch the countryside speed past her compartment window, she had formed another theory. If she was right about Florence Waverley having been kidnapped and about her husband having been forced to hand over secret naval documents for her safe return, she supposed that whoever was behind the plot was now trying something similar with her and her family. In Waverley's case, his patriotism had proven too strong, but surely even the most patriotic mother could not allow harm to come to her children if by her own actions she could prevent it. Was that what Raskin had in mind for her? Did he now mean to use her to obtain the same kind of naval intelligence they had previously tried to get from Admiral Waverley? Alice was sure of it.

The breeze whipped up suddenly, tugging at her skirt and threatening to steal away her new straw boater. She held on to it and took a deep breath as she set her bicycle against the pier railing. Then she collected her handbag from the handlebars and made her way between the kiosks that fronted the pier, towards the hotel, crossing Marine Parade and then Clarence Lawn, not daring to stop until she was inside the hotel; otherwise, she thought she might lose the courage to go on again.

Inside the Burlington Hotel, the lobby was colonial in style, with latticed wainscoting and parlour palms here and there in brightly coloured ceramic pots. Alice made straight for the reception desk and asked to see Mr Raimund Drescher, the head waiter, as Raskin had instructed. A few minutes later, a man wearing a black suit and a light-grey tie came into the lobby and presented himself to her. His thin face wore a quizzical expression.

'I am Drescher,' he said with a clipped German accent. 'How may I be of service?'

He was a short, thin-lipped man with a balding pate, who looked older to Alice than she thought he probably was. She moved closer so that her softly spoken reply could not be overheard, noticing as she did so that he was missing his right earlobe.

'How is your mother?' she said, remembering the lines Raskin had given her. 'I hope she is well.'

Drescher drew an audible breath through his teeth. Then in an equally low voice he said, 'Come with me.'

Alice followed Drescher through a set of double doors and then along a panelled corridor before entering through another door marked 'Private.' Part way along the narrower corridor on the other side, Drescher stopped.

'In here. Quickly.'

Drescher opened another door, and Alice stepped through into a cramped, windowless room—a storeroom, judging from the shelves and crates she could just about distinguish in the low light. Drescher flicked a switch as he closed the door behind him, and an electric lamp came on.

'What is your name?' Drescher asked.

'Alice.'

'Well then, Alice. Did you bring a notepad and pencil with you?'

Alice nodded.

'I must say. You are far prettier than any of the others who have come to enquire about my mother.'

Alice feigned a polite smile, not wishing to offend. That Drescher did not smile as he spoke made her all the more nervous now that she was alone in such a confined space with him.

Drescher edged slowly past her, brushing his arm against her as he went. She watched him go to the back of the room, where he slid one of the crates out from a lower shelf. Then he dropped to his knees and reached for something at the back of the shelf. A moment later he returned with a sheet of paper.

'Raimund Drescher is too smart a man to keep this sort of thing in his room,' Drescher said, handing the paper to Alice.

'What is it?' Alice asked, studying what was clearly a series of crude drawings of ships with letters and numbers written beside them. She put it in her handbag beside her notepad.

'It is a simple identification aid and code sheet. You will use it to identify the ships you see coming and going in the harbour. You must not let anyone else see it. Is that clear?'

'Yes, quite clear.'

'Very well. Write down the identification number from the sheet, followed by the location of the ship and any markings you see. You will also observe the area in general and take note of anything you feel could be of benefit to our cause, come the day.'

'Come the day?'

Drescher grabbed Alice's arm and cast a suspicious eye over her. 'You are either very new to this, or you are not all you seem.' He shook her. 'Which is it?'

'New,' Alice offered. 'I'm very new. You're hurting my arm.'

Drescher gave a condescending scoff as he let her go. 'I refer to the day of the invasion of England,' he said. 'Never forget it.'

The thought left Alice cold. 'I won't,' she said. 'Never.'

'Good. I'll show you back to the lobby. You must be discreet. Keep moving so as not to draw attention. The Admiralty Pier to the west and the Prince of Wales Pier will give you the best vantage points. When your task is done, go home and prepare your report for your agent in the usual way.'

'Music sheets and lemon juice,' Alice said. 'And Raskin showed me a cipher—'

'No names!' Drescher interrupted. 'And especially not that name.'

He rubbed at the lower edge of his right ear, where his earlobe should have been, and Alice knew she was looking at the Dutchman's handiwork.

'Be careful around that one,' Drescher said. 'He is not someone you want to cross.'

Alice swallowed dryly. 'I will,' she said. 'How will I know when my task is done?'

'You will be finished when it is too dark to see,' Drescher said, making for the door.

This time as he passed her, Alice pinned herself back against the shelving so as to avoid contact with him. He went for the light switch and paused, turning back to her, eying her up and down in a way that made her feel all the more uncomfortable.

'Perhaps you need a job?' he said. 'I can find work for a pretty girl at the hotel.'

Alice immediately wondered what would be expected of her in return. 'No, thank you.'

'As you wish.'

Drescher went for the light again, and again he paused. 'You know, if you would like to have dinner this evening, I can promise you the finest dining in Dover, and who knows, maybe a little champagne?'

'I really don't—'

'If you are in no hurry to return,' Drescher continued, cutting in. 'I could even find you a comfortable room here in the hotel tonight.'

Alice felt her skin crawl. 'No, thank you,' she said again, a little firmer this time.

Without saying another word, Drescher switched the light off, and the small room was plunged into darkness. Alice gasped, fully expecting his hands to find her at any moment, knowing she would not be able to call for help and risk discovery. There was too much at stake. As it was, the door clicked open, and instead of Drescher's hands, it was the light from the corridor outside that found her. Drescher poked his head out to make sure the way was clear.

'Come,' he said, and Alice followed him back to the lobby, where they parted company without further discourse.

As Alice reached the main doors, she became aware of a man in a tweed suit and bowler hat sitting by one of the lobby windows. She would have thought he was merely waiting for someone were it not for the way he seemed to study her, to the point of being rude, as she passed him. She was certain she had never seen him before, and his unwanted attention caused her to quicken her pace as she neared the main doors, thinking that she never wanted to set foot in the Burlington Hotel again.

———

Collecting her hired bicycle from the pier, Alice tied her hat beneath her chin and pedalled west into the wind, along Marine Parade towards the esplanade and the piers Drescher had suggested she use to best monitor the harbour activity. Although the day was generally bright, it was still cold enough to keep the crowds away. She saw people on the beach and others strolling along the esplanade as she passed, but not in the numbers she imagined would be there in the height of summer if it was anything like Margate. The people she saw were mostly wrapped in their coats, and she was glad of hers as she pushed her pedals harder and the wind began to bite.

As she circled the inner harbour by Granville Dock and came to Admiralty Pier, the longest of Dover's piers, at over four thousand feet, she slowed, thinking about how Drescher had referred to Raskin as her 'agent' and about how Raskin had told her she was now a 'fixed post.' She imagined that Drescher was another, and she wondered how many 'fixed posts' there were in England, and how many agents. She was now of the impression that a whole network of spies was abroad in England, all feeding information back to Germany and the kaiser through the chain of command that had been established. She wondered then who Raskin reported to. She didn't imagine he reported direct to Germany himself. He was known to her and no doubt many others like her. She thought that anyone reporting direct to Germany would be as far removed from the front line as possible so as to reduce the risk of discovery.

Arriving at the pier walkway, Alice dismounted from her bicycle and leaned it against the iron railings before climbing the steep steps that now forced her to continue on foot. To her right, over a thick wall, was the English Channel, and to her left was the harbour. Immediately below her, she could see the train tracks that had been laid to serve the ships that docked alongside the pier. There was a cross-channel passenger steamer on the other side of the water, alongside the Prince of Wales Pier, but Alice supposed that was of little interest to Raskin and his company of spies. What she was there to record were the splashes of battleship grey—as her father had once told her the colour was officially called—that she could see further along the pier and out in the Channel.

She stopped walking about halfway along the pier and discreetly took out the chart Drescher had given her, using it to identify two types of cruiser and an armed yacht. After noting them down, she went out to the lighthouse at the end of the pier, where the wind became so strong she had to remove her hat altogether or risk losing it to the sea. Looking out into the Channel, she saw an easily identifiable destroyer, which she noted down along with the details of the other ships she had so far collected.

On her way back, the sight of at least three ships out in the Channel stopped her in her tracks. They were coming towards the harbour in a convoy from the west. They were too far distant, and she knew she would need to see them from the side to accurately determine their type, but she thought if she waited, she would soon be able to. She leaned over the wall and rested her chin on her arms, closing her eyes as the wind pinned her hair back. She would have been happy to wait like that for those ships to arrive, had a voice not startled her, reminding her of Drescher's advice to keep moving.

'Do you need any help, miss?'

Alice spun around and felt her cheeks flush with guilt.

'What are you doing out here by yourself?'

The man was smiling at her, and Alice felt no alarm, but she had to think fast.

'I'm planning to paint the harbour,' she said. 'I was just looking for the best composition.'

The man smiled broadly. 'Well, you won't find it looking out to sea.'

'No, I'm sure I won't,' Alice said, meeting his smile. 'I was just resting.'

She bid the man a good day and set off again, thinking that she would make her way to the Prince of Wales Pier and watch the convoy of ships come in from there. On her way back it seemed that every man she passed eyed her with suspicion, and she supposed it was a little unusual for a woman to be out on this particular pier unaccompanied. It wasn't anything like Promenade Pier, where it was common to take casual strolls to the pavilion and back. She saw her bicycle again and descended the steps towards it. Then, halfway down, she froze when she thought she saw the man in the tweed suit and bowler hat from the hotel lobby earlier. He was standing beside a horse and carriage by the pier gatehouse. Alice looked away briefly, trying not to let on that she'd seen him. When she reached her bicycle and glanced over again, he was no longer there.

Alice laughed nervously at herself as she pedalled away, convinced that her imagination was getting the better of her. Just the same, she took a particular interest in looking out for tweed-suited gentlemen as she cycled back the way she had come by the Western Docks, taking only a few minutes to get there.

The railway tracks on the Prince of Wales Pier were on the same level as the walkway, although Alice hadn't seen any trains coming or going from this pier, supposing it was no longer in use. She passed the clock tower that marked the entrance to the pier and cycled towards the passenger steamer she had seen earlier from Admiralty Pier, with its twin funnels. It bore the letters 'SECR,' which she knew stood for the South Eastern and Chatham Railway. Further on, she had to slow for the passengers waiting to board the ship, and then she pushed on to the lighthouse at the end of the pier, knowing that from there she would have the best view of the convoy of warships as they came into the harbour.

Every minute Alice had to wait, the tenser she became. After the first few minutes had passed, she began to ride around the lighthouse, and after that she rode to the steamer and back so as to keep on the move. She was glad all those passengers were there because they gave everyone else something to focus on other than her. When at last the first flash of battleship grey appeared in the mouth of the harbour, Alice stopped pedalling and took out her chart and notepad. A few minutes later she could see all three ships, and she quickly recorded a Dreadnaught class battleship and two destroyers similar to the one she had seen anchored in the Channel, the view to which was now obscured by the harbour's Southern Breakwater.

*Keep moving,* Alice told herself.

She put everything back into her bag and got on her bicycle, having decided she had recorded enough information for now. As she came onto the pier, she saw by the clock tower that it was still early afternoon, so she thought she would go in search of some light refreshment. She could come back afterwards and loiter by the harbour and the docks until sunset, which for Alice could not come soon enough. As she began to pedal, however, she saw the man in the tweed suit again, and she stopped abruptly, causing her brakes to judder. She stared at the man long enough this time to see that he had a crooked nose that appeared slightly squashed on his face, as if he might have been a boxer, or had at least seen his share of street brawls.

He was on foot as before, but this time a moment of startling recognition flashed between them as they locked eyes, and in that moment Alice knew beyond any doubt that he was following her. More alarming was the determination on his face and in his manner as he came directly towards her. It was clear that his intention was to challenge her, and what then? He would discover her treason, and all would be lost. She was trapped at the end of the pier, and there was only one way back.

Alice looked around, quickly weighing her options. They appeared to be few: the sea or the steamer. Then she decided there was one other option open to her. It was bold, but she couldn't see how jumping into the sea would save her any more than she thought she could escape him by boarding the steamer. She turned the bicycle around and began to pedal back to the lighthouse. A quick glance over her shoulder told her that the man in the tweed suit had started to run after her. She kicked harder. She needed speed.

The lighthouse was wide enough so as not to slow her down as she came to it. She kept going, all the way around it, pedalling faster until she was heading back along the pier. The man was less than twenty feet from her now, and Alice gave it everything she had. Faster and faster she went, heading right at him. As she arrived, she saw the troubled look in his eyes just before she ducked her head down. She saw a flash of tweed out of the corner of her eye, and she felt the man grab at her coat, but she was going too fast. His grip gave out, and she was away, pedalling for her life, it seemed. When she chanced a look back, she saw the man pick up his hat and dust it off as he stared after her.

# Chapter Seventeen

It was late evening by the time Alice returned to Hamberley, having taken a hansom cab from the railway station. Thankfully, she saw no more of the man in the tweed suit that day. After leaving the pier, she had cycled away from the harbour, through the town and out the other side, not daring to chance her return train journey so soon after the ordeal on the Prince of Wales Pier. She had feared her pursuer would suspect she had arrived in Dover by train and would go to the main station to look for her, so she had waited almost four hours, counting on the idea that any man's patience would have run out by then.

As the train sped Alice back through the dark Kent countryside, she had plenty of time to reflect on who the man could have been. She thought it unlikely that he had followed her all the way to Dover, so she supposed he must have been watching Drescher at the Burlington Hotel and that he had become suspicious of her when she made contact with him. If the man was on to Drescher, then Alice could only conclude that he must have been a spy catcher of sorts, perhaps working for the Special Branch of the police or for the Secret Service Bureau her father had mentioned after breakfast that morning. Whoever he was, Alice knew she had made a narrow escape.

Hamberley was all but in darkness when she entered. The air was cool and quiet save for the perpetual ticking of the clocks, and she was glad she had thought to take a key to the side door with her, because her parents had clearly retired for the night, and she didn't want to disturb them. She lit a candle from the kitchen and removed her shoes so as to make as little sound as possible. Then she made her way along the corridor that led to the main staircase, wondering how well Chester had recovered and thinking to look in on both of her children on her way to bed.

She was about to climb the stairs when she heard a sound that drew her eye to her father's study. Was it a voice? She thought it was, but she couldn't be sure. She held up her candle and saw that the study door was closed, but there was a faint amber glow filling the gap beneath it. She thought her father must still be up, working late. But whom was he with? She went to the door, proposing to find out and to let him know she was home again, but as she drew closer, she heard the voice again and faltered. It was not her father. She was certain of it. She couldn't make out whose voice it was, but he was talking in whispers, and Alice believed her father incapable of talking so quietly—and why would he in his own home?

Alice pressed her ear to the door, momentarily thinking that spying was becoming second nature to her. She could determine the words that were being spoken, always from that same hushed voice, and she quickly realised that whoever was in the room was talking on the telephone: her father's telephone in her father's study. She thought it must be her uncle. Oscar Scanlon had reportedly taken so many liberties since he and her Aunt Cordelia had taken up residence at Hamberley that Alice supposed he now considered her father's study as much his own as the contents of her father's wine cellar.

*But why is he whispering?*

Alice was intrigued, and as much as she knew it was wrong to remain there, given the late hour and the clandestine nature of the conversation, she felt there was something underhand taking place and considered it her duty to stay.

'I see,' the man said. 'Yes, it's all arranged.'

Alice couldn't fathom what the hushed conversation was about.

'A minor complication,' the voice continued, 'but it's all in hand.'

Alice wondered what was arranged and what was in hand. Was it another one of Uncle Oscar's dubious business deals? What she heard next almost made her drop her candle.

'Come the day, we shall both be very wealthy men. Now I must go.' There was a pause. 'Yes, until then.'

Alice heard the telephone rattle back into its cradle, and she ran silently from the door, blowing out her candle as she went. She quickly found the shadows in one of the alcoves and hid, trying to control her breathing as the study door opened. She wanted to look to see who it was, but she resisted out of fear of discovery. She heard footsteps on the wooden flooring. Then they stopped suddenly, and Alice stopped breathing altogether. She heard another sound then, as though someone was sniffing the air. She realised she could smell it too. Her candle was still smoking. She squeezed the hot wick between her thumb and forefinger, hoping it hadn't already given her away. A moment later the footsteps continued, and she breathed again. When the footsteps were distant, she came out into the dark hall and followed after them.

The squeak of a dry door hinge drew her to the passageway on her right. She saw light spill out from an open door, and then it closed again. It was the door to the games room. She went to it and listened again and immediately picked up another conversation. There were two people this time, and their words were not whispered, but spoken clearly and confidently, without regard for being overheard. It seemed they were playing cards and were soon laughing about something. Alice recognised the voices as those of Oscar Scanlon and Frank Saxby.

She wondered what Saxby was doing there so late and concluded there were any number of reasons. 'Uncle' Frank needed no invite to Hamberley. She supposed that while he was there, her real uncle had enticed him into an after-dinner game of cards to try to win some money from him. It didn't matter to Alice how or why either of them were there. What did matter was which of them had just been in her father's study.

*Come the day . . .*

Those words replayed through her mind, and she wondered whether she was just becoming paranoid, like so many other people in England, about German spies and the threat of invasion. Yet she herself was proof of their existence, if any were needed. Could there really be another spy at Hamberley besides herself? Alice could not deny her own ears, but which of them was it? She turned away from the door and went up to her room, deep in thought. She was unsure of the answer, but she was going to find out.

# Chapter Eighteen

Present day.

Jefferson Tayte awoke from a restless sleep, squinting at the bright sunrise that was pushing through the gaps in the blind at his hotel room window. He rolled out of bed in the Hershey's boxer shorts Jean had sent him for Christmas and made straight for the coffee machine, noting along the way that it was just after eight—Wednesday already. Following the research at Davina's apartment the night before, Tayte hadn't stayed long. His body clock was still running on DC time, and his second glass of Jack Daniels just made him want to sleep. So, as soon as their line of research had been concluded, he'd made his excuses and called it a day, much to Davina's disappointment. Tayte imagined she would have stayed up researching with him all night if he'd had it in him.

As he switched the coffee machine on, his thoughts were already back on the articles he'd read in *The Times* Digital Archive about Admiral Waverley's heart attack and the question of what he was doing at Tilbury Docks in the middle of the night, and of the discovery of his wife's decomposed body, found in the Thames two weeks later. He considered that much speculation, but no solid conclusions, had been drawn to explain with any certainty how their deaths had come about, but he thought it was useful information to have.

The connection to Charles Metcalfe that had led him to the articles had proven tenuous at best—Lord Metcalfe having been called upon to assist in the official enquiry, both as a Lord of the Admiralty and a close friend of the late Admiral Waverley, for whose character Charles Metcalfe had gone on record to defend, stating that Admiral Waverley was as devoted a patriot as King George V himself. In reading the accusations against Waverley, of stealing Admiralty secrets prior to his death, and of the concern over his missing service revolver, Tayte could not help but wonder, given the suspicious circumstances surrounding the death of Waverley's wife so close to his own, whether the Admiral had been put under pressure to obtain those naval documents for someone. He wondered, then, whether there was a connection to Alice. Were the same people forcing her to spy for them?

Tayte decided he wasn't ready to shower and dress just yet, so he slipped his guest bathrobe on, poured his coffee and sat down at his laptop, thinking to move his research on. From his briefcase, he pulled out Davina's photograph of the Metcalfe family-and-friends gathering, which she'd let him hold on to. Standing beside Admiral Waverley was Lord Ashcroft, and the Ashcroft family had interested Tayte, not least because of the young boy standing in front of his father in the image, whom Davina had told him was known as Archie.

Tayte thought a visit to the current descendants of Lord Ashcroft could prove fruitful, so he called up the 1911 UK census to find out where they were living at the time the census was taken. He checked his notebook and saw that he didn't have a first name for Lord Ashcroft, whom he thought was likely the head of the household, so he entered the search criteria for the only full name he did have: first name, 'Archibald'; last name, 'Ashcroft.' In the place-of-residence field he entered 'Kent,' which was where Davina had said she believed the family were from.

Hitting the search button presented Tayte with a single entry that showed a birth year of 1889; the subject's age in 1911, which was twenty-two; and an entry in the district column showing 'Medway,' all of which gave Tayte confidence that he was looking at the right record. He preferred to do his own transcribing where possible, so he clicked to view the original page, knowing such a page often contained more information than could be found on the general transcripts. When he saw that the head of the household was listed as 'Lord Thomas Ashcroft,' and that his profession was listed as 'Royal Navy, Board of Admiralty,' he had no doubt that he was looking at the right family.

Archibald's relationship to the head of the household was recorded as 'son,' which was as Tayte expected. It told him that Thomas Ashcroft's wife was called Lydia and that they had another son, Ernest, and a daughter who was no longer alive in 1911. Several members of staff were also listed on the report, along with a large number of rooms, which said a good deal about the status of the family—again, to be expected for such a high-ranking naval official. For his records, Tayte took a screen shot of the page, which contained so much more information that was useful to someone in his profession, such as the civil parish of each member of the household, as well as the person's place of birth. Then he wrote down the address in South Gillingham as it was recorded in 1911, hoping that the descendants of Lord Thomas Ashcroft still lived there.

He opened another browser and brought up a map application. A few seconds later he was looking at an aerial photograph of a mansion and grounds that were not far from his current location, but he knew it wasn't going to be easy to get in touch with the occupants—he didn't expect to find their number in the phone directory. He reminded himself of the welcome Raife Metcalfe had given him at Hamberley when he'd first arrived in England, and he decided he didn't want to turn up unannounced again this time.

*DI Bishop . . .*

Tayte thought that as Bishop had managed to get him an interview with Reginald Metcalfe at Hamberley the day before, it was worth a phone call to find out whether he could help out again with the Ashcrofts. Tayte checked the time again and thought it a little too early to call to find out, so he made for the shower, thinking that if DI Bishop couldn't help, he'd go along to the address anyway, if only to find out whether the Ashcrofts still lived there.

Two hours later, Tayte was sitting in the front passenger seat of DI Bishop's unmarked police car, briefcase between his feet, heading for an address the Inspector had told him was no more than a fifteen-minute drive into the Kent countryside, to the south of their present location. When Tayte had called, he'd thought Bishop sounded far from enthusiastic about the prospects of visiting the Ashcroft family, but Bishop had offered to see what he could find out. He'd called back an hour later, having confirmed in that time an appointment with the current Lord Ashcroft, who was descended from Archibald Ashcroft's brother, Ernest.

'They're having a tennis lesson until eleven,' Bishop said, chewing on one of Tayte's Mr Goodbar Hershey's miniatures. He pulled the car out of the hotel car park onto the main road.

'It's a fine morning for it,' Tayte said, gazing out the window and up into the blue, wondering what new information he might discover today. 'Did you have any trouble persuading the family to see us?'

'None at all. Once I'd explained who you were and the nature of our visit, I was informed that Lord Ashcroft was only too happy to see us.'

'That makes a nice change,' Tayte said, reminding both of them that his occupational penchant for digging up the past wasn't always welcome.

Bishop laughed under his breath as they continued through Chatham's suburbs in the seemingly ever-present traffic.

'I was hoping to see you today, anyway,' Bishop said. 'With any luck I should have something to show you later.'

'With any luck?'

'It might be nothing, but if it is, how are you fixed this afternoon?'

Tayte thought his schedule was far from crowded. 'No plans I can't change,' he said, thinking that he had to pick his car up from Gillingham Marina where he'd left it because he'd taken a taxi back to his hotel the night before. 'I thought I'd call on Mrs Scanlon at some point. She's understandably keen to help find her husband's killer, and she's proving to be very helpful.'

'Yes, I'm sure she's pinning a lot of hope on your assignment. I do hope all this is leading somewhere.'

So did Tayte. He couldn't miss the sideways glance Bishop had given him as he said that, letting him know that he remained sceptical about the value of Tayte's assignment in his murder investigation.

They turned off the main road, leaving the town behind them, and the landscape seemed to change in an instant from concrete grey to emerald green.

'How long have you been in law enforcement?' Tayte asked.

'I've worked for Kent police since I dropped out of university partway through my second term,' Bishop said. 'I suppose I rejected my further education at Canterbury as a protest against my parents. They seemed determined to dictate the entire course of my life, but I can see now that they meant well. They wanted me to become a barrister, and with a family history embedded in the judiciary for generations, I suppose law at one level or another was always on the cards for me.'

'But you didn't want to be a barrister?'

'I was young. I think I just didn't want to be what my parents wanted me to be. So I chose to help tackle crime at the source—prevention over prosecution, as it were.'

'Well, it's an admirable profession,' Tayte said.

Bishop laughed. 'I wish everyone shared that view.'

They continued in silence for about half a mile, when Tayte's thoughts turned back to the events of the day before. 'Did you turn anything up after the break-ins at Mrs Scanlon's properties?' he asked. 'Any leads?'

'Nothing to get excited about. It's amazing the amount of material our modern forensics teams can gather from a scene, but it takes time to analyse. And even if they do find a match with anything found at the scene of Lionel Scanlon's murder, it only tells us that the same person was likely present at both locations. Unless he's on file, it's unlikely, we'd be able to confirm his identity until we have a suspect to bring in.'

Tayte was beginning to wonder how anything he might uncover by digging up Alice Stilwell's past life might lead to a suspect here in the present, although it wouldn't be the first time that had happened. 'Are you any closer to finding a motive for Lionel Scanlon's murder?'

Bishop gave a wry smile. 'That would be nice, but I'm hoping that's where you come in. His killer clearly wants something he thought Mr Scanlon had with him in his workshop that night. If the same man was responsible for the break-ins, then I have a good idea of his height and build, although both are pretty average, which doesn't help.'

'You've seen him?'

Bishop nodded. 'In a manner of speaking. There are plenty of CCTV cameras at the Marina. The images from the floor covering

Mrs Scanlon's apartment show a man wearing blue maintenance overalls and a grey ski mask, exiting the lift. He collects a fire extinguisher from the rack on the wall and hammers at the apartment door until the lock gives out. Then in he goes. He's inside no more that five minutes before he's seen going back into the lift. Job done.'

'What about the other cameras?' Tayte asked. 'Was he seen anywhere else?'

'Not in any way that he could be recognised. My guess is that he'd checked the camera locations beforehand and planned his exit so as to avoid them. I suspect he changed out of the overalls and removed his mask in the lift.'

'It wasn't covered by the security cameras?'

'No, and he must have known that, too. They're generally not too hard to spot, mind you.'

'I don't suppose he was careless enough to leave the overalls and mask behind?'

Bishop drew a breath through his teeth, shaking his head as he turned the car onto a lane bordered by farmland—wheat still young and green in the sunlit fields. 'No, and he's proving to be anything but careless. The overalls were marina issue, for maintenance staff. They wouldn't have been too hard to pick up, and without the mask he'd have blended right in, even if he was still wearing them when he came back out of the lift. The only other people who show up on the various cameras around the time of the break-in can be accounted for. They're mostly staff and a few people who live at the marina, or have boats moored there. None of the people we interviewed afterwards saw anything unusual. It's like he just vanished, but as I say, you just have to know where the cameras are.'

They reached a junction and turned right, plunging into shade beneath a leafy canopy as the road rose before them.

'We're almost there,' Bishop said. 'Have you got your questions worked out?'

Tayte smiled to himself. 'I don't really work to an agenda like that, but yes, I'm all set. I often find it best just to set the ball rolling and listen. Folks generally like to talk about the past once they get started, and who doesn't like an excuse to get the old family photos out?'

As they came to the brow of the hill and emerged from the canopy of trees, Tayte saw the house they were heading for to their left. He recognised the bold red brickwork and the general landscape of fields and trees from the aerial view he'd seen on his laptop earlier. Drawing closer, he thought that it was not on the same stately scale as Hamberley, but it was nonetheless a fine English mansion, with several thick chimney stacks on two main floors, Dutch gables and a tower-like main entrance that was topped with a pediment.

When Bishop turned the car onto the drive and proceeded past what appeared to be the ruin of the former gatehouse, Tayte began to wonder just how close Alice had been to the young Archibald Ashcroft and how much the descendants of his brother, Ernest, knew about their time together before the First World War. As Bishop stopped the car on the limestone gravel outside the main entrance, Tayte supposed he was about to find out.

# Chapter Nineteen

Tayte and DI Bishop were met on the drive of the Ashcroft residence by a cheerful young member of staff in a smart navy suit. He informally introduced himself as John, and then he escorted them to the rear of the house, where the thump of tennis balls could be heard. John ushered them to a table on the partially shaded terrace behind the house, which overlooked the tennis court and gardens, with an expanse of hazy countryside beyond.

'They should be finished soon,' John said as they sat down. 'Can I get you something to drink?'

'Black coffee, thanks,' Tayte and Bishop said in harmony, and John left them to watch the tennis, which Tayte thought was all very British.

He settled back on the upholstered rattan chair he'd been invited to sit on, and while they waited for their hosts to finish their game, he asked Bishop, 'Are you from Kent?'

Bishop raised his eyebrows and nodded. 'Born and bred.'

'So, are you a Kentish man or a man of Kent? I see there's a distinction, depending on where you were born.'

'I was born near Canterbury, east of the River Medway, so according to folk lore that makes me a man of Kent.'

'And any man born in Kent to the west of the Medway is a Kentish man?'

'Or maid if it's a woman. It harks back to the days of William the Conqueror. The East resisted the invasion, while the West surrendered without putting up much of a fight, so the East came to regard the West as Kent-ish, or so I read.'

Tayte became aware then that the near constant sound of a tennis ball being thumped back and forth since their arrival had stopped. He looked back towards the court to see three people—two men and a woman in their tennis whites—walking slowly up the garden path towards them. They were dabbing at their perspiration with towels as they talked, and judging from his animated arm movements, Tayte supposed the taller, younger of the two men was the tennis coach, finishing off the lesson. The coach broke away before reaching the terrace steps, and Tayte and Bishop stood up as their hosts came to meet them.

'Good morning,' the man said in bright tones, still trying to catch his breath. 'It's another fine one, isn't it? Although I could use a breeze to help cool me down.'

Tayte and Bishop returned his smile. Tayte put him in his fifties. He had short brown hair of a slightly unnatural shade, which was glistening with sweat in the sunlight. Beside him was a woman who appeared a few years his junior, her blonde hair tied up in a ponytail behind her tennis cap.

'Thank you for agreeing to see us, Lord Ashcroft,' Bishop said. Then, as he made to continue, their host stopped him.

'Do call me Brendan,' he said. 'I don't go in for all that peerage puffery. This is my wife, Rachel.'

Everyone sat down, and John arrived with a tray bearing a large cafetière of coffee with all the usual accoutrements, two tall glasses, and a jug containing what appeared to be Pimm's.

'The sun's just about over the yardarm,' Brendan said as he poured his and his wife's drinks. 'At least, it is in the North Atlantic this time of year, which is where the phrase was first coined, and

Pimm's is just the tonic after a gruelling hour on the court. Help yourselves to the coffee, or shall I have John bring some more glasses?'

'Thank you,' Bishop said, 'but not while I'm on duty.'

'Coffee's good for me,' Tayte added as he picked up the cafetière and poured, thinking that a caffeine shot was all the tonic he needed.

'Will there be anything else?' John asked, addressing Brendan.

Brendan began to answer, but his wife beat him to it. 'There's a cardboard box on the landing at the top of the back staircase,' she said. 'Could you bring it out to us?'

'Of course,' John said, and then he retreated back into the house via the terrace doors he'd previously arrived by.

The idea of a box being brought out to them greatly intrigued Tayte. He was already imagining what it might contain, hoping there would be something to help unlock another piece of the puzzle that was Alice Stilwell's life.

'So . . .' Brendan said as they all settled back with their drinks. 'How can we be of service?'

Bishop answered. 'I'm investigating a recent murder that could be connected to events that occurred a hundred years ago.'

Tayte saw that as his cue to join in. 'And I'm trying to put those past events together,' he said. 'Events that appear to centre around a young woman called Alice Stilwell née Metcalfe. Are you still in touch with the Metcalfe family? By all accounts your ancestors were close family friends.'

'Not so much these days, I'm afraid,' Brendan said. 'We cross paths at one function or another from time to time, but that's about it. Associative friendships tend to drift once the root has gone, don't you think?'

'Yes, I suppose they do,' Tayte said, thinking that he hadn't been in touch with Marcus Brown's wife, Emmy, so much since his old friend had died. He made a mental note to correct that, and then he moved the conversation on. 'I've heard that Alice was a close childhood friend of Archibald Ashcroft—your great-grandfather's brother and the son of Lord Thomas Ashcroft.'

Tayte already had his briefcase open on the floor beside him, with Davina's photo at the ready. He withdrew it and slid it across the table, indicating the two young people he was referring to.

'I know the names,' Brendan said, and Rachel nodded in agreement. 'I've no need to tell you that Thomas Ashcroft was a naval man—that much is plain from this picture. You might not know, however, that Archibald followed in his father's footsteps.'

'He died very young, didn't he?' Rachel said. She sounded unsure.

Brendan nodded. 'I believe the First World War took him, although I've never checked. I suppose that's why my great-grandfather, Ernest, inherited all this.' He cast a hand towards the house and added, 'Fate can change with the wind, can't it? For good or bad.'

John came out with the aforementioned box then, and Rachel went to meet him, carrying it the rest of the way before setting it down on the floor beside her chair. Tayte thought it looked like an old hat box, and it was still dusty, clearly having been tucked away out of sight and mind for some years. Rachel sat down again, removed the lid and reached inside, bringing a handful of old photographs up onto the table.

'I knew we had these somewhere,' she said. 'It didn't take long to find them after you called this morning, Inspector.' She began to flick through the images, pausing from time to time to study one. 'Most of them look too recent to be of any interest to you,' she added. Then she set them aside and delved into the box again, bringing up another handful. 'Here we are. This looks more promising.'

She looked one of the photographs over and then passed it to Tayte. 'That's from Granddad Ernest's wedding. September 1912.' She grinned at Tayte. 'I only know that because it says so on the back.'

Tayte turned the image over and read the now faint hand-writing. He considered such thoughtful labelling as something of a gift in his profession; an image and a few well-chosen words, especially names and dates, could confirm so much. Rachel offered up another photograph, and Tayte was pleased to see that whoever had written on the back of the image he was holding had clearly made a habit of it.

'Hubby at the coronation, June 1911,' Rachel read out.

The image was of a proud, if somewhat stern-faced, man in a highly decorated dress uniform, at what was evidently the coronation of King George V.

'The handwriting's the same,' Rachel added, confirming that the inscriptions had been written by Thomas Ashcroft's wife.

Tayte noticed that Rachel's face had suddenly lit up. She had another image in her hand, which she slid across the table. It was the young boy and girl he recognised from the photograph Davina had loaned him: Archibald and Alice, holding hands in front of a merry-go-round. They were a few years older in this image, but the resemblance was unmistakable. The words Tayte read on the back as he turned it over confirmed it, along with the year 1897, making Alice seven years old when the photograph was taken. Tayte squinted at her image, trying to see the resemblance with his client's great-grandmother, but Alice was still too young in this photograph to be sure.

'The boy was just like his father,' Brendan said, interrupting Tayte's scrutiny.

He looked up to see Brendan looking over his wife's shoulder at the next image she was holding. A moment later, Rachel offered it up. It showed a young man in a naval officer's uniform, who looked to be in his early twenties, his abundant smile dimpling his cheeks. In the background a building faced predominantly with Portland stone filled the shot.

'Archie's first day at the office,' Rachel said. 'July 1913.'

'That's the Old Admiralty Building in the background,' Brendan said.

Tayte looked more closely. 'London?'

'Yes, those towers are unmistakable. If the picture were in colour, you'd see them capped with copper, turned verdigris by the weather. It would have been taken from Horse Guards Parade.'

Tayte got his notebook out. When Brendan had said that Archibald had followed in his father's footsteps and joined the Navy, and that he thought he had died during the First World War, Tayte had imagined the sailor had served aboard one of His Majesty's warships. Yet this photograph confirmed that Archibald had served at what was, in 1913, British naval headquarters. He wrote the details down and made a note to look into Archibald Ashcroft more thoroughly when had the chance.

*British naval headquarters . . .*

The discovery prompted Tayte to wonder what the young officer's chief responsibilities were prior to the outbreak of war, and in light of Alice's albeit alleged spy activity, whether he had ready access to information that might prove useful to an enemy. Whatever Archibald's responsibilities, given where he worked, Tayte believed it was highly likely that he did.

# Chapter Twenty

Thursday, 30 April 1914.

Just over a week had passed since Alice had made the discovery that she was not the only person at Hamberley spying for the kaiser. In that time she had travelled to numerous harbours and ports along the South Coast of England, adding Portsmouth, Southampton, Folkestone, and Newhaven to the list of places she had visited at Raskin's behest, to observe and report on Britain's naval activity. Accordingly, she had spent little time at Hamberley, and, day by day, the lie that she was visiting her sick friend in Margate had escalated to the point that her friend was now, as far as her parents were concerned, at death's door. Alice hated lying to her family, and she had come to despise herself for it—and for everything else the people now in control of her life had forced her to become.

The train carrying her home after a thankfully uneventful day in Poole hissed to a stop as it came into the next station. The compartment Alice was sitting in cleared of the middle-aged couple who had been her travelling companions on the London & South Western Railway since Winchester, and she slowly turned her head to the rain-streaked window beside her, noting from the sign on the concourse outside that she was in Woking. She had lost count of how many towns she had passed through. It was already nearly an hour past dark, and she knew it would be very late by the time she was back at Hamberley.

She shifted in her seat, and her focus snapped to the dark reflection gazing back at her. She thought how tired she looked and how changed she appeared even to herself after all that had happened. She thought the old Alice she had known in Holland little more than two weeks ago had now passed beyond both recognition and redemption. Settling back in her seat again, she closed her eyes and forced the only happy thought she could muster into her head.

She saw Chester as she had seen him before she set out that morning, fully recovered, in his little riding breeches, excited to be spending the day with his grandmother and the new pony Alice suspected had been bought for him on account of his recent fever. She pictured Charlotte in the kitchen with Mrs Morris, cake mixture on her nose and a toothy grin on her face, and she was thankful that her mother and the household staff had taken to keeping the children amused during her absence. The images Alice conjured in her mind brought her comfort, but even those happy thoughts were tainted by her situation, because it meant she had not been with her children to share those memories.

Somewhere outside the carriage a whistle blew, loud and shrill, and a few seconds later the train was moving again to the slow puff, puff, puff of the Adams T3 class locomotive that Alice hoped would soon arrive at London's Waterloo Station. From there she would take the London, Chatham and Dover Railway to Rochester and her bed, and she could not wish herself there soon enough. She wondered how many more tasks she would have to endure, and how many more tiresome train journeys she would have to undertake in the process. She closed her eyes more tightly; with the compartment now empty, she thought she would allow the carriage to rock her to sleep until London, but the sound of the compartment door opening caused her to open her eyes again.

When she saw who had entered, all thoughts of sleep left her. It was Raskin, in a pair of loose-fitting trousers and a thick Aran cardigan, as if he'd just stepped off a fishing boat. The Dutchman filled the doorframe to such an extent that he had to stoop as he entered the carriage. He neither spoke to Alice nor looked at her, and the sight of him caused her to catch her breath, more out of surprise than fear—although fear was never far away when Raskin was around.

Alice watched him close the door and turn into the compartment, carrying his hat and coat and a brown leather case, which he placed on the seat beside him as he sat opposite her. He pushed his fair hair back off his brow and settled. Then at last he looked at her, smiling the well-practiced smile that Alice had learned to see through. She glanced at his hat, a navy-blue peaked cap, the likes of which she had seen aplenty around the docks and harbours she had recently frequented. She noticed it was dry, suggesting he had been on the train for some time, because it had been raining for several stops.

'I can see you are puzzled to see me, Alice.'

Alice relaxed her brow, which she now realised was set in a deep furrow. 'Yes,' she said. She was really past caring how this man came and went about his business with such stealth, but on this occasion she had to admit that she was intrigued to understand how he knew what train she would be on, and more importantly, why he wanted to see her before their usual time. It had become routine for her to hand over her report at night below the garden terrace at Hamberley. Surely he knew today's report would not yet be ready.

'How did you know where to find me?'

'Find you?' Raskin laughed softly. 'My dear Alice, I never lost you. I've been in your shadow all day. First to Poole Harbour where you took refreshment at Harvey's Tea Gardens, and then to the quay. As dusk fell, I boarded the train after you, and I have been looking in on your compartment at every stop, waiting for our chance to talk.'

'Why? What about?'

Raskin took an apple from his pocket and began to toss it slowly from one enormous hand to the other as he spoke. 'I have something important to tell you. I must remain in London tonight, so I cannot collect my report in the usual way. I will collect it when we next meet, which I hope will be tomorrow. What I have to say cannot wait.'

He reached into the folds of his coat on the seat beside him and withdrew a curved knife that was about eight inches long. Alice locked eyes on it at once and followed its shining steel to the apple that Raskin began to slice, as if he were carving a fine sculpture. He took a piece of apple to his mouth on the edge of the blade and their eyes met.

'Do you like my knife?' Raskin offered it out. 'It's a whale flensing knife. It used to belong to my father. I'm from a long line of whalers. The handle is made of whale bone and brass. It's very strong and easy to clean.'

Alice did not like it. She had never heard of a flensing knife before, but she could imagine its purpose. She turned away in disgust and looked out the window, but it was so black outside that all she could see was the compartment and the Dutchman's angular features reflected back.

Raskin laughed and continued to carve his apple. 'I have a new task for you, Alice. Something different.'

Alice turned back to him. 'Different?'

'Yes, a very special task, in fact.'

Alice knew she had not been recruited in this manner merely to count ships. She had always known there had to be more to it.

'What is it? What must I do now?'

Raskin sighed as though contemplating how best to tell her. A moment later he said, 'Traditionally, Britain's enemy has been France, and so your sea defences are largely concentrated along the South Coast, leaving the eastern shores of Essex, Suffolk, and Norfolk wide open. We are aware that your government, in conjunction with the Admiralty, have prepared plans for the defences of East Anglia, such that Britain would be better prepared to repel an invasion targeted at England's East Coast by a new enemy.'

'Germany?' Alice said.

'Germany, yes. And Austria-Hungary and Italy. There will be other nations, too. It goes without saying that these plans would be of significant benefit to Germany, come the day.' Raskin paused and leaned forward on his elbows, apple in one hand, knife in the other. 'Put simply, Alice. I want you to photograph them for me.'

Alice's jaw dropped. It seemed laughable to her that she could even get close to such information. Then a terrible thought struck her, and she understood precisely what Raskin had in mind. There was only one way she could do it, and the idea left her numb. She stared at Raskin as he chewed his apple, and then he began to nod slowly, confirming her thoughts, clearly aware that she had just realised what she had to do.

'Your good friend Archibald Ashcroft will help you,' Raskin said. 'I believe he will do anything you ask of him, with a little encouragement.'

Alice was already shaking her head in defiance. 'I won't do it.'

'But you must.'

'How do you know all this? You can't know how Archie feels for me.'

'I am a very good spy, Alice. I know many things. Besides, I heard the two of you talking on the terrace that night I first came to you at Hamberley.'

The idea of the man eavesdropping on her private conversations repulsed Alice, but she thought Raskin would have to understand the depth of Archie's feelings far better than could be gauged by overhearing what was said between her and Archie that night to believe he would betray his country for her. It occurred to her then that someone at Hamberley must have told him that Archie would do anything for her, and she was reminded of the telephone conversation she had recently overheard in her father's study, which had told her she was not the only spy at Hamberley.

'I can't ask it of him.'

'You can, Alice. And you will. Or you know what will happen.'

Even if Archie agreed to it, Alice thought she would sooner leap from the train than use his love for her so cruelly against him, but the thought passed when she considered what would happen to Henry and her children. Their lives were more important to her than the betrayal of a friend or a few secrets that might never come to be of any use to anyone.

'If I do this, will my husband be released? Will all this stop?'

'I cannot say,' Raskin said. 'Such decisions are for others to make. But I am sure it will bring that happy day much closer.'

Alice wondered whose decision it was to make. She wanted to ask Raskin who he reported to so that she might make a plea to him, but she knew she would get no answer from the Dutchman, and her impertinence would only anger him, which was something she did not want to do at any time, let alone while he was holding that awful flensing knife.

Raskin picked up the brown leather case he had been carrying when he came into the compartment. He opened it and withdrew a black metal object that was rectangular in shape and roughly the size of a house brick.

'It's a prototype camera called the Ur-Leica,' he said. 'It was developed last year in Wetzler, Germany, by Oskar Barnack, an optical engineer at the Ernst Leitz Optische Werke. It's really a very clever design. It uses 35 mm cine-film. See how small it is.'

Alice took it with a heavy heart, as though doing so meant that she had now accepted the task. 'It's quite heavy,' she said, but she had to agree that it was small compared to all the other photographic cameras she had seen. She thought her Uncle Oscar would love such a device.

Raskin proceeded to give Alice a few instructions, letting her know how to release the shutter and wind the film on, adding that everything else was set up.

'You will need as much natural light as possible,' he added. 'Use of a flash lamp is out of the question. I'm told the lens is designed to cover a wide angle, so it will be difficult to miss your subject as long as you are not too close. A couple of feet should do.'

'When would you like it back?' Alice asked.

'Tomorrow evening.'

'And where should I take it?'

'I will find you,' Raskin said, and Alice did not doubt him.

Alice alighted from the train at Rochester station, still thinking about Archie and the seemingly impossible task Raskin had set her. She had called Archie from a public telephone kiosk as soon as she arrived in London, saying only that she was in trouble and that she needed his help, and Archie had agreed to collect her from Rochester without a moment's hesitation. Alice never doubted he would come. *He's such a sweet boy,* she thought, wishing now that she had agreed to go for a ride with him in his motorcar when he'd visited Hamberley to see the children previous Sunday. It had been the only day she was allowed off from her spying escapades, and only then because the railway service was generally so poor on Sundays.

Alice came out from the station building and saw Archie's car waiting. It wasn't raining, but she could see from the puddles here and there that it had been, and the yellow and silver Vauxhall C10 had its folding roof up. She stopped and stared into its bulbous chrome headlights for several seconds, wondering how she could go through with this. She had prepared her lines on the train journey and had rehearsed them over and over—lies she knew could not fail to manipulate Archie into doing whatever she asked of him. But even now, she considered whether to just tell him the truth about everything that had happened and leave the rest to chance. She wanted to tell him, but she could not gamble with the lives of her family.

The car's headlights winked at Alice, and a moment later Archie stepped out. She started walking again as he came to meet her, and he was full of smiles, despite the circumstances that had brought them together for this late night rendezvous. It began to rain again as they met, and Archie laughed.

'This isn't at all what I had in mind when I said I wanted to take you for a spin,' he said. 'We shan't see anything of the countryside.'

'I know, Archie. I'm sorry. We'll go for a very long drive together when all this is over, I promise.'

The heavens opened then, and they ran to the car.

'That's a deal,' Archie said. He dashed ahead to open the passenger door. Then he held Alice's hand and helped her inside. 'Mind the running board. It's a little slippery.'

The bench seat inside the two-seater was so narrow that when Archie climbed in beside Alice, his shoulder was pressing against hers. 'It's a little cosy,' he said. The engine was already running. 'Listen to that,' he added. He revved it harder. 'Have you ever heard such a roar?'

'No, I'm sure I haven't.'

They set off for Hamberley, turning out onto the High Street, and when the car had settled into its stride, Archie said, 'Now then, what's this all about? If you're in trouble, Alice, I'm your man.'

'I know you are, Archie, but I really can't tell you what it is just now. I need you to trust me. You do trust me, don't you?'

'Yes, of course, but—'

'Good,' Alice cut in. 'I promise I'll explain everything when this is over. You'll understand then—I know you will. Now drive slowly. There's something I have to tell you. It's the reason I couldn't go for that drive with you last Sunday.' Alice bit her lip then and delivered what she knew would be the first of many painful lies that evening. 'You see, Archie, I was too afraid.'

'Afraid? Whatever of?'

'I was afraid of getting too close to you. Seeing you again after so long brought back such fond memories. I'm afraid my feelings have been very confused of late, but not any more.'

'However do you mean?'

'I think you know what I mean, Archie. You were plain enough about your feelings for me when you rescued me from my father's interrogation that night after dinner, when you took me out onto the terrace for some air. My father was right in supposing that everything is not all it seems between Henry and me.'

'It's not?'

Alice could already hear the hope rising in Archie's voice as he spoke. She despised herself for leading him on like this. 'No, Archie,' she said. 'Henry wasn't delayed on business at all. We quarrelled and I came home to Hamberley with the children. We've quarrelled so much recently.'

'I see,' Archie said.

A single tear fell onto Alice's cheek. She wiped it away and turned to Archie, forcing herself to go on with her pretence. 'Do you, Archie?' she said. 'I wonder if you really do see what I mean.'

Archie shifted in his seat, and Alice noticed that the car had slowed to a crawl. He didn't look at her. His eyes remained fixed on the road ahead as he said, 'Perhaps you should tell me, so there's no misunderstanding.'

'Very well,' Alice said. Then she choked back another tear and delivered the lie that hurt the most, partly because it was no lie at all. 'I love you, Archie Ashcroft.'

Their eyes found one another's in the near darkness, and although Alice couldn't quite make out the dimples on his cheeks, she knew they were there, exaggerated by his smile. All her memories of their happy times together seemed to rush her at once, and she began to shake as she fought to control her emotions.

'I'm sure I've always loved you,' she added, her voice trembling. Then somehow she managed to deliver the remainder of those hateful lines she had practiced on the train, to that sweet boy she knew deserved so much better. 'But if we're to have any future together, there's something I need you to do for me first. Perhaps it's too much to ask of you.'

'Is it worth a kiss?'

'It's worth a hundred kisses, Archie, but not now. When this is all over, I promise.'

'Well, you just name it,' Archie said. He stopped the car and grabbed Alice's hand. 'Nothing's too much for you.'

# Chapter Twenty-One

Friday, 1 May 1914.

Unveiled by King George V in 1911, under the watchful eyes of Kaiser Wilhelm II, London's Queen Victoria memorial stood twenty-five metres high and was made from white Carrara marble and granite. It was the largest statue of any British monarch and was surrounded by ships' prows, and mermaids and mermen in reference to Britain's great naval power. Archie had told Alice to wait for him on the statue steps facing Buckingham Palace at four o'clock that afternoon, and there she had waited with her camera case hanging from her shoulder, growing more and more anxious with every minute that passed beyond the appointed time.

*Where is he?*

It was after four thirty now, and Alice wondered again whether something had gone wrong. Had Archie changed his mind? He hadn't been so keen to help her once she'd told him what she wanted him to do for her, and she knew it was asking a lot of him, despite his obvious feelings for her. Perhaps it had proven too much for him. She certainly wouldn't blame him given what was at stake. When he'd finally agreed to help her, Archie had told her that with his level of clearance it would not be too difficult to access the plans she needed to see. They had agreed that he would bring them to her so she could photograph them, and then he would return them again before anyone noticed they were gone. It was as simple an arrangement as they could devise, but she knew deep down that he had not wanted to do it. She had forced him to choose between her and his country, and as the minutes now ticked by, she started to think that he had made his choice and was not coming.

Alice began to circle the statue, thankful that the day was dry and bright. She took in one of the mythical stone hippogriffs as she passed it: a winged creature that was part horse in the lower section, with the head and torso of an eagle. She eyed its wings and silently wished she had wings of her own so she could fly far away, and for the first time she wondered what would happen if she did. What would Raskin and the people he worked for make of that? Who then could they levy their threats at? A simple irony occurred to her when she thought that the biggest threat to her family might well be herself.

Alice shook her head to rid her mind of such thoughts and gazed out from her elevated position. Being so close to Buckingham Palace, she supposed this was always a busy area, and today was no exception, making it all the more difficult to pick anyone out from the crowd. She continued to pace around the statue, and she had circled it three times before she saw him. He was walking towards her along The Mall, wearing his officer's cap and a long greatcoat, hands thrust deep into his pockets. She went to meet him and noticed he was walking oddly and drawing even more attention to himself by looking over his shoulder every now and then.

'Alice, quickly,' he said as they met. 'Into the park.'

'Is something wrong, Archie? You're later than you said. I was worried about you.'

'I'm fine. I was delayed, that's all. By my conscience more than anything.'

'Why are you walking like that?'

They crossed The Mall into Green Park, beneath the cover of the trees that were not quite in full leaf, and as they moved off the path and away from the other park goers, Archie showed her the reason for his odd gait. He unbuttoned his coat and quickly thrust his hand inside, before the plans he had purloined from the Admiralty Building could fall down altogether. They were wrapped around him and had slipped below his waist.

'I've had the devil of a time trying to keep these things from falling to my ankles,' he said. 'I half expected them to trip me over altogether.'

Alice thought the two of them would have laughed about that under different circumstances. One day she hoped they would, but not now.

'I don't know why we couldn't have done this in St James's Park,' Alice said. 'It's much closer.'

'Too close for comfort. Look, let's get this over with. The sooner they're back in their rightful place, the better.'

'How will you get them back? You can't walk into the Admiralty like you just walked here to meet me. Someone will ask what's wrong with you.'

'I'll take them back in a roll under my arm,' Archie said. 'No one will suspect anything of a naval officer taking charts into the Admiralty building. At least, I hope not.'

'Let's take them further out onto the lawn,' Alice said. 'It's quiet over there, and the light's much better away from the trees.'

When they were out in the open and a good hundred or so feet from anyone, Alice stopped, and Archie started looking around.

'Stop doing that,' Alice told him. 'You'll only draw attention. Here, hand me the plans, and I'll lay them out. It will look as if I'm putting a blanket down, and anyone looking over will think we're having a picnic or afternoon tea in the park.'

Archie opened his coat, and Alice slid the plans out. They sat on the grass, and Alice unbuckled the leather camera case. Despite telling him not to, Archie still kept looking around, as though he was expecting the First Sea Lord himself to walk up and collar him.

'It's going to be all right,' Alice reassured him.

Archie just smiled nervously as she lined up the first section. She recognised part of the coastline of East Anglia, which was drawn out like an ordnance survey map, with contour lines and numerous numbers and symbols scattered here and there, along with a good many other things she didn't understand. Of particular significance was the port of Harwich in Essex and mention of a Harwich Force. She got to her knees and hovered the camera above it, a few feet away as Raskin had instructed. She pressed the shutter release button and then did so again for good measure before moving on to the next section.

'Hurry it along, Alice, please,' Archie said. 'I'm a nervous wreck.'

'I'm almost finished. Pretend to laugh as though I just said something funny.'

'What? No. Please, just hurry up.'

Alice could feel her own heart thumping as she took the last of her photographs and sat down again. She put the camera back into its case, and she thought Archie couldn't have collected the plans together again quickly enough. He rolled them up and got to his feet.

'Look, don't think it rude of me, Alice, but I don't want to hang around.'

They started walking back to the path and the gate they had entered by, and Alice slipped her arm through his. The gesture was partly for show, but she had to concede that a bigger part of her wanted to.

'Will I see you tomorrow?' Archie asked.

Alice was more concerned about when she was going to see Raskin again. 'I don't know,' she said. 'Everything's so complicated.'

'And this trouble you're in—'

'Do you mind if we don't talk about it just yet?' Alice cut in.

'No, I suppose not. All in good time, eh?'

Alice had no idea how she was going to explain herself to Archie when all this was over, or whether he would understand, let alone forgive her for what she had done. She would at least have liked to remain friends, but she knew she no longer deserved such friendship. They arrived at the park gate and parted company with nothing more than a half smile between them.

'Good luck,' Alice whispered, and she watched him head back along The Mall, striding now like the naval officer he was, with the plans for Britain's defences of East Anglia tucked neatly under his arm.

When Alice could no longer see him, she turned away and headed back into the park. It was a pleasant afternoon, and she thought a gentle stroll before heading back to Victoria railway station would be a good tonic for her nerves. She kept to the path now, ambling as though without purpose. A gentleman in grey with a tall top hat tipped it towards her as he passed in the opposite direction. She passed two nannies who had stopped beside their perambulators to chat, both of whom paused to wish her a good afternoon. Her thoughts drifted to better times—to when her own life had been as calm and carefree. She recalled numerous afternoon walks with her own perambulator, first when Chester was born and then with Charlotte. She found herself smiling at her memories, and she had become so caught up in the daydream that she almost bumped into someone.

'Do excuse me,' she said, stepping aside.

But the man did not excuse her, and it was only when he stepped with her to block her way that Alice looked up and took full measure of him. She recognised him at once. It was the man with the crooked nose who had pursued her in Dover. He wore the same tweed suit and black bowler hat.

At the sight of him, Alice startled, but she did not freeze. She turned and ran, holding the camera case as she went. Out of the corner of her eye, she saw the man reach for her. She felt a tug at her shoulder as he grabbed her arm and pulled her back to him.

'You're not getting away from me this time!'

Alice struggled. Her arm began to slip out of her coat, but she could not free herself. With her other arm she took the camera off her shoulder and swung it wildly. The man ducked and his hat flew off, but his grip held.

'I know what you've been doing. You're coming along with me.'

Alice knew she could not let that happen. She struggled all the more, twisting and pulling against his grip until the buttons popped from her coat, and she slipped free of it. At the same time the man staggered back under his own force and fell to the ground. Alice ran for the trees then, aware that the disturbance had drawn attention.

'Come back here!'

Alice looked over her shoulder and saw he was close. She reached the trees, not really knowing what to do now she was there. She just kept running, hoping to make the far gate before he caught up with her again. She thought she could lose him in the streets, but he was closing fast. She knew she wouldn't make it.

'You're only making this worse for yourself!'

Given what Alice had done, she couldn't imagine how her situation could be any worse. She would be shot for high treason for all she had done. The man sounded very close now, and Alice knew it would soon be over. But then she heard another voice that was followed by a heavy thump. She slowed and turned, and there was Raskin. The thump she had heard was the man in the tweed suit as he crashed to the ground following the blow the Dutchman had given him.

'Chasing ladies in the park is not a very admirable pastime,' Raskin said to the other man, who was already on his feet again.

'You!'

Raskin nodded. 'You've wanted me for a long time, haven't you? Well, here I am.'

Alice thought the other man looked suddenly terrified. His eyes were wide, his skin pale, despite the chase. He looked as though he was about to run for his life, but Raskin lunged at him with great speed, both hands catching him around his neck. Alice swallowed dryly as she watched the smaller man pull something from inside his jacket. It was a knife. Its blade jabbed at Raskin, and the Dutchman caught the other man's wrist, twisting the knife away until the man dropped it and cried out in pain.

'Go!'

Alice knew Raskin was shouting the command at her, but fear had rooted her to the spot. She realised then that she was not afraid for herself, but for the man in the tweed suit. Raskin hit him to the ground, and before he could recover, Alice saw another flash of steel as Raskin pulled out his flensing knife. The curved steel shone brightly as Raskin leaped onto the man with murder in his eyes, and at last Alice ran.

# Chapter Twenty-Two

Present day.

Standing in the front porch of a flat in Gravesend, ten miles northwest of Chatham, Jefferson Tayte continued to catch his breath as he watched DI Bishop knock on the door again. The lift was out of service, and they had to take the stairs—all ten flights to the top, which Tayte thought was typical. When Davina had checked her records for Dean Saxby's contact details, as she had told Tayte she would, she had found nothing, suggesting that no business had been conducted during Dean's visit with Lionel Scanlon on the day Davina had seen him at the workshop—at least, none that Lionel had recorded. Locating this descendant of Frank Saxby had then fallen to Bishop, who had received his details while they were visiting the Ashcrofts earlier that morning. Both men stepped back as a shadow appeared beyond the privacy glass and the front door opened. Dean Saxby was expecting them.

'Mr Saxby?' Bishop said with a businesslike smile. He showed his badge. 'Detective Inspector Bishop. We spoke on the telephone earlier. This is Mr Tayte. He's assisting with my investigation.'

Tayte gave a nod, noting the close-cropped hair and the sagging sports pants and T-shirt the man before them was wearing, thinking that he understood now what Davina had meant when she'd said that Dean Saxby hadn't looked like their usual type of client.

'Sure. Come in,' Dean said. 'You wanna cuppa? Kettle's just boiled.'

'Coffee, thanks. Black, no sugar,' Bishop said.

'Same here,' Tayte added.

They were shown into the sitting room, where tired furniture seemed to sigh at them as they entered. The wallpaper was peeling back, the carpet was close to threadbare in places, and the air was heavy with the odour of stale cigarettes.

'Make yourselves at home,' Dean added. 'I won't be a mo.'

Tayte sat beside Bishop on the sofa with his briefcase and continued to take the place in; the old-style cathode ray tube television set and the faded prints on the walls, telling him that Dean Saxby was either down on his luck or that he cared little for his surroundings. He was gone no more than a minute. When he came back and handed out the drinks, he sat in one of the armchairs opposite them and put his feet up on the low table that stood between them.

'So, what's this about?' Dean said. He laughed to himself. 'Not in any trouble, am I?'

'Not at all,' Bishop said. 'I'm hoping you might be able to help me out, that's all.'

Bishop relayed everything Tayte had told him—everything Davina had said about the day she had seen Dean Saxby visiting her husband at his workshop a month ago.

'Can you tell me why you went to see Lionel Scanlon?'

'I knew this was about that,' Dean said. 'I read about his murder. I didn't have anything to do with it, if that's what you think.'

'I don't think that, Mr Saxby. I'd just like to know why you went to see him.'

'I had something to sell that I thought he'd want to buy.'

'What were you trying to sell him?'

'An antique cigar case. Solid silver.'

Tayte looked around at the décor again, and he couldn't help but wonder what a man who lived in a place such as this was doing with an antique silver cigar case.

'It's been in the family ages,' Dean added, answering Tayte's thoughts. 'I needed the money.'

Bishop glanced at the photograph on the mantle that was above a plastic, plug-in fireplace. 'Kids draining the coffers, are they,' he said, half jokingly. 'I know all about that, believe me.'

'I'm divorced,' Dean said. 'It's the maintenance and lack of work that's keeping me in this dump.'

'Do you mind if I ask what do you do for a living?'

'Electrician. Contracts mostly. There's not much work about at the moment.'

Tayte sat forward then, and he looked at Bishop as if to ask if he minded him asking a question. Bishop nodded back at him.

'Why did you take the cigar case to Lionel Scanlon?' Tayte asked. 'You said you thought he'd want to buy it, but why him? There must be plenty of other places more local you could have taken it to.'

'I took it to Lionel Scanlon because I thought he'd pay the best price. I said I thought it belonged to one of his ancestors.'

Hearing that aroused Tayte's interest further. 'Do you know which of his ancestors?'

Dean nodded. 'Someone called Oscar Scanlon. Him and my great-great-granddad knew each other.'

'Frank Saxby?'

'That's right,' Dean said, eyeing Tayte quizzically, as if to ask how he knew. 'The cigar case must have changed hands at some point. Maybe he won it off him.'

Bishop came back into the conversation. 'So you thought Lionel Scanlon might like to have it back in the family and would pay extra for it?'

'I did. Only he didn't want to pay much for it at all—the cheapskate.'

'Did you sell it to him?'

'No,' Dean laughed. 'Not for the price he was offering.'

'Can we see it?' Tayte asked.

Dean shook his head. 'Sold it last week.'

Bishop drew an audible breath and Tayte understood why. Without the cigar case, Dean Saxby could have just made the whole thing up.

'Who did you sell it to?' Bishop asked.

'There's a place on Northfleet Hill,' Dean said. 'Can't remember the name.'

'Did you get a receipt?'

'Probably, but I didn't keep it. I had the cash. What was the point?'

Tayte stepped in again. 'How do you know Oscar Scanlon and your great-great-grandfather knew one another?' He was keen to find out what Dean Saxby knew about his ancestors.

'There was an old photograph of two men inside the case. It had their names on the back. That's how I matched the inscription, "O.W.S". I've no idea what the "W" stands for.'

'Do you still have the photograph?'

Dean shook his head again. 'Sorry. I sold it with the cigar case. Apparently it made it more valuable.'

'Provenance,' Tayte said. 'Do you have any other old photos? Was anything else handed down to you?'

'I wish,' Dean said. 'I was lucky to get the cigar case.'

'That's too bad. Do you know much about Frank Saxby?'

'No. I was just told who the man in the photo was.'

Bishop sat forward then, as if he were about to stand up. 'It's just a routine question,' he said, a little ominously, Tayte thought, 'but before we go, can you tell me where you were on the night of Friday the 23rd of May—the night Lionel Scanlon was murdered.'

Dean Saxby scoffed. 'I knew that was coming.' He paused. Then he began to shake his head. 'No, I can't. I was probably here, as I am most nights—and days, come to that. I already told you I wasn't getting much work.'

Tayte could see that Bishop's question with its possible implication was angering their host. His tone had changed, and his arms were now tightly crossed around his chest.

'Would you have been with anyone on that Friday night who could vouch for you being home?' Bishop continued.

Dean scoffed again. 'No, it's just me. I can't afford to go out and find a girlfriend, if that's what you mean—let alone afford to keep one.' He shot forward to match Bishop on the edge of his seat. 'That doesn't mean I killed anyone.'

'Calm down, Mr Saxby. As I said, it was just a routine question.' Bishop offered him a calming smile as he rose to leave. 'Northfleet Hill, you said?'

'That's right. Silver cigar case. You can go and ask the dealer if you want.'

'Thank you for your time, Mr Saxby,' Bishop said, and as Tayte followed him out, he knew the Inspector fully intended to.

'Come in, Mr Tayte. Have a seat.'

An hour after leaving Dean Saxby's flat, DI Bishop ushered Tayte into a small office at the North Kent and Medway Division police headquarters. Tayte sat at one end of the desk, facing a window that looked out onto a featureless part of the building and the car park below. As Bishop put his coffee down and lowered himself into his chair, Tayte offered him a chocolate to go with it.

'Don't mind if I do,' Bishop said, dipping his hand into the proffered bag of Mr Goodbar miniatures. 'I think you've given me a taste for these.'

They had gone straight to the police station after their last visit, picking up a sandwich for lunch along the way. Bishop had received word that the information he'd previously told Tayte he was hoping to receive had arrived, and Tayte was more eager to see it than ever when Bishop told him it concerned Alice Stilwell. There was a screen on the desk, surrounded by photographs. Bishop switched it on and slid it around so Tayte could see it better.

'So, your wife's in law enforcement, too?' Tayte said, eying a photograph of a woman in uniform beside another photograph of the same woman, this one with two small children in a park somewhere.

'It's how we met,' Bishop said, smiling momentarily at the face in the picture as he spoke. 'She put her career on hold to have a family, but if I know Amanda, she'll be back as soon as they're in school.' He indicated the photograph of the children. 'That's Benjamin—he's quite a handful. Beside him there is Olivia.'

'Great-looking kids,' Tayte offered, thinking that a simple family day out in the park must be a wonderful way to spend some time.

Bishop thanked him, and then he began tapping at the keyboard in front of him. 'Are you familiar with the history of our Secret Intelligence Service, commonly referred to as MI6?'

Tayte sipped his coffee and smiled to himself as he recalled his last visit to England and how he and Jean Summer had encountered one such government agency while helping out with a very different kind of murder investigation. *That was MI5,* he reminded himself, *the Security Service.*

'I've had some dealings with your homeland security,' he said. 'But I'm not too clued up on your secret service.'

'I was surprised how little I knew,' Bishop said, 'so I conducted some research of my own. The SIS began as the Secret Service Bureau in 1909, a collaboration between the Admiralty and the War Office, largely on account of the German threat and the arms race that was going on at the time. Given what you've told me about Alice, I thought there might be some information on her to support the allegations that she was a spy.'

'It would certainly be good to confirm the rumours,' Tayte said.

'My thoughts exactly. I don't know whether it's the same in the US, but government bodies here in the UK have a legal obligation under the Public Records Act of 1958 to place records in the public archive. For reasons of national security, however, the Security Service and the Secret Intelligence Service are exempt. So, the decision on what gets transferred to The National Archives is made on a case-by-case basis.'

'It's no wonder my searches on Alice Stilwell returned so little information,' Tayte said.

Bishop agreed. 'Where information is considered sensitive for whatever reason, it remains out of public sight, under lock and key.'

'How come you've been allowed access to this information?'

'You mean apart from being a detective inspector in charge of a murder investigation?' Bishop said, half-grinning. 'Actually, as the file is just over a hundred years old now, it was up for review. Apparently, a large number of records that have previously been deemed too sensitive to release are being looked at again.'

'Why was it deemed sensitive at all?' Tayte asked, thinking aloud.

Bishop opened a folder on the computer's desktop and clicked on one of the files that appeared inside. 'Let's find out, shall we?'

Tayte edged closer as the file opened, filling the screen with a scanned image of a document bearing the title 'Home Office: Registered Papers, Supplementary.' Below that Tayte read the subheading, 'CRIMINAL CASES: Stilwell, Alice Maria.'

'"Observation,"' Bishop read aloud. '"21st of April, 1914."'

Both men continued to take the document in. Tayte read the account of observations that had been recorded in Dover on that day by a member of the Secret Service Bureau. He read that Alice had been seen meeting with a German waiter who was already known to the SSB as Raimund Karl Drescher, a man who was himself under observation for spying. The account stated that Alice had left the hotel where Drescher worked and had proceeded to Dover harbour, where she had loitered suspiciously for some hours. The account ended with a brief summary of how the SSB officer had attempted to confront Alice to enquire into her purpose there, stating that Alice had then wilfully evaded him so as not to expose that purpose.

'That's very interesting,' Tayte said. 'I wonder how they knew that the person they were observing was Alice Stilwell.'

Bishop closed the file and opened another. 'I suppose they must either have already known or had collated the information afterwards, once Alice's identity was discovered.'

The next file was dated a few weeks later, and it explained precisely how the SSB came to know who Alice was. The report was similar to the first, but two further incidents were logged, of Alice having been observed loitering at England's southern ports, where it was thought she was engaged in monitoring the movements of British warships, helping to provide the enemy with an account of Britain's naval strength and placement. Scans of several train ticket stubs were also attached, and Tayte imagined they must have been found at Hamberley at some point. Reading on, he saw that no attempt had been made to question Alice on these occasions, presumably because the purpose of her activity was now obvious to the SSB. On these further occasions, the task was not then to engage, but to follow.

When Bishop opened the penultimate file, Tayte saw that on 30 April 1914, the SSB had been successful. Hamberley was mentioned, as was Admiral Lord Charles Metcalfe, and Tayte thought this was why the records had been classified as sensitive material and not transferred to the public archive. The Metcalfe family held high positions in the Admiralty and the British government. At the very least it could have caused the family public embarrassment and perhaps even provided a motive for blackmail, making it a potential threat to national security.

Tayte was already wondering what was in the last file, and he felt certain it would offer more incriminating evidence against Alice. That she was spying against her own country now seemed irrefutable, although he had yet to understand why. Bishop was about to open the file when Tayte's phone started playing the theme from *Guys and Dolls*. He quickly took it out.

'Sorry,' he said, checking the display. 'It's Davina Scanlon. I'd better take it.' He pushed a button and pressed the phone to his ear.

'JT,' Davina said. 'I hope I'm not calling at a bad time.'

Tayte thought she sounded bright about something. 'No, that's okay,' he said. 'I'm with DI Bishop, going through a few files.' He cast a glance at Bishop and smiled apologetically. 'Is everything okay?'

'Yes, I'm perfectly fine. I went back to the house today to finish tidying up. I've found something I think you should see. It might be important. I was wondering if you were free to come over and take a look.'

'What is it?'

'It's a telegram. I think it's better that you come and see it. Perhaps you could bring me up to date on how your assignment's going at the same time.'

'Sure,' Tayte said, thinking that his assignment was suddenly on a roll. 'How about I come by later this afternoon?'

'Great. I'll be waiting.'

The call ended and Tayte slipped his phone back inside his jacket. 'She has a telegram to show me,' he said to Bishop, wondering why she thought it could be important and what bearing it might have on his assignment.

Bishop drained his coffee back. 'Seems we're keeping you busy between us.' He eyed Tayte seriously. 'I'm going to need something from you soon.'

Tayte nodded that he understood. He had to find the connection to Lionel Scanlon's murder, or their collaboration was over. Bishop turned back to the screen and the last of the SSB files on Alice Stilwell. This file was different from the others—that much was apparent to Tayte as soon as the scanned document image appeared on the screen.

'It's an arrest warrant,' Bishop said. 'Special Branch, Metropolitan Police.'

'May 2nd, 1914,' Tayte said. 'We're getting closer to the date Alice is supposed to have died. This warrant was issued just under a month before the *Empress of Ireland* sank.' He looked quizzically at Bishop. 'How come the Metropolitan Police were involved?'

'The Secret Service Bureau had no powers of arrest, which is still true of the SIS today. They worked in conjunction with special branches of the police service, assisting with investigations and dealing with arrests. The Metropolitan Police in London had the largest Special Branch, so I'm not surprised to see they issued this warrant.'

Tayte read on and learned that the warrant for Alice's arrest had been issued on grounds of high treason and in connection with the murder of a Special Branch detective in Green Park, London, on the day before the attempted arrest was made. That the arrest had not been successful was evident from the events that followed; otherwise, Tayte suspected that given the enormity of her situation, Alice's name might have appeared alongside Carl Lody's on the list of executed spies he'd previously seen.

*High treason and murder . . .*

Tayte thought back to Lord Reginald Metcalfe's reaction to seeing the photograph of Alice he'd shown him on his visit to Hamberley the day before. In light of this new information, Tayte began to re-evaluate his earlier thoughts about the lengths to which such a family might go to protect their good name and family honour. Reginald Metcalfe was surely too old and in too poor a state of health to have acted directly, but Tayte supposed now that this obviously wealthy man could have been behind Lionel Scanlon's murder. And he could just as easily have sent someone to run him off the road after his first visit to Hamberley.

Tayte didn't voice his thoughts to Bishop; it was mere speculation for now. He gazed at the window and wondered what further discoveries he was going to make about Alice Stilwell, and he began to think over what he knew about the journey she had made, which had taken her to Canada in 1914. That Alice was in Quebec on 28 May and that she had boarded the *Empress of Ireland* was a fact he could bank. The reason she had fled from her home, and from her country, was now also clear to him from the records Bishop had just shown him. And they had also provided him with the date on which Alice's journey to meet that voyage had begun: 2 May.

What puzzled Tayte about Alice's journey now was why she was returning to England. She had made it out of the country. She was as safe from prosecution as could reasonably be expected as long as she managed to keep a low profile. Surely a better journey, and one which he knew she had later made, was to make her way south into America, leaving the British Commonwealth behind for good. But the *Empress of Ireland* had been bound for Liverpool. Alice was returning, then, to certain arrest and probable execution. Yet still she had intended to return.

Tayte gave a thoughtful sigh as he turned back to Bishop and thanked him. He collected his briefcase and rose from his chair, his thoughts drifting ahead to the telegram Davina had told him she'd found. He was keen now to go and see it. Perhaps it would unlock another piece of the puzzle that was Alice Stilwell's life. He knew there had to be more to her story than he'd so far been able to uncover, and he reminded himself that something must have happened to instil the belief in Alice that when she returned to England, she would do so in the knowledge, or at least the hope, that she could return safely to her family—to her children—without the threat to her life that had taken her to Quebec in the first place. But what?

# Chapter Twenty-Three

Saturday, 2 May 1914.

The day after Alice Stilwell met Archie in London, it was Oscar Scanlon's birthday. He was drunk by lunchtime, and Alice couldn't wait to get away from the dining table, having heard enough of the man's bad jokes and having seen enough of his nauseating behaviour at being the centre of attention to last her a lifetime. Her father and Frank Saxby had already managed to escape. Saxby had arrived at Hamberley earlier that morning in part by invitation to the birthday lunch, and Alice thought that he and her father must have had some business to discuss because they had taken themselves off to the library and did not want to be disturbed.

Alice could not chase the memories of the past twenty-four hours from her mind, no matter how hard she tried. On her return to Hamberley the night before, the feelings she had somehow managed to keep in check on the train journey home finally overcame her, and she was physically sick. She lay awake most of the night, thinking about the poor man who had chased her in Green Park, knowing he was only doing his duty and that her criminal actions, even if they had been forced upon her, had likely led to his murder. She supposed he was dead because she knew Raskin could not let the man live, although she hadn't waited to see him go to work with that hideous flensing knife of his.

*I know what you've been doing . . .*

Those words haunted Alice. She wondered who else knew, and more importantly whether the authorities knew who she was. If they did, then she supposed they would come for her soon enough, and she was resolved to go quietly now to meet her fate, not least because she could see no way through this living nightmare that her life had become. She had not seen Raskin again, and that at least was a blessing. He had not come to her for the camera as she expected he would, and she supposed it was because he was lying low after what had happened.

Alice forced a polite smile and rose from her seat. 'Do excuse me,' she said. 'I've been feeling light-headed all morning and need to rest.' It was a lie, even if she did have good reason to feel unwell. She turned to her mother, who was sitting beside Aunt Cordelia. 'Would you mind looking after the children?'

'Of course not, dear. It must be all the travelling you've been doing this week. How is your friend, the poor thing? Is she much improved?'

'Yes, very much,' Alice said.

She ran a hand over Charlotte's hair as she passed her, and then over Chester's, dragging her feet as she went.

Oscar Scanlon stood up as she left. 'Make sure you come down again in time for the cake,' he called after her.

Alice kept up her pretence until she reached the top of the main staircase, and then instead of turning left towards her room, she turned right towards her uncle's. She had been away from Hamberley so much that past week that she had not had time to follow up on her plan to discover whether it was Oscar Scanlon or Frank Saxby whom she had heard on the telephone the night she returned from Dover. She was all the more keen now to find out who it was. It was no secret that Oscar Scanlon was bankrupt, and Alice supposed he might be doing it for the money, or at least for the promise of some great fortune 'come the day.'

Alice reached his room and opened the door, confident that he would not leave the dining room until the last drop of wine had been wrung from the decanter, which was still half full. She stepped inside and pulled the door to behind her. It was a tidier room than she'd imagined, perhaps because she knew her uncle did not share it with her Aunt Cordelia. She had no idea why that was, but the situation afforded him greater opportunity for secrecy.

After taking the room in briefly, she went to the mahogany chest of drawers beneath the window and opened each drawer tentatively, as though expecting something unpleasant to jump out at her. She found shirts, neatly folded; an assortment of undergarments; several ties and a box of cufflinks. The wardrobe yielded nothing out of the ordinary either. There was writing paper and ink on the table, but on closer inspection of the nibs, Alice found them to be bone dry and only slightly stained, as though rarely used. After checking beneath the mattress and under the bed, she decided that if her uncle was a spy, then he, like Raimund Drescher at the Burlington Hotel, kept the tools of his trade elsewhere. There wasn't so much as a sniff of lemon juice in the air, which was more than could be said for her room.

Alice went back to the door and checked to make sure the way was clear. She could hear her uncle's voice all the way from the dining room, delivering a terrible rendition of a new song she'd recently heard called 'You Made Me Love You (I Didn't Want to Do It).' She imagined only her Aunt Cordelia remained in the room with him and that her mother had, thankfully, taken the children off somewhere else.

Alice slipped out onto the landing and quietly clicked the door shut behind her. When she reached the top of the stairs she relaxed again, and she began to think about Frank Saxby. She supposed there was little chance of finding out whether he was the other Hamberley spy, and she had the idea then to wait until afternoon tea, when they would all be gathered again for the cutting of her uncle's birthday cake. She started down the stairs, thinking that she would ask a few well-chosen questions. It occurred to her that all she had to do was to fit the words 'come the day' into an otherwise innocent sentence and see who reacted. It wouldn't prove anything, but she thought it would be a good place to start.

She was almost at the last step when she heard a door open along the passageway to her right. She thought it must be her father and Frank Saxby coming back from the library, so she ran back up the stairs and hid behind the banister. It was only once she was there, peering down through the rails, that she realised she wasn't doing anything wrong. She watched them pass by, heading towards the dulcet tones of Oscar Scanlon, and she noticed that Saxby wasn't wearing his jacket. She was sure he'd had it on when he left the dining room earlier, in which case he must have left it in the library. As soon as they were out of sight, Alice went down the stairs again, taking them two at a time. Then she made for the library, thinking it was at least worth having a look through his pockets for incriminating evidence.

The library door was not quite closed. Alice pushed it open and entered into a sunlit room that was several degrees warmer than the hallway. Her father often used the library in the afternoons because his regular office faced east, whereas the library windows looked to the west, catching the afternoon sun and making the room brighter and warmer in the cooler months. She saw Saxby's jacket hanging on a chair by the desk and went to it. Two weeks ago she would have thought it appalling to go through another person's pockets, but now she did so without apprehension or guilt.

In one pocket she found a train timetable and a used steamship ticket to Bruges. In the other were some keys and a white paper bag containing a few pieces of toffee. She tried the inside pocket and found two tickets to a play by George Bernard Shaw called *Pygmalion*, which Alice knew had opened just last month at His Majesty's Theatre in London. There was nothing incriminating at all given that Frank Saxby was a businessman who inherently travelled a great deal.

Alice heaved a sigh as she put the items back. Then as she slid her hand into the inside pocket to return the play tickets, she felt something catch against her fingernail. She felt inside the pocket again, sure that she hadn't missed anything, but there was definitely something else there. She felt over the jacket and confirmed that it contained something rectangular within the lining. Looking more closely at the inside seam, where the outer cloth met the silk, she found a slit, and her pulse began to rise. There was another pocket—a secret pocket.

What Alice withdrew from that secret pocket made her jaw drop. It was a notebook. She opened it and saw page after page of jumbled letters and numbers arranged in blocks of three. She saw it at once for what it was: a cipher like the transition cipher Raskin had told her to use. But this was not the same. When she tried to switch the letters around in pairs the result still made no sense. This was clearly a variant of the cipher she had been using, and it was something far more complex. It would take time to work it out, but Alice was confident she could do it now that she knew how these things worked.

The library door began to open then, and the sound made Alice jump. In that same instant she wheeled around, picked up a book at random, and slid the notebook inside.

'Alice?'

Frank Saxby was standing by the door.

'Whatever are you doing in here?'

Alice swallowed dryly. 'I came in for a book,' she said, stepping away from the desk. 'I've been reading a lot lately.'

She made for the door, and Saxby met her halfway.

'What are you reading?'

Alice had no idea which book she'd picked up. She held it out for Saxby to see for himself. He reached for it and held it firmly as if to take it from her, but Alice did not let go.

'*The Influence of Sea Power upon History, 1660–1783* by Alfred Thayer Mayhan.' He gave a small laugh. 'Seems an odd reading choice for a young lady?'

Saxby was still holding the book, and Alice was now holding her breath. Their eyes met, and caught as she was in his inquisitive stare, she was lost for words.

Eventually, she managed a smile. 'Well, I am an admiral's daughter,' she said, and Saxby smiled back at her.

'Indeed you are, Alice.' He let go of the book at last. 'I forgot my jacket.' He indicated it with a nod of his head, and Alice glanced at it. When she looked at Saxby again, he was still staring at his jacket.

'I must be going,' Alice said. 'I don't want to miss the birth-day cake.'

Saxby stepped towards the desk. 'Wait a second. I'll come with you,' he said, but Alice was already heading for the door, wishing it was several feet closer. She reached it at a painfully normal pace, and when she was on the other side, she ran.

'Alice!'

She ran faster, emerging from the corridor into the main hall.

'Alice!'

Saxby was out in the corridor now, and Alice kept going. She crossed the main hallway into another passage, heading for the voices ahead of her. They were coming from the front sitting room. A second later she burst in and was glad to see everyone already gathered for the cutting of Oscar Scanlon's cake.

'Alice, you made it!' Scanlon said, full of exuberance and slurring his words.

Alice forced a smile and tried to control her breathing as she went to her parents and stood next to them by the fireplace.

'Are you feeling better, dear?' her mother asked.

Alice nodded, and then her attention was drawn sharply to the door as Frank Saxby came in. He was wearing his jacket now, and he looked red-faced and angry. Their eyes locked, and there was no question in Alice's mind that he knew she had discovered him—the other Hamberley spy. She wondered what type of spy he was, and she doubted a man of his standing would be assigned the kind of tasks she had been engaged in. Neither could she imagine Saxby taking his orders from Raskin, as she did. She doubted that Saxby was an agent, either, so close to the area the Dutchman operated in. It dawned on her then that Frank Saxby was in all likelihood no mere spy at all, but a spy-ring leader. His notebook could prove it, she thought, but that was of little concern to her now. Whatever his role, Alice had found him out, and the only question on her mind now was what he was going to do about it.

Several uncomfortable minutes passed in general conversation that both Alice and Frank Saxby avoided. The cake was cut with great pomp and ceremony because Oscar Scanlon insisted on cutting his own birthday cake, handing each piece out himself and exhibiting great flair as he did so on account of the amount of wine he'd drunk. Alice was sitting beside her father on one of the settees, with Chester and Charlotte to the other side of her, wondering how she was going to escape this new predicament she now found herself in. She had decided that staying close to her father was best for now. Her mother was on the other settee with Cordelia and Oscar Scanlon, and Frank Saxby was sitting opposite Alice with nothing more than a low table laid out with the tea between them.

She was still clutching her book, cake balanced on her knees. Everyone was eating the cake except Saxby, who kept looking at

Alice, and he would often catch her stealing glances at him. She grew nervous when Saxby sat up and edged forward on his seat.

'What's that you're reading?' he asked her.

The question was unexpected given that he had already asked Alice that in the library, but she couldn't very well let on.

'It's a book about naval warfare,' she said, and her father eyed her curiously.

'I thought it was about time I took an interest.' She turned to Chester, who was busy devouring his cake. 'If I don't, I shall have little to discuss with my son in a few years.'

Her father laughed. 'It's a fine book, although you might find it a little heavy going.'

'May I see it?' Saxby said. He stood up and leaned over the table, his arm outstretched.

Alice hesitated, but how could she deny him? She offered the book, and Saxby took it from her. He sat back with a satisfied grin on his face, opened it and guardedly flicked through the pages. Then Alice watched his grin dissolve. The notebook was no longer there.

Saxby shot a knowing look at Alice. Then he scoffed as he rose again and handed the book back. 'I'm afraid it would be too heavy going for me,' he said, and then everyone laughed except Alice.

Several more minutes passed, and gradually everyone began to stand up and move about the room, chatting in small groups and laughing at the children every now and then as they chased one another and ran rings around them. Alice remained close to her father, and Saxby remained close to Alice. She couldn't think how this was going to end, but it took a natural course when someone suggested a game of charades, which prompted Lord Metcalfe to pull out his fob watch.

'Heavens! Look at the time,' he said to Saxby. 'We've kept you too long. I'm afraid if you don't hurry, you'll miss your engagement. Four o'clock, didn't you say? It's five and twenty minutes to, now.'

'It's really nothing important, Charles.'

'Nonsense. I won't hear of it. Business is business after all.'

Saxby gave what Alice thought sounded like a deflated laugh. 'Yes, you're right of course,' he said. 'Business first. Thank you all, as always, for your hospitality.'

Alice watched her father place a hand on Saxby's shoulder. He led him towards the door, and they continued to talk about things Alice could no longer hear. It didn't matter to her what they were saying, just as long as Frank Saxby was leaving Hamberley.

An hour after Saxby left, Alice was in her room, packing a small travelling case. She had no idea where she was going, only that it was now too dangerous for her to remain at Hamberley. She had left the sitting room soon after Saxby had gone, and she'd spent most of the time since then poring over his notebook. She already knew that swapping the first two letters around yielded nothing legible, so she tried swapping the first and third letters, but that didn't work either. She went through several such transpositions before she came around to thinking that the code produced by the cipher might also have been reversed, so she began again on a small sample of text.

It was when she read the code backwards, swapping the first and third letters that she began to see words she recognised. Once she had completed the first page, it became clear to her that it was an address book, containing an entire network of spies for all she knew. She was even more convinced now that Saxby had to be the leader of this spy ring. She supposed there must be others, too, each controlling an area of England, with Saxby in command of the Southeast.

Alice knew the significance of her discovery and she knew that Saxby would do just about anything to get his notebook back. She finished packing the last of her essentials and placed the Ur-Leica camera on top. Together, they put her in as strong a bargaining position as she could hope for, and she planned to use them to get her husband back and end all this. Henry would know what to do from there on. She imagined they would go to America and, once there, send for the children. They would be safe enough while she had Saxby's notebook, and she would make a copy and use it to safeguard their future.

She took a deep breath, hands trembling as she closed her case and picked it up from the bed. She paused a moment, still wondering where she would go, concluding that anywhere was now safer than Hamberley. She had a little money—enough to check into a hotel for a few nights while she thought things through. She made for the door, to go to the children to hug them and kiss their sweet faces before she left, but the sound of a motorcar arriving on the drive stopped her. She ran to the window, hoping it was Archie in his little sports car, but the car she saw was not familiar to her. She watched two men get out, and at seeing them, she staggered back with her hand to her face. It was Inspector George Watts and his sergeant—the same two detectives from the special branch of the police service she had met in her father's study the day he was asked to go to London in connection with Admiral Waverley.

Alice bolted from her room, convinced this time that they had come for her as she had feared they would. She had been resolved to go with them if it came to it, but Saxby's notebook had given her new hope. She was out on the landing when they knocked, and she was at the top of the main stairs when the way was cut off by old Mrs Chetwood as she went to answer the door. Alice saw her father then, and she paused long enough to see the front door open. She saw the shorter man with the wiry grey sideburns produce the coat she had wrestled herself free from in Green Park—her coat, which her father would easily identify.

Alice could hear little of the conversation, but she heard her name clearly enough in connection with spying, along with the words 'arrest' and 'murder,' which seemed to ring out with great emphasis and clarity as the detectives came into the hallway. Alice knew she had only a moment to act. She could hear Charlotte's sporadic laughter from below, and she wanted with all her heart to go to her and to Chester. How would he take this news? He was old enough to know what she had done, if not to understand her reasons. Her father would take the news very badly, of that there was no doubt. She was discovered, and she knew now that her only hope lay with the release of her husband. He was the only person who could confirm her fantastical story.

Alice turned away and walked at a clip back the way she had come. She turned off the passageway and along another corridor, then through another room and out again by the back staircase. She would use the side door as she often did, and once outside she would run to the bottom of the garden where there was a gate she knew she could climb. In a matter of minutes the detectives and her father would be in her room, and once there they would find everything they needed to secure a conviction against her: the lemon juice and the music sheets, and the report that Raskin had not yet collected.

But in a matter of minutes, Alice would be gone.

# Chapter Twenty-Four

Present day.

Jefferson Tayte was sitting on a bench in a colourful garden that backed on to Foxburrow Wood, where the dappled shade from a cherry tree standing in the middle of the lawn cast ever shifting swatches of light and shade in the gentle summer breeze. He heard a door close towards the house, and a few seconds later Davina Scanlon reappeared through the rose arbour that was part way down the garden path. She was wearing a white summer dress and sandals, and was carrying a wine cooler and two glasses. Tucked beneath her arm was a large, clear plastic envelope, which Tayte thought had to contain the telegram she wanted him to see.

'It's too nice an afternoon not to have a little glass of something cool,' she said as she approached. She set everything down on the small foldaway table in front of them. 'You will join me, won't you?'

'Sure,' Tayte said, and as Davina sat beside him, he thought the bench suddenly felt too small. He shifted along as best he could, but it made no perceptible difference.

Davina poured their drinks, and they settled back. 'So what have you been up to since I last saw you?'

Tayte would rather have talked about the contents of the clear envelope that was now tantalisingly within reach on the table, but it seemed only reasonable to bring Davina up to date on his progress first, so he told her about his visit with the Ashcrofts that morning, and then about Dean Saxby and the reason he'd said he went to see her husband on the day she bumped into him. He concluded with the records he'd seen in DI Bishop's office, confirming that Alice had indeed been wanted by the British government for spying.

'I knew it,' Davina said. 'A rumour like that has to be founded in truth, don't you think?'

'No smoke without fire,' Tayte said. It was a well-coined phrase, but following the smoke in his case had often led to results.

'It sounds as if you're making good progress,' Davina said. 'Do you want to see what I've found?'

Tayte snorted. 'Are you kidding?'

Davina leaned forward and picked up the folder, crossing her legs as she sat back again, revealing more of her slender thigh through her half-buttoned dress than Tayte felt comfortable being so close to. She slid the contents from the folder and passed the telegram to him.

'I'm sure you'll find the date very interesting.'

Tayte's eyes found it immediately. In the top right-hand corner he read, 'Sent date: 29 May 1914.' Below the date, in bold typeface, was the heading 'The Marconi International Marine Communication Company Ltd.' Further down he read, 'Origin: *Empress of Ireland.*'

Tayte said what he was thinking. 'That's the date the *Empress* sank.' He thought back to his conversations with Emile Girard in Quebec. 'So, it had to have been sent between midnight and around one thirty.'

'I knew you'd like it,' Davina said, clearly sensing Tayte's excitement.

Tayte's eyes dropped to the message section, and he read it aloud with great interest, taking his time over the words. 'To: Frank Saxby. Notebook in care of Ms Phoebe Dodson.' It gave an address in Charlesbourg, Quebec City, and a sender's name that sent a tingle running through him. 'Albrecht,' he said, narrowing his eyes.

'Does the name mean anything to you?'

Tayte reached down beside the bench and pulled his briefcase up onto his lap. 'Yes, it does. At least, I've seen it before.' He pulled several documents out and began rifling through them. 'Here it is.' He showed Davina. It was the extract from the first-class cabin allocations Emile Girard had given him, showing which cabin Alice's husband Henry was in and whom he was sharing it with.

'Mr W. Albrecht,' Davina said with a raised brow. 'What does it mean?'

'Right now, I don't know, but it has to mean something. The man sharing a cabin with Alice's husband sent this telegram to Frank Saxby soon after the *Empress of Ireland* departed Quebec.'

'So, Alice wasn't sharing a cabin with her husband?'

'No, and I've thought that odd since I first checked the passenger lists and saw that Alice wasn't even in first class. She was travelling on the deck below in second.'

'That is odd. I wonder who Phoebe Dodson is.'

Tayte had been wondering that, too, and he thought the address in Quebec City was telling. Alice had fled England at the beginning of the month, so it stood to reason that she had been staying somewhere local until her planned return at the end of that month.

'Perhaps Phoebe Dodson gave Alice lodgings while she was in Quebec,' Tayte said. 'Maybe she was a friend or family member, or just the owner of a boarding house where Alice sought refuge before her journey back to England. That's if she has anything to do with Alice at all.'

Tayte thought about the message that had been sent in the telegram, and he wondered whether it was in some way connected with his earlier supposition that something had to have happened to change Alice's intended plans after the ship set out for Liverpool—besides the ship's unpredictable sinking. He read Frank Saxby's name again and took Davina's photograph out from his briefcase to take another look at him, wondering how this friend of the family and one-time business partner of Oscar Scanlon could be involved. Right now the potential reasons seemed boundless. He went back to the telegram and read the message again, focusing now on the notebook it mentioned as he tried to figure out why it was so important to Frank Saxby that he should get a telegram about it from the *Empress* at such a late hour.

'Have you seen this telegram before?' Tayte asked. 'Do you have any idea how your husband came by it?'

Davina shook her head. 'No, I've never seen it, and I can only imagine it must have been handed down through Lionel's family for some reason—it's hardly the kind of thing you just come across, is it? Perhaps Oscar Scanlon got it from Frank Saxby at one time or another.'

Tayte agreed that it seemed a likely explanation, but why? He voiced his thoughts. 'Why did Oscar Scanlon want it at all? And why bother to hand something like that down through the family? It's not your typical heirloom.' Just the same, he would have thought the telegram harmless enough were it not for the fact that it had belonged to a man who had recently been murdered, and it clearly held some importance to Lionel Scanlon, or why else keep it?

'I don't know,' Davina said, 'but do you think it's possible that whoever killed Lionel was after the notebook it mentions? Maybe his killer thought my husband had it.'

'I wouldn't rule it out,' Tayte said, thinking about the police investigation and wondering whether the notebook could be the connection he was looking for. 'We know that whoever did kill your husband is looking for something. Why else go over your properties like that?'

They both sat back with their thoughts and their wine, Tayte contemplating this new discovery and its possible implications, thinking that further research into Frank Saxby was now a high priority. Davina, it was soon apparent, was thinking about something else entirely.

She reached for the wine bottle. 'Would you like to stay for dinner?' she asked as she topped up their glasses.

'Well, I don't know,' Tayte began, but Davina cut him short before he had the chance to raise an objection.

'Surely the idea of a bit of company and a home-cooked meal is more appealing than eating alone at the Holiday Inn?'

Tayte couldn't argue with that, and he didn't try to. He began to wonder whether there was something wrong with him—why couldn't he just relax around people and fit in? He knew he had to take control of that if his relationship with Jean was to have any future. He laughed at himself. 'I'm sorry,' he said. 'Why don't you ask me that again.'

'Okay.' Davina repositioned herself on the bench as if she'd just sat down. Then turning to Tayte, she said, 'Would you like to stay for dinner this evening?'

Tayte laughed again. 'Sure,' he said. 'Dinner would be great.'

'Perfect. Actually, I do have an ulterior motive for asking you. I thought we could crack on with the research together.' She took Tayte's wine glass from him and set it down with hers on the table. 'Shall we go inside and get your laptop out? You said you had several lines to follow. Where do you want to start?'

'With Archibald Ashcroft. He's been on my mind since I visited with the Ashcroft family this morning.'

That the young naval officer was somehow involved with Alice in her hour of need seemed only logical to Tayte, given what he'd learned. He also thought that Alice might have needed help to evade the authorities, and who better to turn to than her childhood friend, whom for all Tayte knew, given his connection to the Admiralty, was already deeply involved in her plight.

# Chapter Twenty-Five

Saturday, 2 May 1914.

At seven thirty in the evening on the day Alice Stilwell fled Hamberley, she was sitting at a small oak table in a dimly lit corner of the Three Gardeners public house in North Street, Strood, which was just across the River Medway to the north of Rochester. It was a lively place, but not so busy that she couldn't see who was coming and going. She thought most of the patrons were regulars because everyone seemed to know everyone else, and now and then someone would look over at her as if to ask who the stranger was. She hadn't given much thought to it before now, but she supposed she was an odd sight to be sitting in a public house unaccompanied. She felt suddenly self-conscious and nervous enough to set her fingers tapping on the table. She caught another man's eye then. He was staring at her from the bar, and she turned away, wishing that Archie would soon arrive.

Not knowing whom else to turn to, Alice had taken a motor-taxi straight to Archie's address in South Gillingham, but he wasn't home. 'Not back from London,' his mother had said as she invited Alice in to wait. But supposing those now after her would second guess she would go to Archie, she had declined. Instead, she had left an urgent and cryptic message, asking that Archie meet her as soon as possible at the place where they'd had their first proper drink together, knowing that Archie would easily remember how they had once sneaked off to the Three Gardeners when they were younger, not daring to do so locally in case anyone recognised them.

Alice had a glass of vermouth in front of her, just as she had back then. She had almost finished it by the time Archie walked in, still in his uniform and with an eager expression on his face as he looked around for her.

'I came as soon as I got your message,' he said. 'What's that you're drinking?'

Alice told him, and a few minutes later he came back from the bar with a fresh vermouth for her and a pint of bitter for himself. He set them down and lowered himself into the chair opposite her.

'What's happened, Alice? Perhaps if you opened up to me more, I could help.'

'I will, Archie. I'll tell you everything,' Alice said, glad to have someone to tell at last, hoping that by doing so she would find some degree of relief from the anxiety she had kept locked inside her all this time.

Over their drinks, Alice explained everything that had happened, saying how Henry and her children had been abducted in Holland, and about the Dutchman and how Chester had been poisoned. She told him all about the spying she had been forced to do before coming to him for his help in getting the photographs Raskin wanted. She paused at that point, and from her travel bag she showed Archie that she still had the camera, letting him know that she now had no intention of handing the film over.

'I suppose someone must have followed me home after one of my tasks on the South Coast,' she said. 'They must have been watching Hamberley after that, and then they followed me to London. I'm scared, Archie.'

Archie placed a hand on hers to comfort her. 'Of course you are, Alice, but try not to worry. I'm here now. I'll see you're all right.'

He withdrew his hand again. 'Actually, I'm surprised I've not been arrested by now. Whoever followed you must have seen me bring those plans to you.'

'I'm sure,' Alice said. Then she told him what had become of the man who had followed her, bringing him up to date with everything that had happened since they'd parted company outside Green Park, including how she had uncovered Frank Saxby when she found his encrypted address book.

Archie went quiet for several seconds, then said, 'So, everything you told me when I collected you from the train station the other night—that was all lies?'

He made it sound as cold as it really was, and Alice didn't know what to say.

'I thought it was rather too good to be true,' Archie continued, 'Still, I suppose I must have wanted to believe you.'

'I don't expect you to forgive me, Archie, but I am sorry. Really I am.'

'"Sorry" doesn't really cut it, does it?' he said, turning away.

'Archie, please don't turn your back on me. I know I don't deserve your help, but I've no one else to go to.'

Silence fell between them, and Alice sensed that Archie was considering the matter. A moment later he turned back to her, took a big gulp of his drink, and said, 'I can't say it doesn't hurt, Alice, but I can hardly leave you to the wolves in your hour of need, can I?' He forced a half smile. 'Now we'd better keep moving forwards. This is serious business. Any delay could prove disastrous.'

Alice gave a solemn nod, thinking it was as well that she had married Henry and not Archie, because she knew now that she didn't deserve a man like Archie. She finished her drink and moved the conversation forward as Archie had suggested.

'Looking at it now,' she said, 'I suppose Frank Saxby was well placed to set all this up.'

'He's a scoundrel of the highest order,' Archie said. 'Just say the word, and I'll box his ears for you.'

Alice placed a hand on his. 'No, Archie, it's much more complicated than that.'

'Then you'll have to turn yourself in and tell the authorities everything you've just told me. They'll soon break Saxby down, and they'll see how you were forced to do these things. I'm implicated now, too. I'll come along and face the music with you. You won't be alone.'

Alice smiled kindly at him. 'You're very sweet, Archie. But I've given that a lot of thought, and I can't do it. You see, Frank Saxby is just a part of a much bigger network. It's too dangerous, for Henry and the children, and besides, who would believe me if Saxby didn't confess?'

'Then what do you propose to do?'

Alice produced Saxby's notebook from her coat, which was on the back of her chair. 'I'm going to use this to bargain with.'

Archie flicked through it with a puzzled expression on his face.

'It's all in code, but I can read it,' Alice said. 'For all I know, it could be an address book with the contact details of all the spies operating in the Southeast of England.'

'Then you'll need some time,' Archie said. 'And you'll have to get out of the country, for a while at least. I've heard a thing or two about these Special Branch detectives and about the Secret Service Bureau they collaborate with in these matters. They won't stop until they've caught up with you, especially since you say one of their number has been murdered. Have you got your passport document?'

Alice nodded. 'But where shall I go?'

'I know somewhere safe. We'll check you into a hotel or a guest-house for the night, and I'll call for you in the morning.'

'I can't ask you to get any more involved in this, Archie.'

'Look, Alice, I said if you were in trouble I was your man, and I meant it. Do you have paper and a pencil?'

Alice did. She gave him her notebook, and he began to write.

'We'll go for that long drive you promised I could take you on,' he said. 'I'm going to take you to Liverpool, where you can board a steamship for Canada.'

'Canada?'

Archie nodded and showed her what he'd written. It was an address in Quebec.

'Who lives there?' Alice asked.

'Long story, but in a nutshell, it's my sister, Phoebe.'

Alice looked surprised. 'I didn't know you had a sister called Phoebe. You've never mentioned her.'

'No, well I wasn't allowed to. No one in the family was supposed to talk about her. I only found out she existed myself a few years ago.'

'But why?' Alice asked. 'Why wasn't anyone supposed to talk about her?'

Archie scoffed. 'To avoid a scandal. That's what I was told. You see, Phoebe's really my half-sister. Her surname's Dodson. Same father, different mothers.'

'I see.'

Archie nodded. 'Precisely. Quite an indiscretion on my father's part. I don't know the full story, but I did want to know my half-sister, so I found out where she and her mother lived, and I went to see them.'

'And they won't mind me just turning up?'

'No,' Archie said, shaking his head as though there was no question about it. 'We've kept in close contact. Phoebe's heard so much about you already, you'll be just like old friends when you meet.' He laughed to himself. 'For heaven's sake don't tell her everything about me, will you?'

Alice could only manage the slightest of smiles in return. 'I shall simply tell her what a wonderful man you are and leave it at that,' she said. 'But what about Chester and Charlotte? I can't leave them behind.'

'You have to, Alice—for now at least. You'll be caught for sure if you try to go back for them. Don't worry. I'll see no harm comes to them. Besides, I shouldn't think Saxby or any of his cronies will make a move while you've got that notebook of his. You'll have to make a copy. Then once Henry's safe, let Saxby know you'll use it if he doesn't leave you and your family alone.' Archie paused to finish his bitter. 'You know, you should use it anyway once everyone's safe. Bring the scoundrel to justice and the whole spy ring down like a house of cards.'

'I aim to,' Alice said, 'but first things first.'

'Yes, of course. Have you eaten? Would you like to?'

'No, thank you. I'm not hungry.'

'No, of course not,' Archie said. 'Silly of me to suppose you were.' He stood up. 'Come on, let's find you somewhere to stay.'

# Chapter Twenty-Six

Sunday, 3 May 1914.

They left for Liverpool early the next morning, following a 1910 publication of the *Duckham's Motor Map of England and Wales*. It was a bright start to the day, but Archie kept the Vauxhall's top up until they were twenty or so miles clear of London, heading north-west through Hertfordshire, to give them better cover until they were well on their way. From then on, they had the sun on their faces and the wind in their hair as mile after mile of open country-side sped past them. They had their coats on to keep warm as it was still cold for the time of year, and Archie had thoughtfully brought along some provisions and a blanket for Alice, together with one of his mother's silk scarves, which she wrapped over her head and tied beneath her chin.

Not wanting to lose any more time than was necessary, they stopped only to refuel from the petrol cans Archie had brought with them for the journey. Towns and villages came and went with the hours that passed in conversation, which largely concerned their years growing up together. It was a welcome escape for Alice. They had to raise their voices to hear one another over the beat of the exhaust and the engine tappet noise combined with the buffeting wind, but Alice knew that despite her circumstances, or perhaps because of them, she had not felt so at ease in a long time. When they weren't talking, Archie would turn to her every now and then and throw her a dimpled smile as if to suggest he was having the time of his life.

By mid-afternoon they were in Staffordshire, and Archie suddenly shifted gear and put his foot down. The Hele-Shaw multiplate clutch hissed as it engaged, and the acceleration came as a shock to Alice, causing her to clutch at the air in front of her as she tried to hold on to something.

Archie eyed her with a wide grin. 'I've had her up to sixty-five miles an hour before now.' A moment later he eased off, and the car began to slow down again. 'Perhaps not today, though, eh? We've got almost a hundred miles still to go. Better not push her too hard.'

They passed through Stafford and were in open countryside again, where there were few other motorcars to be seen among the usual horse drawn conveyances they passed. A few miles on, Alice became concerned about one other car in particular that she thought she'd seen before, some twenty miles back, which she had now seen twice since leaving Stafford.

'Archie, I think we're being followed.'

Archie looked over his shoulder. 'I can't see anything.'

Alice looked again. 'It's dropped back now, but I'm sure I've seen it before. It's dark red with a cream-coloured roof. Do you think the authorities are on to us?'

'I shouldn't think anyone would have followed us this far,' Archie said. 'If it was the police or the Secret Service Bureau, why haven't they stopped us?'

'Yes, I suppose you're right. It's probably nothing to worry about.'

They continued for several miles, and Alice kept looking back, but she saw nothing more of the red and cream car. She supposed her nerves were getting the better of her, and she wished the journey were over. As the tappet noise from the engine continued to play its repetitive tune, she began to daydream, and on any other Sunday her thoughts might have been happy ones. Instead, she thought about her father and wondered what the police had told him and what he had made of it all. She wondered whether he had told her mother and how her absence would be explained to her children. She could have cried just thinking about Chester and Charlotte and what they would think of her. She knew she had to succeed in getting Henry back and, in doing so, put everything right again.

'I need to put another can of petrol in,' Archie said, stirring Alice from her thoughts. He pointed to a road sign ahead. 'Look there's a village coming up. Perhaps we can get a spot of tea.'

'Yes,' Alice said. 'Tea would be lovely.'

They approached the village of Turnfield by what was little more than a rough track through farmland that shook the two-seater Vauxhall and its occupants all the way to the village High Street. They crossed a narrow bridge over a tinkling stream, and looking around, Alice thought the population of Turnfield couldn't have been more than a few hundred people. As the car continued at a crawl, winding around one corner and the next, they passed a few slate-tiled cottages and an elderly man with his dog. Further on, they came to a few more buildings and a church that seemed far too big for such a small village to have all to itself.

Archie laughed. 'I don't think we're going to find a Lyons tea shop here.'

'No, it doesn't look as though we will,' Alice agreed. 'It's very quaint, though.'

When the few buildings petered out, indicating that they had already passed through the village of Turnfield, Archie stopped the car behind a horseless cart, and they got out. He was smirking as he took out one of the two-gallon petrol cans he'd brought along and began to fill the fuel tank. 'It seems even the horses get Sundays off in this sleepy little place.'

'Maybe the next town isn't too far,' Alice said.

'I'm sure it can't be, but there must be somewhere here to get a cup of tea.' Archie finished refuelling and put the can back. 'Look, why don't you sit tight while I run back and have a quick scout about. We passed a couple of lanes back there. It's worth a look.'

'All right,' Alice said. She got back into the car. 'But hurry back.'

'I will.'

Alice watched him go until he disappeared around a corner and she could no longer see him. She didn't think he would find anywhere for refreshment here, but as Archie had said, it was worth a quick look now they were there. A couple of minutes passed, and she soon began to hear an unmistakable sound over the trickle of the stream. It was another motorcar, the engine note growing louder, as though it were coming towards her. She looked back, expecting to see it, afraid that it would be the same car she had seen before. But the sound stopped. She wanted to go and look, but she resisted, too afraid to in case she was right, and they were being followed.

A few more minutes passed, and then she saw Archie coming back, and she laughed nervously to herself. She got out of the car and went to him. Then as she drew closer, she knew something was wrong. He was clutching his side, staggering with every other step. She ran to him.

'Archie!'

He smiled at her, but she could see the pain in his eyes. His lower lip was bleeding—his nose, too.

'Archie, whatever's happened?'

'No joy with that tea, I'm afraid.'

Alice helped him back to the car.

'On my way back I saw that car you mentioned. You were right, Alice, but it wasn't the police or the Secret Service Bureau.'

He looked down as he brought his arm up, and in his hand Alice saw Raskin's flensing knife, the curved steel no longer gleaming, but nonetheless bright with blood.

'Where is he?' Alice asked, panic in her voice as she looked back.

'Don't worry. He won't bother you again.'

'What happened? Is he dead? How did you get his knife?'

'That car caught my eye first—a Mercedes. Then I saw the driver, and I realised who he was from what you'd told me in the Three Gardeners last night. How stupid of me not to think I'd be followed. I led him straight to you.'

'Don't be too hard on yourself, Archie. I'm sure you wouldn't have seen him unless he wanted you to.'

'No, perhaps not. Well, he must have known who I was because he came straight at me, and we went at it like bare-knuckle prize fighters for a few minutes. He was no boxing man, but he took his punches better than most I've seen, and he gave better, too. We wound up further back by the little bridge we crossed on the way through. I thought I had the upper hand at one point, but then he produced this knife.' Archie tried to smile again as he added, 'I thought that was hardly fair.'

'However did you best him?' Alice asked. She couldn't imagine how any man could, as proficient at boxing as Archie was.

'I'm not entirely sure I did.'

He pulled one side of his coat open.

'Oh, Archie, you're bleeding.'

'I'm sure it's nothing. Just a flesh wound. The fella made the mistake of leaving his knife in my side when he lunged at me with it. I turned away, and I suppose it was caught through my coat. He came back for it without hesitation, but I must have landed a lucky blow as I returned it to him. I left his body by the stream.'

'We must get you to a hospital.'

'There's no time, Alice. If you're delayed, the authorities will catch up with you for sure. They may already have people at the major seaports looking out for you.'

'Yes, but all the same I—'

'Please Alice, I won't hear another word about it.'

'You're too stubborn for your own good, Archie Ashcroft. Did anyone see you fighting?'

'No, I don't think so, but we'd better move on. Someone's sure to wonder whose Mercedes that is back there. It won't be long before someone raises the alarm. Just help me into the motorcar, will you? I can manage from there.'

———

They picked up the main road again, and however much Alice tried to engage Archie in conversation, he became very quiet. By the time they had travelled another fifty miles and were not far from their destination, Alice thought he had begun to look very pale, but however much she tried to persuade him to stop and seek help, he would not do so.

'I'll take myself off to the hospital when we reach Liverpool,' he kept saying. 'Once I know you're safe.'

They crossed an inland tributary of the River Mersey, with a couple of hours of daylight to spare, and they were soon on the outskirts of Liverpool, where the vista changed from one of nature and agriculture to industry.

'Nearly there, Alice,' Archie said, struggling now to maintain his usual upbeat tone. 'I shouldn't think you'll get a crossing tonight, but there should be something tomorrow. We'll find you a guesthouse until then. Something low key.'

'And then you'll go to the hospital?'

'I will, Alice. That's a promise.'

They continued in silence for several minutes, over cobbled streets that caused Archie to wince and clutch his side every now and then. There were shops to either side of them, the pavements busy with people moving beneath awnings that advertised the shop-keepers' wares. A moment later a horse and cart overtook them.

'You're driving very slowly, Archie. People are staring.'

'Am I? I hadn't noticed.'

'Please let's go to the hospital.'

'I'm fine, Alice. Please don't fuss.'

'You really don't look fine, Archie.'

His mouth was open as if he was struggling for breath. His eyelids were half closed, and his face was glistening with sweat. A moment later, Archie slumped over the steering wheel, and the car veered towards an oncoming tram.

'Look out, Archie!'

He sat up again, his face now pallid and drawn. He turned the wheel in time to avoid a collision.

'I'm sorry, Alice. I've let you down. I don't think I can go much further.'

Alice shook her head. Tears welled in her eyes. 'No, you haven't, Archie. You'll be fine. Pull into the next street, and stop the car. I'll get help.'

Archie turned the car off the main road, along a narrow street lined with terraced houses. He stopped the car.

'I think it's too late for all that, Alice.'

'No, it isn't. Don't say such things.'

Archie opened his coat, and with what strength he had left, he reached inside.

'Here, take this.'

It was a fold of banknotes.

'I won't,' Alice said, choking back the tears she knew were not far away.

Archie managed one of his dimpled smiles even now. He pressed the money into her hand. 'You'll need it,' he said. 'Please take it.'

The first tear broke as Alice took the money, knowing he was right. 'Archie, I'm so very sorry. I should never have involved you.'

'What, and have me miss the best day of my life just for spending it with you?'

Alice began to sob. 'We'll have many more days together. Better days.'

'I'd like that.'

His eyelids began to flutter, and Alice soothed his brow. 'I do love you Archie.' She meant every word. 'I've always loved you.'

She kissed his lips for the very first time, knowing it would also be the last. When she withdrew, Archie smiled at her again, and they continued to gaze into each other's eyes for several seconds. Then Archie drew a sudden breath and sighed, and he was gone.

# Chapter Twenty-Seven

Monday, 4 May 1914.

At ten o'clock the following morning Alice Stilwell was sitting in a specially soundproofed telephone kiosk waiting for her long distance, person-to-person call to be connected. She had spent the night in cheap accommodation above a public house in Bootle, not far from the docks, where she had slept for no more than three hours at most. She couldn't stop thinking about Archie, and neither did she want to. She kept seeing his ghostly face as he sat lifeless in his little yellow motorcar, and she would never know how she managed to leave him there to be discovered by strangers or how she had the strength of will to keep going and not once look back. With every step she took she had wanted to, but she had known if she had that she would have broken down and would never have regained the strength to keep walking. She would never forgive herself for his death, any more than she would forgive those who were ultimately responsible.

She supposed it would not have been long before Archie's body was discovered. The story was no doubt already on the cover of the local, if not national, newspapers, but Alice had avoided them all. She could imagine well enough the headline concerning the mystery man who had been found dead in his motorcar; a mystery man, for now at least, because she had taken anything she thought could be used to identify Archie, and she thought it would take time to find out who he was from his motorcar registration. Then the people hunting her would realise that Archie had taken her to Liverpool to make her escape, and after that it would not be long before they checked the ships' registers and knew her destination. They would surely send a telegram to Quebec, and the Canadian authorities would be waiting to arrest her as soon as she stepped off the ship. But they would have no more than a written description of her, and she would have plenty of time on the voyage ahead to alter her appearance and plan how best to disembark unnoticed. She would have to be careful, and she knew it would be dangerous, but what about her life since Holland had not been?

The first thing Alice had done that morning was to purchase a second-class ticket aboard the White Star Line's RMS *Laurentic*, a triple-screw steamer with a single funnel and twin masts that was leaving that afternoon and was expected to make the journey in thirteen days. It was not a particularly fast crossing, and she had been told that if she cared to wait, there were larger steamers that could make the journey to Quebec in a week, but Alice did not care to wait in Liverpool any longer than she had to. She had thought to use an alias for her departure, but she knew her passport document would give her away if she had to present it.

She heard another crackle in the earpiece she had pressed to her ear as another connection was made further down the line, and she felt suddenly nervous.

'Hello?'

This was not a telephone call she wanted to make, and certainly not today, but she knew she had no choice. Having lived in America with Henry and the children, she understood that once she crossed the Atlantic Ocean, there would be no opportunity to do so. Henry had often said how he welcomed the day that transatlantic telephone calls were possible and how good it would be for business, but that day had not yet arrived.

Alice heard a further series of clicks in the earpiece, and then the female voice of the distant operator said, 'I'm connecting you now.' A few seconds later Frank Saxby came on the line, and hearing his voice again made Alice's skin crawl.

'Hello? Alice? Are you there?'

He sounded faint, and knowing they were many miles apart made her feel a little easier about what she had to say.

'Yes, Mr Saxby. I'm here.' She could no longer think of him in first name terms, let alone the 'Uncle' Frank she had once trusted.

'Good,' Saxby said. 'I was hoping you would get in touch.'

Alice mocked him. 'Please don't lie to me, Mr Saxby. I know you sent your Dutch friend after me.'

'Yes, of course you do,' Saxby said. 'How is he?'

'If he were well, do you suppose I would be talking to you now?'

Saxby didn't answer.

Alice had had plenty of time to think about the reason Raskin had been sent after her, and she fully believed that since her activities had been discovered by the authorities, the Dutchman had been sent not only to recover Saxby's notebook but to kill her, and in doing so, guarantee her silence. Her cover was blown, and what further use was she now? She had become too big a risk and was now a threat to their entire operation.

'Look, where are you?' Saxby said. 'Everyone's worried about you. Won't you come back, so we can talk about all this before it gets out of hand?'

Alice wanted to scream down the telephone line. 'As far as I'm concerned this has been out of hand since you had my family kidnapped.'

'Yes, I suppose it has. Well, I'm sure we can help each other now. You have something I want, and I can get what you want.'

Alice was counting on it. 'I'm not coming back,' she said. 'We'll do this my way, or I'm taking your notebook straight to the authorities. And you must stay away from my children. Do you understand? I know how to decipher your code. It really wasn't hard for me to work it out.'

Alice heard an awkward laugh from Saxby then. 'Come now, Alice. Let's not be rash, eh? Tell me what you have in mind.'

'An exchange. My husband for your notebook and my silence.'

'And what about those photographs you took? I'd like those, too.'

'No, they're not part of the bargain,' Alice said, thinking about Archie again and how she had told him she had no intention of handing the film over. At least that was one promise to him she could keep.

'Very well,' Saxby said, 'but how can I be sure of your silence?'

'You'll have to trust me. You know I won't do anything to endanger my family.'

'I see. So, if you go to the authorities, my associates or I will come after you and your family. On the other hand, if anything untoward happens to your family, then you will go to the authorities?'

'Yes, that's it precisely.'

'Do you intend to make a copy of my notebook?'

'I do. And I'm going to make arrangements so that if anything happens to me, either before or after the exchange, it will be sent to the authorities with a letter explaining everything.'

The call went quiet again. All Alice could hear for several seconds was the ever present sound of static on the line. Then Saxby said, 'Well played, Alice. I really don't have any choice in the matter, do I?'

'All I want is my husband back,' Alice said. 'And I want my children to be safe.'

There was another pause.

'Very well,' Saxby said. 'An exchange it is. Do you have somewhere in mind?'

'I'm leaving the country,' Alice said. She saw no reason not to tell him now. 'As soon as I've made arrangements for my return, I'll send a telegram stating where and when the exchange is to take place.'

'Then I shall wait with great anticipation to hear from you again,' Saxby said.

Alice was about to end the call, but there were questions burning inside her that she had to ask.

'Why are you doing this? I mean, how could you?'

'I'm a businessman, Alice, and I'm a survivor. Many people believe a great war is coming, and I thought it was time to choose sides.'

'So you sold yourself to Germany? What of loyalty?'

'Loyalty?' Saxby scoffed. 'I'm afraid this great country of ours turned its back on us Saxbys a long time ago. My family went to India to help build the British Empire, and what thanks do you suppose they received?'

Alice didn't answer.

'They were slaughtered, Alice, all but my father, who was just a small boy then. And all for want of a relief column that was never sent. Where was their country's loyalty to them when they most needed it?' Saxby laughed sourly. 'No, I'm afraid I have very little loyalty in me.'

'Well, what of friendship? You've been a close friend of my family's since you were a boy. Doesn't that count for anything?'

'Like I said, Alice. It was time to choose a side, and some paths once taken are impossible to deviate from. Now I think we've chatted long enough. I shudder to think what this telephone call is going to cost you.'

Alice didn't care what it cost. She had enough money—Archie had seen to that—and this was unquestionably the most important conversation of her life. She was about to ask Saxby why he'd chosen her, and whether it was because of her closeness to Archie, just so that she could use him to get the defence plans they wanted, but as she started to speak, she knew any further questions would have to wait. The call had already ended.

# Chapter Twenty-Eight

Present day.

An early start to another bright new day saw Jefferson Tayte at one of his most frequented locales—the churchyard. This particular churchyard belonged to a flint-and red-tiled church of early twelfth-century origin called St Peter's, which was located in the village of Bredhurst, South Gillingham, no more than two miles from the Ashcroft residence Tayte had visited the day before. He was standing beside a family burial plot in God's Acre—as he'd been informed this particular churchyard was commonly known—surrounded by trees and encircled by a low wall, the dewy grass at his feet dampening his loafers.

The research he and Davina had conducted at her home the day before, during what had turned into a pleasant evening of good food and good company, had revealed much about Archibald Ashcroft—who, as well as Davina and the lengthy meal she had prepared, had dominated the evening, leaving no time to explore any of the other lines of research he wanted to follow. By the time Tayte went back to his hotel, later than he'd planned to and accordingly ready for his bed, he had discovered all he thought he could hope to about the young naval officer. It had become apparent that Archibald had not died during the First World War as the current Lord Ashcroft had supposed, but had instead died the day after the warrant had been issued for Alice Stilwell's arrest, which threw the timing of his death into an entirely different light.

Tayte continued to gaze upon the nautically themed burial plot before him, taking in the large stone anchor that formed the cross, and the depiction of a ship's sail being blown on a heavenly course by a cloud of angels, thinking that although it was good to talk to the family, it was also vital to back things up with hard facts. His eyes drifted back over the faded but legible inscription he'd gone there to see: 'Archibald Ashcroft. 1889–1914. Died May 3rd. Age 25 years.'

This revelation had led Tayte to wonder whether Brendan Ashcroft's mistake over the year Archibald died had been forced in an attempt to throw him off the scent. Surely Brendan had visited the family burial plot before and knew precisely when Archibald died. Although, Tayte had to concede that this was an old family plot, long since full. If Brendan were even the type to visit his family's graves with any regularity, he would likely now do so at the crematorium.

Had Archibald's involvement with Alice—and more importantly, the threat of his own activities coming to light—caused Brendan Ashcroft to take steps to keep the past buried? Tayte wondered whether the notebook mentioned in the telegram Davina had shown him might contain something to implicate Archibald more directly in crimes against his country, but it was a fanciful thought. Protecting the memory of the dead, or the reputation of the living, still seemed to Tayte too weak a motive for murder a hundred years on, although it was a possibility he could not rule out.

The close proximity of these incontrovertible events—of Alice's attempted arrest and Archibald's death—had led Tayte and Davina deeper into the circumstances of his demise, and by the end of the evening Tayte had formed a clear picture in his mind, leaving him in no doubt that Archibald had aided and abetted Alice, borne as his actions surely were out of their long-standing friendship and, in all probability, his deeply affected love for her.

From various newspaper archives such as *The Times* and the recently defunct *Liverpool Daily Post*, Tayte had learned that Archibald's body had been found on the outskirts of Liverpool, in a car that later proved to be registered to him. Tayte had read how he had died from blood loss following a stab wound, and much mystery had surrounded the piece for both the newspaper reporter and Tayte. Then Tayte found a later report that connected Archibald's murder to another murder, discovered that same day in a village not far from where Archibald's body had been found. This other man had suffered a similar knife wound, thought to have been inflicted by the same weapon, but which was more instantly fatal. He carried no identification papers and was travelling in a car registered to an untraceable alias, which had only served to deepen the mystery further.

Knowing all that Tayte now knew, he saw it as far less of a mystery. It seemed clear to him that Alice and Archibald had been pursued. The fact that this other man was not a policeman or an officer from the Secret Service Bureau—who would have been carrying identification papers if he were—told Tayte that they were being pursued for reasons other than arrest. Their pursuer had clearly caught up with them, for what good it did him, and a fight had ensued. Tayte couldn't help but wonder whether the reason Alice and Archibald were being pursued at all was because of the notebook he had come to believe Alice was carrying with her when she fled to Quebec.

Details of the final part of Alice's journey had been provided by the Outbound Passenger Lists for Britain: 1890–1960, which he had searched online towards the end of his evening with Davina. The pertinent record told Tayte that Alice had sailed on the RMS *Laurentic* from Liverpool, having departed for Quebec on the third of May, the day after Archibald had died. This left no question in Tayte's mind that Archie had helped Alice make her escape and had paid the ultimate price for doing so.

Tayte checked his watch and turned away from Archibald's resting place. He popped a Mr Goodbar miniature into his mouth and made his way back out along the path and through the gate to his car. He had two meetings planned for that morning. DI Bishop had called to say that Dean Saxby wanted to see him, and Bishop thought Tayte might like to go along. The second was a meeting with Lady Vivienne Metcalfe. A highly unexpected phone call the night before had left him with the promise of seeing someone who held a key piece of the puzzle, and she had said to meet him at the Historic Dockyard Chatham at eleven.

It felt to Tayte as though there were twice as many steps in the stairwell to Dean Saxby's flat as there had been the day before. He was always a few paces behind DI Bishop, and as they neared what he hoped was the top, he had the feeling that Bishop had slowed down for him.

'What does he want to see you about?' Tayte asked, panting.

'He said he had some information that could be useful to my case. Lord knows why he couldn't have told us yesterday. I expect we're wasting our time, but you never know.'

They reached another level where the stairwell flattened out, and Tayte was relieved to see the number 9 on the door that led out to the flats on that level. One flight to go.

'I checked up on him,' Bishop said. 'He was arrested for domestic violence last year—put his wife in hospital, but she dropped the charges.'

'I guess that explains the divorce.'

Bishop agreed. 'At least she had the good sense to end their marriage.'

They reached the top floor and left the stairwell, pacing out onto the balconied walkway that looked down over the rooftops of the terraced houses below. Tayte drew a deep breath, filling his lungs with fresh air to clear out the tang of ammonia that was prevalent in the stairwell from countless dried urine stains.

'Are you telling me that,' Tayte asked, 'because you think Dean Saxby's violent nature has a bearing on the case?'

'No,' Bishop said, 'but my experience won't let me ignore it. And what if Lionel Scanlon's murder was nothing more than a burglary attempt gone wrong after all? Whether it's connected with your assignment or not, if he thought there was money to be made from it, I'd say that Dean Saxby had a pretty strong motive given his impoverished circumstances, and he clearly has a temperament for violence. That said,' Bishop continued, 'he does seem to be on the level. I followed up on the sale of that cigar case yesterday afternoon. It checked out.'

They reached the door to Dean Saxby's flat, and a moment later they were invited in. No refreshments were offered this time.

'So what did you want to tell me?' Bishop asked him. 'You said you had some information about the Scanlon case.'

'That's right.' Dean paused. His eyes flitted back and forth between Bishop and Tayte. 'Before I tell you'—he stopped again, as if he was having difficulty with what he wanted to say—'I read about a reward.'

'Did you now?' Bishop said, throwing Tayte a cynical glance. 'When was that?'

'How do you mean?'

'I mean, when did you read that a reward had been offered.'

'Yesterday, after you left. I thought I'd look into the murder some more. Amazing what you can find on the Web. Why does it matter when I read about it?'

Bishop smiled to himself. 'It just strikes me as an odd coincidence that you—a man who's obviously short of money—should suddenly have something to offer my case less than twenty-four hours after reading about the reward. Why didn't you say what you had to say yesterday?'

'It didn't come to me at the time—not until after you left.'

'No, of course not,' Bishop said, and Tayte noted the sarcasm in his tone, even if Dean Saxby didn't.

'So, if what I'm about to tell you leads anywhere,' Dean said. 'I'll get the reward, right?'

'Possibly, yes. If it leads to a conviction.'

Dean smiled to himself. 'Great,' he said. 'Lionel Scanlon was in the middle of a phone call when I went to see him. The door wasn't locked, so I went in. He was standing behind his desk in his overalls, talking on one of those old-fashioned phones with the curly wire. He put his hand up to stop me approaching, which I did, but I could hear most of what he said. He said he couldn't find it, whatever "it" was, and that he needed more time. The conversation must have become heated then, because Scanlon couldn't seem to get a word in edgeways, and I could hear the other voice in the speaker for the first time, not that I could make anything out. Before the call ended, though, I did hear the name "Metcalfe."'

'Metcalfe?' Tayte repeated, unable to stop himself.

Dean nodded. 'That's right.'

'Did you hear a first name?'

'No, that's it.'

'And there was no mention of what Mr Scanlon couldn't find?' Bishop asked.

'I just said that's all I heard. Maybe it's not much, but it could lead somewhere, right?'

Tayte thought it certainly tied in with the idea that Lionel Scanlon's killer was looking for something. *Metcalfe* . . . The name offered several candidates, and foremost in Tayte's mind was Raife, but he still couldn't discount Lord Reginald Metcalfe either.

'Well, thank you for the information,' Bishop said. He made for the door, and Tayte followed him.

'So, you'll let me know about the reward,' Dean called after them.

They paused in the cramped hallway, and Bishop turned back and said, 'Of course, but I wouldn't hold your breath.' He had a foot outside when he turned back again and asked, 'Just for the record, could you tell me where you were on Tuesday last, up until lunchtime? That was only two days ago. I'm sure you can remember.'

Tayte thought back and quickly realised that was when Davina's house and apartment were broken into.

'Here we go again,' Dean said. 'I've just helped you out, and you're still getting at me. Why do you want to know this time? Someone else murdered, was there?'

'Just tell me where you were, Mr Saxby, and we'll be on our way.'

'I told you yesterday. I've got no work on. I made a few phone calls to see if I could get any, as I do most mornings, and then I played some Xbox and watched the telly.'

'Thank you,' Bishop said, forcing a smile. 'That's all I wanted to know.'

---

HM Dockyard Chatham, as the dockyard was once called, had served the Royal Navy for more than four centuries before the last hammer fell in 1984. In its heyday it provided jobs for ten thousand workers across a four-hundred-acre site. Now known as the Historic Dockyard Chatham, it was an eighty-four-acre Georgian maritime museum, home to three historic warships and an important trove of British naval history.

As he stepped out into the late morning sunshine, Tayte had his head down in the information leaflet he'd been given along with his admittance ticket. He was looking at the map that had thoughtfully been printed on the back of the leaflet, searching for the Wheelwrights' restaurant. That was where Lady Metcalfe had said she would meet him, adding that the dockyard would be easy for him to find and that she didn't think it was a good idea for him to return to Hamberley. Tayte suspected the reason was also because Lady Metcalfe didn't want her husband to know she was talking to him.

He looked up from the map to get his bearings. There were covered slips ahead, and on his right there were several long huts—one of which, according to the map, was the restaurant, which he soon found a few doors down. As he made his way inside, he was glad that Lady Metcalfe had chosen to meet him at the dockyard, or he might otherwise never have seen it. He supposed Alice must have visited many times herself, given who her father was, and he tried to imagine the dockyard as it had been then—fully functioning and unknowingly preparing for war.

Tayte thought the interior of the Wheelwrights' had a cafeteria feel to it. It was long and narrow, the walls and vaulted ceiling painted chalky white, the bare wooden tables set along the side walls and in a continuous line down the centre, perhaps to represent a ship's mess. It was quiet. Lady Metcalfe was easy to spot, sitting in a pale peach summer coat at one of the side tables, beneath one of several windows that ran the length of the building.

Tayte fixed his best smile as he approached, and at the same time he noticed the brown envelope in front of her. 'Lady Metcalfe,' he said. 'I can't tell you how excited I've been since I got your call.'

'I just want to know the truth,' Lady Metcalfe said, dispensing with the formalities. 'The idea of a traitor in the family is doing nothing for my husband's health.'

Tayte was about to offer an apology for stirring up the past as he had, but Lady Metcalfe continued without pause.

'Did Alice Stilwell die when that ship went down in 1914, or didn't she? Was she spying, and if so, why? I refuse to believe that a young girl with such a patriotic upbringing as Alice would have received from her father would do such a thing willingly.'

Tayte didn't believe it either. 'I've seen proof that confirms Alice was wanted in connection with spying,' Tayte said. Diplomatically or otherwise, he chose not to tell her that Alice had also been wanted in connection with murder. 'As for the rest . . .' he paused. 'All I can say is that I'm still working on it.'

Lady Metcalfe placed a hand on the envelope before her and slid it across the table. 'Maybe this will help answer my first question.'

Tayte opened it. When he saw the edges of two old photographs, the corners of his mouth curled into a smile. He held his breath as he withdrew them and set them down in front of him. One image was of a family gathering at Christmas time, showing several happy-looking people in front of the tree. He had no difficulty picking Alice out, or her father, whom he recognised from Davina's photograph. The second image was a full portrait of Alice Stilwell—or Dixon; it no longer made a difference. He knew right there and then that he was looking at the proof he needed. He'd studied the photograph his client had given him of Alice Dixon enough times to need no further confirmation. They were without question one and the same person.

Just the same, for Lady Metcalfe's benefit Tayte went into his briefcase and found the image. He set it down beside the others and let his smile flourish. There were perhaps a few years between them, but in those years Alice had changed little. He turned the photographs around.

'I think that does indeed answer your first question,' he said. 'No, Alice Stilwell did not die in 1914.'

Lady Metcalfe studied the photographs in silence for several seconds, and Tayte could see that the stark comparison between the images had taken her aback. He supposed then that she had likely come to him hoping for a different outcome. Perhaps she had hoped to prove his assignment folly, and that realising it as such, he would pack his bags and go home again—and for her husband's sake, stir the Metcalfe family past no more.

'Would it be okay with you if I held on to these photos for the time being?' Tayte asked. 'I'll be sure to return them once my assignment's finished.'

The sudden change in Lady Metcalfe's expression told Tayte that she wasn't keen on the idea. 'Well, I . . .' She paused as if weighing up her answer. Then she seemed to change her mind. 'Yes, I suppose that would be okay.'

'Thanks,' Tayte said. 'I'll take good care of them.' He gathered the photographs together and put them in his briefcase. 'Now only one of your questions remains to be answered. Why did she do it?'

'And *how* could she do it?' Lady Metcalfe said. 'I mean, how could she go on with her life, letting her children believe she was dead?'

'That's a question I'd like the answer to myself,' Tayte said, coming to realise now that things must have become very desperate for Alice.

'They were adopted,' Lady Metcalfe said. 'Did you know? Their grandparents, Charles and Lilian Metcalfe, looked after them at first, but they eventually made it legal.'

'Yes, I was aware of that from my earlier research,' Tayte said. He went to get up. 'Can I get you a coffee, or maybe some tea?'

Lady Metcalfe glanced over at the self-service counter and then turned back to Tayte. 'No, I don't think so,' she said, as if the crockery, let alone the contents, fell too far short of her expectations. 'I must be getting back to Reginald.' She stood up and Tayte stood with her. 'If you should find out why Alice did what she did, you will let me know, won't you?'

'Of course.'

'Very well then. Good luck, and goodbye for now.'

With that, Lady Metcalfe left, and Tayte went to the counter and bought himself a large black coffee, which he sat and drank while he thought about Alice and the facts, as he saw them, of the closing stages of her journey. He took out the photographs of her again, and beneath them he set out several other documents in chronological order, hoping that they might help him to understand what had happened in those scant hours between the *Empress of Ireland* leaving Quebec and the disaster that awaited her.

The first record showed that Alice had boarded the *Laurentic* on 3 May, bound for Quebec. That leg of the journey seemed straightforward enough. She had arrived in Canada and had in all likelihood stayed with someone called Phoebe Dodson. The second record he set down showed that Alice had boarded the *Empress of Ireland* on 28 May for the return journey, which told Tayte that Alice had intended to return to England, presumably because at that point she had found a way to stay her execution and get her life back.

The next record was for Henry Stilwell's entry on the ship's passenger list, which told Tayte that Henry was travelling in separate accommodation to Alice. Next to that record he placed another, which showed that Henry was sharing a cabin with a man named Albrecht, which Tayte thought was surely a German name. He also thought that had to hold some significance.

The last document he set down was the telegram Albrecht had sent to Frank Saxby, longstanding friend of the Metcalfe family. He knew it would be difficult to find out who Mr W. Albrecht was, but Saxby remained high on Tayte's list of people to look into further. As was Henry Stilwell. He still couldn't fathom why Alice and Henry were travelling in separate cabins, and in different classes, aboard the *Empress of Ireland*. He imagined then that Henry had not been with Alice when she boarded the ship, which led him to wonder where he had been all this time and what had kept them apart during what was clearly a most difficult time for Alice. The questions dominated Tayte's thoughts as he continued to sit and drink his coffee. Whatever the answer, one thing was certain—they had been brought together again for that ill-fated voyage aboard the *Empress of Ireland* on 28 May 1914.

# Chapter Twenty-Nine

Quebec City, Canada. Thursday, 28 May 1914.

The twin-funnelled ocean steamer RMS *Empress of Ireland* was the pride of Canadian Pacific's twenty-vessel-strong White Empress fleet. Built in Scotland and launched eight years earlier in 1906, she was 570 feet in length with a beam of almost 66 feet. She boasted an average speed of eighteen knots, allowing her to cross the Atlantic in less than a week.

Alice Stilwell was standing on the shelter deck, dressed in a white lace tea gown and boater hat, waving back at the many people on the pier who had come to wish their friends and family bon voyage. The Salvation Army had struck up a hymn she recognised called 'God Be with You 'til We Meet Again,' which she began to hum along to. It seemed that everyone on the pier had a Union Jack flag, which they waved enthusiastically as the air filled with cries of 'Goodbye!' It was almost four thirty in the afternoon. In a matter of minutes, the ship that had helped settle Canada would cast off and embark on its ninety-sixth voyage.

Archie's half-sister, Phoebe, had wanted to come to the pier to see Alice off, but Alice had asked her not to. She knew she could not trust Frank Saxby, despite the warnings she had given him about turning his notebook over to the authorities, and she did not want to put anyone else at risk. She had been on her guard since she arrived at Quebec Harbour earlier that afternoon to watch the *Empress of Ireland* arrive from Montreal.

When Alice had gone to the address Archie had given her, Phoebe had welcomed her just as he said she would, and it was easy to see the family resemblance in her. It had saddened Alice to the point of wanting to stay somewhere else at first, simply because Phoebe reminded her so much of Archie, but Phoebe would not hear of it once she knew who Alice was.

'Archie's childhood sweetheart,' Phoebe had called her with a grin, and Alice couldn't bring herself to tell her that Archie was dead. It was selfish of her, she knew, but she also thought that telling her might jeopardise her situation, and she knew Archie would not have wanted that, so she made up some story instead, which just made her feel worse. But Phoebe and her family were very kind, realising that Alice must be in trouble to have come to them in such a manner, and they didn't pry. Alice would tell them everything one day, and hopefully soon, and then if Phoebe could find it in her heart to forgive her once the full story was known, it was her hope that they would take comfort in one another over Archie's death. She knew she owed everyone the truth, and she longed to tell it, but if she was to be believed after all her deceit, she needed Henry, without whom she felt she was beyond redemption.

Alice had bought her return ticket to Liverpool soon after she arrived in Quebec off the *Laurentic* eleven days earlier, having allowed what she considered to be enough time for Frank Saxby to arrange for her husband to board the ship and make the crossing with her. She was travelling second class and had been informed that she would be accompanied by 170 members of the Salvation Army, who were on their way to an international conference in London.

That same day, with her ticket bought, she had gone to the local telegraph office to wire Saxby the particulars of her journey, thinking to fabricate her address on the telegram so that no one would know where to find her, at least until she was aboard the *Empress*. She had not yet seen Henry, but as passenger numbers were close to the liner's capacity of almost sixteen hundred, she supposed it was unlikely she would, especially as she was certain he would be travelling first class and would therefore be on the upper deck. That's if he were aboard at all. Sending a false address on her telegram had meant that she was unable to receive any confirmation.

Two long and deep blasts from the ship's horn heralded the *Empress of Ireland*'s departure, and the shouts from the pier grew louder, until very soon the fourteen-thousand-ton ocean liner began to move. As the ship headed further out onto the St Lawrence River, and as Alice slowly followed the other passengers back inside, she felt a burst of excitement ripple through her at the thought of seeing Henry again. Had the six weeks that had passed since Holland changed him? She supposed not, unless Raskin had lied to her, and Henry had been mistreated all along. She began to worry about him again and wished it were closer to six o'clock than it was to five. That was the time she had stated on her telegram. All she had to do now was to find the grand staircase where she had said they would meet, and wait for him to show. She thought it would be easy enough to find, and she had chosen it because she supposed it would be a busy thoroughfare at any time of day. She wanted to meet Henry somewhere public in case Saxby thought to double-cross her.

As she moved into one of the oak-panelled vestibule areas, which were served by staircases connecting the decks, she thought she would go to her cabin first and ready herself for dinner, which, according to the itinerary, was to be served at seven. She wondered whether she would dine with Henry tonight, and she hoped she would. She had bought a new dress in Quebec for the voyage, something in pale blue silk she thought Henry would approve of, and she wanted to wear it for him. She smiled to herself as she entered into one of the narrow passageways that led to the cabins, thinking he would hardly recognise her in the simple, working-class clothes she had become accustomed to, and rather fond of wearing, in his absence.

As Alice ambled along and the throng of people gradually thinned, she thought about her previous voyage from Liverpool aboard the *Laurentic*. It was not as grand a liner as this, but then this was not as grand as many of the White Star Line's flagships, such as the *Lusitania* and the ill-fated *Titanic* that had ended her maiden voyage so tragically two years before. Alice could recall each of the thirteen days she had spent aboard the *Laurentic* with great clarity, even though every new day came and went much like the last. She recalled them so well because they were not pleasant days. She had kept to herself most of the voyage, and she had passed much of her time on deck staring at the horizon and wishing she could undo everything that had happened that spring. The journey had afforded her plenty of time for reflection—plenty of time to wrestle with her demons—and she had cried herself to sleep most nights over Archie's death. Then somewhere in the middle of the great Atlantic Ocean she found the strength to look forward—to having Henry back and seeing her children again, and to once more living the happy life she had known.

Towards the end of the voyage, she had cut her hair extra short to help disguise herself, and she'd made the acquaintance of a group of women who were returning to Quebec, having previously travelled to England as activists in support of the women's suffrage movement. Alice had fitted right in, and once she had earned their confidence, she had spun them all a story about an abusive husband she was running away from, and how he would have people waiting for her in Quebec to take her back to him, where he would surely imprison her so that she could not run away again. Alice had gained their sympathy all too easily, and she had safely disembarked the RMS *Laurentic* in the middle of the group, cradling her belly so as to give the impression that she was heavily pregnant, when really it was her own dress she carried in a bundle beneath the clothing she had borrowed. If the authorities had seen her, there would have been little about her to recognise from any written description they might have had, and perhaps because she had been veiled by so many citizens of Canada returning home, she managed to slip through without challenge.

Alice reached her cabin, having followed the signs along several narrow passageways that were lined with handrails in case of rough seas, and she went inside. It was a small space, but it looked comfortable, and she had very little with her by way of luggage. There was a single, narrow bed with a curtain and rail, a small sink and a mirror, and a chair in the corner beneath the porthole. It would service her needs, but she didn't expect to spend much time there, as the ship boasted a second-class music and reading room and several lounges, not to mention the promenade decks. Alice did not delay. She washed and changed, and after one last look in the mirror, she put her straw boater back on—which was something she was sure Henry would not approve of, but which she had become rather attached to—and went to find the grand staircase.

———⌣———

Alice caught her breath when she saw him again. She arrived at the grand staircase with its wide, sweeping oak handrails in time to see him coming down from the first-class accommodations. He wore the same light-grey sack suit and felt Homburg she had last seen him wearing in Holland, and she thought he looked well despite everything he must have been through. He began to look about as he descended the stairs, and Alice supposed he was just as excited and nervous as she was.

There was another man with him whom Alice took an immediate dislike to. He was about the same height and build as Henry, dressed in a navy-blue suit with a white flower in the lapel. Unlike Henry, who was clean shaven, the other man had a thin black moustache. Someone passed by in front of her then, blocking her view momentarily. Then once he had passed, Alice saw that Henry was looking right at her. He smiled and quickened his pace as she went to him.

'Alice!'

They fell into each other's arms, and he kissed her, and in that brief moment all her troubles seemed to melt away, if only for a moment.

'Oh, Henry! I thought I would never see you again.'

'I never doubted it,' Henry said with that soft American accent Alice so adored. 'You and I were meant to be.'

Alice smiled at the notion. 'How have you been?'

'I guess I can't complain. They fed me well enough, and I was able to take regular exercise. Worrying about you and the children was the hard part. How are they?'

Alice didn't want to ruin their reunion by telling Henry that Chester had been poisoned. She decided to save that for later. 'They're both fine,' she said. 'At least they were when I last saw them. That was three weeks ago now. They're at Hamberley with my parents.'

'Then I'm sure they're still fine,' Henry said. 'I won't ask you how you've been, Alice. I know all this must have hit you hardest.' He stepped away. 'Just look at you. Whatever have you done to your hair?'

'It will grow back.'

'Yes, of course it will, but I barely recognise you. You're so thin, and your eyes . . . I don't suppose you've been sleeping at all well, have you?'

Alice shook her head.

'Well, just you let me do the worrying from now on. Until this is over with anyway—then neither of us will have to worry about a single thing again, I promise.'

The man who had arrived with Henry stepped beside him then, stopping their conversation. When he spoke, his accent reminded Alice of Raimund Drescher, the head waiter she had met in Dover. He got straight to the point.

'Do you have the notebook?'

'This is Herr Albrecht,' Henry said. 'I don't think for a minute that's his real name, and we're not exactly on first-name terms. He's from Germany, as is no doubt apparent.' He lowered his voice then and leaned closer to Alice. 'He's not much of a swell, if you know what I mean. He doesn't say much, but he's been easy enough company so far.'

'I don't want him around us,' Alice said, throwing the man a distasteful glare.

She was surprised to see that Henry only had one escort, but then again, they were aboard an ocean liner. Where could they go? And she couldn't discount that there were not others like Albrecht aboard the *Empress*, who were not yet known to her or her husband.

'I don't suppose we're going to have much say in the matter,' Henry said. 'Not yet anyway. Have you got this notebook he's after?'

Alice addressed Albrecht directly. 'I don't have it with me, Mr Albrecht. I wanted to make sure my husband was safe and well first.'

'But it is aboard the ship?' Albrecht said.

'Yes, of course,' Alice replied. 'I've hidden it where you won't find it, so there's no use searching my cabin. You shall have it as soon as I'm ready to give it to you.'

The German's lips twisted into an amused smile, as if he knew he had no choice but to play along. 'And when will that be, Mrs Stilwell?'

'Once I know that no one can get on or off this ship until we reach Liverpool.'

'But how can they?' Henry asked. 'I mean besides jumping overboard.'

'The navigation pilot. Before I came aboard, I learned that he would be going ashore at Pointe-au-Père near Rimouski, when they'll also exchange the last of the mailbags. That's usually sometime after one o'clock in the morning.' She turned to Albrecht. 'And that's when you shall have the notebook. I'll bring it to the music and reading room on this deck at one fifteen.'

# Chapter Thirty

They took dinner in the second-class dining saloon, which was full and loud with conversation. Henry had wanted to see if they could buy Alice an upgrade to first class, but she wouldn't entertain the idea. After everything that had happened since Holland, she hardly felt she deserved such comforts as she already had.

'I've heard the second-class meals aboard the *Empress* are as good as many first-class meals on some other ships,' she had said to appease Henry. 'The only difference here seems to be the quality of the upholstery.'

'Come now, Alice,' Henry had replied. 'I'm sure the whole experience in first class is entirely more agreeable. But have it as you wish.'

Much to Alice's dismay, Herr Albrecht had insisted on joining them, which limited the conversation, as Alice did not want to say the things she would otherwise have said to Henry in front of him. As far as Alice was concerned, it was some small grace, though, that Albrecht hardly spoke a word all through the dinner, which he seemed to eat with unsettling precision, as though performing some delicate operation.

At around nine o'clock, and with dinner almost over, Henry leaned closer to Alice and spoke softly to her so that Albrecht couldn't hear him.

'Do you want to get out of here—just the two of us?'

'Very much,' Alice said, supposing her body language throughout the meal could not have made her wishes any clearer.

Henry winked at her. 'Then be ready.'

The bottle of wine they had been served earlier was still more than half full. Albrecht had shown no interest in it, and Alice and Henry had consumed very little; their own glasses had barely been touched. Henry picked the bottle up and poured no more than a drop into Alice's glass.

'Rumour has it that the distinguished British actor Lawrence Irving and his wife are travelling with us,' he said. He spoke loudly now, as if trying to draw attention to himself. 'First class of course. If there's any truth to it, I shall have to seek them out before we reach Liverpool.'

Alice followed the wine bottle as Henry pretended to top up his own glass. 'I didn't know you liked the theatre,' she said, going along with the conversation that Albrecht seemed entirely disinterested in.

'I can't say that I do really, but they're sure to be interesting conversationalists.'

With that Henry put the bottle down and tipped it over with a clatter as it crashed onto Albrecht's dessert plate. The wine gushed from the bottle in crimson waves that soaked both the tablecloth and Albrecht's suit, causing him to leap to his feet.

'You clumsy American!'

'I'm awfully sorry,' Henry said. He stood up and offered Albrecht his napkin as he called out for the waiter.

Alice sensed that the time to run was coming soon. Her eyes found the nearest exit, and she readied herself.

'Here, let me,' Henry said.

He made to mop up the wine with his napkin. He leaned towards the German as a member of the crew came over to assist, and at that moment Henry shoved Albrecht back over his chair.

'*Go!*' he called to Alice.

She was already on her feet. She turned and ran, and then she felt Henry grab her hand. He pulled her towards the exit, and Alice couldn't stop herself from laughing as he led her along the oak-panelled passageway beyond, neither of them having any idea where they were going.

'*Stop!*'

It was Albrecht, already in pursuit. Alice turned and saw that he was not far behind them.

'Quickly, down here,' Henry said, and they descended a stairway to the third-class level on the main deck.

With the number of passengers in third class being roughly equal to twice that of the rest of the ship, they now found themselves moving at a much slower pace. It became noticeably warmer, too, and given away by their apparel, Alice was soon conscious of being stared at. They ran into another narrow passageway, and very soon Alice could hear music. It grew louder when they came to the third-class dining saloon, where a supper of gruel, cabin biscuits and cheese was being served—the third-class passengers having already taken their main meal of the day. They pressed on and came to another tight passageway, and after that they arrived at the source of the music: the Salvation Army band were giving a concert.

'I'm getting very hot in this gown,' Alice called.

'Let's go back up then,' Henry said, and they took the next staircase they came to.

'We could go to your cabin,' Alice said when they reached the next deck.

Henry laughed. 'I share a twin with Albrecht. He's sure to look there.'

Alice paused briefly to get her bearings. 'My cabin's this way,' she said a moment later.'

There was a commotion below the stairs then, and someone called, 'Hey, mind where you're going!'

'Come on,' Alice said, and this time she led the way, taking them along another passageway, and then another that was more familiar to her. 'It's just along here.'

They were no more than twenty paces along the passageway that led to Alice's cabin when the German caught up with them again. 'Come back!' Albrecht called.

Alice didn't think she could run any faster, but they didn't stop. She knew her cabin was just out of sight around the corner, and they reached it with moments to spare. Alice pulled Henry in after her and quietly closed the door, just before she heard Albrecht pass by on the other side. Henry was smiling so much he looked as if he was about to laugh. Alice put a finger to his lips, and Henry kissed it. Then he kissed her hand, and very soon they were locked in a tight embrace.

'Do you suppose he'll leave us alone?' Alice asked. She took off her hat and put it down on the dressing table.

'Well, he can't very well go around knocking on all the cabin doors. Especially as it's getting late.'

'We'll have to be quiet then in case he's listening for us.'

Henry's smile was suddenly full of romantic intent. 'I didn't plan on doing much talking.'

He pulled Alice onto the bed, but she sat straight up again.

'I'd just like to talk. Do you mind? Can we hold each other for now and talk in whispers? There's so much I want to tell you, and we've only a few hours before we have to go and meet that awful man again.'

Henry sat up beside her and wrapped his arms around her. He kissed her again. 'All right, Alice. Anything you like.'

Alice wanted Henry to know everything that had happened since they'd last seen one another, so she started at the beginning, from when they'd left the Hotel Des Indes as a happy family on that bright morning in The Hague. By the time she reached the part where she made her telephone call to Frank Saxby to set up the exchange, it was as if an immeasurable weight had lifted from her, not least because with Henry beside her she could finally see an end to the nightmare she had been living these past six weeks. She could see that Henry was perturbed by what she'd told him.

'That's too bad about your friend Archie. I didn't really know him, of course—I'm sure we only met once or twice—but he seemed like a decent fellow.'

'Yes, he was,' Alice said thoughtfully.

Henry got up and went to the porthole. He opened it wide and took a deep breath. 'And Chester made a full recovery?'

Alice nodded. 'Yes, it was just a terrible scare, that's all—a warning.' She paused before adding, 'We're not supposed to have the portholes open once we're underway.'

Henry stuck his head through the opening and looked out. 'Most of the other portholes are open.' He turned back to Alice. 'Do they expect us to suffocate in our sleep?' He came back to the bed then and sat down again. 'Saxby should answer for what he's done. You say you made a copy of this notebook of his?'

'Yes, I copied the exact code into another notebook, and then I deciphered everything I could and wrote that down separately. I've told him it will be sent to the authorities should anything happen to us.'

'Smart move,' Henry said. 'But who could you trust with something like that?'

Alice told Henry all about Archie's half-sister, Phoebe, and how she'd been staying with her in Quebec City these past eleven days.

'I didn't know what else to do,' she added. 'I'm sure it's safe enough.'

'Well, just the same, I think we'd better place it with an attorney for safekeeping as soon as possible.'

'Of course,' Alice said. 'If you think it's for the best.'

They spent the next hour talking about what they would do when they arrived in Liverpool, and as Alice had hoped, Henry reassured her that once he corroborated her story and told the authorities he'd been kidnapped, everything would be okay. The rest would fall into place, he told her, and the Dutchman would be held to account for the murder in Green Park, albeit posthumously. Henry put her mind to rest further by saying that they had almost a week to go over what they would say to the authorities and to her father when the time came, insisting that she leave any further worrying to him.

'Do you know why this has happened to us?' Alice asked. Following her telephone conversation with Saxby, she had continued to wonder at the reason, and she had come to think that perhaps it wasn't because of her connection to Archie and the defence plans he had access to. Surely Saxby would not have given the photographs up so easily if it were. 'While you were being held, did anyone explain why they wanted me to spy for them?'

'They told me everything,' Henry said. 'I suppose they didn't think it mattered whether I knew or not since they weren't about to let me go until it was all over—that's if they planned on letting me go at all.' He paused and looked into Alice's eyes. 'It was never about you, Alice. It was your father they wanted.'

'My father? How do you mean?'

'I mean they were going to use you to get your father to become a mole for them. They were planning to force him to hand Admiralty secrets directly to them. Seems they've been trying to get a British admiral in their pockets for some time now.'

'Admiral Waverley,' Alice said to herself. She had already thought as much. Now Henry had as good as confirmed it. Waverley's wife had surely been kidnapped in an attempt to force the admiral to spy for them. But it had all gone terribly wrong. Then they had looked to her family. 'But how did they expect to use me to get information directly from my father?'

'You were being set up. They had you spying here, there, and everywhere, didn't they? You were getting deeper into trouble, and they could prove everything you'd done. They planned to turn you over to the authorities unless your father cooperated, and if they did that, as you're still a British citizen, you would have been tried and executed for high treason. They would have had your father on a lead for as long as they wanted. You can't undo the things you've done, and as I'm the only one who can prove you were set up, I suppose I would have had to disappear at some point.'

Alice thought about everything Henry had said, and it all made perfect sense to her now. She was just another pawn in their high-stakes game.

'So when the police came to arrest me, their plan became useless,' she said. 'I suppose that's why Raskin had to kill that man who came after me in London. He wasn't just protecting me. He was trying to protect their entire blackmail operation. Only it was already too late. The police knew who I was and what I'd been doing.'

'Well, I'm glad it's turning out differently to how they planned it.' He checked the time on his pocket watch. 'I'd better be going,' he added. 'It's after midnight, and I think I ought to patch things up with Herr Albrecht before you see him again. He's sure to be mad, and I've got to share a cabin with him tonight.'

Alice was alarmed at the thought of Henry leaving her again so soon, even if it was just for an hour. 'Really, Henry? Must you go?'

Henry laughed. 'You'll be just fine,' he said as he rose. 'Besides, you'll need some time to fetch that notebook from wherever it is you've hidden it.'

Alice spun around and took up her boater hat from the dressing table. She turned it over and showed Henry the lining. 'I had it with me the whole time,' she said, smiling as she slipped the notebook out.

Henry gave her a grin. 'I can see you've picked up a few tricks while I was away.' He opened the door to leave. 'You've become a proper little spy, haven't you?'

Alice frowned. 'Don't say that, Henry. I despise all of it.'

'I'm sorry. I didn't mean anything by it.' He brushed her cheek with the back of his hand. 'Tuck that notebook back inside your hat. I'll see you at one fifteen.'

# Chapter Thirty-One

Present day.

Following his meeting with Lady Vivienne Metcalfe at Chatham's historic dockyard, Jefferson Tayte spent the remainder of the morning ambling with his thoughts as he took in such attractions as the Old Ropery and the Smithery, and the three warships now in permanent dry dock at the museum as part of the core collection of the UK's National Historic Fleet: HMS *Gannet*, HMS *Cavalier* and HMS *Ocelot*, an Oberon-class submarine commissioned in 1964 and the last warship to have been built at Chatham. Tayte was heading back into the Wheelwrights' restaurant for lunch, having just left the *Ocelot*, when his phone rang. He checked the display. It was Davina.

'Guess what I've found?'

Whatever it was, she sounded excited about it, and Tayte supposed the reason had something to do with Phoebe Dodson. During dinner with Davina the night before, she had asked whether she could help out with the research more directly than she felt she had been, so they had agreed she should take Phoebe Dodson from the list of names and connections still to be explored.

'You found something?' Tayte said. 'That's great. What is it?'

There was a pause. Then Davina said, 'Let's meet up and talk about it. I've made some printouts I want to show you. Where are you now?'

Tayte told her, adding, 'I was just about to grab some lunch. Then I thought I'd go over my research into the *Empress of Ireland* in case I've missed anything. I was heading back to my hotel when I'm finished here.'

'Great,' Davina said. 'I've still got a few things to check myself. Why don't we meet in the hotel bar at six o'clock this evening? That should give us both plenty of time.'

'Sure,' Tayte said, 'six o'clock it is. I'll see you then.'

The call ended and Tayte continued into the restaurant, which by now was moderately busy with lunchtime trade. He made straight for the self-service counter, grabbed a tray and got in line behind two other people, and when his turn arrived, he ordered a hearty-looking dish, which the lady behind the counter told him was called Lancashire hotpot. He found a quiet table at the opposite end of the restaurant and fired up his laptop. As he began to eat his meal, he started browsing the Web, looking to expand his understanding of the *Empress of Ireland* disaster in the hope that something might strike a chord with the question he'd been ruminating on most of the morning: what had happened after the *Empress of Ireland* left Quebec to affect Alice's plans to return to England? As he began to read, he was quickly reminded that over a thousand passengers and crew had lost their lives that night, and now he saw that only 4 of the 138 children aboard had survived. It was a heartbreaking statistic.

He came across a number of survivor accounts, and of particular interest was Grace Hanagen, daughter of the Salvation Army bandmaster, not least because at seven years old she had been the youngest survivor, and when she died in 1995, she was also the last. Tayte read how she had refused to sleep in a berth by the porthole in the family's second-class cabin because she believed that that was where the water would come in. If the account was true, Tayte thought how prophetic the young Grace had been.

He followed another link, this one taking him to a Web page containing some of the more notable figures who had died that night. He read about Henry Lyman, a millionaire from Montreal, who had married late in life because he had spent so much of it looking after his sick mother and only felt free to do so after her death. He and his wife were said to have been travelling to Europe on their honeymoon, and neither had survived.

Perhaps most famously was the account of the dramatist and novelist, Laurence Irving, and his actress wife, Mabel Hackney. They had been touring Canada with Irving's production troupe, the majority of the troupe having followed to England on the White Star Line's RMS *Teutonic* because there had not been enough time for the entire troupe to pack up and meet the voyage. Tayte thought the obvious: if only Irving had not been in such a hurry to return to England and had instead waited with the rest of the troupe.

Tayte turned to the newspaper archives with a broad search for articles mentioning the *Empress of Ireland* in 1914, and he was soon reading an extract from the *New York Times*, printed on 5 June. The headline read, 'EMPRESS WIRELESS HAD ONLY 8 MINUTES.' The account that followed was from the radio operator Ronald Ferguson, who had managed to get an SOS call out in that short time before the water had flooded the stoke room, causing the dynamos to fail, cutting all power. He read how those eight minutes had been vital in securing aid from two nearby ships, the *Lady Evelyn* and the *Eureka*, without which many more lives would have been lost.

For all Tayte read, while it helped to build a picture of events in his mind, it didn't help to answer his questions, so he steered his thoughts back to Alice. He wondered somewhat fancifully whether she had met any of the people he'd just read about, whose lives had hung in the balance with her own on that cold and foggy night.

He clicked on another article, and for the umpteenth time he saw the words 'Fourteen minutes' in reference to the time it had taken the ship to sink after she had been struck by the Norwegian collier. He couldn't imagine anything having happened during those last minutes aboard the *Empress* to change Alice's plans about returning to England. In that short time, he imagined everyone's efforts would have been focused solely on trying to stay alive, or trying to help their loved ones. Whatever had happened to change Alice's mind about returning to England had in all probability been determined before the SS *Storstad* struck its fatal blow.

Tayte sat back and stared up at the vaulted ceiling. He closed his eyes and went through his logic again. Alice was returning to England—of that much he was certain, as she couldn't have known the ship was going to sink. Had it not, the *Empress of Ireland* would have arrived in Liverpool, where either the authorities would have been waiting for her or would soon have caught up with her and made their arrest. That told Tayte that when the ship left Quebec, Alice must have had hope that she would be able to return to England and to her family rather than to a death sentence. But somewhere in that brief time before the *Empress* sank, that hope had been dashed. Something had changed, leaving Alice in a desperate situation, feeling that she had no other choice than to leave everything and everyone she knew and loved behind, to feign her own death and start her life over.

# Chapter Thirty-Two

RMS *Empress of Ireland*. Friday, 29 May 1914.

The second-class music and reading room on board the *Empress of Ireland* was located in the aft section of the shelter deck behind the dining saloon. It was plushly carpeted, with panelled walls and ceiling, and the seating, although not finished in leather as Alice imagined it would be for the first-class passengers, looked nonetheless clean and comfortable. It was a well-lit room, despite the portholes that were now black against the night and the recently arrived fog that was common to the St Lawrence River in late spring, when the warmer air meets the river's icy meltwater.

Alice arrived later than agreed. She had waited until the ship had picked up speed again after the navigation pilot had alighted at Pointe-au-Père, indicating that the *Empress of Ireland* was now on her way out to sea. She moved further into the room and saw Henry and Herr Albrecht sitting in a pair of armchairs that were facing an upright piano. They were the only people there, most other passengers having turned in for the night. Both men rose, and Henry smiled. Herr Albrecht, now in a fresh three-piece suit that was almost white, did not. He checked the time on his pocket watch.

'I was concerned you were not coming, Mrs Stilwell. It is now close to one thirty.'

'I'll make no apology to you, Mr Albrecht. Here, I have your notebook.'

Alice was no longer concealing it. She stepped closer to Albrecht and saw his eyes grow bright with anticipation as she handed it to him.

'Now you have what you want,' she said. 'I trust you'll leave my husband and me alone for the remainder of the voyage?'

Albrecht did not answer right away. He flicked through the notebook, and Alice thought he looked pleased with what he saw. A moment later he stepped back and slipped it into his jacket pocket. When he withdrew his hand again it was holding a Luger semi-automatic pistol.

'Now wait a minute,' Henry began, but Albrecht cut him short, aiming the pistol at him.

'Silence!' Albrecht waved the muzzle of his pistol towards the door. 'Move! Both of you!'

'Where are we going?' Alice asked.

'Outside for some fresh air.'

They passed no one as they were led the short distance out onto the promenade deck, where the foggy night air was bitterly cold. At that moment the ship's horn sounded three short blasts, momentarily drawing everyone's attention. The *Empress* appeared to slow, but Alice was afforded no time to wonder what it meant.

'Stand by the rail, both of you!' Albrecht ordered. 'That's it. Now turn around and face me.'

Albrecht's Luger was trained on Alice now, and his intentions could not have been clearer. He was going to shoot her and throw her body into the cold St Lawrence River. Alice knew then that she had made a grave mistake somewhere, but she could not fathom where. The copy she had made of Saxby's notebook was supposed to protect her, and yet here she was facing certain death at Albrecht's hand. The only possible answer came to her then, and it made

Alice feel so light-headed she thought she would faint. She turned to Henry.

'Tell me you've not told him where the other notebook is.'

There was no need for Henry to answer. As soon as Alice finished speaking, she knew in his eyes that he had. She had been betrayed, and by the one person she should have been able to trust implicitly. Now, with the location of the second notebook known to Albrecht, it would be a simple matter to send a message via the ship's Marconi wireless system. Long before the *Empress of Ireland* reached Liverpool, Alice had no doubt that the packet she had left in Quebec with Phoebe would be on its way to Frank Saxby. And then what of Phoebe?

'You've killed us both,' Alice said under her breath. Confusion engulfed her. She wondered how she could have been so foolish as to trust anyone. But *Henry*? How could he? She stared into his eyes. 'Running away from Albrecht earlier,' she said. 'Going to my cabin where we could be alone to talk . . . that was all just an act to have me tell you where the copy of Saxby's notebook is?'

Henry gave a solemn nod, and Alice stepped away from him, no longer feeling the cold, but shaking nonetheless from the shock of this unforeseen development. Everything that had happened since Holland flashed through her mind.

'So you've been in on this from the beginning? You're one of them?'

'I'm sorry, Alice.'

Alice shook her head, disbelieving even now in the face of her husband's own admission. 'But why?' She had to ask the question, even though she knew no answer could ever be justified.

'I never told you this,' Henry said, 'but my father was born in Stuttgart, as was his father. My grandparents moved to America when he was just a small boy, to save their business. My family's allegiance has always been to Germany.'

'So all this was for Germany?'

'Yes, for Germany. And for you and the children, Alice. We were all going to live such wonderful lives in my father's land, come the day.'

Hearing those words from Henry's lips made Alice feel sick to her stomach. 'Don't say that, Henry. Not you. I can't bear it.' She wondered how this man she had loved could have become so deluded and so arrogant as to suppose she wanted any of this—that everything he had put her through was ultimately for her own good. 'Was our marriage all just a part of Saxby's plan? It *was* his plan to get my father to spy for the kaiser, wasn't it? Tell me you didn't instigate this.'

'I married you because I love you, Alice. Frank Saxby may have made the introductions, but—'

'Don't say any more, Henry. You've already said enough.' A bitter tear fell onto Alice's cheek, and she felt a rage like nothing she had known before rise from within her. 'Poor Archie is dead because of you. They poisoned our son, Henry! Our own son! They might have killed him, too!'

'Chester would not have been harmed.'

'Really?' Alice glanced at Albrecht, and then at the pistol he still had trained on her. 'And I suppose I wasn't meant to be harmed either? You clearly don't know these people as well as I've come to.'

'It was never supposed to be like this, Alice. Really it wasn't. You have to believe me.'

'I don't know you any more, Henry. You're a monster! How could you?'

'This is all very amusing,' Albrecht cut in, 'but I really must insist you both stop talking now.'

'This wasn't part of the plan,' Henry insisted.

'The plan changed, Mr Stilwell.' Albrecht turned to Alice. 'If you had only carried out your instructions and nothing more, I am sure it would not have come to this. Now I am afraid I have my orders.'

'Albrecht, please!' Henry pleaded. 'We can work something out.'

'You know it is for the greater good. She knows too much.'

Albrecht aimed the Luger more precisely at Alice. Then as he went to pull the trigger Henry ran at him, and both men crashed onto the deck. The crack of the pistol's report was accompanied by the sound of two more blasts from the ship's horn, and it seemed to Alice that time had frozen around her. The *Empress* had stopped moving altogether now and was dead in the water, wrapped in the clinging fog.

'*Run!*' Henry shouted, but Alice could not move.

There was blood on the deck, and she knew at once that it was Henry's. He had stopped the bullet that was intended for her. She watched him grapple for the pistol, throwing punch after punch at Albrecht, who seemed to take the assault without so much as flinching. Another shot was fired, and this time it was followed by the sound of splintering wood. Alice could not bear to watch, yet she was unable to take her eyes off the two men as they wrestled and fought for control of the Luger, like two wild animals fighting over their kill. A second later, Albrecht smashed the butt of the pistol hard into the side of Henry's head.

'*Henry!*'

The blow instantly gave Albrecht the upper hand, and now Alice knew she had to move before it was too late. She ran along the promenade deck until she could barely make out who was who through the thickening fog. She found a door and opened it, and then she stopped as the crack of another gunshot rang out between the decks. She turned to see the veiled silhouettes of both men now standing just a few feet apart. She saw Henry stagger to the rail. Then just as Henry was about to collapse, she watched Albrecht lunge at him with both hands, sending his limp body over the side of the ship.

⌣

Alice looked on in shock, just long enough for Albrecht's eyes to find her in the gloom. She was mesmerised by his white suit, which was now covered in Henry's blood, and the sight of it seemed to make Henry's death real to her, as if what she had just witnessed had only now registered. Her eyes filled with tears. Then Albrecht raised his pistol towards her as he came after her, and without thinking Alice found herself running again, into an open vestibule area, and then along one of the many narrow passageways. She was desperate to find a member of the ship's crew. She had to raise the alarm, but where was everyone? She turned a corner and ran into one of the ship's stewards. He grabbed her arms as they collided.

'Steady on, miss!'

'Please, you have to help me,' Alice said, breathing hard. 'There's a man chasing me. He has a pistol. He just killed my husband!'

'Now take it easy, miss. You've had a bad dream. That's all it is.'

'I wasn't dreaming. Now let go of me. You must get help.'

'I can see you're upset about something, but I'm sure—'

'Look, there he is in the passageway,' Alice cut in. 'Let go of me!'

She tried to pull her arms free, but the steward's grip was too strong. They began to struggle.

'I told you to take it easy, miss. Now if you'll just wait until the gentleman arrives, I'm sure we'll soon have all this sorted out.'

'Why aren't you listening to me?' Alice yelled.

Albrecht was almost upon them, walking at a steady pace now and smiling as if there had indeed simply been some misunderstanding on Alice's part. The steward's expression changed to one of fear, though, when he saw the blood on Albrecht's suit. His grip lessened and Alice kicked him in the shin as she pulled herself free. They were close to a staircase that led down to the main deck. She took it just seconds before Albrecht arrived, shoving his way past the steward.

Alice ran wildly along the first passageway she came to, having no idea where it led. There were cabins to her left and she thought to bang on the doors, hoping someone would come to her aid, but with Albrecht so close behind her, she knew that any help would come too late. She tried anyway, and as she did so the entire ship seemed to shudder and roar with a sound that was like nothing Alice had ever heard. She used the handrails to steady herself—she almost fell down. Looking back, she saw that Albrecht had stopped. He was looking around as if wondering, as Alice was, what had just happened.

The cabin doors began to open then, and people in their night-clothes started pouring into the passageway, expressions of confusion hanging on their faces.

'What was that?' someone said. 'Did you hear that?'

'I felt it all right,' another man said.

Alice kept going, pushing past the other passengers now as she tried to stay ahead of her pursuer. The sleeping ship seemed to have come awake now, and Alice recalled the blasts she had heard from the ship's horn earlier. She thought the *Empress of Ireland* must have run aground—that a navigational error had been made since the pilot who knew the St Lawrence River had left the ship. She took another passageway, and further ahead she heard a call that contradicted her thoughts.

'Everyone on deck! The ship is sinking!'

It was one of the crew, alerting the passengers. Alice looked back for Albrecht. Beyond the half-dozen or so passengers between them, she saw a man with a suitcase, blocking the passageway as another man tried to fight his way past. She saw Albrecht further down and knew that the commotion would hold him back. Her immediate concern now turned to finding a life vest. She had to get out onto the main deck.

'This way! Keep coming!' someone called.

Alice continued to move with the crowd. No more than a few minutes after impact, the ship listed to starboard, and people began to scream. Through an open cabin door, she saw someone trying to escape through a porthole. Then without warning, the *Empress of Ireland* was plunged into darkness.

'Stay calm!' a voice in the distance urged, but by now the frightened passengers were in a state of sheer panic.

Alice felt an elbow thrust into her side as someone scrabbled to get past her in the darkness. The shouting and screaming masked any useful instruction. She had no choice but to move with the masses, and she had no idea how long it was before she felt the first blast of cold air on her face. Her hopes lifted. There had to be a doorway close by that led onto the deck. She had no idea where any life vests were. There had not been time to acquaint herself properly with the ship or the correct procedures to follow in such an event. She supposed her own life vest was in her cabin, but what use was that to her now. She had seen the lifeboats, but the ship was listing so fast now that she supposed there might not have been time to launch them all.

Alice had no idea how she made it out onto the main deck, and with nothing more to guide her through the darkness than the person in front of her, but she was glad to be there. She gasped for breath as soon as she felt the damp night fog against her skin again, but she understood that she was by no means out of danger. The cold river could not be survived for long, and the fog would surely hinder any rescue attempt.

She found one of the pillars that connected the main deck to the shelter deck above, and as the ship continued to roll onto its starboard side, she held on for dear life. All around her and beneath her were cries of panic. Below the wailing, she could hear a constant rumble as though gallon upon gallon of water was surging throughout the entire ship. She had no further concern for Albrecht. He would neither follow her nor find her now—if he made it out of the ship at all.

She climbed the port side rail as it continued to rise beside her, and suddenly the deck slipped away beneath her. The screaming intensified then until the night was filled with the sound, and Alice was thankful that she could see little of what was happening in the near darkness. She climbed further until she was able to sit on top of the rail, and she gasped as she felt someone grab her ankle. Then a split second later that person was gone.

Alice sat there for no more than a minute. The Empress seemed to shift violently, and Alice knew the ship was about to go down. She clung ever more tightly to the rail, knowing she would soon have to jump, and at the same time she thought she might be sucked down with the hull if she failed to time it right, or perhaps there was no right time. A moment later all decision was taken from her as the entire stern of the ship rose out of the water and something unseen came at her out of the darkness. It caught her on the side of her head and she was thrown into the icy river.

Then, for Alice, the darkness was absolute.

# Chapter Thirty-Three

Present day.

In the Wheelwrights' restaurant at the Historic Dockyard Chatham, Jefferson Tayte had become so immersed in his research into the *Empress of Ireland* disaster that he'd completely lost track of time. He looked up from his screen and pinched his eyes, noting as he did so that there were now very few people there, the lunchtime trade having long since dissipated. He picked up his coffee cup and went to take a sip, but it was empty, the cup stone cold in his hand. He was currently reading a particularly harrowing newspaper extract from the *Chicago Tribune* dated 1 June 1914, the headline to which read 'FRANTIC CROWDS VIEW LINER DEAD.' It carried the subtitle 'Body of Sir Seton-Karr Identified at Quebec from 188 others. MANY NOT RECOGNISED.' He put his cup down again, still too engrossed to get another refill, and continued to read.

*Women Victims Found Stabbed; Men with Knives Gripped in Their Hands.*

*Quebec, May 31.—[Special.]—The British flag was at half mast and the city was in mourning when the 188 bodies of victims of the Empress of Ireland disaster recovered from the St. Lawrence river reached here from Rimouski today.*

The coffins were placed in a pier shed. They formed three rows. All day long the identification went on. Frantic relatives were on hand to do their mournful task. Upon many of the crude coffins was written 'Do not shed tears over me,' but hundreds wept nevertheless.

While there were more than 125 bodies that had not been identified, many survivors and relatives of victims left here tonight. They gave up hope of finding the bodies. They telegraphed relatives that the bodies they sought were not recovered. A few, however, went to Rimouski in the hope that more bodies might be picked up and that they might find the ones for which they were looking.

*Women Victims Found Stabbed.*

A glance at the bodies taken in a walk along the line revealed the story of the collision and the incidents following.

Almost every body bore marks of violence inflicted by contact with parts of the wrecked ship or in struggles in the water. There were bodies of women whose heads were split open or gashed. It is possible that women running from their staterooms in the darkness following the collision ran against stanchions or were hurled against the walls of the sides of the alleys. The wounds also indicated that some of the women had been crushed when the collier buried its steel nose in the side of the Empress.

Officers in Rimouski have said also that the bodies of the women showed that several of them had been stabbed, that bodies of men had been found with knives in their hands. At any rate, it was apparent by a glance at the shrouds that had been placed on the bodies of both the men and the women that there were other wounds not disclosed on the faces.

*Charges Brutality to Sailors.*

Victor Vancoster, a Belgian, who was aboard the Empress, charged today that sailors who were in the life boats kicked him in the chest when he tried to climb in.

*Walter Erzinger of Winnipeg, a first class passenger, also said he saw fighting between sailors and second or third class passengers in the water.*

*In the pier shed this morning were black, brown, and white pine coffins containing the 188 bodies, less than one-fifth of the victims of the collision between the Empress of Ireland and the collier Storstad. Twenty five of the coffins contained the bodies of babies.*

*Pathetic Attempts at Identification.*

*At the heads of the coffins stood lines of men and women, many of them survivors, looking for relatives and friends. As coffin lids were lifted they crowded close to view the bodies. One lid would be dropped with a low toned 'No' and a searcher would raise the lid of the next coffin just dropped by another ahead.*

*Suddenly a low moan of a man or the muffled scream of a woman broke the silence. 'O, Mary!' 'My husband!' or some name of endearment was uttered.*

*A stalwart man bent forward and kissed the forehead of his wife. A woman would fall fainting on the lid of the coffin she had just raised. Thus it went on all day long until forty-eight bodies were identified.*

*A man would find the bodies of his wife and children. A woman would identify the body of her husband. In the hunt for bodies of the victims there was no distinction of class. Every person, whether finely dressed or roughly clad, took his turn in the line that moved constantly from coffin to coffin, but the great majority of persons were disappointed in their search.*

*Identifies Salvation Army Victims.*

*Major J. M. McGillivray of the Salvation Army was at the pier to make identification of members of his band who had perished. He explained that 175 persons connected with the army had sailed on the*

*Empress and only 25 had survived. Of the victims, he identified sixteen, but said that many were so badly disfigured that it was not possible to recognize them.*

*While stories of premonitions are always told after every disaster, McGillivray told a story about Mrs Nettice Simcoe, a major in the army, that could not be ignored.*

*'Mrs Simcoe told me on the morning that the Empress sailed,' he said, 'that the night before she had dreamed about crowds of people in mourning. She told the story to several members of the army at breakfast, and as a result of her story several army men did not sail.'*

*Furthermore, Edward Gray, solo cornetist, had a similar premonition. As a result, he made his will and left it with his fiancée.*

*In addition to the 188 bodies recovered here today, twenty-one had been identified at Rimouski and shipped to the homes of relatives. This makes 209 bodies recovered out of a total of 957 passengers. The probability is that the remainder never will be recovered, for the current of the St. Lawrence will sweep them out into the Atlantic.*

Tayte had to swallow the lump in his throat when he'd finished reading. He knew his imagination could not come close to the horror experienced by the passengers and crew of the *Empress of Ireland* towards the end of her last voyage.

*Women victims found stabbed. Men with knives gripped in their hands . . .* The obvious connotations were unthinkable.

Tayte screwed his face up as he wondered what he would have done under such circumstances. Could he bring himself to kill someone he loved, to spare that person the horror and suffering that might otherwise ensue? He shook his head to dispel the terrifying images those words had trapped inside his head. A moment later he snapped his laptop shut and stood up, suddenly craving some fresh air and an open space. He checked his watch as he collected his things together and put them away. It was almost three. He figured he had time for a quick stroll by the river before heading back to his hotel to meet Davina.

———~———

The lounge bar at the Holiday Inn was modern and spacious, with alternating brown and white leather seating and accents of apple green. The floor-to-ceiling windows were bright with sunlight, giving the interior an airy feel. Tayte entered at a pace, knowing he was running close to twenty minutes late. When he saw Davina, he slowed down, not wanting to arrive out of breath, and he immediately noticed that she'd come dressed for dinner, in heels and a knee-length black dress. They greeted one another, and Tayte set his briefcase down by the seat next to hers.

'Sorry I'm late,' Tayte said, still breathing harder than he wanted to be. 'I got stuck into some research when I got back. You know how it is.' He noticed that her highball glass was almost empty. 'Can I get you another drink?'

'Thank you,' Davina said. She finished her drink and handed it to Tayte to take back to the bar. 'Gin and tonic with ice and lemon, and don't worry about being late. I'm sure you had a good reason.' She seemed to stare at Tayte then. A moment later she smiled and pointed to the left side of her mouth. 'You've got something on your face. Is that chocolate?'

Tayte felt his cheeks flush as he wiped it off with the back of his hand. 'I have some in my briefcase if you'd like one,' he said, more out of embarrassment than anything else.

'No, I'm fine. Thank you.'

'Yes, of course you are. I'll just get us that drink.'

Tayte returned a few minutes later, set Davina's drink down and followed his Jack Daniels into his seat. They touched glasses, and then they both began to speak at the same time. They laughed about it, and Tayte settled back with his glass.

'Go on,' he said, still smiling, thinking how much more relaxed he felt in Davina's company than when he'd first met her. 'Ladies first.'

'Oh, I do like a gentleman,' Davina said. 'I was going to ask how your day was. Turn up anything good?'

'You could say that. A few things in fact.' Tayte reached into his briefcase and showed Davina the photographs of Alice that Lady Metcalfe had let him hold on to. 'It's proof that Alice and my client's grandmother were one and the same person,' he added, once he'd finished explaining how he came by them.

'You must be very pleased,' Davina said, 'and I'm sure your client will be thrilled.'

Tayte nodded, subconsciously chewing at his lower lip, knowing there were still gaps in the story he hoped to take back to America.

'You don't look very pleased,' Davina said. 'What is it?'

Tayte snapped out of his thoughts and gave voice to them. 'I want to know why Alice feigned her death when the *Empress* sank. It's been puzzling me since I realised she must have found a way to undo the mess she was in. She was all set to return to England, but something happened after the ship set off to change that. I've formed a few ideas. I even have one pretty sound theory, but I can't prove anything.'

'Well, let's hear it,' Davina said. 'You never know, it might lead to something.'

'Henry Stilwell,' Tayte said. 'Alice's husband. I've been wondering where he'd been through all this—why he hadn't boarded the *Empress* with Alice, and why they weren't sharing a cabin on the voyage. I've held the opinion that someone like Alice wouldn't have spied on her country without good reason, and I've found no such reason. She came from a respectable, patriotic family. She had no motive that I can see to have spied against her country. And yet, I've seen the proof that tells me she did, so I have to assume she was forced.'

'By the Germans,' Davina said.

'Yes, and with a husband and a young family, I don't think it would have been too difficult to find ways to persuade her.'

'So, do you think Henry wasn't able to board the ship with Alice because he'd been kidnapped?'

'I did, but now I'm not so sure. Since leaving the dockyard this afternoon, I'd come to think that Henry was travelling in a different cabin to Alice's, with this man called Albrecht from the telegram, because he was Albrecht's prisoner. Henry, then, was Alice's get-out-of-jail-free card if you like, because once they reached England, he would be able to explain everything. I figured that's what must have changed that night.'

'Because Henry died when the ship sank?'

'That's one possibility, but I've also come to think that Alice had lost all hope by that point.'

'How do you mean?'

'I've looked into Henry Stilwell some more. I'd only had call to cover the basics about Alice's husband before I left home—just enough to know who his parents were and that they lived in New York. Henry was an only child, and with the two Stilwell children having been adopted by Alice's parents, there were no descendants in America I could go and see. When I got back to my room earlier, I started over with the US census reports and found Henry listed in 1910, age twenty-six, son of Randall Stilwell, who was the head of the household at the time. From there I went back to 1900, and that's when things got interesting. You see in 1900, Henry's grandmother was still alive and living with the family, only she wasn't listed as Stilwell. She was listed as Steinwall.'

'German?'

'A surname of German origin, certainly, but I wanted to be sure, so I went further back. The 1890 census shows that her husband, Henry's grandfather, was still alive and was then the head of the household, so presumably he'd died or had otherwise left by 1900. His name was also Steinwall, and his place of birth was shown as Germany, confirming it.'

'So Henry was of German descent,' Davina said, and Tayte could see she was thinking over the implications, just as he had when he'd first made the discovery.

'It was common for foreign immigrants settling in America to change their names to avoid prejudice, even before the Great War, particularly for families in business as the Steinwalls were. It could mean nothing, of course, but Henry's Germanic roots are a hard fact to ignore.'

'It has to mean something,' Davina said. 'Suppose Henry and this Albrecht were associates? Perhaps Alice had boarded the *Empress* hoping to be reunited with her husband, only to be betrayed by him.'

'That's an interesting theory, too,' Tayte said. 'And one which might certainly have dashed Alice's hopes if she believed her husband would corroborate her story.' Tayte finished his drink. 'But it is just a theory. Right now I don't see how we can know for sure.'

A slow smile spread across Davina's face. 'I think once you've heard what I turned up today, you'll agree that it's more than just a theory.'

Tayte was more intrigued than ever now to find out what she had discovered, but he thought they would need another drink to go with the explanation, and both their glasses were empty.

'Hold that thought,' he said. 'Let me get us another drink first.'

When Tayte came back from the bar, Davina's handbag was open, and there were two folded pieces of A4 paper on the table, which Tayte supposed were the results of Davina's research.

'Phoebe Dodson,' Davina said. She sat up and eyed Tayte seriously. 'I've been looking into her most of the day, and I strongly believe she was murdered for the notebook mentioned in that telegram.'

'Murdered?' The word struck a familiar chord in Tayte's ear.

'Yes, and it also seems clear to me now that my husband was killed for the same reason. Because someone wants this notebook—now as then.'

'Two murders motivated by the same object a hundred years apart?' Tayte said, as much to himself as to Davina. He thought back over some of his more adventurous assignments and knew it wouldn't be the first time. 'What did you find out?'

'I began in the usual way, looking for Phoebe's details in the birth, marriage and death indexes. From the International Genealogical Index I found that she was born in England, right here in Kent, which piqued my interest. I could find no record of marriage, so I moved on. Then I saw when she died.' Davina paused to sip her drink. 'It was in 1914.'

Tayte's interest had more than piqued. He sat forward. 'When in 1914?'

Davina looked at him assuredly, as if to suggest that what she was about to tell him would knock him for six. 'Phoebe died on the 2nd of June 1914.'

The information certainly knocked Tayte back into his seat. He scrunched his brow, scarcely able to believe what Davina had just told him. 'That's just four days after the telegram was sent.'

'I know, and I couldn't believe it was simply a coincidence, so I kept digging.'

'Do you know how she died?'

Davina nodded. 'There wasn't time to wait for a copy of her full death certificate from the relevant authorities in Quebec.'

'The Directeur de l'état civil,' Tayte said. 'I'll put a request in anyway, for my records.'

'Yes, good idea. It should also confirm who Phoebe's father was. Unless Lord Thomas Ashcroft was shrewd enough to keep his name off it.'

'Thomas Ashcroft? Archibald's father?'

'The very same. At least, I believe he must have been Phoebe's father. I turned to the newspaper archives once I felt I'd gone as far as I could with the various genealogical indexes. I thought that if the timing of Phoebe's death was connected to the telegram, her death would likely be unnatural and thus newsworthy. At least if not, then I thought I might find an obituary in the newspaper archives—which I did.' Davina reached forward and picked up one of the pieces of paper she'd previously set out. 'Here it is,' she added, handing it to Tayte.

Tayte unfolded the sheet of paper and saw a printed screenshot of the original copy from the obituaries section of North America's oldest newspaper, the *Quebec Chronicle*, which Tayte now knew of as the *Chronicle Telegraph*, following a merger between the two newspapers in 1925. It was dated 15 June 1914. He read it and quickly discovered that the obituary was not for one person, but two: Phoebe Dodson and her mother Irene, both having died on the same day.

'See who was in attendance,' Davina said.

Tayte scanned ahead and saw the connection. 'Thomas Ashcroft,' he said. 'So it's possible, even likely, that Phoebe Dodson was Archibald's half sister.'

'Which explains why Alice went to Quebec when she went on the run.'

Tayte gave a thoughtful nod as he lingered over the obituary. 'Two deaths on the same day,' he mused. 'The plot thickens, doesn't it?'

'Perhaps not too much,' Davina said. 'I kept digging in the news-paper archives, and it didn't take long to discover the cause of death.' She handed Tayte the other piece of paper. 'It's a bit of a shocker.'

Tayte unfolded it and studied it in silence for several seconds. This copy was from a newspaper Tayte was less familiar with: The *Quebec Daily Mercury*. It was dated 3 June 1914—the day after Phoebe's death. He read the headline aloud. 'BLAZE AT CHARLESBOURG HOME KILLS TWO.' He read on and his face had drained of expression by the time he'd finished. The report was a detailed and harrowing account of the events that had led to the discovery of the charred remains of two women found huddled together in an upstairs closet while their house burned around them.

Tayte heaved a thoughtful sigh. 'Did you find anything else—anything to suggest it was arson? There's a gap of almost two weeks between the fire and the funeral. I'm sure there must have been an inquest.'

Davina shook her head. 'No, that's all I could find. When you put it all together, though, it looks pretty conclusive, doesn't it?'

'Yes, I'd say it does,' Tayte said, making a mental note to have a look for an inquest report himself before he turned in for the night.

He thought about Frank Saxby then. 'As well as looking into Henry Stilwell, I also looked into Frank Saxby some more before I came down from my room. It's why I was late.'

'What did you find?'

'Not much beyond what little we already know, but what else I did find is interesting. According to the indexes, Francis Edwin Saxby, as he was christened, died August 5th 1914—the day after Britain declared war on Germany.'

'That is interesting,' Davina said. 'Do you know how he died?'

'Not yet, but I've requested a copy of his death certificate. Maybe it will tell us something, although it's going to take time to come through.'

Tayte reached into his briefcase and took out the Metcalfe family-and-friends photograph. Studying it again, he was reminded of Oscar Scanlon and the failing business partnership Davina had told him about, and of the shoe factory fire that had taken several lives. He thought that if Saxby was behind the death of Phoebe and her mother, then such a modus operandi was perhaps not unfamiliar to him—not if the accusations of causing the factory blaze for the insurance money were true.

'You see now why I think Phoebe was murdered for the note-book mentioned in the telegram,' Davina said. 'And why my earlier theory that Alice was betrayed by her husband might hold some truth.'

Tayte didn't need Davina to spell it out for him. 'Given the gravity of her situation,' he said. 'Alice wouldn't have given Phoebe's details to anyone other than Henry, and certainly not to Albrecht. But it was Albrecht who sent the telegram to Saxby. Ergo, Henry must have told him after getting the information from Alice.' He slapped his palms on his armrests. 'And that's what changed after the *Empress* left Quebec. Alice was betrayed by the one person who could have saved her—her own husband, whose allegiance clearly rested in his deep rooted love for Germany over the love he felt for his family.'

It upset Tayte to think that a man could put anything before his family like that. It made him think about his birth mother again, and the reason she had abandoned him. 'For the child's own protection,' was all she had said. Clearly she thought him to be in some kind of danger all the while he was with her, and he now began to see Alice's situation in a similar light.

*But why had Alice never gone back for her children?*

Tayte figured there must have been plenty of good, if painful, reasons to Alice's mind, and he supposed now that that was probably also true of his own mother, unless of course his own mother, for reasons he didn't like to think about, had been unable to return for him.

'What about the timing?' Davina said, cutting into Tayte's thoughts. 'How do you suppose Saxby could have reached Quebec so quickly? The fire only happened a few days after the telegram was sent. He can't have taken a ship in time, and transatlantic flight wasn't an option then, was it?'

'No, but I don't believe Saxby would have tried to go himself,' Tayte said. 'And neither did he have to. If my thinking around Saxby and his notebook is on the right track, I'd say he already had a network of people to call upon from all over the world, ready and willing to do whatever it took to get that notebook back to him.'

'Spies?' Davina said.

'It all fits, doesn't it? It's clear that Alice got hold of a notebook that belonged to Frank Saxby, which he desperately wanted back. She was being forced to spy on her country, and there's Saxby in the middle of it all. I can only believe from all this that Alice came to learn more than she should have about the people who were pulling her strings. The only questions in my mind now are what was written in that notebook, and why would anyone kill your husband for it today?'

'Whoever did kill Lionel must have thought he had it with him that night.'

'That telegram certainly could have led someone to believe he did. Perhaps Lionel had shown it to someone.'

'I suppose it's possible, but I can't think who would be interested in seeing it, or why.'

'Any of the Metcalfe family?'

Davina smiled. 'You're clutching at straws again, JT. If you're suggesting Raife Metcalfe, I should remind you that he and my husband didn't really get on with one another, and Raife was with his wife and me at dinner the night Lionel was murdered.'

Tayte gave a thoughtful nod, wondering perhaps whether the telegram and the notebook were somehow behind the reason why Lionel and Raife fell out. But as Davina had just reminded him, Raife had a solid alibi that night. He wondered then who else had both the motive and opportunity, and he figured it had to be someone Lionel knew. He thought about Dean Saxby. There was no question that he and Lionel Scanlon were acquainted. His story about the cigar case had checked out, and he'd even provided Bishop with information he hoped would prove useful to the case, if only for the reward money. But had he told them everything about what happened the day he went to see Lionel Scanlon?

Tayte couldn't dismiss the fact that Dean Saxby was Frank Saxby's great-great-grandson, either. Items that appeared to be connected with Lionel Scanlon's murder had been handed down through the Scanlon family, so why not the Saxby family, too? Was there something else from the past that Dean had neglected to tell them about? His and Lionel's ancestors had been business partners, and their partnership had literally gone up in flames, claiming the lives of several factory workers. Did a motive for murder exist somewhere in the ashes? Tayte heaved a sigh and concluded that the only way he had any chance of working out who had killed Lionel Scanlon was to first understand why, and to do that he needed the notebook, to understand what it contained.

'If the notebook still exists today,' Tayte said, 'and someone clearly seems to believe it does' where could it be?' He was thinking aloud, but he thought that if Davina had any ideas he'd be glad to hear them. 'How could a notebook survive for a hundred years? What kind of environment is conducive to protecting something like that in the longer term?'

The most likely answer came to both of them at the same time, perhaps because such things were always on Tayte's mind on account of his profession, and because of the research he and Davina were currently embroiled in.

'An archive,' they said, turning to one another as they spoke, wearing similar expressions that were as much to suggest it was obvious.

'Or it could just as well be tucked away in a box in someone's attic,' Tayte added.

'Yes, it could,' Davina agreed. A moment later she laughed to herself. 'Actually, my husband would have favoured that answer. "It's amazing what you can find in the forgotten spaces of the world" he'd say.' She laughed again. 'Plenty of which has ended up in his workshop over the years, I can tell you.'

That notion set Tayte wondering. 'Do you think the notebook could be tucked away somewhere at your husband's workshop?'

Davina shook her head. 'It's possible, but I shouldn't think so. It's the only place associated with Lionel and me that hasn't been broken into since Lionel's murder.'

'Perhaps by the time the killer left your husband's workshop, he already believed it wasn't there, but I don't see how he could be certain.'

'No, and nothing much was disturbed that night, although I'm sure the police searched the place quite thoroughly. They can't have known what my husband's killer was looking for, though.'

'Do you want to go and take a look?'

'Why not?' Davina said. 'We've a few hours of daylight left, and it's too early to eat. You don't mind if we have dinner again this evening, do you?'

'Not in the least.'

Tayte picked up his drink and finished what little was left. He hadn't imagined he'd be going anywhere else that night, other than to his bed, or he'd have had a cola. 'I'll get reception to call us a taxi.'

# Chapter Thirty-Four

By the time they arrived at the workshop-cum-warehouse where Lionel Scanlon had once breathed new life into the old furniture it had been his passion to restore, the sun had dipped below the woodland trees that backed on to the old building, casting the yard before it into shadow. Tayte and Davina left the taxi and crossed the yard to the click of Davina's heels as she tried to keep pace with Tayte's long strides. Taking the area in, he thought it no surprise that Lionel Scanlon's killer had gone about his nefarious business unseen. The woodland shielded the building on one side, and to the other a flyover gave few people cause to pass by. There was a street where the taxi had dropped them off, but it was quiet and set far enough back as to be of little concern to anyone intent on breaking into the property. They reached the gate-like double doors, and Davina unlocked the deadbolts and the heavy padlock that secured them.

'You go first, JT. There's a light switch just inside on your right.'

Tayte entered and found the switch. When the lights came on, he almost jumped out of his skin as an eight-foot-tall grizzly bear swiped a claw at him, or so he'd imagined for the briefest of moments.

'Sorry,' Davina said, turning off the alarm. She looked as if she was trying not to smile. 'I should have warned you. Lionel picked him up at auction, goodness knows how many years ago, and we've been stuck with him ever since.'

'Not much call for antique taxidermy in the Medway area?'

'You could say that.'

They moved further into the high-ceilinged building, which seemed to accommodate more floor space than had been apparent from the outside. Looking around, Tayte saw a potential Aladdin's cave of treasures, few items of which he imagined held much value to a burglar in their present state. It was mostly furniture, with other large items such as antique fire surrounds and chandeliers, old picture frames, and an assortment of stone carvings in various states of disrepair. All of which must have aroused their buyer's interest at some time, but which—like the bear—had yet to find another home.

'I've not been down here much since it happened,' Davina said. 'Apart from anything the police might have disturbed, everything should be the same as it was when Lionel . . .' She paused, unable to finish the sentence.

Tayte rested a hand on her shoulder, trying to comfort her. 'It's okay,' he said, knowing how difficult it must be for her to come back to the scene of her husband's murder—to stand so close to where Lionel was killed. 'We don't have to do this if you don't want to.'

Davina sniffed. 'No, I'll be fine, and I do want to. I have to face up to it.' She moved further in, brushing a hand gently over the things she passed, as if stirring fond memories.

'Where do we start?' Tayte said, looking around at all the possible places a notebook could be hidden.

'Why don't we take half the room each? You go that way, and I'll look over here.'

'Sounds like a plan.'

Tayte moved off to his left as Davina began to rummage among the things to his right. He came to a trunk, which he opened and found empty. He felt around inside it and tapped the base, hoping to discover whether it had a secret bottom, but he quickly decided it did not. It was beside a tall set of drawers—a Wellington chest that, as with everything else, had seen better days. He removed the drawers one at a time in case anything had been taped to the back, but he found nothing. Moving on, he put his hands inside every opening and drawer he came to, scrutinising everything in his path until an hour or more had passed in fruitless pursuit of a notebook he was fast coming to believe wasn't there.

'I think you were right,' he called to Davina. 'There's not much else I can check this side.' There were several other items, and he continued to explore them, but he knew it wouldn't take more than ten minutes to satisfy himself that they had gone there in vain.

'Same here,' Davina said as she came over. 'Still, it was worth a look.'

Tayte was standing beside a motley collection of antique photographic equipment, some of which he thought must date back to the late 1800s. There was an assortment of smaller cameras, all chipped and tacky with dust. The jewels of the collection—if such a comparison could be made in their present state—appeared to be a pair of mahogany and brass bellows cameras on wooden tripods, complete with dark cloths hanging off their backs.

'Lionel had a passion for collecting old cameras at one time,' Davina said. 'He wound up with far more lost causes than he could ever hoped to have restored.' She picked one of them up—a Kodak Box Brownie—and opened the case. 'He had his great-grandfather to thank for that.'

'Oscar Scanlon?' Tayte said with interest.

Davina nodded. 'Lionel told me once that Oscar had a studio in Maidstone. Some of his equipment remained in the family and was handed down, sparking Lionel's interest.'

Tayte went to one of the tripods and put his head under the dark cloth. He turned the camera to Davina as he looked into the apparatus, and saw her upside down, which amused him enough to draw a small laugh.

'I'm sure the camera on that other tripod used to belong to Oscar.'

Tayte studied it briefly. Then he threw the cloth over his head as he had before. 'Now hold perfectly still, ma'am,' he said in an old Wild West accent, playing the part of the kind of photographer he imagined would have used such equipment back home. When he couldn't see an image, upside down or otherwise, he came out from under the dark cloth, thinking the front lens cap must have been on, but there was no cap.

He threw the cloth forward over the camera body, exposing the back. It was a wet plate camera, and he thought an old plate must have still been in there, obstructing the view, but there was no plate either. The back was exposed, and now he could clearly see the problem. Inside the body of the camera was a cloth parcel, which he took to contain no more than a collection of items necessary for the camera's upkeep—until he removed it and unwrapped the material. It was a set of photographs.

Davina came closer. 'What is it?'

'I don't exactly know,' Tayte said, studying the first image. Whatever it was, it was incomplete. He looked at the next image, which was similar. 'Words,' he added. Then as he looked at another image, he felt a tingle of excitement run through him. 'I think they're photographs of a document.'

He went to a nearby pedestal desk and spread the photographs out on the faded leather inlay. There were twenty images in all, and they didn't appear to be in any kind of order, but some clearly had edges, like the pieces of a jigsaw puzzle. He went through them and sorted those with edges from those without. Distinct corners could also be seen, and he was quickly able to put them in place, using the orientation of the words to guide him. When he'd matched the left side, he could see that the image coming to light wasn't so much a document, but another, much older photograph of a document.

'It looks as though someone's taken all these pictures to magnify the original,' he said as he continued to set the pieces of the puzzle in place. 'Lionel?'

'I suppose so, or perhaps his father. I've never seen them before.'

The image forming in front of them was not that clear, but it was legible. Judging by the paper and the degree of fading, Tayte thought the photographs must have been taken during the 1970s or 1980s, and it seemed likely that they were taken in order to preserve and expand the original, which by now might otherwise have perished. It led Tayte to wonder, as he had with the telegram, why the original had been preserved at all, and why it had been kept in the Scanlon family all this time.

He found another match and turned to Davina. 'Most secret,' he said, drawing her attention to the words.

Davina leaned in and set another piece into place in the bottom right-hand corner. It contained a signature. '"Charles Metcalfe,"' she read. '"For and on behalf of the Board of Admiralty."'

'So the clues reveal themselves,' Tayte said under his breath.

Davina looked puzzled. 'How on earth did Lionel come by such a thing?'

'I think that signature goes some way to explaining it. Oscar Scanlon was living at Hamberley when this document was signed. Perhaps it was drawn up and signed at Hamberley, or maybe it was with Charles Metcalfe at his home at some point—long enough for Oscar to take a photograph of it, as has clearly happened.'

Tayte was more intrigued than ever now to know why someone had gone to such lengths to keep the image of this particular document in the family. He continued to put the photographs together, and once the outside of the puzzle was complete, it was only a matter of minutes before the full picture could be seen. Tayte's eyes were immediately drawn to the name near the top of what was evidently a photograph of a naval court of enquiry—a court martial, where after the outbreak of war, civilians could be tried under the Defence of the Realm Act. It showed a schedule and a summary of evidence against Francis Edwin Saxby, who, on 20 July 1914, was charged with high treason for spying. On the right-hand side it showed a verdict of guilty and the sentence of 'death by being shot,' together with another signature confirming that the sentence had been carried out on 5 August 1914.

'Oh my goodness,' Davina said, as she seemed to realise what she was looking at. 'This explains the significance of Saxby's date of death, doesn't it?'

'Yes, it does,' Tayte said, wondering whether Alice had played an anonymous hand in Saxby's arrest. Perhaps she had tipped off the authorities at some point. Tayte liked to think she had, and he couldn't imagine Alice would sit back and let the man go unpunished for what he had done—and what he might have gone on to do if she had not. However the arrest came about, Frank Saxby had clearly been uncovered for the spy he was.

Tayte began to read the summary details, which was heavy going given the quality of the images and their disjointed nature. The summary of evidence showed that following Saxby's arrest on Tuesday, 7 June, various incriminating items were found at his home, such as the materials required to write invisible messages and an envelope bearing an address in Antwerp, Belgium, that was known to the Secret Service Bureau as that of Mr Dierks, one of several men involved in the recruitment of spies for Germany's spy network. Also found was an Enfield revolver with thirty rounds of ammunition. Tayte came to another section that detailed a further discovery made after Saxby's arrest.

'The notebook,' Tayte said. He pointed to one of the photographs below the section he'd just been reading. 'It's mentioned right here.' He read out the salient points. '"A coded notebook containing names and addresses was also found on the suspect's person."'

'Names and addresses,' Davina repeated. 'Do you think that's what my husband's killer is after?'

'It's possible, but only his killer or the notebook itself can tell us why, and I think I now know where it is.'

'You do?'

'Yes, and it's no wonder I couldn't find anything when I looked online, given its "most secret" classification. This was all carried out *in camera*—a private court martial led by Admiral Lord Charles Metcalfe, presumably because he wanted to oversee Saxby's punishment personally because of his betrayal not only to his country but to the man who had been his lifelong friend. There's only one place that notebook can be—the non-public Security Intelligence Service archive in London. The notebook should still be there, along with all the other evidence against Saxby.'

'But if it's non-public, how can we get to see it?'

Tayte smiled. 'DI Bishop,' he said, thinking about the file on Alice Stilwell that Bishop had previously been granted access to. 'He's conducting a murder investigation, and that notebook would appear to be a vital piece of evidence. The time that's lapsed between then and now is also in our favour.' Tayte started gathering the photographs together. 'I'll call him first thing in the morning and explain everything. Maybe I can accompany him to London to see it.'

# Chapter Thirty-Five

By three o'clock the following afternoon, Tayte was back at his hotel, waiting for Davina to pick up his call so he could share his good news with her. DI Bishop had just dropped him off after their trip to the government's SIS archive in London that morning, and he was keen now to get to work on bringing whoever was responsible for Lionel Scanlon's murder to justice. The call rang for the umpteenth time, and he was about to hang up when a breathless voice answered.

'Hello.'

'Davina? It's JT.'

'JT! Sorry about that. I had my hands full. I was just taking some boxes out to the car. How did it go?'

'It went very well,' Tayte said. 'Inspector Bishop made a few calls, and I imagine a bunch of other people made a few more calls. It was pretty much as I said last night. The release of information is considered on a case-by-case basis. As Frank Saxby's file contained information that was deemed useful to a current murder investigation, that was all the justification needed to see it. Everything the SIS had on Saxby was waiting for us in a reading room outside the SIS archive when we arrived. I have the notebook with me now.'

'They let you take it out?'

'Yes, they did,' Tayte said, studying it again as he turned it slowly in his hand. It was a tan, softback notebook that had no remarkable features other than its condition. It was a hundred years old, but it looked like new thanks to the way it had been stored all this time.

'The writing inside the notebook isn't Saxby's,' Tayte said, thinking back to the reading room where he and Bishop first made the discovery. 'Given what it contains, I don't doubt that it was originally penned by Saxby, but this version was most definitely written by someone else.'

'How can you tell?'

'Do you remember that one of the incriminating pieces of evidence against Saxby was an address written to someone in Belgium called Dierks?'

'Yes.'

'Well, that was proven to be Saxby's handwriting. I've seen the original letterhead, and that handwriting is very different to the handwriting in the notebook. The style is unchanged from start to finish, too. There's usually some degree of variation in notebooks, which are typically added to over time. This one appears to have been written in one sitting.'

'As would happen if someone was making a copy?' Davina said.

'Precisely.'

'Do you have any idea who wrote it?'

'I believe Alice must have,' Tayte said. 'We know Phoebe Dodson had it when the *Empress of Ireland* left Quebec. Given what we now know, an educated guess is that Alice made the copy and left it with Phoebe for safekeeping should anything happen to her. I suspect she had the original on board the ship with her and that it perished when the ship went down, which would have made this copy all the more important to Saxby. He must have known he had no chance of getting the original back when he heard that the *Empress of Ireland* sank.'

'So what does it contain?' Davina asked.

'Names and addresses mostly. It's all written in code, but it was deciphered a long time ago. I have a decoded transcript to go with it—the handwriting is different again, so I guess it was penned by someone who worked for the government. The addresses are scattered all over the country.'

'A spy ring?'

'Could be. It doesn't say, but I imagine those names and addresses were checked out at the time.'

'Do you think someone's after the names and addresses now?'

'I can't see why after all this time,' Tayte said. 'But then again, right now I don't know why else anyone would want it.'

'You said it *mostly* contained names and addresses. Was there something else?'

'Yes, there was. There's a further section of code at the back that no one seems to have been able to crack, apart from a few seemingly random words, that is. The transcript shows the exact same letters and numbers. That's why I have the book now. Knowing what I know from my assignment, Bishop thought I was best placed to have a go at making sense of it all—to try to understand how it could be a motive for your husband's murder.'

'Well, two heads can be better than one,' Davina said. 'Why don't we have a look at it together?'

'I was hoping you'd say that. I told Bishop you might be able to help. Maybe there's something about your husband that will register with you when you see it. Where are you?'

'I was just on my way out. I'm taking a few paintings down to the marina. I thought the apartment could use a new look. After that, I thought I'd spend the rest of the afternoon on the boat. Why don't you meet me there in an hour or so?'

'Great,' Tayte said. 'I'll—'

Davina cut in. 'Before you go, I wanted to tell you that I found a receipt earlier this morning. It's probably nothing, but I thought you should know about it. It was handwritten and paid in cash to Saxby Electrical.'

'Saxby?' Tayte repeated. 'Dean Saxby carried out electrical work for you?'

'For my husband at the workshop, apparently. I didn't know anything about it. It was just a few days before Lionel was killed. Didn't Saxby mention it when you went to see him?'

'No, he didn't. Have you told Inspector Bishop?'

'Not yet. I've been too busy with my boxes, and then you called.'

'I'll let him know,' Tayte said. 'Hold on to that receipt. I'm sure he'll be interested to see it.'

'Of course. I'll see you shortly then.'

———

Striding along the pontoon boards towards the *Osprey* at Gillingham Marina an hour after his phone call with Davina, Tayte was in high spirits, subconsciously whistling a tune from *Calamity Jane* because the wind had picked up. A keen gust flapped at his jacket and tousled his hair, causing him to look out across the estuary towards the eastern horizon. A grey cloud bank was building, perhaps heralding an end to the sunny days he'd become accustomed to since arriving in England. He was in high spirits nonetheless because he was thinking about Jean. It was close to four o'clock on Friday afternoon, and within twenty-four hours he knew she'd be back in London. He was buzzing at the thought of speaking to her again, but on the inside he remained nervous about what she was going to say, and whether or not she wanted to see him again. As he approached the *Osprey* and tried to refocus his thoughts, he hoped those grey clouds were not an ill omen.

'JT!'

Davina appeared on the deck of the *Osprey* and began waving at him, full of smiles and looking very nautical, Tayte thought, in a striped blue sweater and white jeans.

Tayte stepped aboard. 'Looks like the weather's set to change.'

'I know. Still, we've had a good run.' She extended a hand to steady Tayte aboard. 'We might as well go straight below,' she added. 'It looks like rain. That weather front will be here before we know it.'

'I think I just felt a spot,' Tayte said as he ducked his head beneath the beam and followed Davina down the steps into the main cabin.

'Have a seat,' Davina said. 'Did you manage to tell Inspector Bishop about that receipt I found?'

'Yes I did. I called him right after you told me. He said he was going to talk to Dean Saxby again, to find out why he didn't mention it.'

'Good,' Davina said. 'What can I get you to drink? There's a bottle of Rioja open if you'd like some. I'm afraid I don't have any tea or coffee aboard.'

'Do you have any soda?'

'Can of Coke?'

'Perfect.'

'You don't mind if I stick to wine, do you? I've already had a glass.'

'No, not at all,' Tayte said as he opened his briefcase and found the notebook. He threw Davina a smile. 'It's your boat.'

Davina set their drinks down and sat beside him. 'I can't tell you how excited I've been since you called. Is that it?' she added, eying the notebook as Tayte brought it into view and set it down on the table.

'That's it,' Tayte said. 'It's quite unremarkable, as I said.'

'It's the contents that matter. People have died because of it—Phoebe Dodson and perhaps poor Lionel.'

Tayte picked up his drink and downed half of it in one go. He opened the notebook. 'Let's take a look then, shall we? Hopefully we can work out why.' He went back into his briefcase and found the deciphered transcript, which he set down between them. 'The contents of the notebook itself won't mean much,' he added. 'This transcript, on the other hand, shows all the names and addresses. Do any of them mean anything to you?'

Davina looked through them, shaking her head between sips of wine.

'Maybe they meant something to your husband?' Tayte said.

Davina came to the last name and address and dismissed it. 'It's possible, but I don't recognise any of them myself.'

'That's too bad. There doesn't seem to be any commonality among them, either. No repeat names, and geographically they're all over the place. I thought about looking to see if there was a family history connection between them. Maybe the census would tell us something about these people that's not evident from their names and addresses alone.'

Tayte finished his drink and held the can up to get the last drop.

'You were thirsty,' Davina said. 'Would you like another one?'

'Thanks, but that's my quota of sugary beverages for today.'

Davina just smiled and sipped her wine. 'You said on the telephone that there was a section of code that hadn't been deciphered.'

Tayte nodded and flicked to the back of the notebook. 'Here it is. It's mostly numbers, as I said.'

Davina studied them. 'There are ten blocks,' she said a moment later. 'They all appear to be the same length.'

Tayte already knew as much. 'These letters beside them have been deciphered, but the words they form appear to be random.' He read a few out. 'Fortissimo. Antelope. Wedgwood. The numeric code would probably make sense of them if it could be worked out, but as things stand, we've no way of knowing what it means.'

Davina looked up from the notebook, and she looked somewhat apologetic as she said, 'Oh, I know what it means.'

'You do? That's great.'

'Is it? I'm afraid you won't think so when I tell you *how* I know.'

Tayte's eyes narrowed on her. 'How do you mean?'

Davina sighed and shifted along the seat, moving away from Tayte. 'I suppose I do owe you an explanation,' she said. 'You've been very kind, and so helpful. When I first met you I thought you might prove too clever to fool, but thankfully I was wrong. I've had you fooled from the beginning—you and the police.'

Tayte's brow set into a deep furrow. 'So you were behind all this—the break-ins at your homes and everything else?'

'Yes, I was. I thought the break-ins would help to draw suspicion away from me, and I wanted to let you and Inspector Bishop know that someone was looking for something. Clever, don't you think?'

'Wait a minute,' Tayte said. ' So you killed your own husband?'

'Not personally, no. I had a watertight alibi, remember? But yes, I was responsible. I wasn't as close to Lionel as I might have led you and the police to believe.'

'So you had someone else kill him? Was it Dean Saxby?'

Davina laughed to herself. 'No, he had nothing to do with any of this. When I recalled his visit to the workshop, I thought he could make for another useful distraction to the Inspector's investigation, but that's all it was.'

'Then who did kill your husband? Why?'

'For this notebook, of course,' Davina said, tapping it with a fingernail. 'I've been leading you towards it all this time, dropping clues in your lap—the telegram and those photographs of Lionel's. I planted them in his workshop for you to find, and I led you to believe it was your idea to go there to look for the notebook. I knew it wasn't there, but I also knew that the document shown in those photographs would tell you where it was.'

'So you knew where it was all along?'

'Not to begin with, but we soon worked it out, or rather, Lionel did. Getting access to it was proving to be the difficult part.'

'Which is where I came in,' Tayte said, an air of defeat in his tone.

'Your arrival was as manna from heaven to me,' Davina said, smiling broadly. 'At first I just wanted to stop you. I knew when and why you were coming to England from the messages you left on my husband's answering machine, so I had someone look out for you at Hamberley, where it was obvious you would go. Then I had you run off the road. I thought if that didn't seriously injure you, or even kill you, then you would at least get the message and back off. But I'm glad you proved to be the stubborn type.'

'You still haven't really told me why you had your husband killed or who did it.'

'You're not the patient type, though, are you?' Davina drank some more of her wine, as though they were still two people enjoying a sociable afternoon together. 'It's really very simple. Lionel discovered that I was having an affair. We argued and he told me he had the notebook, saying that I wasn't getting a penny. I believed him, so I set up his murder—to shut him up about the affair and to get the notebook for myself. But Lionel didn't have the notebook, of course, so I devised my little plan to get it through you.'

Tayte scoffed. 'So this is about money? Why am I not surprised?'

'It really is the root of all evil, isn't it?' Davina said. 'Which brings us back to the un-deciphered code at the back of the notebook. That's the important bit.'

'So what is it?'

Davina laughed to herself, as if the idea of what the code represented excited her. 'It couldn't be cracked because it's not code at all,' she said. 'They're account numbers. The random words beside them are access codes.'

'And they were hiding in plain view,' Tayte said to himself as his eyes drifted back to the notebook. 'Their meaning obscured by all the code around them.' He turned back to Davina. 'What are bank account numbers doing in a spy's notebook?'

'Among other things, I'm sure,' Davina said, 'Frank Saxby was also a fundraiser. The names and addresses at the front of the notebook are for those people who donated to the cause.'

'To Germany?' Tayte said, getting the picture.

Davina nodded. 'If you did check the census, you'd find that they all lived in grand homes with numerous members of staff to wait on them. They were wealthy British families who supported the kaiser and who gave generously to help fund Germany in the arms race. But the money Saxby raised didn't all find its way to Germany. He was skimming a large percentage off the top for himself, which he exchanged for gold that he tucked away in Switzerland.'

'And you think it's still there now?'

'I don't see why it shouldn't be, and we had to find out, didn't we? Saxby was arrested and executed soon after he recovered the notebook. He had little to no chance of doing anything with the contents of his Swiss bank accounts, and he would have had no reason to think he had to until it was too late.'

Tayte eyed Davina quizzically. 'How do you know all this? It was a hundred years ago.'

'Family stories,' Davina said. 'The telegram and the original photograph of Frank Saxby's court martial document weren't the only things passed down to Lionel. You see, Oscar Scanlon was Saxby's accomplice—or so the story Lionel told me goes. Together they would identify wealthy families with reason to support Germany, offering them security and position under the kaiser's rule when the inevitable war was won. But of course when Saxby was arrested,

Oscar lost access to the notebook. Apparently, Saxby was paranoid about anyone else getting hold of the information, so he insisted on keeping the details on his person. Presumably, he didn't trust Oscar enough to let him have his own copy.'

Davina's handbag was beside her on the seat. She reached into it and produced an envelope, which she held up for Tayte to see. 'Oscar also handed this down. I suppose he thought it was all part of the legacy that would convince subsequent generations of Scanlons that the story about the kaiser's war-fund gold was true.'

Tayte squinted at the postmark. The letter was from Canada, dated 20 May 1914.

'It's a letter from Alice Stilwell to her father,' Davina said, withdrawing it again. 'Oscar must have intercepted it at Hamberley before it reached him. Oscar really was the devious type, wasn't he?'

'Can I see it?' Tayte asked. From the date he knew that Alice must have sent it soon after she arrived in Quebec, and as it was addressed to Alice's father, Tayte supposed it was an explanation about everything that had happened. As assignments went, it was a priceless record.

Davina seemed to think about it. Then she said, 'No, I don't think so.'

A wry smile spread across Tayte face. 'You're playing it very cool for someone who's just admitted all this to me. Presumably you're doing so because your scheming isn't over yet?'

'No, not quite,' Davina said. 'I have to fool Inspector Bishop a little longer, and you're going to help me with that, too.'

Tayte laughed at the idea. He was about to ask how, when a sound from the boat's bow drew his attention. It sounded like a door being opened and closed. He whirled around to see Raife Metcalfe coming towards him, his perennially sour expression fixed on Tayte every step of the way. Tayte thought he was imagining things at first. He certainly felt confused all of a sudden. When he realised he wasn't hallucinating, he sprang to his feet—at least he tried to, but he found he had little control of his legs. He felt dizzy, as if he'd had too much to drink, and why were his eyelids beginning to feel so heavy?

'I'm afraid I've been a naughty girl again,' Davina said, pulling Tayte's attention back to her. 'Are you familiar with Rohypnol?'

Tayte tried to say that he'd heard of it, but his words were so slurred he could barely understand them himself.

'I slipped some pills into your drink,' Davina continued. 'It's commonly known as the date-rape drug for obvious reasons.' She leaned towards Tayte then and caressed his cheek. 'Don't worry. You're not really my type.'

Tayte tried to get up again, but all he managed to do was fall off his seat.

Raife caught him and sat him up again. 'Mr Tayte,' he grinned. 'I can't tell you how much I've been looking forward to this.'

# Chapter Thirty-Six

Aboard the *Osprey*, Tayte was aware that his left cheek was stinging. His eyes peeled slowly open to see Davina sitting across the table in front of him, right before she slapped his face again. Tayte's eyes opened more fully. He felt disorientated and confused.

'Davina. Where am I?'

'You're on my boat. Don't you remember?'

Tayte drew a deep breath and thought about it. He looked around at the semi-familiar interior of the main cabin as he tried to recall when he'd been there before. Then snippets of information flashed back at him from somewhere deep within his subconscious, and he knew his life was in danger. His initial instinct was to get as far away from Davina and her boat as possible, but the drug Davina had slipped into his drink had fully incapacitated him. He literally felt as if he were glued to his seat.

'I think I might have given you too much Rohypnol,' Davina said. 'I was beginning to think you were out for good.'

Tayte felt himself drifting out of consciousness again. Then the boat slapped a wave and gave him a jolt. He was aware of the engine noise then, and he wondered why it hadn't registered before. They were moving at speed, or were they? Everything was so unclear.

'Raife's taken us out of the estuary. The sea's a little choppy,' Davina said, confirming his thoughts. 'It won't be long now, though.'

'Where are we going?' Tayte asked, but he figured Davina couldn't have understood a single slurred word he'd said, because she didn't answer.

A moment later, as though she'd been waiting for Tayte to regain consciousness all this time just so she could continue to gloat, she said, 'Now then, what was I saying?' She paused. 'Oh yes, I remember. I was about to tell you how you're going to help me fool the police. You can see now that you never really had a choice in the matter, can't you?'

Tayte wanted to tell her that she wouldn't get away with it, but by the time the words had formed, he'd forgotten them again.

'I expect you're still wondering who killed my husband and who ran you off the road,' Davina continued, as though unable to stop the ego trip she was on, filling the time until they reached their destination by revelling in how clever she had been.

Tayte didn't even try to answer. He'd heard enough.

'Do you remember Luca?' Davina said. 'You met him the other day at the Marina restaurant. He would have done anything for me—for the promise of my affection and another night in my bed.' She paused and opened Tayte's eyelids more fully, as if to make sure he was still paying as much attention to her as he was able to. 'Don't get me wrong,' she added. 'The affair I told you about earlier wasn't with Luca—I was just using him. I was having an affair with Raife. That's why Lionel didn't want to go to the restaurant with us the night he was murdered. He'd not long since found out about our affair, so you can see why I had to shut him up, can't you? As soon as Raife found out that Lionel knew, he wanted to take care of the matter himself, but that wouldn't have been very clever, would it?'

Davina leaned across the table and slapped Tayte's face again. His eyes shot wide open, and he managed to shake his head, albeit slowly. He heard himself moaning something, but he couldn't understand what it was.

'I'm surprised you didn't try it on with me,' Davina continued. 'I'm sure most men would have in your situation, and it's not as if I didn't give you enough opportunity.' She smiled to herself. 'Don't you like women? Or perhaps there's someone special in your life, is that it? Are you that rare, faithful type?'

Tayte didn't try to answer her. Jean Summer was none of her business, and he planned to keep it that way.

'Anyway, here's how you're going to help me one last time,' Davina said. 'I've made up a little story for the police. It tells how you came here with the notebook and that Luca must have been watching the boat, having seen me come aboard earlier. When we went below deck, Luca must have crept aboard and listened to our conversation until he was satisfied we had the notebook. At that point he burst in, wearing the same grey ski mask caught on the marina's CCTV cameras after I had him break into my apartment. He was brandishing a knife exactly like the one that was found at the scene of Lionel's murder. Can you see where this is going yet?'

Tayte didn't care. He just wanted to sleep.

'So at knife point,' Davina continued, 'Luca made you take the boat out to sea. I'll say that when he ordered you to stop the boat, you managed to run back inside and grab the notebook, using it to distract Luca long enough to gain the upper hand. You flung the notebook into the sea and charged at Luca.' Davina paused for thought. 'Yes, that should work fine,' she added, as though she were narrating her story to Tayte just to make sure there were no holes in it.

Tayte wondered where Luca was. He figured he already had to be aboard the boat. He managed to ask the question, and his words were heavily slurred as before, but he knew Davina understood him this time.

'Where's Luca?'

Davina looked over Tayte's shoulder towards the *Osprey's* bow, from where Raife had earlier appeared. 'Luca had already played his last part for me before you came aboard,' she said. 'The promise of another small sexual favour was all it took to get him down here, and Raife was only too happy to take care of him. Poor Raife needs the money, you see. He's afraid he'll be broke when his grandfather dies and leaves everything to his wife and her son.'

Davina cast her eyes around the cabin. 'The rest of the story goes that you fought one another from bow to stern while I sat huddled in a corner out on deck, too scared to move. I see you both come out from the main cabin again, and now Luca has been stabbed with his own knife. I say you must have turned it on him, being the stronger man, and now you appear to have the advantage. But in the last moments of the fight you go overboard, while Luca bleeds out on the deck and dies. You and the notebook are lost to the sea, where you drown. The police have their killer, and the case is closed.'

Through Tayte's blurred vision, he saw Davina smile and clap her hands together, as if she had never been more pleased with herself.

'So, what do you think?' she asked.

Tayte thought her story sounded as watertight as the *Osprey's* hull. He also thought that if he went into the sea in his present state he would sink helplessly to the bottom and drown in seconds. The boat slowed suddenly then, and he found himself falling forward, causing Davina to put her hands out to prevent him from face-planting the table.

'We're stopping,' she said. 'Ready to play your last part?'

Seconds later, the boat was still and silent, pitching and rolling with the waves. Then Raife came below. Somehow Tayte didn't seem to care what was going to happen to him now—another effect of the Rohypnol. He felt Raife pull him from his seat and lock his burly arms around his chest. Then Tayte was half on the floor and Davina was at his feet. She lifted them and Tayte was suddenly floating, up through the cabin door and out onto the deck where rain lashed at his face in the fading grey of the late afternoon.

'Ready?' Raife said to Davina.

A moment later, Tayte heard Raife groan, and then Tayte was hauled up onto the side of the boat, where Raife's strong hands held him steady as the boat rose and fell.

'You'll make a fine meal for the fishes before your body's found,' Raife said to him.

Tayte opened his eyes and saw Davina again. Her face held no expression as she spoke to him for the last time.

'I wasn't going to play the hypocrite and tell you how sorry I am that it had to end this way, JT. But I came to like you more than I wanted to, so a part of me really is sorry—for what it's worth.'

With that she stepped closer, and as Raife loosened his grip, Davina shoved Tayte's chest, sending him overboard into the sea.

# Chapter Thirty-Seven

St Lawrence River. Friday, 29 May 1914.

At two o'clock on the morning the *Empress of Ireland* sank, Canada's St Lawrence River was barely above one degree Celsius. At such a low temperature, those who are able to survive the cold shock response following their initial plunge into such frigid waters are faced with hypothermia, the debilitating effects of which can take hold of a person in less than ten minutes, rendering that person incapable of survival unaided. Alice Stilwell was a young and healthy woman. She was unconscious when she hit the water. Within seconds she was gasping for air, drawing deep, uncontrollable breaths—hyperventilating.

Her eyes quickly found a thick section of wooden beam floating nearby—perhaps the very beam that had struck her. All around her, she could hear people splashing and crying out for help. The fog limited her view, but as it rolled and shifted, she could make them out now and then: some people clinging to debris as she was, others treading water as they looked for something to hold on to. A greater number than she cared to think about were just floating lifeless, their ghostly faces as ashen as the fog. She could see no trace of the *Empress of Ireland*, and she sensed the ship was already on the riverbed. For the second time that night, she wondered how many lifeboats had been launched before it became too late to do so.

A minute passed, maybe two or three, Alice couldn't be sure. She was surprised she no longer felt cold. She had imagined the sensation would be akin to a thousand daggers constantly stabbing at her skin, but she could feel little now beyond a slight tingling on the soles of her feet. A few minutes more and her breathing slowed, and she found it a challenge to move her legs. All around her the night gradually became quieter, and it seemed somehow peaceful to her in its way. Her grip on the beam that was helping to keep her afloat was rapidly weakening. Where were the lifeboats? Why wasn't she calling for help?

As the beam began to drift away from her, Alice knew why she did not call out. It was because she had already come to terms with her death, knowing that it would be better for everyone if Alice Stilwell died right there in the St Lawrence River. Even if she survived the night and returned to England, she would return to her immediate arrest. Since marrying Henry, she had held dual citizenship. As a British citizen under the protection of the Crown, as Archie had pointed out, she would be tried and executed for high treason for all she had done. With Henry dead there was no one left to corroborate her story. She would tell it, but who would believe such a fanciful account from a woman who would surely say anything to avoid the hangman's noose or the firing squad's bullets? With Henry dead, her own fate had been sealed, and if she was going to die anyway, then she would do this one last honourable thing for her family.

Without Alice Stilwell there could be no trial. Her father would receive the letter she had sent to him, explaining everything, but would he believe her? It pained Alice to think that he would not— that he would go to his grave believing his daughter was a traitor. But at least she would bring no public disgrace upon him or the family name. No ruinous scandal would ensue.

As Alice took one last breath and began to drift beneath the water, she thought about her children and smiled. Above all, she would gladly embrace death for Chester and Charlotte. They would not grow up in the shadow of having a traitor for a mother, and neither would they see her executed as one. Even if by some miracle she managed to stay the executioner's hand, she understood now that all the while she lived, she would be a threat to her children. Frank Saxby would never let the matter rest; he had shown her as much when he sent Raskin and then Herr Albrecht to kill her. He would not hesitate to threaten her children again to get what he wanted from her, and if not him, then it would fall to another of his many associates to do so.

*Frank Saxby* . . .

As Alice sank lower and began to fade from the world, she knew her death was close at hand, and in those last moments she was consumed with hatred for the man who had taken everything from her. Wherever she looked in that black abyss, she saw his likeness, laughing and mocking her in his triumph. He had taken everything. She began to convulse as her lungs cried out for oxygen. She started thrashing and kicking as she fought the urge to open her mouth and put an end to her torment. Then a white light appeared above her, and instinctively Alice tried to kick her legs—to reach out for it, believing that if she could reach it in time, she would be reborn. Saxby had not yet taken everything, and she would be damned if she would let him. She would have the world believe that Alice Stilwell died when the *Empress of Ireland* sank. But she would live on to spite him. The water splashed above her, and she saw a hand reach down through the light. She grabbed it, accepting that in doing so she would have to endure the pain of giving up those she loved, knowing that she would never be able to return to her old life again.

# Chapter Thirty-Eight

Present day.

Tayte managed to stay afloat no more than a minute in the cold sea off the Medway estuary where the *Osprey* had left him. As soon as he hit the water, all he could see was the stormy sky above and the sea rolling around him, further disorientating him. He held his breath as time and again the sea crashed over him, taking him under and tossing him around as if his life had already left him. He willed his legs to kick beneath him—to tread the water—but they would not. A high swell took him under again, and before long he felt his breath run out. Slowly, he began to let it go, and he watched the bubbles rise, wishing he could go up to the surface with them, but he knew now that the only way for him was down, and the more air he exhaled, the deeper he sank.

*This wasn't supposed to happen . . .*

Tayte thought about Jean then. He couldn't bear the idea of things ending this way between them. He imagined she would miss him, or at least he thought she would miss the idea of him, despite everything. It was no consolation to him, though, in his last moments to know that she would be the only person in the world who would. He tried to clear his mind, which had become surprisingly lucid since hitting the water, in spite of the debilitating sedative Davina had given him. He closed his eyes, and it was as if the sea were suddenly filled with light. He opened them again and thought he must be close to death because he could see the guiding light—the one all the stories told you not to go towards.

But very soon, Tayte had no choice.

There was a splash above him, and a moment later he was no longer alone. He saw a diver's mask and a pair of eyes staring back into his. Then both men were rushing up through the water towards the light. Tayte felt his face break the surface, and he gasped for the air that was howling down around him, flattening the sea. Above him he heard the drone of a helicopter, and then he was flying above the sea, being winched to safety. He didn't know whether to laugh or cry. The emotions that rushed out in that moment were a mixture of both. He was alive.

Below him now he heard a voice over a megaphone, drowned out as it was to some extent by the rotor blades spinning above him as the winch continued to pull him up. He turned towards the indistinct voice below and saw another spotlight shining onto the *Osprey* from a vessel that had moved alongside it. The *Osprey* was not as far away as he'd imagined. He saw Davina and Raife out on deck. Then he saw several police officers boarding, some with guns drawn.

*About time,* Tayte thought as the helicopter moved closer to the boats, heading towards land. The air-sea rescue helicopter above Tayte directed its own spotlight onto the vessels, floodlighting them as it went closer, and in that moment Tayte saw Davina look up at him. Their eyes met, and with a scornful glare Tayte ripped his shirt open and pulled out the concealed wire he'd been wearing since he left Bishop earlier that afternoon. He held it out for Davina to see, knowing that it had picked up every damning word she'd said.

As the helicopter passed beyond the vessels and Tayte was hauled inside, his thoughts drifted back to the previous afternoon when he'd met Davina at his hotel. It was there that she had tripped herself up, although Tayte hadn't realised it at the time. It was not until he was back in his room after visiting Lionel's workshop that he knew she had lied to him about her research into Phoebe Dodson. Aside from the practice of following up other people's research, he had also wanted to look for details of the inquest he knew must have been held following the house fire that had taken Phoebe's and her mother's lives.

What Tayte found was that the newspaper report Davina had apparently printed off, concerning the house fire in Charlesbourg, did not exist in any online archive today. The *Quebec Daily Mercury* ran from the early 1800s to the 1950s, but Tayte had discovered that—possibly due to fire or other environmental damage—archives only existed for the newspaper between 1870 and 1903, meaning that it was impossible to find such an article from 1914 and print it off today, as Davina had said she had done. The copy she had shown him then could only have been made from an original copy of the newspaper, which had to have been another of the legacy items handed down through the Scanlon family. Davina had therefore had it all along.

Having explained all this to DI Bishop on the way to London the following morning, the pair had hatched their own plan to sign the notebook out of the SIS archive and to use it to draw Lionel Scanlon's killer out. Tayte had readily agreed to wear the microphone and transmitter that would be used to record his conversations. Then he had called Davina and dangled the bait, knowing that Bishop and his team would be watching and listening, and that all the required services would be on standby, ready to act when the right moment came—before any harm could come to Tayte.

As the air-sea rescue helicopter reached land, heading for a hospital, Tayte thought he would have to have a word with Detective Inspector Bishop about his timing as soon as the opportunity arose.

# Chapter Thirty-Nine

Following a restful night under observation in a hospital bed, where he'd slept like a baby, courtesy of the acute sedative Davina had slipped into his drink the day before, Jefferson Tayte spent the morning with DI Bishop at the police station. He had gone there to give his statement, but he'd found he couldn't recall much of what had happened during the time between stepping aboard the *Osprey* and waking up at the hospital.

'Don't worry,' Bishop had said. 'You and Davina played your parts well.'

Bishop had then taken Tayte into another room, where he'd played back the recordings from the wire Tayte had been wearing. It had filled in the blanks in his memory caused by the Rohypnol, and all Tayte had to do then was confirm that he had gone aboard Davina's boat that afternoon and that it was his voice on the recording.

'What's going to happen about those Swiss bank accounts?' Tayte asked, having been reminded of the war-fund gold Frank Saxby and Oscar Scanlon had reportedly secreted away.

'Who knows?' Bishop said. 'They'll be checked out, of course. If there is anything there after all this time, one thing's for sure. Neither Davina Scanlon nor Raife Metcalfe will see a penny of it.'

'Where are they?'

'Safely locked away for now. Raife Metcalfe still hasn't said a word, but Mrs Scanlon made a full confession during the night.'

Tayte didn't see how she could have done otherwise. The charges ran the entire gamut of murder-related crimes, including planning and sanctioning Lionel Scanlon's murder, attempted murder in Tayte's case, and actual murder in the case of the young restaurant manager, Luca. With everything that was said on the recordings, and with Luca's dead body found in one of the cabins, the evidence against them was undeniable.

Bishop had also apologised to Tayte for not intervening sooner than he had. 'Once the *Osprey* left the marina,' he'd said. 'I had to hold the team back so as not to be seen. It put a few minutes distance between us. Then when the *Osprey* stopped, you were in the water before we could get close enough to prevent it.'

Tayte had learned that he hadn't actually been in the water anything like as long as he felt he had. The helicopter had moved in as soon as Davina had pushed him overboard. Raife had then started the *Osprey* up again in an attempt to make an escape, which, along with the current and the sea swell, was why Tayte quickly lost sight of the boat.

'All's well that ends well,' Tayte had said, and then he'd turned his thoughts back to Alice Stilwell and the further business he felt he had to conclude before his assignment was over.

The letter Davina had shown Tayte—the letter Alice had sent to her father soon after arriving in Canada off the RMS *Laurentic*—had been found alongside the notebook in Davina's handbag. Tayte had read it in Bishop's car on the way to Hamberley. He felt he had a duty to set things straight for the Metcalfe family, as Lady Vivienne Metcalfe had previously asked him to when she'd brought the photograph of Alice to him. So the letter had finally arrived at Hamberley, albeit a hundred years late, but Tayte felt that in this case it really was better late than never.

With the entire household still in shock over the murder and attempted murder charges brought against Raife Metcalfe, Tayte had read Alice's letter to Lord Metcalfe in the hope that it would offer him some degree of reconciliation with the memory of his grandmother. The letter contained Alice's full account of what had happened in the spring of 1914, from that fateful day in Holland to her arrival in Quebec, and the hopes she carried with her of seeing Henry again, of returning to England and to her children, not as a criminal, but as a mother who had been forced to act as she had for the safety of her family. Tayte had also felt it his duty to remind Reginald that had Alice not done the things she had done, he might never have been born.

Tayte and Bishop left Reginald Metcalfe in his chair by the window, to ponder over the contents of the letter in silence and to draw whatever conclusions he wished to from it. Another record had been set straight as far as Tayte was concerned—the past repaired. The Metcalfe family now knew the truth, and Tayte could do no more than that. It was just after midday when Lady Metcalfe showed them out, offering her thanks as they walked—thanks for what she believed would now bring peace to her husband's mind over the former black sheep of the family, if not over his grandson's arrest.

'Only too happy to help,' Tayte said with a smile. Then as the doors to Hamberley closed, he ambled back to the car with Bishop beneath a blanket of low grey cloud that looked settled in for the day. It was time to leave the past to memory again and move on.

'I found out what that phone call was all about,' Bishop said. 'The call Dean Saxby said he'd overheard at Lionel Scanlon's workshop.'

'You did?'

Bishop nodded. 'Lionel was talking to Raife Metcalfe's wife, Miranda, about the items of antique furniture the Scanlons were trying to acquire for them. Apparently, the conversation became heated when Lionel said he was having trouble finding one of the pieces and wanted more money for his trouble. Miranda Metcalfe said she remembered the conversation clearly.'

'What about that receipt for electrical work? Did you find out why Dean Saxby never mentioned it?'

'Yes I did,' Bishop said. 'I'm paraphrasing here, but he told me he spent an afternoon doing some re-wiring work for Mr Scanlon shortly after he went to sell him that cigar case. He told me he didn't mention it because he thought it would strengthen their association and implicate him in the break-in at Mr Scanlon's workshop before he was killed. He knew I'd find his arrest record and his history of violence, and with the poverty-line lifestyle he was leading, he thought I'd try to pin the break-in and subsequent murder on him. The newspapers reported that Mr Scanlon's murder was suspected at the time to be the result of a burglary attempt gone wrong. Dean Saxby must have read that and panicked.'

'Well, you got your case solved in the end,' Tayte said.

'Yes, and I want to thank you, Mr Tayte. Your assignment played a key role after all. I really wasn't expecting anything to come of it.'

Tayte offered the Inspector a smile. 'Team effort,' he said. 'I couldn't have done it without you.'

'Why do you do it?' Bishop asked. 'I mean, what motivates you to keep delving into the past lives of people you've no relation to?'

'We all need to make a living.'

Bishop scoffed. 'Don't give me that. It's not about the money with you, I can tell. You wouldn't have offered to put yourself in harms way like you did if it was just about earning a crust.'

'No, perhaps not,' Tayte said, thinking over the question again and finding no single answer. He wanted to say that he had to delve into the lives of other people's families because he didn't have one of his own to delve into, but thanks to Marcus Brown and the contents of the safety deposit box he'd left him, that was no longer true. They reached the car, and Tayte followed his briefcase into the passenger seat.

'Well, whatever drives you,' Bishop said, 'you've got quite a story to take back to your client. I'm sure she'll be chuffed to bits.'

'Yes, I'm sure she will,' Tayte said, 'And I can let her know about her extended family, too. Being connected to British aristocracy always goes down well. I don't know whether either side will want to get in touch, but I'll certainly offer to open the door for them.'

'That's a nice gift to be able to give to people.'

Tayte smiled. 'Maybe that answers your question. Maybe that's why I do what I do.'

Bishop started the engine and the car began to move off, gravel crunching beneath the tires. 'I suppose you'll be heading home now.'

*Home* . . .

Tayte thought about Jean and reminded himself that home was where the heart is. 'No, not just yet,' he said, knowing she would be back in England in a few hours. When he'd thought he was going to die in the sea off the Medway estuary, all he could think about was Professor Jean Summer. He'd known then that she'd already had a profound impact on his life. When he'd been in life-threatening situations before, it had always been the need to find his family that had made him want to survive. Now it was Jean.

'I'm hoping to spend a few days in London,' Tayte said as he gazed thoughtfully out of his window at Hamberley for the last time.

He had decided not to wait for Jean's phone call. He was going to meet her at the airport. He had to see her again, if only to say good-bye. If it was over between them, he didn't want to find out down a phone line. He recalled one of Marcus Brown's many pearls of wisdom then. It was a line his old friend had been fond of telling him.

'The past is already written, Jefferson. The future, on the other hand, is a story yet to be told. So write it well.'

'And then,' Tayte continued, smiling to himself as he began to dream about that possible future, 'who knows?'

# Epilogue

'That's good coffee,' Tayte said over the rim of his cup as he took the first sip. He knew it was useless small talk, meaningless words to fill the space between all the important things he wanted to say, but now that he was with Jean again, he simply didn't know how to get to them.

Tayte had been waiting for her at the arrivals gate at Heathrow Airport when she came through. He had flowers in his hand, and because of the cellophane wrapping they came in his palms were clammier than they usually were whenever he was nervous about something. He'd been glad to see that Jean was alone—no Nigel on her arm—and just seeing her again reminded him of what a fool he'd been. There had been smiles between them as they greeted one another and Tayte took her bag, but no kisses.

'That call I told you about—the lead I've been waiting on,' Tayte said as he set his coffee cup down again. 'It came through about an hour ago.'

'That's great,' Jean said. 'I'm pleased things are working out for you.'

Reading between the lines, Tayte couldn't help but think that she meant *even if things aren't working out for us*. 'It means I won't be heading back to America just yet,' he added, and his heart sank when he heard Jean sigh from behind her coffee. She looked far more serious than he wanted her to.

'Look, JT, ' she said. 'I told you I had some thinking to do—'

'Just don't say anything hasty,' Tayte cut in, afraid she was about to deliver the punchline to their all too brief relationship.

'I've been thinking about it all week, JT. I'd hardly call that hasty.'

'No, of course not,' Tayte said. He paused and took another sip of his coffee. 'So, what do you think?'

'I think you're about to bury your head in your research again, and I know how important it is to you, but I don't think there's room in your life for both of us.'

Tayte felt his shoulders slump with his hopes. A part of him knew she was right.

'It has to be all or nothing,' Jean added. 'It's the only way I can see our relationship working, because if there is to be any future for us, I can't be shut out of your life again like that.'

Tayte let go of the breath he was holding.

'I've decided I want to help you find your family.'

'You do? Are you sure?'

'For better or for worse, but you have to let me into your life, absolutely, or you have to let me go. Do you think you can do that?'

'Absolutely,' Tayte said, and he couldn't have held his smile back if he'd tried.

'Good.' The corners of Jean's mouth began to lift at last. 'Now come here and give me a kiss, you great lummox!'

As Tayte leaned across the table and kissed Jean full on the lips, he only hoped she hadn't let herself in for more than she'd bargained for. Wherever his own family history was going to take them, his mother's parting words forty years ago told him it was into a past she had wished to protect him from. Whether for better or for worse, he expected it was going to be a bumpy ride.

# Acknowledgements

My thanks to Emilie Marneur and the Amazon Publishing team; to my editors, Katie Green and Jill Pellarin, and everyone else who has been involved in the publication of this book; and as always to my wife, Karen, for so much more than I can put into words.

# About the Author

*Credit: Karen Robinson*

Steve Robinson drew upon his own family history for inspiration when he imagined the life and quest of his genealogist-hero, Jefferson Tayte. The talented London-based crime writer, who was first published at age 16, always wondered about his own maternal grandfather—'He was an American GI billeted in England during the Second World War,' Robinson says. 'A few years after the war ended he went back to America, leaving a young family behind and, to my knowledge, no further contact was made. I traced him to Los Angeles through his 1943 enlistment record and discovered that he was born in Arkansas . . .'

Robinson cites crime writing and genealogy as ardent hobbies—a passion that is readily apparent in his work.

He can be contacted via his website www.steve-robinson.me or his blog at www.ancestryauthor.blogspot.com.